DONATO & DAUGHTER

A Creative Kind of Killer

Razzamatazz

JACK EARLY

DONATO & DAUGHTER

E. P. DUTTON   NEW YORK

Publisher's Note: This novel is a work of fiction. Names,
characters, places, and incidents either are the product
of the author's imagination or are used fictitiously,
and any resemblance to actual persons, living or dead,
events, or locales is entirely coincidental.

Published in the United States by E. P. Dutton,
a division of NAL Penguin Inc.,
2 Park Avenue, New York, N.Y. 10016.
Published simultaneously in Canada by
Fitzhenry and Whiteside,
Limited, Toronto.

Library of Congress Cataloging-in-Publication Data
Early, Jack.
  Donato and daughter.
  I. Title.
PS3555.A693D66   1988   813'.54   87-24368
ISBN 0-525-24625-8

Designed by Mark O'Connor

10 9 8 7 6 5 4 3 2 1

First Edition

*For Charlotte Sheedy, who believed before it began
and kept on believing.*

Acknowledgments

I wish to thank the following people who made this book possible: ex-policeman Tony Dellaventura and my anonymous friends at the Fifth.

And for help, faith and support beyond any call: Linda Crawford.

DONATO &
DAUGHTER

One

Detectives Michael Donato and Frank Moore had caught the squeal. As they pulled up in front of 609 East Sixth Street, Donato jumped from the unmarked car and started toward the dilapidated building.

"Christ, Mike, what's your goddamned hurry?" Moore called, slamming his door. "This is a DOA."

"Yeah, I know."

Donato was always in a hurry when he thought he might see her. He hoped he could get in and out before she arrived. It wasn't likely, but he'd try anyway.

People were standing around in a knot, blocking the outside stairway. Donato felt someone touch his arm and jerked away, his right hand automatically going to his hip where his .38 was holstered.

The man who had touched him was short and dark. Above his lip, a thin mustache looked as if he'd drawn it on with an eyebrow pencil.

"Whass gon' on? Hass somebody been kill'?" the man said. There were large sweat stains under his arms even though it was a cool April day.

This was Donato's precinct, the Ninth, and he knew most of the junkies, robbers and con men on these streets. He'd seen this guy around, but so far he was clean. "Who're you?" he asked.

"Me?" He stabbed his chest with his dirty thumb.

"Yeah, you."

"Me?"

Moore grabbed the little man by the front of his yellow shirt. "Yeah, you, fuckface. Who are you?"

"My nam'?"

Moore twisted the shirt tighter. "I'm not fooling, slimeball."

"Hey, man," a woman yelled, "that's po-lice brutality."

There was a chorus of agreement.

"C'mon, Frank, let's go," Donato said quietly.

Moore ignored him. "I asked you who you was."

"I'm juss on the si'walk."

"What the fuck's that supposed to mean, 'I'm juss on the si'-walk'?" he mimicked.

"Let him go," Donato said. "We've got other fish to fry."

Reluctantly Moore released the man. "Don't be here when I come out. You hear me, asswipe?"

"I dinn do nothin'."

Donato took the cracked cement steps two at a time. A middle-aged, uniformed cop, arms crossed over his chest, stood at the top. "What've we got, Schwartz?"

"A homicide, Sergeant," he said, swallowing hard. "A woman. Christ, it's awful."

Ron Schwartz almost had his twenty; he'd seen everything. Donato took what he said seriously.

"Where is it?"

"Fifth floor, right rear."

The sergeant nodded his thanks and stood back while Schwartz opened the door. The smell of urine and sweat hit Donato across the face like a snapped towel. He never got used to it.

"How can people live like this?" Moore always said the same thing when they entered the filthy, crumbling buildings in the East Village.

Donato didn't bother to answer. They both knew how. Deserted women on welfare with four kids and old people subsisting on dog food didn't have much choice. Neither did junkies. Donato guessed that the squeal was drug-related. Routine for this part of New York City. It was hard to care about one junkie killing another or a dealer getting offed by one of his customers. As far as Donato was concerned, they were doing the city a favor. A picture of Rich flashed in his mind, and he shook his head to dislodge it.

On the ground floor, the apartment doors were open a crack. As Donato came abreast of the one on the right the door opened. A tall black woman, dirty hair hanging in hanks around her drawn face, stepped into the hall. Attached to her mother's jean-clad leg like a third appendage was a child, her lip puffy where she'd fallen or been hit.

"C'n I ax you somethin'?"

"What?" Donato noted the tracks on the woman's arms.

"What's goin' down here?"

"Take the kid inside and close the door," he said.

"Why can't you answer me? I be just as good as you." She thrust out her chin defiantly.

"This has nothing to do with equality, ma'am. Take the kid inside. Now!"

She jumped, pulled the girl in with her and slammed the door. Donato heard her say, "Honky motherfucker."

Moore took a step forward ready to kick the door, but Donato stopped him and, smiling, said in a singsong voice, "Sticks and stones, Frank." The smile faded. "C'mon, cut the bullshit." He was sick and tired of having to control his partner. Moore's hair-trigger temper had gotten him to the Ninth six years before, and he hadn't made his way out yet. But hell, he wasn't doing much better. It had been four for him. Donato suddenly realized he'd been thinking about retirement daily for the last year. Something better give soon because he didn't know how much more he could take of the Ninth, the scumbag precinct of Lower Manhattan. He started for the stairs.

Donato was a much bigger man than Moore, almost six-two and weighing one-eighty-five to Moore's five-ten, one hundred sixty pounds. At fifty-five, Donato had fifteen years on him, but it was Moore who was puffing by the third landing. Donato felt he was in as good shape as he'd been thirty-three years before when he'd graduated from the Academy. And women told him he was just as handsome, maybe more. The gray temples and salt-and-pepper widow's peak did the trick. Recently a woman perp had told him he looked like Richard Conte, the old movie actor. He'd rented *House of Strangers* from his video club that night and decided she'd been right. Except he was taller than Conte. And older.

As they climbed the stairs, they ignored the tenants who peeked out at them from their apartments. At the fifth floor, they walked down the dark, smelly hall. A rookie they didn't know was stationed outside the door to the victim's apartment.

"Sergeant Donato and Detective Moore." They withdrew their leather cases and flashed their gold shields.

"In the bedroom," the cop said. He looked shaky.

"You okay?" Donato asked.

The rookie nodded, his eyes reflecting the horror he'd seen.

"First DOA?" Moore asked.

"Yeah, first one." He ran his thumb and forefinger over his blond mustache.

Donato clapped him on the shoulder and gave him a reassuring squeeze. "What's your name?"

"George Kelley."

"Okay, Kelley, try to relax. Who found the body?"

"The lady in there." He jutted his chin toward the opposite door. "I told her to wait in her apartment."

"How'd she find her? She have a key or what?"

Kelley looked scared. "I don't know," he said softly.

"You shoulda asked her," Moore said, an edge to his voice.

Donato said, "Got your memo pad, kid?"

Kelley nodded and slapped at his back pocket.

"You take any notes?"

"Yeah."

"You should've asked her how she got in."

"Yeah, I should of. I . . . when I saw the . . . the deceased I . . . I don't know I just . . ."

"Next time don't forget," Donato said gently. "You didn't touch anything, did you, Kelley?"

"I didn't touch nothing," he said, as if shocked that he should be asked about such a rudimentary rule.

"You look for a suspect when you came on the premises?" Moore asked.

"Yeah."

Donato examined the lock; then he and Moore entered the apartment.

The expected stink of decomposing flesh was absent. Whoever she was, she hadn't been dead long. This wasn't the apartment of a

[4]

junkie. It was too neat, too homey-looking. Maybe it belonged to a dealer, but the big ones didn't live in this neighborhood and the ones who did were hooked. Donato was almost certain this wasn't a drug hit.

The furniture in the living room was worn but clean. A black, foam rubber couch sat against the right-hand wall, a low, wooden coffee table on brass legs in front of it. An issue of *Newsweek*, the *New York Times* and several copies of *Commonweal* lay on the table. Donato picked up the newspaper and looked at the date: April 3, 1985. Yesterday's paper. There were no ashtrays. On the left wall was a built-in floor-to-ceiling bookcase housing hundreds of books as well as a stereo and two speakers. Donato ruled out burglary.

Two sling chairs, one green, one yellow, faced the couch. On the wall between two clean windows was the LOVE poster by Sister Corita.

"Looks like a goddamn sixties apartment," Moore said.

"I was just thinking that." Donato knew they were stalling. It didn't matter how long you had, you never got used to it. You pretended, even made jokes sometimes, but viewing a corpse was always grim. Moore moved toward the door off the living room and Donato followed.

The room was a shambles. A pine dresser was overturned and a mirror on the closet door was shattered, one large shard hanging precariously from the upper left-hand corner like a huge loose tooth. Clothes were strewn around the room, and bits of paper littered the floor. Above the bed the glass was smashed on the framed portrait of Jesus Christ, the inevitable bleeding heart the color of raw meat. On a marble-topped nightstand was Graham Greene's *The Heart of the Matter*. The clean white sheets had been torn, and slashed by a knife.

She faced them, half on the bed and half off. The torso and head were not visible. Her legs were spread and bent at the knees as though she were waiting to receive a lover. Around one ankle were her underpants and panty hose. She wore no shoes. The blue skirt was bunched at her waist. Blood stained the sheet between her legs. Heavy bruising on her thighs showed she'd fought her attacker.

They walked around the end of the bed. Donato heard something crunch under his shoe. He moved his foot. It was a piece of purple glass. When he leaned over to get a better look, he observed that it was a bead his weight had cracked. There were more scattered nearby.

On the other side of the bed, her torso hung down, and the top of her skull rested on the floor as if she were going to try a headstand.

Below the backward arch of her body was a large, dark pool of blood. Her pink, short-sleeved blouse had been ripped open. There were multiple stab wounds in her stomach. Flung out behind her, her arms showed no track marks, but were bruised from her death struggle. Defensive wounds showed on her palms. On the left hand, the fourth finger was missing.

"Where is it?" Moore asked.

"Don't see it," Donato answered. Lack of blood told Donato the killer had hacked it off after death.

They glanced at each other. This was a new one, but they'd seen things equally horrifying.

Around her throat was a broken, purple-beaded necklace. The killer might have tried to strangle her with it, Donato thought, and when it had snapped, used his knife.

The woman was white with short, curly, ginger-colored hair. Her eyes were closed. She was thirty-five or so, he guessed. About the same age as Dina.

The sound of shuffling feet drew the detectives' attention to the bedroom door. The forensic team had arrived.

"Give us another minute," Donato said to the man in the doorway.

"We'll start out here. Anything special we're looking for?"

"Everything and anything."

"Right."

"Whadaya think, Mike?" Moore asked.

"She's no junkie. Maybe somebody was looking for something."

"Just in here?"

It was true. Only the bedroom had been ransacked. "Yeah, you're right."

"Anyways, this looks like a sex crime. Jesus. What kind of weirdo cuts off a finger?" Moore asked rhetorically.

Donato felt his insides plummet. Usually it was serial killers who did bizarre things. He bent down, knees cracking, and took a closer look at the necklace. One part was behind her head, under her neck. With his ballpoint pen, he coaxed it out. At the end of the chain was a small silver crucifix. The beads were sections of a rosary.

"Where was her God when this happened?" Moore said bitterly.

Donato, who'd left the church thirteen years earlier when his son died, had nothing to say. He rose and went to the window, took a pair of surgical gloves from his pocket and slid them on. Carefully pushing aside the clean, white cotton curtain, he checked the lock. Closed.

The view was the back of another building. There was no dust or marks on the sill.

Crossing the room, his foot kicked something that slid across the floor and stopped near the end of the bed. It was a Catholic prayer book. Or had been. The volume lay open, its pages ripped from the spine. He picked up a few of the confettilike papers, identified them as pieces of the torn pages, then dropped them, watching as they fluttered back to the floor.

At the open closet he joined Moore. Dresses, skirts, blouses and jeans hung a uniform one inch apart. Most of the clothes were dark, and there weren't many of them. On the floor, a pair of tired blue sneakers was lined up neatly next to a pair of black loafers. He thought of his wife's closet and the rows of shoes she had, almost all gifts from the old man. God, how he hated the son of a bitch.

"Well," Moore said, rubbing a hand across his pockmarked face, "she wasn't no snappy dresser, that's for sure."

"And she wasn't living with a man either. But the finger," Donato said thoughtfully. "If she was separated, the husband might have done it, chopped off the wedding ring finger as some kind of symbolic gesture."

"Could of been a new guy jealous she was still wearing her ring. Just because no guy lived here don't mean there wasn't one."

"I don't see a weapon, do you?"

"Maybe it's under her."

"Maybe. Let's get out of here, let forensic in."

The small living room was jammed. All the lights were on, and flashbulbs popped as pictures were taken of every corner and every piece of furniture. Some of the people were powdering surfaces for prints. When they went into the bedroom, they'd repeat the procedure, adding other tasks such as measuring blood spills and searching the sheets for semen. Back at the lab, they'd go over the woman's clothing like children picking at scabs.

Donato noted that she hadn't arrived, but neither had anyone else from Homicide South. He'd better face it—there was too much to do; he wasn't going to get away without an encounter. He told Moore to check out the hall closet, then said to forensic, "Okay, men, you can go in now."

"Thanks a bunch," said a blue-eyed, blonde woman Donato had never seen before.

"Sorry, I didn't notice you."

"Yeah, sure."

"Look, I said I was sorry," he snapped. "I was thinking about the victim, not you."

"Okay, forget it," she said, chagrined.

Donato was pleased he'd gotten the desired effect, then promptly felt guilty. It was Dina he was angry with, not this woman. He gestured dismissively and grunted something that could be taken as an apology.

After checking out the two living room windows, which were locked, Donato went into the small, windowless kitchen. He opened the refrigerator: a carton of milk, an open can of Martinson's coffee, chicken or tuna salad in a plastic wrapped dish, half a bagel. She didn't eat much, or maybe just not at home.

At the sink, he poured out the milk, peered inside the carton. Empty. He took off the top of the coffee can and shoved a hand down inside, felt around, dumped the contents on the small counter. Nothing. It was what he'd expected, but he needed to be sure.

When he'd been through the two cabinets and satisfied himself that nothing was hidden anywhere, he walked over to the bathroom. As tenement bathrooms went, this one was a pretty good size. Many apartments had bathtubs in the kitchen, toilets in the hall. But this bathroom had it all: toilet, sink and a bathtub with claw feet. The floor was made of hexagonal tiles, the walls, halfway up, of rectangular ones. Everything sparkled. Donato pulled back the Charlie Brown shower curtain. For a moment, he wondered if the victim had had a child but then remembered his twenty-five-year-old niece's penchant for Snoopy cards.

A dripping green washcloth hung over the bathtub faucet. Donato made a note in his pocket memo. The cloth could have been used by the killer to wash away blood. There were no traces of it in the tub. Later, hair samples would be taken from the trap in the drain.

He popped open the medicine chest. It contained a bottle of Listerine, Colgate toothpaste, dental floss in a Johnson & Johnson red-and-white container, three disposable razors, a nail file, a tweezers, a stick of Mennen deodorant and a package of super Tampax. The razors might belong to a man, but Donato doubted it. Anyway, there was only one toothbrush. There were no creams, no lipstick, no eyeliner or shadow. She used no makeup. But maybe she kept her makeup in her purse. He hadn't seen a purse and made a note to look for one.

It was possible that a man had lived here and cleaned out his stuff after killing her, but Donato felt in his gut that that wasn't what had happened. He'd never known a husband or lover to kill in this fashion: rape and mutilation. He was sure she'd been raped. Still, the trail of blood on the sheet between the woman's legs puzzled him. Surely, at her age, she hadn't been a virgin. Maybe she'd been raped by something other than a penis. It wouldn't be the first time.

Since he'd been sent down from the One-Nine four years ago, he'd encountered women defiled by everything imaginable. Uptown, where he'd spent most of his career, they had a little more class and usually raped with what God gave them. The bastards. Jesus, he had to get out of this precinct.

"Anything?" Moore asked, standing in the doorway.

"Might be something in the bathtub trap or in the washcloth. How about you?"

"Nothing to write home about. And no men's clothing." From his memo pad, he began reading what he'd found in the hall closet. "One woman's gray cloth coat, one woman's tan raincoat, a pair of galoshes—when's the last time you saw galoshes, Mike?—a black umbrella, a tennis racket . . ."

"A tennis racket?"

"Yeah. What's the big deal?"

"I don't know. It just seems out of place."

"You gotta live on West End Avenue to smack a ball around?"

"Can it." Since Donato had joined the Ninth, and he and Moore had become partners, it had been clear that Moore resented the fact that Donato had a rich wife. In the old days, a lot of cops found it humiliating to have their wives work or to live on money they might have, but those days had been over for a long time. He had never felt that way. Although he resented gifts from Renata's father, her money was something else. He would have been stupid to adopt any other attitude.

Still, he wondered if he would have tried to go beyond sergeant if they'd had to live on his salary alone. The fact was, sergeant was all the responsibility he wanted. It gave him an edge, but it left him in the action. Sitting behind a desk, playing politics, would have wiped him out years ago. He considered himself fortunate that he had a rich wife.

"What else?" Donato asked.

"A vacuum and . . . a pair of crutches." He looked up and smiled.

"Always save the best for last, don't you, Frank?"

"That's me, Mike, just one helluva fun guy. Found her purse in the closet, too. Nothing much in it." He consulted his pad again.

"One hanky, one ballpoint pen, half a pack of Chewels cinnamon gum, a change purse with eight dollars and seventy-two cents, an ID folder with a driver's license and a picture of an old man and woman. Probably her parents. A religious card . . . you know, one of them Virgin Mary things. No address book. That's it. And Sellon found her shoes under the bed. No mystery there."

"How about the finger?"

"Not yet."

"Weapon?"

"Nothing."

"Okay." Donato started out of the bathroom but stopped when he heard somebody say:

"In the back, Lieutenant."

He watched the new arrivals pass by the bathroom, and he felt himself stiffen as if someone had shoved a pole down the back of his jacket.

"Keep your cool, Mike," Moore said.

"Yeah, sure." Pushing past his partner, he headed for the bedroom. He didn't know why he was doing it—he could've gotten out, left Moore to deal with things. But it had been a while, and he found himself wanting to see how it made him feel, face to face.

The lieutenant was standing at the other side of the bed, looking down. And then she glanced up, and they were staring into each other's eyes.

Donato had to admit police work hadn't made her any less attractive. At the outset, he'd been sure there would be a hardening of her features, maybe a coldness in her eyes. But he'd never been able to see it, couldn't see it now. Her face was heart-shaped and she wore her wavy blonde hair loose to just above her shoulders. The brown eyes were deep-set, expressive, honest. Her nose was almost straight, a slight bump in the bridge giving hint of her Italian ancestry. And her mouth still turned up, two half moons at the corners. Maybe being a cop didn't affect women the same way it did men. All the cops he knew, including himself, had become cynical after just a few years on the Job.

She was wearing a tan skirt and a red silk blouse. Her jacket was dark brown and made of soft leather, the collar and sleeves stylishly pushed up.

"Hello, Donato," she said.

"Lieutenant." He pulled off the rubber gloves and shoved them in his jacket pocket.

"Any thoughts?"

"Probably nothing more than you've surmised yourself."

"Let's hear it anyway."

"It's not a drug hit, and I think she lived here alone."

"The missing finger?"

He told her their ideas.

"Forced entry?"

"Nothing through the windows unless one was open and the killer shut and locked it afterward, but there were no marks or disturbed dust on the sills. And no marks around the lock on the door, but it's flimsy; plastic easily could've been used to gain entry."

She nodded, then turned away and began talking softly to John Pesetsky, the detective who stood beside her.

It was a bigger exchange than they'd had in a long time. Donato felt pleased and that surprised him. Watching her, he realized, with a sudden thump of his heart, that he missed her. And then everything came back to him, one scene after another, like a kid's flash cards. His feeling of warmth changed abruptly, and all the anger and bitterness returned.

She crossed the room and stood next to him. "Anything in the bathroom?"

"A wet washcloth." He realized they were facing the dead woman, both of them looking at her open legs. Donato was embarrassed. This was one of the things he didn't like about women in police work. It was bad enough with strangers, but to stand there with his daughter was almost more than he could bear.

"Is there anything else, Lieutenant, because if not I'd like to . . ."

Kelley, the young cop at the door, was suddenly beside them, his face flushed, beads of sweat on his forehead. "Lieutenant," he said nervously, "I think you'd better come outside."

"What's up?" she asked.

"There's a guy says he knows the victim. She's a sister," he said softly.

"Whose sister?"

"No, Lieutenant, not *whose.* She's *a* sister. A Catholic nun."

Two

"Where is this guy?" Dina Donato asked.

"Out in the hall, Lieutenant."

"Come on, Pesetsky," she said. "You too, Donato."

In the hall Kelley gestured to a man leaning against the wall opposite the victim's apartment. He was tall and thin, and his clothes hung on his frame as if he'd recently lost weight. Even so he was fashionably dressed in tan pleated trousers, a pink T-shirt and a collarless brown linen jacket. His dark blond hair was slicked back, no part. Dina thought he had a handsome face: blue eyes, straight nose and a square chin like a Frye boot.

Kelley introduced them. "This is Bob Briney."

Dina said, "I'm Lieutenant Donato, and these are Sergeant Donato and Detective Pesetsky."

Briney looked at Dina and then Mike as if he were trying to see a resemblance.

At times like this, Dina wished she hadn't kept her maiden name. If she'd wanted to take a stand, remain independent, she should have used Fiorentini, her mother's name. It was too late now. "Mr. Briney," Dina said, "Officer Kelley tells me you knew the victim."

"Yes. She's Sister Honora . . . I mean, she was," he corrected.

"Have you been inside the apartment?"

"Ever or today?"

"Today."

"No."

Pesetsky picked it up. "How'd you know who's in there? Who was killed?"

"I . . . I assumed," Briney said.

"How do you know the deceased?"

"We were friends."

"How did you meet?" Donato amplified.

"I can't remember. It was a long time ago."

"Were you her lover?" Pesetsky put in.

"No. I'm a priest."

The detectives glanced at one another.

"Don't any of you wear clerical garb anymore?" Dina asked.

"Most do. The St. Luke's order is fairly progressive."

"Were you her lover?" Pesetsky repeated.

The priest's full mouth tightened. "I told you, I'm a . . ."

"That doesn't automatically rule you out," Donato interrupted.

Father Briney took a deep breath. "I've taken a vow of chastity, Sergeant," he said, annoyed.

Dina looked at him coolly. "When's the last time you saw Sister Honora?"

"I think it was two days ago. Yes, that's right, it was Tuesday. Father Coughlin was sick, so I said the eight o'clock mass as well as the seven. She always comes to that. Sister Honora. She always comes to the eight o'clock mass."

Dina noted that Briney was having trouble speaking of the victim in the past tense. "And that was the last time you saw her? You didn't see her yesterday?"

"No. Father Coughlin was better and I wasn't around yesterday."

"Why not?"

"I had a personal day. My mother's sick. I went to visit her. She lives in Massachusetts. Sheffield."

Dina said, "What time did you go and when did you come back?"

"I left right after the seven o'clock mass, and I came back about eight last night."

"Can you prove that?" Donato asked.

"I guess so." Briney moved back against the wall in small jerky motions.

"You guess so?" Pesetsky said.

"Well, sure. Yes. Sure I can prove it." He nodded up and down as if he were trying to convince himself as well as them.

"So then," Dina said, "the last time you saw Sister Honora was at the eight o'clock mass on Tuesday morning."

"That's right."

"Did you talk to her?"

"Yes. After the mass we talked a minute or two."

"What about?"

"Dave Koutek. A boy in the neighborhood who'd gotten in trouble again."

"What kind of trouble?" Donato asked.

"Police trouble. Narcotics."

"Why were you talking about him?"

"He's one of ours. A group of kids we were working with, Sister Honora and I."

"Did Sister Honora have a family?"

"A brother. James Dunn. He lives on Staten Island where Sister Honora grew up. He's a lawyer."

"Great," Pesetsky said under his breath.

"Will you identify the body, Father?" The appellation felt awkward to Dina, as if she were back in grammar school.

The priest hesitated.

"We could wait for her brother," Dina explained, "but having you do it now will make things move more swiftly."

"I understand."

As they went into the apartment, she wondered how the priest would react when he viewed the body. It would be kinder to warn him, but she wasn't in the business of being kind. The important thing was to observe him at the scene of the murdered nun. In a world where nuns could be murdered, priests could be killers.

At the door to the bedroom, they met one of the assistant medical examiners.

"How long has she been dead, Goode?"

"Want my guesstimate?"

She stopped herself from rolling her eyes heavenward. Greg

Goode was not a favorite of hers. He was the kind of man who would say: have some *horses ovaries* instead of hors d'oeuvres.

"I figure between fifteen and seventeen hours. She's already coming out of rigor."

Dina did a fast calculation. "So that would be somewhere between four and six P.M. yesterday."

"Don't count your chicks, Lieutenant. It's not over 'til the fat lady sings."

"I'm approximating. Cause?"

"Multiple stab wounds to the heart. But don't quote me. Could be arsenic and old lace, for all we know." He grinned, showing pink gums. "Gotta be a good girl and wait for the autopsy report."

Dina checked a flare of anger, thanked him, and she, the two detectives and Father Briney went into the bedroom. When Donato and Pesetsky moved aside, exposing the nun's open legs, the priest stumbled backward as though he'd been slapped. His eyes grew wide, then he immediately shut them, his mouth trembling.

"Father," Dina said.

His eyes still closed, he said softly, "I can't."

"What d'you mean?" Pesetsky asked.

The priest's face grew pallid.

"Father," Dina said louder. "Are you all right?"

He nodded, turned away from the body and slowly opened his eyes. "Can't she be covered?" he asked her.

"No, not yet."

"There should be some dignity. A little dignity at the end of your life."

"I'm sorry," Dina said. "We have to do it this way. Could you go to the other side so you can see her face?"

Father Briney gratefully agreed. He followed Dina around the end of the bed, then looked down at the woman's face, the mutilated hand. He slapped his palm across his mouth as though he were holding back vomit, then sucked in air, his shoulders sagging.

Donato said, "You all right now?"

He nodded.

"Is it Sister Honora?" Dina asked.

"Yes. Yes, it's she." He made the sign of the cross in the air.

Touched by his obvious pain, Dina guided him out of the room, past the crowd in the living room and back to the hall.

Slumping against the dirty wall, Briney said, "Who could do such a thing?"

"That's what we're going to find out. And you can help. For starters, you can sit down over a cup of coffee with Detective Pesetsky and give him the names of everybody who knew Sister Honora."

"But there are hundreds. Boys and girls from the center."

"What center?"

"HAFH. Home Away from Home."

"It's on St. Mark's Place," Donato supplied.

Dina nodded. She knew the place but had never been inside. It was for runaways, drug users.

The priest went on. "People come and go there all the time. They reach out for help, shelter, food; then most of them disappear. It would be impossible to remember them all."

Dina said, "Do the best you can, Father."

"I'll try."

"Good."

Pesetsky and the priest started toward the stairs.

"Father?" Dina called. "Where do you buy your clothes?"

He looked down at himself as though his outfit were as surprising to him as it was to the lieutenant. "Unique," he said. "It's on Broadway."

She nodded. "Did Sister Honora ever wear a habit?"

"I've never seen her in one."

"Thanks."

When they were gone, Dina and her father were left in the hall. She couldn't remember the last time she'd been alone with him or how long ago she'd seen him at all. He looked good. Maybe there was a little more gray in his hair, but that was the only sign of age. In spite of what he ate and drank, she knew how well he took care of himself— working out twice a week and running two miles a day, a regimen not typical of the average cop. But then Mike Donato was not an average cop.

Your average cop, for instance, didn't study painting whenever he got the chance. She wondered if he was painting now, taking classes. She couldn't bring herself to inquire.

"Who found the body?" she asked him instead, the noise spilling from the apartment making her shout.

"Woman across the hall."

"Has anyone talked to her?"

"Just the first cop on the scene, Kelley. He didn't get the particulars."

"So let's do it."

"Why don't I get Moore to go with you?"

Dina felt the slight as keenly as if he'd turned his back on her. She searched his eyes and found them cold. More than four years had gone by since the Peak case, when Captain Crider had let slip the truth, and Donato obviously hadn't softened at all. As if his lies to her had been her fault. But had *she* softened? Was she ready to give an inch? Still, she was willing to work with him. He was one of the best cops she knew.

There weren't many like her father, and it was wrong, no matter what he'd done, that after twenty-nine years with the department he'd been dumped into the Ninth. Especially when everything had been so circumstantial.

"No, don't get Moore," she said, rapping on the door. "You'll do."

"Who is it?" The woman's voice was shaky.

"Police. We'd like to talk to you."

They listened to the sounds of city living, locks opening, chains dropped. The woman kept one chain on as she peered through the crack between door and frame. "You have identification?"

Dina reached in her pocket and showed her gold shield. "Lieutenant Donato. And this is Sergeant Donato."

"All right." The woman undid the last chain and stepped back. The apartment was a mirror of the victim's, but the furnishings were from another age.

The place reminded Dina of her grandmother's home on Mulberry Street. The same immaculate, but worn, white curtains, the sagging couch, the easy chair, the inevitable television on its metal stand. Pervading the air was the smell of frying onions, a touch of garlic. It was as if she'd known this woman all her life.

"What's your name?" she asked.

"Mrs. Baum." She pulled her gray cardigan tighter as though she were cold.

The woman was about seventy, Dina guessed, younger than Grandmother Donato, but she looked older. The lines and creases of a harder life were etched in her face.

"We'd like to ask you a few questions," Dina said. "Can we sit down?"

She nodded. "You want a glass a tea, maybe?"

"No thanks. We don't have much time."

Mrs. Baum waved a hand toward the couch. "Sit, sit." She took the chair, perching on its edge as if ready for flight.

"We understand you found the body, Mrs. Baum. Could you tell us about that?" Dina asked.

The old woman shook her head and gave a sigh of despair. "I never seen nothing like that in my whole life," she said to Donato. "Not even in the camps. Maybe there was something like it but I never seen it. I wish I'd never gone in there."

Donato said, "Why *did* you go in?"

"The door was open. Not much, but enough."

"Enough to make you concerned," Dina added.

"That's right." She stopped and stared at Dina. "You're a policeman?" she asked.

Dina felt her back tighten. She said yes. "Mrs. Baum, tell us what happened when you saw the open door."

"I peeked in. It wasn't open much, maybe two, three inches. I didn't see nothing, nobody was in the front room. I called her. Once, twice, three times. Loud. I thought I should go in, but for a minute I got scared. What if somebody was in there robbing and who knows what. But then I thought maybe Sister Honora was in trouble. Tied up maybe. The robber came and went and left her with a thing . . . a gag in her mouth. I had to do something."

"You didn't think of calling the police?"

"Not then. I wish I had." She began to rock slightly as though to soothe herself. "I pushed back the door and went in, still yelling her name. 'Sister Honora, Sister Honora,'" she demonstrated. "There was no answer. Then I went to the bedroom. The worst mistake I ever made." Mrs. Baum shut her eyes. When she opened them, she seemed startled to see the two detectives in her living room, as if they'd just materialized.

"Mrs. Baum, did you know Sister Honora very well?" Dina asked.

"Everybody in the building knew her. She was a good lady. Always trying to help everybody." She sighed. "What kind of a person would do such a thing?"

Again, Dina thought. It was what they always asked. After thirteen years she still didn't have an answer. "Was it usual for Sister Honora to leave her door unlocked?"

"I said she was good, not stupid. You couldn't. Not here. The junkies would come in like vultures and steal everything that wasn't nailed down. But one thing she wouldn't do, and I yelled at her over and over, whoever was at the door she'd let in."

"What do you mean?"

"Me, I ask who's there? The person says and then I look with the chain on. If I don't know them from Abel, they stay out. Sister asks and if she knows them, they come in. No chain. I told her it was foolish but she laughed and said God would protect her." Her shoulders heaved. "Some protection."

"You mean she opened the door to anyone without keeping a chain on as you did when we knocked?"

"That's right."

"But only if she knew the person?" Dina asked.

Mrs. Baum shrugged. "Anybody could say they were anybody, couldn't they?"

Dina said, "Yes, but then the person would have to know who *you* knew."

"Ahh, yes, I see. So you think who got in, who did this, was somebody she knew?"

"Possibly," Dina said. Or who knew *her*, she thought. "Let me get this clear, Mrs. Baum. Would Sister Honora open the door to a total stranger? A name she'd never heard before?"

"No. This much of a saint she wasn't."

If Sister Honora's killer was known to her, that would make their job much easier.

Donato said, "Why didn't you tell the first officer on the scene that she was a nun?"

"I tried, but he didn't want to hear nothing from me, told me to go in my apartment and lock up. Lock up he didn't have to tell me."

"Did everyone in the building know she was a nun, Mrs. Baum?" Dina asked.

She shrugged. "I think they probably did." She leaned toward them, whispering conspiratorially. "I don't bother with most of them. They're not a nice class of people. Not like it used to be when Mrs. Rosenberg was down the hall, the Merenskys below, Hannah and Abe Werthman on my head," she pointed toward the ceiling. "Now we got the Spanish and the Negroes. Not that I got a thing against them for their race. Nice ones I'd have to dinner . . . but here . . . no. Here they're bums sticking needles in their arms. My son Sidney says, 'Ma, why don't you move in with me and Comfort.' Is that a name? Comfort? How could I live with anybody named Comfort? But I don't tell him that. I say, 'Sidney, this is my home and here I am and here I stay.'" She nodded her head once for punctuation.

Dina had heard this rap before. Slightly different, an Italian accent instead of this one, but the message was the same. Her grandmother didn't want to leave her home either.

Donato said, "Do you know if Sister Honora had any enemies?"

"Who would be her enemy, a nun?" A lock of white hair slipped over one eye. With a flourish she pinned it back into her bun. Again she lowered her voice. "They don't need enemies to kill. Bums."

Dina rose. "Thank you, Mrs. Baum. If you think of anything that might be important, contact Sergeant Donato at the precinct or me. This is my number." She handed the old woman a card.

Mrs. Baum read the card, then looked from Dina to Mike. "You're married?"

"No," they both said at once.

Looking uncomfortable, Donato moved toward the door.

"So, nu?"

Dina said, "He's my . . . I'm his daughter."

"Yes," Donato said, "I'm her father."

"Nice," Mrs. Baum said. "You watch out for her then. That's nice."

Neither responded. Out in the hall, they threaded their way through the cops and technicians to the fifth-floor landing.

"What do you think?" she asked.

"I don't think it's the priest."

"No. One of the kids from the center?"

"Maybe."

"You don't think so."

He shook his head. "Not really."

"It's too ritualistic, isn't it?" She couldn't bring herself to say they might have a serial killer on their hands. "There's always her brother."

"I wouldn't put money on it."

"But you would put money on it being someone she knew?"

"Or *thought* she knew. That sort of rules out a serial, don't you think?" he asked.

She understood he was wishing, as she was. "Might. Let's hope."

"The best bet is somebody in the building."

"I'm sure that'll be it," she said, not sure at all. "Rudolph and Vicarel have been canvassing the building since we got here. Maybe they have something by now."

"Right." He turned to go down the stairs.

Dina put a hand on his arm.

He looked startled.

"We should talk," she said. "About us."

"We *have* talked."

"Again. We should talk again."

"Why?"

"Because," she said tightly, "you're my father and I'm your daughter." She felt as if she were begging, and it made her angry. He was the one at fault.

Donato said, "The facts are still the same, *Lieutenant.*"

"You're so damned stubborn," she said, ignoring the jab at her title.

"That's where *you* got it from. Do you need me for anything else?"

He always had to have the last word. "No. Let me know if you get any leads," Dina said brusquely. She watched him go down the stairs, head up, shoulders squared, as if nothing had happened between them.

Had he always hidden his feelings? she wondered. She remembered the death of her first dog, Lucky, when she was four, and how her father had told her about it and held her, crying almost as much as she did. Could that have been the last time she'd seen him show emotion? There was Rich's death, of course. He'd broken down then. But what about the years in between?

Good cops didn't show their feelings. Wasn't that what she'd been taught? So why should she criticize her father? If you were going to turn off feelings, you couldn't be selective: closed at work and open at home. She'd found that out herself. Oh, God, Liam, she thought, if only we could have had a second chance. But nothing would have changed. It was only with her son that she was still vulnerable. Oh, yeah? What about Donato? He'd always gotten to her and just proved he still could. After all this time, after everything that had happened, she continued to want his approval, his love. What a joke.

The sound of running feet broke her reverie. She looked down the well of the stairs and saw her father rushing up toward her, his mouth slightly open, face growing pink.

"What is it?" she called.

He waved a hand, signaling that he'd talk when he got to her. Looking down at the top of his head, she saw that he'd lost more hair since the last time she'd noticed. It touched her, made her want to kiss the tonsured spot, but the impulse quickly passed.

"Another murder," he said, puffing a bit, as he reached her. "Fifty-fifth Street in an open parking lot."

Dina wondered why he'd race back to tell her about a murder that wasn't in their jurisdiction. "I don't get it."

He leveled his gaze at her, their eyes connecting. "This one," he said, "was wearing her habit."

Three

Donato pulled his tan Chevy into a lot on Mulberry Street. He felt like hell. It was Friday afternoon and he'd been working for thirty-one hours straight. When he was younger he could work forty-eight, sometimes seventy-two hours without a break and still stay up for another ten or so, eating a big meal at Puglio's with Johnny Amato and Pete Gould, then knocking back some boilermakers at The Kettle of Fish and finally crashing at his mother's, not wanting Renata to see him that way. Now Amato was retired and Gould was dead and he didn't give a damn how his wife saw him.

Billy the Kid, his blue eyes speed-bright, appeared at Donato's side. "Hey, Sarge, how long you stayin'?" He clicked out the words, his mouth dry from drugs.

"An hour, maybe more."

The Kid gave him a salute, opened the car door and slid behind the wheel.

"You take it easy," Donato warned.

"Don't worry, Sarge."

Donato watched him ease the car into a space that looked too small for a Volks bug, let alone his Chevy. Billy the Kid had an eye, all right. He gave the Kid the OK sign and started up the street.

In early September, for the Feast of San Gennaro, Mulberry, between Canal and Broome Streets, was festooned with glittering gold and silver decorations stretched between the buildings like sparkling laundry. But on this April afternoon, the street looked drab, slightly defeated.

This was where he'd grown up, where his mother still lived. Except for the Chinese working their way across Canal, and some fancy new Italian restaurants, it hadn't changed much. The tenements were still the same, chunks of brick and cement filthy from the exhaust of cars and trucks. Old women sat on the steps in front of their buildings exchanging gossip, keeping an eye on the neighborhood. His mother was not among them. She never had been.

Donato turned in at his mother's apartment house. Mrs. Rossi, her face a map of lines like tributaries of a river, sat on her once pink pillow, talking to Mrs. D'Annunzio, an ancient, wizened crone. As they spoke their hands jabbed and sliced the air like birds gone mad.

"*Buon giorno, signore.*"

"*Buon giorno, Michèle,*" they chorused. "*Come sta?*"

"*Molto bene, grazie. E lei?*"

"*Bene.*"

"*Bene.* You go see your mama?" Mrs. D'Annunzio asked.

Donato nodded. It was the same conversation they'd had since he'd married and moved out at eighteen.

"Good boy," Mrs. Rossi said and patted his arm as he passed by them. "Good boy to his mama."

"*Sì, sì, bene.*"

As Donato opened the front door, he heard their clucking tongues and knew they'd soon be reviewing his mother's life, hoping that this time they'd understand, make some sense of the woman they barely knew, the woman they called the Contessa behind her back.

He walked down the dimly lit hall, stopped at the foot of the stairs and leaned heavily against the newel post. The horror of what he'd seen in the last thirty-one hours had caught up with him. The MO of the second murder had been the same as the first. He could still see the second nun, her habit bunched up around her waist, underwear torn away, legs bruised. The bodice of her habit had been ripped apart. Defensive wounds laced her palms, and her ring finger was missing, as Sister Honora's had been. Both nuns, as was customary, had been wearing wedding bands. This one, Sister Angelica, had been propped up against a chain-link fence in a parking lot on East Fifty-fifth, her rosary wrapped around her throat, multiple stab wounds in her chest and stomach. But this murder was even more shocking than the first. Donato suspected it was because she was in her habit, the crisp white wimple around her face still intact. He recalled how he'd wondered about the nuns when he'd been a boy. Were their heads really shaved? Did they pee like everyone else? What did they wear under their habits? Donato found himself thinking of Joey Loprete.

Joey's claim to fame had been doing anything on a dare. Once Big John Orsi challenged him to sneak into the living quarters of the nuns who taught at Sacred Heart and to spend the night under Sister Regina's bed. Joey did. But about two in the morning, he had a sneezing attack, and Sister Regina, thinking the sound she'd heard was from a spiritual presence, jumped from her bed, fell to her knees and started to pray. Then she saw Joey and fainted. Joey's father had punched him all the way from Spring Street down Mulberry to Canal where they lived. But that didn't stop Joey. He took the next dare that came along and kept on taking them until one got him killed, when he tried to cross Manhattan Bridge by way of the cables and fell two hundred and fifty feet into the cold black water of the East River.

Donato remembered Joey had told him that when Sister Regina undressed she did it in such a way that no part of her body was ever exposed. Even *she* was not supposed to see her nakedness.

But Sister Angelica had been exposed to the prying eyes of dozens of investigators, the modesty she cherished in life replaced by seeming abandon in death.

Donato ran a hand over his jaw and felt a stubble of beard. In his long career, he'd seen murders more grotesque than these: bodies black with the long wait until discovery, stomachs exploded by the body's gases, maggots feasting, children tortured. Still, there was something about these murders that transcended all other homicides. It didn't matter what religion you were. The rape and murder of a nun made a chilling statement. It said: all bets are off, nothing is simple, no one is safe.

Slowly, Donato began his ascent. How many times had he climbed these stairs? Thousands, probably. As a kid he'd taken them two at a time. For a moment he wished to be a boy again, telling himself his life was carefree then, but almost at once he realized he was rewriting history. His teens had not been particularly happy. There were the daily humiliations about his mother, withstanding his brother's rages, and his father's cruelty. Those years had been anything but carefree. Still, he felt a kind of nostalgia for them: the music, the films, the girls.

As he always did, he stopped at the door of his mother's apartment and listened. If he heard music or the radio tuned to the Italian station, he knew she'd probably be in good shape. If there was silence, as there was today, he couldn't be sure of her condition. He used his key and closed the door gently behind him.

The apartment was dark and smelled of must and mothballs. The good cooking smells were long gone. Now she ate frozen dinners, if she ate at all. He tiptoed through the kitchen into the living room. She was there by the shade-drawn window, her back to him. Her hair, white since she was twenty-five, unfastened from the usual bun, hung over her shoulders like a shawl. Donato remembered another April day when he'd come upon her like this. He was fifteen years old, and it was a day that had changed his life.

April 12, 1945. He would never forget that date but for a different reason from most people. It began while he was playing the pinball machine at Fabrizio's Luncheonette. Vinnie Sellito had asked him to join him and his friends at a back table. Mike had been astonished because Vinnie, Doc Mancuso and Joey Loprete were his idols, and they'd never included him before.

Vinnie Sellito, almost twenty, was six-four, weighed two-forty-five and worked out every day at Stumpf's gym. He wore his black hair in a pompadour and had big dark eyes. Flat feet had kept him out of the war.

At eighteen Joey Loprete wore thick glasses, had ears that stood out at almost right angles from his narrow head and showed two long front teeth when he talked. But Joey wasn't afraid of anything.

Mike thought seventeen-year-old Doc Mancuso was a sharp dresser. On that day he wore baby blue, pleated pants and a brown, hand-tailored shirt with the collar over a two-tone, big-shouldered, wide-lapeled jacket. Mancuso's features were thick, his jaw square. The only delicate thing about him were his long, dark eyelashes. Once in a while somebody would say Doc had pretty eyes, but they never said it twice.

They'd ordered Mike a cappuccino and a cannoli without asking what he wanted, which would have been all right except he hated Italian pastries.

"Hey, Mike, don't ya like cannolis or what?" Doc asked.

"I'm not real hungry," Mike said softly.

"Who needs to be hungry to eat a cannoli, right, guys?" Joey said.

Vinnie slapped his big hand on the Formica table. "What's wit you guys, huh? The kid wants to eat the cannoli he eats it. If he don't he don't. Don'tchoo got no manners?"

"What's manners got t'do wit it?" Joey asked.

"Everything. Now take this kid, for a for instance. This kid here's got what they call impeccable manners. His old lady is a contessa or somethin'."

Mike felt the sweat form on the back of his neck. People made fun of his mother, said she was stuck-up and thought she was too good for Little Italy, especially for Mulberry Street. But it wasn't manners that made her seem different. It was the other thing. He hoped the guys wouldn't bring that up. Mike tried to smile, but his mouth felt disabled.

From the jukebox, the voice of Jane Froman singing "I'll Walk Alone" rose above the din of the afternoon crowd and Fabrizio shouting orders to the help.

"And you want to know what else this kid's got besides manners?" Vinnie asked rhetorically. "This kid's got some balls. You wanna know why? Okay, I'll tell ya."

Mike couldn't imagine what story Vinnie would tell that would show he had balls. Instead, fragments of humiliations raced through his mind.

"Once upon a time, like a couple a months ago," Vinnie began, "a couple of Jewboys from Hester Street come up to our turf to look around."

Why would Vinnie tell this story? It made no sense. Mike tried to prepare himself for the inevitable results of the tale.

"These two Heebs had been around here before," Vinnie went on, "and they heard this and that about the neighborhood, like ya do, ya know what I mean?"

Doc and Joey nodded.

Mike studied his cup, the milky froth at the bottom popping small bubbles.

"Their names was Saul and Isidore. Brothers. Big guys. Real big," Vinnie emphasized. "So, anyways, they're lookin' around and who do they bump smack into?" He gestured palm up, as though introducing Mike to a waiting audience. "The kid here who's about five-six and weighs maybe one-twenty. Anyways, when these guys bump into our pal, right away they recognize him as who he is, the youngest son of Ottavia Donato . . . the Martyr of Mulberry Street."

Mike wondered what he'd ever done to Vinnie to piss him off so much he wanted to torture him this way.

"Now nobody's around, it's nine o'clock on a Sunday mornin' and everybody's either sleepin' off the night before or in church. Naturally, these two guys bein' Jews they don't have hangovers and they don't give a shit about Sunday. So right off Saul and Izzy start sayin' stuff to Mike about his mama. Like her bein' crazy thinkin' she's seen Saint Anne in her living room, and sayin' her hands bleed like Christ's and that."

The last time his mother had had one of her visions, she'd been put in Bellevue for two weeks. Mike had visited her, and afterward he'd begun having nightmares about the place.

Vinnie went on. "Then this kid here, this kid with balls as big as a gorilla's, he throws a punch and lands one right on Izzy's nose."

"Nice goin', kid," Joey said, slapping him on the back.

"Yeah, great, Mike," Doc added.

"Hold it, you guys. Don't get too fuckin' excited. That punch was the first . . . and the *last* the kid landed."

"Ahhh," the boys said in unison.

Looking at their faces, Mike suddenly suspected that the whole thing had been planned. But he couldn't figure out why or what they were getting out of it.

"It was a slaughter. Those kikes kicked this kid's ass from one end of the block to the next. But the kid kept swingin' . . . missin' but swingin'. And I'm told he never once called for help. Big balls this kid's got." He clamped Mike's shoulder and gently shook him. "But not too smart."

Surprised at this turn in the tale, Mike looked questioningly at Vinnie.

"You wanna know why, Mike? I'll tell ya. Nobody on Mulberry Street needs to get his brains bashed in by some ugly matzoh-eaters from Hester Street. We're all brothers here. We wanna protect ya. *Capisce?*"

"I'm not sure," he said cautiously.

"What I'm tryin' to bring out, Mike, is that me and the guys are gonna make sure ya never get a beatin' like that again. And we're also gonna make sure nobody hits on ya about yer old lady no more. The only thing is ya gotta help us guys out wit one small thing. What about it?"

Saying yes without knowing what Vinnie wanted him to do was risky but saying no was even worse. "Okay," he croaked.

"Good. What did I tell you guys? This kid's got balls the size of a elephant's. Next Thursday night," Vinnie whispered to Mike, "around one o'clock, me and the boys are gonna pay a little visit to Weiser's Brassiere Company. We got the word that Weiser's gets their payroll Thursday afternoon for Friday, and old man Weiser keeps it in his right-hand desk drawer. Now this is where you come in, Mike. There's a small window in the back of this place on Suffolk Street that they always leave open. None of us big lummoxes could get through it, but you could do it like that." He snapped his fingers. "We boost ya up, and ya go through this window in no time. And then ya come round to the front and open the door and we're home free. Ya wanna know what's waitin' up there in that desk? Twenty-five hundret smackers. Divided four ways that's ahh . . ." he started counting on his fingers.

"Six hundred twenty-five," Mike said.

"Look at that, you guys. Ya see how smart the kid is?"

"Yeah, a regular adding machine," Doc said.

Vinnie continued. "Six hundret twenny-five a piece. Ya could do plenty wit' that kinda loot, right, kid?"

Mike had been taught never to steal. It was the Eighth Commandment, and besides, it would kill his father if he got caught, not to mention the beating he'd give him.

"Now if yer scared a gettin' caught, Mike, don't be. That's what's so good about this. We ain't gonna get caught. But in case—I mean ya gotta plan for all kinda stuff, right?—so if ya get caught yer a juvie. Under sixteen. They give ya a kick in the ass and send ya home. Now us it would be different, so ya can see we're the ones takin' all the chances because we really like ya, Mike."

He knew this didn't quite add up but said nothing.

"And here's the beauty part, kid. Old man Weiser is the grandpa a Saul and Izzy." He tipped back his chair, balanced it on two legs, a huge smile cracking his handsome face. "Let's shake on it, you skinny guinea."

Mike did as he was told, knowing that nothing could be worse than shaking on something and then going back on it. His life wasn't going to be worth living if he didn't keep his pledge.

Donato always remembered that when he'd left Fabrizio's that day he'd gone to Sacred Heart Church and prayed for guidance, then to Mr. Georgi's for lentils that his mother wanted. But the grocer was closed so he went around the corner to Vicelli's. He was shut too. Then he saw that most of the stores in the neighborhood were closed. When he got to his building, Mrs. D'Annunzio and Mrs. Campisi were blocking the stoop and crying. Too frightened to ask what was wrong, he pushed his way past them. Inside he took the stairs two at a time, ran down the hall and burst into the apartment.

His mother was sitting there at the living room window, her back to him. Was she having one of her spells? He prayed it wasn't so. "Mama?" he said tentatively. When she turned, he saw that tears streaked her cheeks.

"Mama, what's wrong?"

"*Michèle, mio bambino*," Ottavia Donato whispered.

"What is it, Mama? Why is everyone crying?"

She opened her arms and Mike knelt by her side. Pulling him closer, she crushed his face to her bosom.

He hated it when she did that. Each time he thought he would suffocate. Annoyed, he struggled to get free. "*Che cosa, Mama?*"

"*Presidènte,*" she said. "*Morto.*"

"President Roosevelt?"

"*Sì.*" She let him go, pulled a white lace handkerchief from her sweater pocket and dabbed at her blue eyes, the color of worn beach glass. Then the thumping and dragging sound of crutches made Ottavia jump to her feet. She smoothed down her hair and started for the kitchen.

This wasn't the first time Mike had seen a look of fear pass over his mother's face when Steve was around. Since his brother had come home from Europe, he was a different person. There were even times when Papa seemed afraid of him.

"*Stèfano,*" Ottavia said, "*tu fame?*"

"No," Steve snarled at her. "You think that's all there is to life, eating?" Disgusted, he thumped his way to a kitchen chair.

Mike leaned against the open door frame. Steve was six-four, and Mike remembered his father saying, "The boy is all legs." He wondered if Steve ever thought about that now. His dark good looks had changed since he'd gone away. The mouth that was once so appealing turned down now in a bitter, rigid set.

Steve sat down, his stump sticking straight out, the trouser pinned up as though waiting for the day when he would retrieve his leg. He had refused a prosthesis. When he held out the crutches, his mother scurried over to take them from him. It angered Mike to see how nervous she was around Steve, behaving as though she were an indentured slave.

"You've been crying," Steve accused. "What the hell do *you* have to cry about?"

She turned away and leaned his crutches against the wall.

"I asked you a question."

"*Basta, Stèfano.*"

"*Basta,*" he mimicked. "She cries and I sit here with half a leg." There was no room in Steve's life for any misery but his own.

Ottavia brought her hands together as if she were a supplicant. "*Dio . . .*"

"Oh, shut up," Steve yelled. "Don't give me any of your bullshit religion. I don't want to hear any God's will crap."

"*Sì. Sì, Stèfano.* Don't be bad."

Steve laughed harshly. "Don't be bad, the bitch says."

Mike hated it when Steve used language like that to his mother. "Shut up, Steve," he said, unable to stop himself.

"What did you say, you little punk?"

"You heard me."

"If I had two legs, you wouldn't talk to me that way."

"If you had two legs, *you* wouldn't talk that way. It's not Mama's fault you lost your leg," Mike shouted.

"Is it *my* fault, huh? Whose fault is it then? Huh? Answer me that, you little fucker."

"*Basta, basta,*" Ottavia ordered, clutching her apron as if it were a lifeline.

Mike wanted to kill his brother, to charge across the room and strangle him. But at that moment, his father came home.

"What's going on, eh? I hear you down the hall." Rosario was a tall man with broad shoulders and huge hands. His nose was large but straight, and a black mustache drooped around the corners of his upper lip like Spanish moss. He turned to Mike. "Answer."

Mike shrugged.

"No give me that," he said, shrugging in imitation.

"*Basta, Rosy,*" Ottavia said. "No more."

"*Stai zitta,*" he said to his wife. "Mike, what happen?" His brown eyes, like two small chestnuts, flashed.

Mike knew it was useless to tell his father they'd been fighting because of Steve's language. The man refused to hear anything against his eldest son.

"*Niènte, Papa,*" Steve interceded and pointed toward his crutches. Rosario brought them to him.

They watched in silence as Steve hoisted himself with his

crutches, then slowly thumped his way across the linoleum toward the front door.

"Where you go, Stèfano?" Rosario asked.

"Out."

Mike felt a surge of anger, knowing he could never get away with talking to his father like that. But Steve could do no wrong. And that had been true even before the war.

When Steve was gone, Rosario turned to Mike. "You pick on your brother, a war hero?"

Sick to death of the war hero, and fed up with always taking the blame, he said, "Papa, Stèfano says terrible things to Mama."

Rosario's hand flashed across Mike's face, sending him reeling backward into his mother and onto the floor. "You go to you room! Now!"

He started to tell his father to go to hell, then thought better of it. Rosario was too big to fight with. Instead, he ran down the hall, slamming the door behind him.

Throwing himself across the bed, he furiously pounded his fists into the pillow, but the act only served to frustrate him further. Then, slowly, he began to smile as he remembered Vinnie's proposition. With six hundred and twenty-five dollars, he could get away from both his father and Steve. He didn't like the idea of leaving his mother, but that couldn't be helped. And if he was caught stealing? Papa would be ashamed in front of friends and neighbors, humiliated. A beating would be worth that. His decision was made. On Thursday night he'd climb through the bathroom window at Weiser's.

Donato remembered that night in sharp detail. He'd crawled through the window, slowly made his way toward the front door, then tripped the alarm. Panicky, he'd become lost trying to find his way out. When the two cops found him, he was under a long table partially hidden by a mound of brassieres.

Sal Prato and Jack Breen were the cops. They'd shoved him into their cruiser and played tough, trying to get him to rat on Vinnie and the others. When he wouldn't, they drove off in silence. Donato recalled how scared he'd been, shaking in the backseat, knowing he was going to jail, but more afraid of what his old man would do. The planned humiliation for his father was forgotten.

Prato and Breen had driven him to Prince and the Bowery, where they parked.

"If we book him he'll end up in Sing Sing for a nice jolt. One, two years, maybe," Prato said.

"But I'm a juvenile," Mike protested.

Breen smiled, turning toward him. "What's the matter? Yer friends tell ya nothin' would happen to ya 'cause yer a juvie?"

Prato laughed. "They saw you comin'. But ya seem like a good kid. I never seen ya before. Ya got a sheet?"

Mike shook his head.

"Somebody got ya into this and left ya holdin' the bag thinkin' ya'd keep yer mouth shut and take the fall," Breen said.

Even if that were true, Mike knew his life wouldn't be worth living if he ratted on Vinnie and the others. Whatever the two cops dished out he was ready to take. "So what's gonna happen?" he asked, trying to sound like he didn't care.

"Nothin'," Breen said.

"If you go up, sure as shit yer gonna come outta there hard as last month's salami," Prato explained.

Breen went on. "We ain't in the business of making criminals, kid. And that's what would happen if ya got sent up. So we're gonna let ya go."

Mike couldn't believe it. "How come? What do I have to do?"

"Jesus, we're not all crooks, ya know," Prato said. "You don't have to *do* nuttin'. It's what ya *don't* do. Ya don't hang around no more wit bums, and we don't never pick ya up again, 'cause if we do yer gonna get the treatment, and I don't mean maybe."

Breen jumped out and opened the back door. "Get the hell out."

It was that night, when he was running along Prince to Mulberry, that he made his decision to become a cop. He'd always thought cops were the enemy, rousting kids and making collars to fill their quota. But Prato and Breen had been square with him, and he saw that cops could be the good guys. He would always feel indebted to Breen and Prato. Being a cop, despite everything that had happened to him, was the most important thing in his life.

Donato stared at his mother's back. "Mama?" he said.

The old woman turned, her face heavily lined, the faded blue eyes sunken in a field of olive skin. But even now it was easy to see that she'd once been beautiful, her aristocratic features evident. Donato could not remember her without the white hair. But he'd seen pictures. As a child, he'd loved poring over the old black photograph album.

Even though some of the pictures, taken in Florence, were out of focus, faint, he could see how lovely she was, smiling, radiant. In many she was with her father, looking up at him with adoration. There was only one picture of her mother, who'd died giving birth to Ottavia. She was a regal-looking woman, her aquiline nose the one Ottavia would inherit. Other photos showed his mother with her cousins. Then, in her teens, she was photographed more and more with one handsome boy. Donato had always suspected his mother had had a crush on him, but whenever he asked about this boy, his mother would wave a dismissive hand refusing to answer.

And then there was the wedding picture. She had been sixteen when she'd married his twenty-eight-year-old father. In this photograph, she was somber, her eyes joyless, almost fearful. Over the years, Donato had been able to piece together that the marriage was arranged because her father had lost his money and didn't know what else to do with his only daughter. Rosario Donato had been to America, made some money, come back for a wife and chosen Ottavia. It was clear to Donato that his grandfather had made a terrible mistake because, as far as he could see, Ottavia had never been happy with her husband. Donato often wondered if the early marriage to someone she considered beneath her, a common peasant, had begun her disintegration.

Or had it happened at Ellis Island, when the big crane lifting his mother's trunk from the ship to the pier had dropped it into the water? She'd told him that story over and over when he was a child, stressing that she'd arrived in America with only the clothes on her back, her valued possessions gone to a watery grave.

Then again, maybe something had transpired when he was three and she'd taken him to Italy for two years, leaving Rosario and Steve behind. No one ever mentioned those years in Florence. The one time he'd asked her about it, she'd slapped him (something she never did) and told him never to question her about it again. Although he had no clear memories of that time, he suspected that she'd tried to leave her husband but was unable to make it on her own in Italy.

It galled him that he'd probably never know what had finally tipped the balance for her. All through his teens, he'd longed for the mother he'd had until the age of five. Now he tried to love her as she was even when she made it difficult.

"*Buon giorno, Michèle.*" She smiled and held out a trembling hand to him.

He leaned down and kissed her cheek. "How are you, Mama?"

"*Sta bene.*"

"You didn't do your hair today." He tried to make it sound like a comment rather than a judgment.

She pursed her lips and shrugged.

Are you sure you're okay?"

"*Sì.*"

"Did you have lunch?"

"*Sì.*"

Donato raised the shade, pulled up the worn green hassock and sat at her feet. He took her hand in his. They stayed that way for half an hour, not speaking, looking out the window. When Donato got up to leave, she squeezed his hand and said, "Saint Anne come to me in the night, Michèle. She say to me very dangerous for you now. You be careful."

"Yes, Mama," he said dutifully. He'd long ago given up trying to liberate her from her fantasies. She needed her visions, her imagined stigmata, just as he needed his painting. Neither of them hurt anyone, so what the hell?

"There." She pointed toward a corner of the room. "She stand there. You be careful."

Donato nodded.

Ottavia smiled and closed her eyes. "*Bene,*" she said softly. "*Bene.*"

Donato kissed her good-bye.

Driving uptown Donato put his mother out of his mind, making room for thoughts of his daughter. She looked good. Until seeing her again, he hadn't realized how much he ached for her. Losing Rich was bad enough. He hadn't wanted to lose Dina too.

He should have told her the truth from the beginning. But he'd wanted to protect her. Stupid. You couldn't really protect your kids from anything once they were grown. They were out there on their own, face-to-face with life. That was the way it was supposed to be. Nobody had protected him and he'd done all right. Why the hell had he thought he had the right to shield his daughter from the truth about her own brother? No wonder she was angry with him.

Dina had always been up-front, saying what she thought, knowing what she wanted and not afraid to ask for it. When she was thirteen, she wanted to leave the Catholic school for the public one. Renata was dead set against it, but Dina had laid out her case like a lawyer presenting a brief. She'd been so serious, as if her very breath depended on the outcome of this decision. Having made her case, she'd stared at them, face set, waiting for their answer. He'd agreed, but Renata stayed firm: *the best education was to be had in Catholic school.*

Another kid might have tried to use her father to change her mother's decision. Not Dina. She never resorted to tricks or manipulation. She'd simply kept after her mother month after month, coming up with one new reason after another, until Renata was convinced. It was that quality that made her such a good policewoman. But, oh, how he'd been against her joining the Force.

She'd accused him of chauvinism and, sure, that was part of it. He'd been on the Job for a long time when the department's change in qualifications allowed women on the streets, in action. He was used to working with men, and the few occasions he'd had to work with a policewoman made him uncomfortable. But his reluctance for his daughter to become a cop was purely selfish. He didn't want anything to happen to her. It was that simple. No, not that simple. It was true that he wanted to protect her from harm but there was another ingredient in the mix. Donato didn't think he could survive another loss.

Of course he hadn't said that. People thought all Italians were easily able to show their emotions, but it wasn't true. Not for him, at least. So he'd just played stubborn, let her think he was all the things she called him, hoping in the end she wouldn't defy him. But he should have known better. Dina would always do what she wanted.

On Eighty-first between West End and Broadway, Donato found a parking place. Frank said he had the Midas touch when it came to parking. He got out, locked up and started toward West End, where he'd lived almost all his married life. The place was about to go coop, and Renata was going to buy. Coops on West End Avenue were not attainable on a detective's salary. He supposed if he'd "used his potential," as Renata always said, he might have become an inspector and be making a decent salary. But the four brass stars on his uniform would have been the only shining thing about him. Still, it would be a far cry from the shit of the Ninth.

He opened the front door of his building and walked to the elevator in the back. Jimmy, the operator, was sitting on his camp stool reading *People* magazine. Reluctantly, he put it down and got into the car. They asked each other how they were and each of them said fine. When they got to eleven, Jimmy missed the floor by a few inches and jerked the car down. He went too low and jerked it up again. He'd been operating the elevator for more than twenty years, but he couldn't ever get it right.

Donato walked down the hall toward his apartment. Renata would be out shopping or playing bridge with some of her friends. He was glad. In sixteen hours, he had to go back on duty, and if she'd been home, they'd more than likely get into some hassle. That's all they seemed to do lately. Right now the only thing he could think about was his king-size bed. He unlocked the door, shut it behind him and walked down the hall toward the kitchen. He hadn't eaten anything since the night before. Remembering he'd stashed a salt bagel from H&H in the freezer a couple of days ago, he could almost taste it. Good with some chopped liver he'd also bought. When he turned into the kitchen, he gave a little start. Dina was sitting at the counter.

"Hello, Donato," she said. "Want a cup of coffee?"

Four

He looked so surprised Dina almost laughed. But the purpose of her visit was anything but funny. "I made a pot of coffee."

"I don't drink it anymore. Gives me heartburn." Donato opened the refrigerator and pulled out a carton of milk. Taking a glass from the cupboard he went back to the counter and sat across from her. "This is what I drink now, milk."

It seemed strange. He'd always had a cup of coffee in his hand. He even had it as a bedtime drink. Rich used to say he was the only man he knew who used coffee for a sleeping pill. She remembered having her very first cup with him. Her mother thought twelve was too young, so they'd kept it from her.

"Bet you're thinking about that secret cup of coffee I let you have when you were little," he said.

She was momentarily startled that he'd read her mind, then

recalled that he'd always done that. They'd been so close. "You're a regular Houdini, Daddy." It just slipped out. She hadn't called him that for years.

"Houdini didn't read minds," he said quickly, trying to cover the intimacy.

"Whoever," she said, and looked down at her shoes. Did he always have to correct her? Couldn't he ever just let something go?

"I didn't know you still had a key."

"I didn't know I was supposed to turn it in," she said sharply.

"Take it easy, kiddo."

She felt a wave of delight. It'd been eons since he'd called her kiddo. They were even now.

"I was making a comment, that's all. Don't be so sensitive," he added, distancing himself from her.

"I'm not," she insisted. But she was. She could have kicked herself for allowing his remark, innocent or not, to get to her.

"You were always like that," he said. "Too sensitive about everything."

It was true. As a child, her feelings had been easily hurt. Especially by him. But that was the part he didn't know. When it came to a kid down the block calling her a name, he was her champion, priming her on how to overcome her thin skin, fueling her with self-worth so name-calling wouldn't mean so much. Don't be so sensitive, he'd say; words can't hurt you. But when he'd get mad at her, tell her she was dumb or had two left feet, she'd bite the inside of her cheek and make her eyes go flat so he wouldn't see that his remark meant more, hurt more, than anything anyone else could possibly say to her.

"I don't know how you can expect to be a good cop," he said, "and be so damn thin-skinned."

She swore she wouldn't pick up the bait. Besides, she really wasn't that way anymore. Liam could testify to that. The Job had had its way with her, like any other cop. "I just thought maybe you resented my having a key," she said carefully. She had to watch herself if she were going to get what she wanted.

Donato shrugged.

She lit a cigarette. "You don't smoke anymore either, I noticed."

"Six months."

"Have you stopped drinking, too?"

"I've cut down."

Dina wondered if there was something wrong with him, giving

up smoking and coffee, and it frightened her. She couldn't remember his ever being sick, not even for a day. Mike Donato was supposed to live forever.

"So, what are you doing here, Lieutenant? I can't believe you've come to inquire about my vices." He took a large swallow of milk.

"Do you have an ulcer?"

"No. I like milk. Maybe when you're my age you'll like milk too. They say that when you get old you start being a baby again." He raised the glass as if it were proof.

She wanted to pat his hand but didn't. How easily they'd once touched each other. "You're not old," she said.

"I'm getting there, kiddo."

He *had* aged, she thought. There were darker circles around his eyes, deeper lines from nose to mouth. But he was still a looker. In college, her closest friend was madly in love with him. "You'll never be old, Donato."

For a moment, she thought she saw a glimpse of love, the way he used to look at her when she was a child. But then it was gone, and she wondered if she'd just wanted to see it.

"Look," he said, "if you've come here to talk about . . . any of it, I'm just too tired."

"So am I," she snapped, immediately regretting it. Why had there always been these flash points between them? Was it because they were so different, or too damn much alike?

"Well, what are you doing here, Dina? If you came to see Renata, she probably won't be home until six or seven."

"I know that," she said. "I came to see you."

"So, you're seeing me. What's up?" He finished his milk and set the glass on the counter with a bang.

It had been stupid to come here with some fantasy of reconciliation, a hope of putting the lies, as well as the judgments, on the shelf at least. Worse, she'd come harboring an illusion that a common cause could bring them together, if only for a while. But as long as Donato clung to his position of the injured party, getting to neutral ground was all but impossible.

She grabbed her purse and stood up. "Nice seeing you, Donato . . . as usual."

He laughed. "Pig-headed," he said.

"Why don't you call me a few more names . . . just let 'er rip!" She tried to push past him, but he blocked the doorway. "This is stupid," she said, experiencing the kind of fury she felt with no one else. Then she reminded herself that there was a real purpose to her coming here. She backed up, leaned against the edge of the stool, started right in.

"There's a lot of heat coming down because of these killings. Archbishop O'Connor's been on the phone to the mayor, and the mayor's been on the phone to the PC, who's been on the phone to Halliday, who's been on the phone to Captain Crider. Since we have murders both up- and downtown, Halliday wants me to form a task force to go after the killer. You know how the CD is. He wants to show them we're really doing something."

"So?"

"I want you on the team." She could feel her heart slamming around in her chest. They hadn't worked together since her early years. And then *he* was in charge.

Donato rubbed his eyes. "Who've you got so far?"

She ran down the six names for him.

"Why don't you get Art Scott for the eighth slot?"

"If you turn me down, I'll ask him."

"Scott's good."

"You're better."

He leaned an elbow on the counter and rested his chin on his fist. Then he started gnawing on a finger, something he did when he had to make a decision. She didn't want to rush him, but she didn't want him to think about it too much either. Having her be his boss might be intimidating, emasculating or some damn thing.

She lit another Carlton.

"You ought to quit."

"I have."

"Try again."

"Soon as this case is over. So what do you say, Donato?"

"It wouldn't work. You and me."

Why had she bothered? All it had gotten her was replays of nasty old games and feelings she'd prefer to keep submerged. But she'd been thinking of him, as well as of herself and what was best for the task force. She wondered if he understood. "You know what this could mean to you, don't you?"

"I don't need you to throw me a bone, Lieutenant," he flashed.

"I'm not throwing you a bone," she assured him. "I need you." That was true. The team she'd picked was tops, but it would be even better with her father. "You'd be second whip."

"Wouldn't that look like nepotism?"

"Since when would that be new in the Department? Anyway, who cares?"

"That's the trouble with you, Dina. You've always gone your own way, done anything you wanted, no matter what the consequences."

"If that's true, I learned it from you." She stubbed out her cigarette as if she were trying to murder it.

"What *I* did wasn't self-serving."

"Wasn't it?" she asked acidly.

He ignored her remark. "If you'd thought about anyone but yourself, you'd still be with Liam. You'd be making a proper home for Cal instead of having him grow up with a bunch of baby-sitters."

"Oh, Christ," she said. "You haven't changed one bit."

"Who said I had?"

"I'd hoped. Well, this is where I came in." She grabbed her cigarettes from the counter and started for the kitchen door.

He put out a hand and intercepted her. "You see, Lieutenant, it couldn't work."

"It could work if you'd stop judging me."

"And what about your judgments?"

"I haven't any." A lie.

"No?"

After a moment, she said, "You should've told me, Donato. You should've told me the truth."

There was no need to say what she meant. They both knew.

"You've never understood," he said sadly.

"And I never will understand why you lied to me about Rich's death."

Donato winced.

"Even after all these years, you can't bear to think about the truth, can you?" She experienced an incomprehensible flood of pity for him.

"I guess you'd better go," he said.

She reached out to touch him but he pulled back.

"Oh, hell," she said. "Goddamn it to hell."

Dina sat in her Ford, cooling down. Why did it always go that way? The few times over the last four years when either of them had tried for a truce it had invariably ended with one of them walking out. Each had such a strong need to be right. Liam had always said, "When I'm wrong I'm wrong, and when I'm right who cares?" She'd tried to look at life that way, but it was hard. Especially with her father. And particularly about Rich's death. She would never believe that he'd had a right to keep the truth from her. It wasn't as if she'd been a child; she was in her last year at Hunter, for God's sake.

Would she have joined the Force if she'd known? Her impetus had come from a desire to memorialize Rich. When her father had opposed her, she'd been floored.

"You must be kidding," he'd said.

"Why would I kid about something so important?"

"I thought you were going to be a lawyer."

"I will be. I'll go to school while I'm working."

He laughed derisively. "Do you have any idea how tough that is? I've seen *guys* collapse under the weight of that kind of schedule."

His emphasis didn't escape her. "And some who haven't?"

Reluctantly, he admitted that was so. "It's a tough life, Dina. You don't know what you have to do. The stuff you see. The scum you have to deal with."

"When Rich told you he was going to join, you clapped him on the back and shook his hand."

"That was different."

"Because he was a man and I'm not?"

"Dammit, yes."

She appreciated his honesty. At least she knew what she was up against. "You've always told me I could be anything I wanted. Since I was five you've been telling me that."

"And you can. Did I ever say you shouldn't be a lawyer?"

"No. But I want to be a cop, too. For Rich."

"What do you mean, for Rich?" His eyes reflected the deep hurt of his son's death.

"Oh, Daddy, he wanted you to be proud of him so much. I have to do it for him. He'd want me to."

"That's bull, Dina. Rich didn't want to see women on the Force anymore than I do. Forget it. You're not cut out for the life . . . just drop it."

After that, her motive had changed from memorializing her brother to defying her father. She was determined to prove him wrong, to show him that she could be a good cop, maybe better than he was.

Dina lit a cigarette. So she'd opposed him, become a cop *and* a lawyer. And what had she proved? That she could do it. She wasn't even sure if he thought she was a good cop. Just because she'd made

Lieutenant meant very little in his book. Donato's standards were high. Rank was meaningless to him. If it was his approval she'd wanted, she'd never gotten it . . . probably never would.

But what about her approval of him? When she recalled the cover-up of Rich's death, it made her furious. They'd said that he was shot in the line of duty, that he was a brave young police officer, a hero. Cops sticking together. Then they'd given him the full treatment, a police funeral, the casket closed because of his wounds.

Well, he'd been shot all right but not in a shootout like the two other cops buried that day. He'd killed himself. Put the gun in his mouth and pulled the trigger because he was hooked on heroin and couldn't face the consequences.

Her adored brother had been a junkie, and she'd never guessed, never known how sick he was. How many nights had she lain awake wondering if she might have helped him if she hadn't been so involved with school, so focused on Liam? Too damned many to count.

At the time of Rich's death, she'd been twenty-one, and it was eleven years later when Captain Crider let slip what had really happened. Maybe she wouldn't have been able to handle the truth when Rich died, but her father had had no right to make that decision for her, or for her mother. Dina couldn't forgive him until she understood. Or maybe until he apologized.

She started the car. The hell with it. It was fruitless to go over and over the same ground. She pulled out onto West End Avenue. What she should do now was go home, try to get some sleep before six when she was going to meet with the men and women who were to be in her task force.

But she wasn't tired. The words she'd had with her father had gotten her adrenaline going again. Damn Donato. She really needed him. Maybe if she hadn't gotten into . . . but he'd started it. He'd purposely caused the argument to show her that they wouldn't be able to work together.

Turning the corner, she headed east toward Columbus Avenue. Images of the dead nuns popped into her mind like pornographic pictures. By this point in her career, she'd believed she was inured to brutal murders, but each time she thought of the slain women she felt weighed down, as if she were wearing a wet woolen cloak.

What had triggered the killer? If he was, perhaps, a fallen-away Catholic carting around the bitter detritus of his religious training, why had he exploded now? Or had he murdered before? Another state, another country? If not, if this were new, had he simply passed a nun on the street, unlocking some unwarranted, unforgiven punishment he'd hidden away in his psyche for years? From past experience, Dina knew the reason could be as simple as that or incredibly complex.

Bulletins with the killer's MO had been sent by computer to all the major cities. Background checks on people in the building where Sister Honora was murdered were being run. Neighbors within a two-block radius were being questioned about what they might have seen or heard, as well as being checked through Records to see if any of them had a sheet. Some of them would, and then they would need to establish alibis. A six-block radius was being searched for the murder weapon.

Uptown, the same things were taking place in connection with the murder of Sister Angelica. All the machinery was working, but it was now over forty-eight hours since the first murder. As the clock ticked away, it became easier for the killer to elude them. Still, they might get lucky.

Heading downtown toward her precinct, she decided to stop off in the East Village and check out Home Away from Home, the place where Sister Honora had presumably spent most of her time, and her last day alive.

The main street in the East Village was St. Mark's Place. Between Second and Third avenues, it had a collection of boutiques, two bookstores, a number of restaurants, and the community center that housed HAFH. Time seemed to have stopped on this block. Here Dina always felt she was back in the sixties, a teenager, hanging out with the hippies, drinking espressos, trying pot. She'd come a long way since then, but St. Mark's Place hadn't.

Inside the HAFH quarters, Dina found a large room badly in need of paint. Old couches and worn chairs had been arranged in what looked like an attempt to give the place a cozy feeling. It didn't work. A few kids occupied the seats, smoking and talking. They were dressed in clothes from the forties and fifties, and a few had dyed their hair in bright colors. She approached a boy sporting a pink mohawk.

"Excuse me," she said.

The boy, who couldn't have been more than fourteen, looked up at her with a surly expression. "Yeah?"

"Are you a member of HAFH?"

He snickered and glanced at his friends, then back at her. His brown eyes were dead, like two bullet holes. "There's no members, lady. You don't join nothing."

"Do you like it here?"

Lighting a cigarette, he blew a plume of smoke in her direction. "Who wants to know?"

She ignored his question and turned to a small girl with freckles across her nose. Her hair was green on one closely cropped side, and on the opposite part, which hung past her shoulder, purple.

"What's your name?"

The girl looked at her suspiciously. "Sunshine."

It was like naming a fat person Tiny. "How long have you been here?"

"In the world?" the girl asked snidely.

"Here. At the center." She tried not to show her annoyance.

"Today?"

"Don't give me a hard time," she said.

"Why not?" asked an overweight girl with no eyebrows.

"Who are you?"

"Lily. What're you hassling us for?" She poked a black boy next to her and gave him a nod.

Dina watched as the boy walked to the back of the room and went through a madras-draped doorway. In a moment, he returned with a tall, thin woman in her forties. Her blonde hair was short and frizzy. A pair of half-glasses hung around her neck on a brown cord. She was dressed in a white, long-sleeved blouse and a loose denim jumper. In other circumstances, Dina might have thought she was pregnant.

"I'm Sister Margaret. May I help you?" she asked energetically.

Dina showed her shield and explained why she was there.

"Shoulda known," Lily said disgustedly.

The others murmured agreement.

Sister Margaret asked Dina to accompany her to the other side of the room.

"The children are very upset about Sister Honora's death," she said.

"I'm sure they are." It was hard for Dina to think of her as a nun. The ones she'd known had all worn habits and seemed ancient, arid. This woman was vital. "Can you tell me if any of them are known to be violent?"

"You don't suspect the children, do you?"

"A month ago, I arrested two children who'd murdered an old man for six dollars. The kids were ten and twelve."

Sister Margaret closed her eyes for a moment as if she might erase the ugliness of Dina's words. "What is it you want?" she asked, a slight churlishness creeping into her voice.

"I'd appreciate it if you could make up a list of any of the children you think might be violent."

"Oh, no. I couldn't do that."

"We're dealing with a homicide, Sister," she said, feeling impatient but keeping it in check. "A very brutal homicide. You may be in danger yourself. Who else works here besides you and Father Briney?"

"No one. It was just the three of us. Now there are only two," she said, as if it had just occurred to her.

"When was the last time you saw Sister Honora?"

"On Wednesday. She left about three."

"Did she always leave at that time?"

"I've been asked these questions before, you know."

Dina forced a smile. "Yes, I know. And you'll probably be asked them again by someone else, maybe even me."

"We all left at different times depending on our schedules, what was going on."

"Was she supposed to leave at three that day?"

"No. She said she wasn't feeling well. She was only going to stay another two hours so I told her to go." Sister Margaret's eyes sharpened, as though she'd suddenly seen something in a new way. "Maybe if I'd told her not to—"

"Don't do that to yourself," Dina interrupted. "It can only hurt you. Besides, this doesn't seem like a random killing, considering the murder of the other nun. Is there any chance that Sister Honora was meeting someone and using illness as an excuse?"

The woman's lips compressed into a tight line. It was the way Dina remembered nuns' mouths.

"Sister Honora was not a liar, Lieutenant."

"I'm sorry. I have to ask." How many times had she apologized to people, explaining herself, her work? "Did she ever mention anyone she regarded as an enemy?"

"She loved everyone."

That, Dina thought, was probably what had killed her.

She continued questioning the nun about Sister Honora's life but learned nothing more. "I'd like you to make up that list of possibly violent kids," she said finally.

"But I'd be betraying them. Most of these children never trusted anyone until they came here."

"Sister Margaret," Dina said wearily, "I don't want to take you into the station for questioning, but if you don't cooperate that's what I'll be forced to do."

The woman bit at her top lip. "All right," she sighed. "I'll try to do it."

"Don't *try*. Do it."

"You're a hard woman," Sister Margaret shot back, her hand immediately flying to her mouth as though to stem the harsh evaluation.

Dina was surprised to be wounded by the nun's assessment.

"I'm sorry, I shouldn't have said that. I'm sure you're just doing your job."

Sister Margaret wouldn't have said she was hard had she been a man. Dammit, she *was* just doing her job.

"I'll send someone for the list," Dina said curtly. "Thank you for your cooperation." She'd be damned if she was going to give Sister Margaret absolution.

Back on the street Dina crossed to the downtown side and decided that as long as she was here she'd look up Florida Bob, one of her snitches. She'd met him years ago during a plainclothes detail in Times Square, when Florida Bob was a pitchman for the game of Fascination. He'd been working the parlors on Broadway and Forty-second Street, had been for eleven years.

"I like the feeling it gives me," he said. "Like I'm in control. I'm watching the boards, watching the assholes throwing their balls, and I'm telling them what's going down. And then, too, I'm getting the assholes in there, which I'm promising it's gonna be good, that it's easy to win. I tell 'em what kinda shit they're gonna go home with. And all the time I'm legit. See what I mean?"

When Florida Bob wasn't pitching, he was pulling cons. He was strictly a small-time grifter, nothing bigger than a thousand-dollar score at one time, and that was rare.

Dina found him in a back booth at Augie's, reading the *Post* and sucking on a Ballantine. As usual, he wore his uniform of a tight black T-shirt and weary jeans. In his early sixties, his skin was deeply tanned, and his face had taken on the look of the carved coconuts tourists brought back from Hawaii. He'd gotten his nickname because no matter what time of year it was, Florida Bob was always tan, and also because as long as anyone could remember, he'd been planning to move to Florida. He'd never been there.

"Hey, Lieut," he said, as she slid into the booth across from him, "how ya doing?"

"Okay. How about you?"

"Can't complain. Ya see this?" He held up the paper. The headline read SISTER SLASHER UPTOWN, DOWNTOWN.

Both press and cops seemed to have a need to give murderers appellations, the way teens christened cars or families named summer cabins: Cozy Cottage, Mouse House, Buoys and Gulls.

"Yours?" he asked, raising one silvery eyebrow.

"Yes."

"Hey, I don't know from this, Lieut."

"I thought you might hear something."

"Hey, not me. This is outta my line, which I thought ya knew. Ya wanna hear about somebody doing Twenties or Three-Card Monte ya come ta me. But murder? No way."

"Sometimes you hear things."

"Yeah, sure. But this gotta be a loon, wastin' two sisters. That's sacrilege."

"One of the nuns worked down here at the center across the street. You ever go in there?"

"You kidding? Me? What would I go in a joint like that for?"

"Maybe you could start," she said.

"Ah, come on, Lieut. Gimme a break. That's strictly for the rummies and kids."

Dina slid a twenty across the table. "I just want you to keep your eyes and ears open."

Florida Bob put his hand over the bill, and it disappeared as if he'd performed a magic trick. "Lieut, here's the thing the way I see it. To me, I truly believe this asshole's gotta be mental, ya know what I mean? And a thing like this he does it alone. He don't talk ta nobody. Nobody talks ta him. So there's nothin' for me ta hear."

Dina slipped out of the booth. "Hang around the center. Make friends with some of the kids." She knew he was good at that. Everybody liked Florida Bob. "But don't pull any cons on them."

"Hey, Lieutenant, would I do that to little innocent kids?"

She looked directly into his eyes, said nothing.

"Okay, okay. I'll give it a shot. I hear anything I'll get in touch. 'Course I might not be around too much longer. I got something goin' which might take me ta Florida. Strictly legit, Lieut," he added quickly.

She wasn't interested in the scam, whatever it was. "This is important, Bob."

"Hey, I know that. I'll do my best, but it's a unlikely situation."

Dina said good-bye, left the bar and walked toward Second Avenue. Her father's words about Cal kept nagging at her. Donato never forgot that his mother, unbalanced as she was, had always been there when he came home from school, and his wife had done the same for their children. But Dina's life was more complicated. She had nothing to be guilty about: she spent as much time with her son as she could. Donato could just stuff it.

Gem's Spa, on the corner of Second Avenue and St. Mark's, was the neighborhood sundries store. It boasted a really good egg cream and carried every magazine imaginable. The phones were on the outer wall of the St. Mark's side. She dropped in a quarter, dialed the Sixteenth Precinct, and asked for Art Scott. The desk sergeant told her Scott was on vacation and wouldn't be back until Monday. She ran the disconcerting news over in her mind as she called her own precinct to check in. Captain Crider told her Halliday had been trying to reach her all afternoon. He wanted to see her forthwith.

"What about?" she asked.

"Your task force."

It was typical of Halliday. He gave her a free hand, then wanted to meddle before she'd even begun.

"Better get down there on the double," Crider said.

After she hung up, she went into the store, had a chocolate egg cream, smoked a cigarette and looked through *Us* and *The Atlantic.* Then she bought *The New Yorker,* walked slowly back to her car and headed downtown to One Police Plaza.

The Chief of Detectives, Hugh Halliday, was a lean man in his middle forties. His once blond hair was a pallid gray, and his long nose had been broken more than once. Blue eyes under bushy eyebrows were cold and forbidding. He wore a charcoal gray suit, a pale pink shirt and a red tie with a dark gray stripe. His gold tiepin was a bar with a musical clef. He sang in a barbershop quartet.

Dina didn't like Halliday. At first she'd been taken in by his Irish charm, but that had changed as she got to know him and watched him relish Donato's reassignment following the Peak case. She knew Halliday didn't like her much either, and it wasn't just because she was Mike Donato's daughter. He simply didn't care for women who weren't enamored of him.

Leveling a gelid gaze at her, Halliday toyed with a paper clip, unbending its curves. "I'd liked to know who you've picked for your task force," he said.

She gave him the names. "I tried to get Art Scott for the eighth, but he's on vacation."

His eyebrows shot up. "Not your father?"

The question unnerved her. That wasn't good. Dina wanted always to be in control around Halliday. "No, not my father."

"You two still at each other?" he asked with an arrogant smile.

It was common knowledge in the department that she and Donato weren't on good terms, but not many knew why. She wondered what Halliday had heard. "I don't know what you mean," she answered. She hated the thought of his knowing anything about her private life.

"I think you do. You shouldn't let personal grievances interfere with your work. Donato's a good detective despite what happened on the Peak case. I had no choice but to reassign him, you know. In fact, you might say I protected him."

It was true that things could have been much worse for her father if Halliday had made public Donato's part in the Peak case. On the other hand, the less fuss the better for Halliday's image. If he was trying to make her believe what he'd done was altruistic, he wasn't succeeding. She said nothing.

Irritated by her lack of response, he said abruptly, "I'm recommending you make Donato your eighth man."

Dina hadn't asked for a recommendation and she didn't want Halliday muscling in on her assignment. She also didn't want him to know her father had refused her. "I'd prefer someone else."

"Can't you two put your differences aside?" he asked. "I don't have to tell you what an important case this is."

"No, you don't." Dina watched him smooth out the paper clip so that the metal formed a straight line. She wondered what he'd think if he knew she wanted his job. Halliday prided himself on being contemporary, but she knew it would never occur to him that someday a woman might be chief of detectives.

"So that's it then," he said. "I recommend that you ask Donato to complete your team."

"Are you ordering that I ask Donato?"

"I'd rather think of it as a suggestion."

She'd had Halliday's suggestions before; this was an order. It was too late now to tell him she'd already asked Donato and been refused. She'd have to pretend she was following orders, tell her father and let him handle Halliday. "I'll ask him."

"Good. And remember . . . we've got a savage killer on our hands." Dina watched as Halliday switched gears and went into the

"Chief Who Cares" mode. "This is a man so deranged, so immoral, that he'd interfere with a woman of God without a thought. To get him we've all got to pull together."

Dina wanted to throw up.

"You and Donato have to put the safety of these nuns before your own . . . difficulties. Do you know what I'm saying, Lieutenant?"

"I think so, Chief."

"Good." He picked up a sheaf of papers and riffled them as though he were about to begin working.

Dina didn't stay to see the "Chief with Important Work" expression. She'd had enough.

The squad room in the First Precinct looked like every other squad room in New York. It was a large rectangle, fenced and gated as if the employees needed to be penned. The blue paint was peeling, and the neon light gave off a sad glow. Desks were shoved together toward the middle. The detention cage was on the left wall; the fingerprint desk in the back of the room. On the right was a small kitchen, and next to that was the lieutenant's office.

Dina sat at her desk waiting for her task force members to arrive. She'd tried her father several times, but there was no answer. Later, she'd phone Crider and ask his advice about an eighth member. The captain was a good man, and she'd have no problem telling him what had taken place with Halliday and that her father had refused her request.

There was a short rap on her door. It was John Pesetsky. In his late thirties, divorced, the father of two, Dina liked him because he was thorough. A good detective went over and over things, even when it seemed useless. Pesetsky was that kind of cop.

Three others arrived. Marv Lachman was single and the youngest at twenty-nine. People smiled when they looked at him, because his hair was brown and his mustache red. Two years before he'd been given his shield when he'd risked his life by staying with a woman trapped beneath the debris of a fallen building until she could be rescued. Lachman wasn't afraid of taking risks, and that made him invaluable.

Judy McCarthy and Dina had been at the Academy together and were close friends. They'd been among the first women to make detective first grade. Several times Judy had been offered modeling jobs but turned them down. All she'd ever wanted to be was a cop, much to her family's horror. She was a brilliant interrogator: something about her made criminals and witnesses alike tell more than they'd intended.

Roy Bobbin was black and the oldest at forty-nine. He'd done his twenty and more. Happily married, he was the father of five. Bobbin was a huge man, but graceful, and handled himself with ease in tight situations. Nothing ever ruffled him.

The last two, Bobby Keenan and Alma Delgado, squeezed into her small office.

"We'll meet at the One-Three on Twenty-first Street after this," she told them. That was the main office, the Bureau of Manhattan Detectives. Everything was available to them there, and the offices were far more spacious.

Keenan was almost a stranger to Dina. The one time she'd met him she hadn't been impressed. He'd seemed arrogant and too aware of his good looks. But Pesetsky said he was a crackerjack detective so she'd put her personal feelings aside. If Halliday knew that, he'd think she was a good girl.

At thirty-six, Keenan was a six-footer with a solid build. Blue eyes flecked with green were both sensual and sad. When he looked at her, she felt uncomfortable. A dark smudge under his left eye could have been dirt or a fading bruise; she couldn't tell.

Alma Delgado was thirty-two and the first member of her family to graduate from college. She was short, five-four, and very thin. Dina used to wonder if she were an anorexic. But then she met Delgado's family at a cop picnic. Both male and female Delgados looked as if they were made of kindling. Delgado was tenacious and amazingly agile.

The task force members had been culled from precincts all over town. Dina was convinced they'd make a terrific team. She told Pesetsky and Delgado they'd be partners, paired Lachman with Bobbin and Keenan with McCarthy.

"Okay, let me tell you what we have so far. It's not much. Forensic is still making tests, but the preliminary . . ."

The phone rang.

Dina looked through the glass into the squad room. She'd asked to have her calls held. Paul Bishop had the phone to his ear and was motioning for her to pick up. Perturbed, she lifted the receiver.

"What is it?" she snapped.

Bishop said, "Listen, I'm sorry to interrupt, but the call's from . . ."

"I said I didn't want to be interrupted for *any* reason."

"Yeah, I know, Lieutenant, but it's your dad. He said it was important."

Immediately she thought of Cal. "Put him on," she said. Her hand felt sweaty on the receiver. "Yes, what is it?" she asked abruptly.

"If the offer's still good," Donato said, "I'd like to join the team."

Surprised, she was silent for a moment, then asked him where he was.

"On Thirty-eighth and Ninth."

She knew he'd walked there from West End Avenue. Walking and thinking it over. That had always been his way. "Okay," she said. "I'll expect you in fifteen minutes." She hung up. It was what she had wanted and now she felt scared.

The six detectives waited expectantly.

"That was Mike Donato," she said. "He's joining the team."

They were silent. All of them knew that Dina and Donato barely spoke and hadn't worked together for years.

Bobbin broke the silence. "Who will Donato partner with, Lieutenant?"

She hesitated only a moment. "Me," she said. "Donato will partner with me."

Five

When he stepped out of the shower, he could tell he felt much better than he had. A workout for half an hour on his Nautilus had done the trick. Spending most of the day with Tyler Mead, a client, always took it out of him. Mead lived on the North Fork of Long Island, and whenever he came in to the city, he wanted to "do the town." Doing the town consisted of going from bar to bar and swilling down cuba libres. The last time Mead had been in, at the end of the evening, he'd stopped on every street corner and yelled out, "Hello, New York, Tyler's here!"

Displays like that were embarrassing. One of the reasons he liked living in New York was that you could remain anonymous if you wanted. It hadn't been like that in Grand Haven, Michigan, where he'd grown up. There, everybody knew what you were doing every minute. He smiled. Well, not *every* minute.

Vigorously, he rubbed the thick maroon towel across his back from shoulder to waist. At thirty-eight, he didn't have an extra drop of fat on him. Besides his workouts at home, he played racquetball every Tuesday evening and swam several times a week at his health club.

At least he'd been able to get out of seeing *Oh! Calcutta!* with Mead. Instead, he'd had lunch with him at Sardi's. He'd lied to Mead just the way he'd lied to his wife, using one as an excuse with the other. He needed time to himself. By Thursday night, he'd been so beat he'd fallen into bed without even eating, and then he'd had Mead all day today. There'd barely been a moment for reflection.

In the bedroom, he took a black Ralph Lauren polo from the second drawer in his chest, put it on and then pulled on a pair of white carpenter's pants over his jockey shorts, finally strapping on his Rolex. He put on white socks and slipped into a pair of black Reeboks. After they were tied, he brushed his gray-streaked blond hair straight back, then shook his head so the hair fell casually from a left-sided part. Grinning, he scrutinized his even white teeth in the mirror, making sure there were no unsightly snippets of food remaining, although he'd brushed and flossed half an hour before.

It was funny, but after all this time he still got a surprise when he looked at himself. He continued to expect an awkward, slightly plump teenager wearing glasses to look back at him. But what he saw was a man with a straight nose, flawless skin, and blue eyes that were large and thickly lashed, the brows perfectly arched, as if they'd been tweezed.

By his second year in college, he'd begun to change, and by his junior year, girls were going crazy over him. Yet year after year his good looks continued to astonish him. He'd read somewhere that very fat people who'd lost enormous amounts of weight continued to think of themselves as fat no matter how thin they got. He supposed his insecurity about his looks was similar.

In the beginning, his wife had nagged him, wanting to see what he'd looked like when he was a kid, but he told her there'd been a fire in the house in Grand Haven and all the pictures had burned. When his mother met her, she went along with it because she did anything he asked her to. It was a good thing the old man was dead because he'd never gone along with anything that was his son's idea. He constantly told him that he was shiftless and a dreamer and wouldn't amount to anything. Well, he'd fooled the old shithead . . . fooled him in several ways.

He walked down the hall to the kitchen. From the refrigerator, he got a bunch of organically grown carrots. Standing at the pine counter he chopped off the ends, tossed them into the sink and pushed down on the garbage disposal, listening as it voraciously sucked in the carrot ends.

After running water over the carrots, he fed them one by one to his juicer. Like Christians to a lion, he thought. Finished, he poured himself a glass of juice and leaned against the counter while he drank it.

He liked being in the apartment alone. Smiling, he thought about how he'd maneuvered the whole thing: getting his wife to take three vacation days from her PR job, and taking the girls out of school, promising to give them extra time to make up for the previous weekend. Then at breakfast on Wednesday morning, the day they planned to leave, he'd dropped his little bombshell.

"I'll come out late Friday night," he'd said.

"Oh, sure," she sulked. "Just like you drove out last Friday night."

"I couldn't help that," he said. "I had to work."

"I don't understand what a financial consultant does on weekends. I mean, the Exchange is closed, so what do you do?"

"I don't only work during trading hours. Christ, you ought to know that by now." He patted his lips with the yellow linen napkin.

"What I know," she said incisively, "is that you promised me and the girls we'd have a long weekend together before the tourists come and it takes twelve minutes to turn onto the Montauk Highway from your own street."

"I shouldn't have promised. I'm sorry. I can't help it that Mead's coming in on Friday."

"Oh, fuck Tyler Mead."

Then he'd calmed her down, telling her he'd keep his promise to drive out on Friday night. Living with her was becoming harder all the time. Still, it was important that he stay married, particularly now. Being married and the father of two girls was good for his image. The company expected that. He didn't mind sharing the apartment with the girls, but his wife made demands. It had been hard enough all these years, playing the game, servicing her. Even before the accident he was having trouble. Now it might be impossible. The accident.

An image flashed in front of him like a colorful slide. He felt himself stir. Quickly, he erased the picture, finished his juice, rinsed the glass and put it in the dishwasher. He picked up his set of keys from where he'd tossed them when he came in and went to his study. From now on he'd have to be more careful about the keys. He couldn't just leave them lying around as he had in the past. No one, to his knowledge, had ever used them, but he couldn't take chances anymore.

His office, which he'd decorated himself, was done in shades of blue. An indigo velvet couch was against one pale blue wall. The matching easy chair, with a chrome standing lamp next to it, faced the couch. His desk was white, the armchair chrome and navy. Near the desk was a white, four-drawer filing cabinet.

Before he sat down, he locked the door. Even though no one was home, he wanted to get himself into the habit. There'd been several occasions when his wife had knocked once, then barged right in. Sitting in his comfortable chair, he stretched out his legs. He wanted to delay as long as possible. It was something he'd always done.

On hot days, when he was a boy and dying of thirst, he'd buy a cold Coke at the candy store on the corner, bring it home, put it in the fridge and sit daydreaming on the back steps, forcing himself to wait until he couldn't stand it any longer. Then he'd grab the Coke and slug it down, almost choking himself. Often, he did the same thing when he had to pee. He'd wait until it became so painful he'd cry. But when he'd finally allow himself to go, he'd shudder with pleasure.

He glanced at his filing cabinet. No, he mustn't think about that yet. Postpone. Delay. He'd think about his wife. That was bound to keep the other in check.

From the beginning, he'd had to pretend with her. As if he were preparing for a role, he'd watched other men with their wives, studied them until he knew what to say, how to touch, when to give in, hold back. It was the same in everything he did. In his college drama club, the others had called him a quick study. What no one understood was that after years of perfecting his imitative skills to get along in life, learning a part for a play was nothing.

The hardest part with his wife was having to fuck her. Still, he'd managed. Then that stupid accident, one thing leading to another, and suddenly he remembered. It wasn't that he'd forgotten, how could he have? He simply hadn't thought about it for almost twenty years. The total recall had rendered him impotent and the third time it happened she became upset.

"*Again?*" she'd said.

"I'm sorry, baby," he lied, trying to sound and look like Steve McQueen at his most boyish.

"This is getting me suspicious."

"What's that mean?" He wanted to smash her face with his fist.

"Are you seeing someone else?"

He started to laugh and rolled off her, the laughter coming in wave after wave.

"What's funny?" she asked, hurt.

He couldn't stop.

"You've never been much good," she lashed out defensively, "but this is ridiculous."

He stopped. "How would you know if I'm good or not?" They'd met and married young. She'd been a virgin.

"How do you think?"

He knew she was trying to make him jealous. She wasn't the type to cheat, but if she had he couldn't have cared less. He'd turned over, and she'd left the room and hadn't come back. The next morning he learned she'd slept in the guest room. He knew how he was supposed to behave, so he went to her and, like Spencer Tracy, asked for her forgiveness and patience, blaming his impotency on business pressures. He learned a lot from movies and television.

Now he glanced at the filing cabinet, then quickly looked away. It was too soon. He counted to a thousand by twos. Next he said the alphabet forward and backward. He counted again, this time to two thousand. Finally, he could wait no longer.

His heart was beating so hard he was frightened for a moment. Rising slowly, he took the keys from his pocket. With a shaking hand, he unlocked the cabinet. Bending down, he pulled out the bottom drawer. Covering his treasure was a plaid scarf, which he slowly removed. The top of the lid said HELLMANN'S MAYONNAISE. Picking up the jar he heard the alcohol slosh from side to side. Not looking at the thing in his hands, he kicked the drawer shut.

Back at his chair, he sat down, eyes closed. When he was settled he rested the jar on his knees. Very slowly, he opened his eyes and sucked in his breath as if what he saw were a surprise: floating in the jar were two fingers, each circled by a gold wedding band.

Six

In a jammed, hot and smoky room at One Police Plaza, Hugh Halliday, his hair freshly trimmed, suit perfectly pressed, faced a group of television and newspaper reporters. Microphones were grouped in front of him like a grotesque bouquet, while cameras turned. Wearing a stylish but sensible mauve suit, Dina stood slightly behind him.

Leaning against a wall in the back of the room, Donato wondered if Halliday would let Dina say anything or if he'd hog the whole conference for himself. Then swiftly, he realized the CD would be handing over this hot potato as quickly as possible. Later, when they'd solved it, Halliday would take the credit.

The Chief of Detectives cleared his throat, touched the knot of his tie as if it were a talisman. "Ladies and gentlemen, I know that some of you believe that we've been avoiding you, and I'll be honest with you—you're right." He laughed but no one joined him. Quickly, he tried to cover his gaffe by creasing his brows, creating an important, serious frown. "For the last forty-eight hours, we've been working around the clock and the truth is, we just haven't had time for this kind of conference. To be perfectly candid, we really haven't had anything to give you until now."

Donato wondered what it was they had to give. Nothing much had come to light since the first few hours after the murders.

"The moment the second murder was discovered," Halliday went on, "I formed a special task force to look into these killings."

Donato smiled at the implication that Halliday was out there, heading things up, running the show.

"As you all know, Thursday morning at six-ten A.M. the body of Sister Angelica was found in a parking lot on East Fifty-fifth Street, and at nine-fifteen A.M. the body of Sister Honora was found in her apartment at 609 East Sixth Street. Each victim had been stabbed repeatedly as well as sexually assaulted." He was silent a moment allowing time for his audience to create a picture, letting the horror sink in. "As I said, I've formed a special task force, and now I'm going to let Lieutenant Donato, who's heading it, answer your questions."

Dina stepped up to the microphones as Halliday slid smoothly into the background. Donato knew she'd faced the press before, but this was probably the most explosive case she'd ever handled. The delicate balance needed to keep the media at bay was not going to be easy.

"I don't have anything to add to Chief Halliday's statement," Dina said. "Let's just begin." She pointed to David George of the *Times*.

"As far as we've been able to ascertain, Lieutenant, you have no suspects. Is that right?"

Donato felt for her. She couldn't lie, but she couldn't say she hadn't the damnedest idea who it might be, either.

"We're putting together our forensic evidence, trying to find out what the victims were doing on the day and night in question, building a picture of the killer," Dina said silkily, and turned away from George. "Ms. Maio."

"How about motive, Lieutenant?" asked Kathi Maio of the *Post*.

"I'm afraid I could only give you conjecture there, but we're talking to everyone who knew the victims even slightly. A motive will surface."

The NBC correspondent, Stan Burns, was next. "So you believe there's only one killer?"

"Yes."

"Could a priest have killed these women?" the *USA Today* reporter, Rusty Burke, asked.

Donato understood why she hesitated. If she said yes, she'd alienate the whole archdiocese of New York. But she'd be lying if she said no.

"Anyone could have killed them," Dina dodged, immediately calling on Jeff Smith of *Newsweek.*

"Were these premeditated murders?"

"It would appear so."

"Then," Smith said contentiously, "there *has* to be a motive."

"I didn't say there *wasn't* one, Mr. Smith. I just said we weren't willing to speculate about it yet." She looked to the back of the room and called on the ABC correspondent. "Can we assume that the police have no solid leads?" Dorothy Nathan asked provocatively.

Dina said, "You shouldn't *assume* anything, Ms. Nathan."

The reporters laughed. Halliday looked irritated. Donato knew it wasn't shrewd for Dina to appear to be a smart-ass. "Do you think the killer will hit again?" Don Doerrer of CBS asked.

Nobody needs this question, Donato thought. If you had a psychopath on your hands, chances were ninety-nine to one that he'd kill again. But who the hell wanted to say that?

"There's no way for us to know what the killer will do next."

"Can you rule out the possibility of another killing, Lieutenant?" Maio asked.

"No," Dina said simply.

"So what's being done to protect other nuns?" David George again.

"We're taking every precaution we can to safeguard them."

"Would you say then," asked Burke, "that the nuns in New York have nothing to fear?"

It was a rotten question, designed to embarrass her. Donato knew if he'd been in her shoes he probably would've popped the guy in the nose and stormed out.

"I wouldn't presume to say that about *anyone* in New York, Mr. Burke."

The reporters laughed again, and this time Donato wished he could applaud.

Dina hurriedly went on. "That's about all we have time for now. But I would like to ask anyone who knows anything about these crimes to come forward. You can be assured the information you give will be confidential."

Dina was driving. Donato had offered to take the wheel, but she'd refused. In the past, Dina had hinted that she didn't like his driving, discounting that it was he who had taught her. She claimed he drove too slowly. Maybe he did. Maybe it was true that as people got older they became more afraid. Less life to live made it more precious.

When he'd turned fifty, he'd stopped finishing books he didn't like. There wasn't enough time. It had nothing to do with being a cop, fearing life could end prematurely. This was an ordinary human feeling, a fear of loss, infirmity. On the other hand, maybe he'd live to be ninety-six and die goosing a girl on the street, like his grandfather. Except he didn't goose girls. But who could be sure what he'd be like at ninety-six?

What he *was* sure of, was that sitting in such close proximity to his daughter made him uneasy. Perhaps wanting to be in on the case may have muddied his thinking. Hoping to get out of the Ninth, he'd tried to bury the hatchet, and now it felt like it was firmly planted in his skull. He'd tried to tell her what a swell job she'd done with the press, but she'd sloughed it off as if his opinion didn't count. How the hell were they going to work together with so much animosity between them?

"This is it," Dina said, as she pulled over.

Donato stared across the street instead of at the convent.

"What is it?" she asked.

"The church," he said. "It's the Little Church Around the Corner."

"Oh, that's right," she said softly. "You were married there."

He turned to look at her. She didn't resemble Renata, but her beauty made him recall his wife's. For a moment, a feeling of love for Renata buoyed his spirits, then made him sad.

They got out of the car and walked up to the secured steel and glass front door of the three-story brick convent. Dina rang the bell.

A clicking sound heralded the unlocking of the door, and she pushed it open. There was a small lobby and a second door. Through a window beside it, they could see a young nun at a desk, a television monitor above her displaying the front entrance.

"They aren't taking any chances," Donato said. It was clear that the Sisters of St. Paul had protected themselves against the outside world before Sister Angelica's murder.

They stood in front of the glass partition and showed their shields. The nun's muddy brown eyes widened, and a blush colored her cheeks as if she were embarrassed. She buzzed them through the second door.

At the desk, Dina said, "We'd like to see the Mother Superior."

"Do you have an appointment?"

"No. It's about Sister Angelica's . . . murder," Dina said, failing to find a more delicate way to put it to this seemingly fragile creature.

The nun blinked and tented her hands on the desk. "It's Saturday," she said, as if murders, like people, should have weekends off.

"Yes, Sister," Donato said gently. "But we need to speak with the Mother Superior."

"Well, if you'll take a seat I'll see if Mother's free."

Four gray metal chairs had been placed against the opposite wall. While they waited, Donato took out his notebook and went over the items presented at the task force's meeting after the news conference.

Sister Angelica had been stabbed with the same type of weapon used in Sister Honora's murder: a long thin blade like a boning knife. She, too, had been raped. Her rosary was tied around her throat after death and her ring finger severed. But the most startling part of the autopsy report was that she'd been killed some time between midnight and six in the morning on Thursday. What was a Sister of St. Paul doing out alone after midnight?

No weapon or severed finger had been found in a ten-block search of drains, catch basins and garbage cans. No witnesses had come forward. That didn't mean there weren't any. It was still early.

A stray blond pubic hair had been found mingled with Sister Honora's. Another, gray, had been discovered in Sister Angelica's. The hairs belonged to the same man. Tests revealed that the killer was a man in his late thirties, early forties and that he was Caucasian.

A green cotton thread had been found clinging to Sister Angelica's habit. In time Forensic would break that down to the type of thread, the origin and the make. But it wouldn't find them a suspect. It was only good if they could match the thread to something in a suspect's wardrobe.

The thrust of the knife showed that the killer was at least six feet tall and that he was strong.

Not much. Thousands of men in New York City could fit the profile they had so far. Donato flipped his pad shut and dropped it into his jacket pocket.

"How many times have you read your notes since this morning?" Dina asked.

"About fifty," he said, smiling.

"And?"

He made a circle with his thumb and fingers. "Zee-ro."

"Me, too. Maybe Pesetsky and Delgado will get somewhere with the HAFH people. Or one of the others will come up with a winner."

Keenan and McCarthy were checking out known blond sex offenders, thirty-five to forty-five, river to river, below Forty-second Street. Lachman and Bobbin were doing the same above Forty-second.

"Yeah, that ought to be rewarding," Donato said sarcastically.

They both laughed, and their eyes met for a moment; then each looked away, Donato fussing with the sluggish crease in his pants, Dina jiggling the car keys in her hand.

"Excuse me," said the young nun behind the desk. "Mother wants to know if you can come back on Monday?"

"No," Dina said. "We can't. Tell her we're investigating the murder of Sister Angelica."

"I did tell her."

Dina and Donato exchanged a look of disbelief.

"Tell her it's extremely important that we speak with her . . . now."

The nun spoke into the phone again but so softly they couldn't hear what she said. She hung up and turned to them.

"Mother will see you in the visitors' room. It's at the end of the hall, the first door on the right."

Walking down the narrow hallway, their arms brushed against each other. Donato moved away, closer to the wall. He felt clumsy, the way he had on his first date with Renata. He'd kept knocking against her, and she'd laughed, saying they were like the bumper cars at Coney Island, taking part of the blame herself.

The door to the visitors' room was open, revealing a brown-striped, foam rubber couch, two brown chairs and a coffee table. The walls were painted precinct blue, and the matching rug was indoor/outdoor carpet. One window had tan drapes and a yellowed shade pulled halfway down. Fluorescent lighting completed the depressing atmosphere.

Donato watched Dina take out a pack of cigarettes and matches, look around for an ashtray, then finding none, stuff the cigarettes back in her leather handbag with a sigh of irritation.

"If you'd quit," he said, "you wouldn't . . ." Her look stopped him midsentence. "Sorry." He'd have to be more careful. If they were going to get through this case together, he couldn't play father.

"Don't you people know that we are in mourning?"

They turned to see a petite woman with blue eyes like marble chips. She was no more than four and a half feet tall, with the scrubbed face of a child. Her arms were crossed, the hands hidden in the sleeves of her habit.

"Are you the Mother Superior?" Dina asked.

"I am. And you?"

Dina identified herself and introduced Donato.

"As I said, we are in mourning for Sister Angelica."

"We appreciate that, Mother, and that's why we must speak with you now. The more we know about Sister Angelica, the sooner we can catch her murderer, prevent him from killing again."

"I see. Well, sit down, sit down." She gestured toward the couch and took one of the brown chairs for herself. Her feet were just able to touch the floor. Draped and hidden under the folds of her robe as she was, her age was impossible to determine.

"First of all," Dina said, "we want to offer our condolences."

"Sister Angelica was a very fine nun. She'd served our Lord for thirteen years."

"How old was she?"

"Thirty-five. I suppose I should say the Lord moves in mysterious ways, but I can't. Most Catholics believe whatever happens is by God's design. I believe God's much too busy to be fussing with every person, every little thing. Death isn't a little thing, you say. True. But God doesn't have time to stop it if it's coming. He takes care of us *after* we die. Sister Angelica was in the wrong place at the wrong time, that's all."

Dina picked up the cue. "About that, Mother, can you tell me what Sister Angelica was doing out alone after midnight?"

"No," she said flatly. "I can't tell you because I don't know."

Donato said, "But you did know she wasn't in the convent?"

"Of course. Nothing the sisters do escapes me."

Donato had no doubts about that.

"Had Sister Angelica left with permission?"

"Oh, yes."

"What time?" Donato asked.

"Three-thirty exactly. Right after school let out. I happened to be downstairs when she left. I even wished her a good day." Her eyes snapped closed as if to block out the irony.

"Where was she going?" Dina asked.

"To her brother's."

Donato consulted his notes. "That would be Bert Harris?"

"Yes." She slid back in her chair, and her shoes hovered over the floor like two black birds.

"How long was she supposed to be gone?" asked Donato.

"Twenty-four hours."

"You mean she was meant to spend the night at her brother's?"

"Yes. She had no Thursday classes."

"Mr. Harris didn't call to say that his sister hadn't arrived or had left his home?"

"No."

Dina asked, "Before leaving here on Wednesday, did she do anything unusual, make or receive any phone calls or letters?"

"I have spoken to Sister Zita, Sister Angelica's direct superior, about those very things, and she assures me that nothing unusual took place on Wednesday or prior to that."

Donato was impressed by the nun's instincts. "What kind of person was Sister Angelica?"

Mother Superior leaned her small head back against the chair, her chin pointing toward the ceiling. "She was very gentle. Very pious. All nuns are pious, but Sister was especially so. Most of them change after the first few years." She brought her head forward and leveled a stony gaze at Donato. "The world creeps in and things change . . . *they* change. We're not a cloistered order, you see. Sometimes I wish . . . well, it doesn't matter now. I'm an old woman, and soon absolutely nothing will matter. How old do you think I am, Sergeant?"

If Donato remembered correctly, Mother Superior was dangerously close to committing the sin of Pride. In his experience, women never asked that question unless they knew they looked younger than they were. "I'd say fifty-eight or -nine."

She smiled, eyes glittering. "What do you think, Lieutenant?"

"I agree with Sergeant Donato."

"I'm eighty," she said. "It surprises you, doesn't it? I've been a nun for sixty-two years, and I look the way I do because I'm happy. I like my work. This is the first time evil has had a direct bearing on my life. Do you two like your work?"

They nodded.

"But day after day you see the worst side of man, don't you? One might say you're intimate with evil."

"That's true," Donato allowed.

"Mother," Dina said, taking back control of the interview, "I know this will seem a strange question, but I must ask it. Did Sister Angelica have any enemies?"

She smiled sadly. "Enemies? Why would a nun have enemies?"

"Aren't you a teaching order?" Donato asked.

"We are."

"A disgruntled student then," Dina explained.

The nun moved forward in her chair, feet planted firmly on the carpet. "Aren't you forgetting that another sister from another order has been murdered as well?"

"There's nothing to say that a child couldn't have moved from one parish to another. It happens all the time."

"Yes, of course, you're right," she conceded.

Dina persevered. "Did Sister Angelica mention any students who were particularly difficult? A student she had to punish, perhaps severely?"

"Were you taught by nuns, Lieutenant?"

Donato watched Dina's face, saw the muscle twitch in her cheek. He remembered when she was eight she'd been furious because Sister Mary Stephen had had the audacity to slap her palms with a ruler. It had outraged him as well. Renata said it was all part of a Catholic education and calmed him down. But Dina had gone on fuming for days, promising that no teacher would ever do that to her again. And none did because Dina made sure she never gave another sister cause.

"Yes, I was," Dina acknowledged.

"We don't use corporal punishment anymore. At least we don't in my order. I can't speak for anyone else . . . the nuns at Sacred Heart."

"Still," Dina said, "there are other kinds of punishment. Humiliation in front of the class . . ."

"Sister Angelica was not that kind of person," she said, nettled.

Donato said, "Please understand, Mother, that we must ask these questions. They may seem absurd to you because you knew Sister Angelica, but we didn't."

Slightly mollified, she said, "I'm telling you she was a fine nun. She had no secrets."

Everyone has secrets, even nuns, Donato thought. "I'm sure that's true. Still, we have to ask."

Mouth tight, she said nothing, knitting her hands together.

"How many people knew where Sister Angelica was going on Wednesday?" Dina asked.

"I did, Sister Zita . . . I don't know. She may have told any number of sisters."

"Is there a priest connected to your order?" Donato inquired.

"Two. Father Paul and Father Sebastian. Father Paul hears confessions and says mass for us in our chapel three times a week, and Father Sebastian says it four times a week."

"How well do you know them?"

Mother Superior looked at Dina coolly. "They have been coming here for over twenty years, if that's what you mean."

"What was their relationship with Sister Angelica?"

She arched faded eyebrows. "Relationship?"

"Yes, Mother," Dina said, unruffled. "Relationship."

"What the Lieutenant means is, was there anything unique between Sister Angelica and either of the priests? A special friendship?"

Dina shot him a malign look. "Or a special antagonism," she added.

"The priests treated Sister Angelica no differently from the way they treated the other sisters," returned Mother Superior.

"We'll have to interview the priests," Donato said. "Will you give us their address?" He was baffled by Dina's obvious irritation with him.

"Certainly. But you're barking up the wrong tree. Sister Angelica was simply in the wrong place at the wrong time, that's all. A stranger killed her. A maniac."

Dina said, "I'm sure you're right, Mother, but we have to eliminate possible suspects. That's standard operating procedure."

"Is there anything else?"

Donato said, "We'd like to see her room, Mother."

"I suppose that's necessary," she concluded, slipping from the chair. "Come with me."

Following her, Donato thought that from the back she looked like a child in costume. At the end of the hall, they went through a swinging door and entered the living quarters. They passed a kitchen where a number of nuns were working. Farther along, the bedrooms began. All the doors were open, and, from what Donato could see, they were more cubicles than rooms. In those that were occupied, nuns were either sitting in straight-backed chairs, reading or kneeling on the floor, backs to the doors, praying. After taking a right turn, Mother Superior stopped.

"This was Sister Angelica's room."

When all three of them stepped inside, Donato saw it would be impossible to move around easily. The narrow bed had been stripped, its nakedness advertising death. A straight-backed chair and a small wooden night table, which held a prayer book and glass, stood next to the bed; a large crucifix hung over it. A modest pine chest was the only other piece of furniture.

Dina went to the chest and opened the top drawer.

"What are you doing?" Mother Superior asked sharply.

"I have to examine the chest, Mother."

"It feels like . . . like . . ."

"A violation," Donato supplied.

"Yes. A violation." She looked at him benignly, as though he were on her side.

"We have to look," he said gently.

She nodded, resigned.

The chest had three drawers. They held underwear, stockings, two cardigan sweaters, several rosaries and a packet of letters from Sister Angelica's mother, father and niece.

"We'll want to take these, Mother."

She stiffened. "Her private letters? What could you possibly find in those?"

"We don't know," Dina said. "That's why we have to read them. They'll be returned when we've finished."

In the closet were a pair of black lace-up shoes, a habit and a black coat. Donato put his hand in each of the coat pockets. He found a tissue in one; the other was empty. There was nothing else to examine.

He turned to the nun. "Is this it? I mean, are there any other belongings of hers that are somewhere else?"

"That's all."

Donato wondered what it would be like to be unencumbered by possessions. Suddenly it seemed appealing.

Mother Superior walked them to the front door.

Donato said, "You've been very helpful, Mother."

"You *will* return the letters?" she said to Dina.

"Yes, of course. Thank you for your time, Mother."

Outside, in the car, Dina whirled in her seat to face Donato.

"How dare you do that?"

"Do what?"

"Explain what I mean. Act like my interpreter. If this is going to work, you and me, you're going to have to stop treating me like a child."

"I wasn't treating you like a child, for Christ's sake."

"You were. What I was saying was perfectly clear. 'What the Lieutenant means . . .' " she mimicked. "Oh, hell."

"Hell's bells," he said.

She looked at him, bewildered.

"Hell's bells. You said that when you were two and a half."

"I did?"

"You did, kiddo." He smiled. "You were building a fort with your blocks, and they all fell down. 'Hell's bells,' you said, 'there goes the whole place.' " Donato laughed, remembering the blonde, curly-headed child looking to him for an explanation. Something inside him swelled, filled him with warmth. God, how he'd loved that kid.

"I said that?"

"Ask your mother. We never knew where you got that expression."

She grinned, the years and angers momentarily shed. Then it was over.

"Let's go back to the shop, compare notes with the others," she said soberly, starting the car. "In the future don't explain me. Get it, Sergeant?"

"Got it, Lieutenant."

Seven

The Caffe Lucca, on the short curving block of Bleecker Street between Carmine and Sixth Avenue, nestled between an optician's storefront and a barbershop, had been a favorite of Dina's and Judy McCarthy's for years. During their months at the Academy, they'd come down to the Village after classes and sit for hours over cappuccinos or espressos and chocolate cake, eclairs or pasticciotto a cremas commiserating over the terrible treatment they were receiving from their male teachers, the humiliations inflicted on them by male classmates. Those six months of training were hell, and they spent a lot of time together. They didn't know then how much worse it would get.

Because Judy lived in Queens and the McCarthys were opposed to her career choice, she spent four or five nights a week at the Donato apartment. They had the room. Rich was dead. And both

Mike and Renata were crazy about Judy. It was as if they'd suddenly gained another child. Not that she replaced Rich, but the feeling of two young people in the house lifted the Donatos' sagging spirits.

After graduation, Judy was assigned to the Twenty-sixth Precinct in Harlem, and Dina to the Twenty-third between Eighty-sixth and One-hundred-tenth, east of Fifth Avenue to the river. It was hard for them to get to the Lucca then, especially when their tours didn't coincide, but they found a way to meet at least once a week, and it was a tradition they still maintained.

From March through mid-October at the Lucca, small tables and metal chairs were tucked behind an iron railing, making it an outdoor café, even though the sun never touched that part of the sidewalk. Still, sometimes the spot was warm enough, and always good for people-watching. Dina and Judy had tried a corner table, but it was too late in the day for leftover warmth, so they'd moved inside. They were both drinking double espressos. No longer kids, they tried to resist the cakes and babas au rhum. But Dina couldn't keep her eyes off the pastry case and wished they weren't sitting so near it.

"Kee-rist, Dina," Judy said, "will you stop it and just have the damn piece of cake you're drooling over."

"I don't know what you're talking about," Dina said, a false haughtiness in her voice.

"I'm talking about that dark thing in the case there. The one with the mocha filling and the thin raspberry strips between the layers. A favorite if I remember correctly. It's called cake, and it's sinful and evil and totally and absolutely divine and I think you should have it."

"I can't," Dina said despairingly. "I just can't. In another month I'm going to have to get into a bathing suit."

"Fine. Then stop staring at it and look at me."

Reluctantly, Dina turned toward Judy and was momentarily startled by her beauty, as if she'd never seen her before. It was funny how, occasionally, you saw someone as you had for the first time.

Surrounded by unfriendly men, feeling frightened and lonely, Dina had been sitting by herself in the Police Academy auditorium, waiting for the orientation to begin, when someone sat beside her. She surreptitiously shifted to see who it was and felt as if she'd been punched in the gut. The woman next to her was breathtakingly beautiful. Dina couldn't recall ever having seen anyone in real life who had skin so smooth, real red hair and eyes the color of ripe limes.

Judy, after introducing herself, immediately began speaking about the risk they were both taking and how they'd have to stick together in this predominantly male, hostile world. It had taken Dina less than thirty seconds to know they'd be friends.

Now, looking at Judy, she still found her impossibly gorgeous. How bizarre it must feel to be collared by her, Dina thought, smiling.

"What's funny?" Judy asked.

"Nothing. Everything. I was just remembering you, us, the Academy, all of it."

"Puh-leeze, give me a break, and let's not go tripping down memory lane."

Dina knew that even though Judy loved the Job, wouldn't dream of doing anything else, she'd also wanted a marriage, children. For a while Judy had thought that the right man just hadn't come along, but now she admitted relationships were too painful for her: lonely as it was to be single, it was preferable to involvement and possible abandonment, as she'd been abandoned by her real father. She had no use for dwelling in the past.

"James Dunn, Sister Honora's brother, was really wrecked, Dina. He said he'd never known anyone like his sister, anyone so selfless, so totally committed to helping other people. Said she'd been like that all her life. Always bringing home strays, that kind of stuff. Funny how some people are that way, isn't it?"

"Could he give you anything?"

Judy shook her head. "He's convinced it's one of the kids Sister Honora worked with. There's nobody in their background, no old enemies or anything like that. The poor guy said he'd been worried about her ever since she'd gone out on her own, living alone. He's the kind of big brother that probably always looked after his sister, protected her and . . ." Judy's thought trailed off as she realized what she was saying. "Oh, kee-rist, Dina, I'm sorry."

"Judy, it's been a long time. I can handle reminders of Rich."

"Yeah, I know, I know. But, what the hell, who needs it, huh?"

Dina had loved Rich, idolized him, and he'd been good to her, too. But when she let the truth creep in, when she didn't have her feeling sentinels in place, she had to wonder if she'd ever really known him, and that scared her. It was best not to think about him at all.

"Anyway, Dunn told me he'd been especially worried when Sister Honora was hit by a cab a few months ago."

"The reason for the crutches?" Dina asked.

"Broken tibia."

"Check on that. The accident. Where it was, the driver, you

know the drill. I take it Dunn has an alibi." They knew now that Sister Honora had been murdered between three and six in the afternoon Wednesday.

"In court until three-thirty and with a client until five-fifteen. Anyway, what would Dunn have to do with Sister Angelica?"

"Maybe he hates nuns because he was in love with his sister." She smiled. They were used to kidding about motives the psychiatrists came up with, although they had to admit how often the shrinks were right.

"As a matter of fact, he isn't married. Cute, too." She wiggled her eyebrows like Groucho Marx.

"Why isn't he married?"

"Too busy, he said."

"What do *you* think?"

"Gay. I said he was cute, didn't I? Isn't that enough proof?"

The great lament between them was that all the single good-looking men in New York were homosexuals.

"What do you think of Keenan?" Dina asked.

"Is he gay, you mean?"

"Yeah."

"I don't think so. No. I'm sure he's not."

Dina was surprised at the relief she felt. She had no problems with gays, couldn't care less, so why should it matter if Keenan was gay or not? "So what do you think of him?"

"Keenan? He's okay. Not my type."

"Judy, darling, I wasn't asking about his sex appeal. I meant as a partner." Was that what she meant? She wasn't sure.

"Oh, a part-ner," she exaggerated. "Make yourself clear, lady. So far so good, but it hasn't exactly been a lifelong relationship. Still, I don't get any chauvy vibes from him. And you, my little chickadee? How's *your* partner?"

Dina reached for her cigarettes. "I think I've made a terrible mistake."

"No!" Judy said sarcastically.

"I must have been crazy to ask him."

"Maybe not."

"Why do you say that?" They hadn't talked about her break with Donato in a long time.

"Because you love him, dopey, and you miss him. Sometimes I think you miss him more than you miss Liam."

"I hardly miss Liam at all," she said.

"That's what I mean. Look, maybe you and Mike can work out your problems, be friends again."

"I can never forgive what he did, Judy."

"People make mistakes, Dina. *Everybody* isn't perfect."

"Like me, you mean. Like I think I am."

"You said it, not me." She swallowed the last of her espresso.

"He did a rotten thing, Judy."

"I agree. He shouldn't have lied to you and Renata, but that was thirteen years ago."

"I didn't know about it thirteen years ago."

"So you've known for four years. What's the difference? I thought it was great that you asked him to be on the task force. Very mature of her, I thought. And I also thought you were asking for trouble. Unless you forgive and forget."

"I try. But it isn't even that. It's that he still treats me like a kid."

"You are. I mean, you're *his* kid. You want to change partners with me? I'd love working with Mike."

"And me with Keenan?" she said, disconcerted.

"How about you and Lachman then?"

"Spare me. Anyway, I can't change partners now. It would hurt Donato's feelings."

Judy smiled knowingly. "Sure. You're right. Better leave things the way they are, see what happens. Anyway, the case is the important thing, and you and Mike will make a dynamite team."

That much was true. And if personal things got in the way, she could always switch later. To Pesetsky, for instance. She was used to him.

"I've got something I want to tell you, Dina." Judy's tone became serious. "Don't look so scared. It's nothing bad. At least, I don't think so. You might, though. You want another espresso?" she asked, stalling.

Dina wasn't tumbling. "What is it?"

"I'm pregnant." Judy's eyes turned a darker shade of green, like sage.

Astonished, Dina stared at her. She had a million questions, but none of them seemed appropriate. How could she have been so out of it that she hadn't known Judy had been seeing someone. Casual sex wasn't Judy's thing.

"So, who is he?" was all she could think to say.

"Who's who?"

"The father?"

Judy shook her head dismissively. "That doesn't matter. I mean, I'll tell you about him, but the father's not the point. I did this on purpose . . . I looked for the right guy . . . don't worry, I checked out his sexual history, no threat of AIDS . . . and then I . . . well, I guess you could say I mated." She grinned. "I'm eight weeks' pregnant, Dina, and I've never felt happier in my life."

Thinking Judy would be leaving the Job, Dina suddenly was overwhelmed by a feeling of loss.

"What the hell's wrong with you? You look like I just told you I was quitting the Force or something."

"Won't you?"

"Of course not, why should I? Did you?"

"But I had Liam," she said.

"Well, you don't now, sport! Oh, Dina, don't be a pain in the ass about this. Don't be mad."

"I'm not mad, Judy. I just . . . I . . . why?"

Judy waved a hand at the waitress and indicated another round of espressos. "I'm thirty-five years old, and time is running out. I'm never going to get married, probably never have a long-term relationship. So why should I punish myself for that and not have what I've wanted since I was five years old? A kid. A kid of my own. I'll be one helluva good mother."

Dina didn't doubt that for a moment. But she knew, too, how hard it was raising Cal without a father. Bringing up a baby alone would be ten times harder. Still, lots of women were doing it.

"Look, I'm not an idiot," Judy said. "I don't think it's going to be a cinch. But after weighing all the possibilities, I decided the pros were worth the cons."

"Why didn't you talk it over with me first?"

"I knew you'd be against it. I knew you'd give me a thousand sensible reasons why I shouldn't do it. True or not true, Lieut?"

She started to protest, then gave it up. "True," she admitted, irritated with herself for being so conventional, so horribly predictable.

"I'll work right up to the end. Inside, the last few months, I know. And I'll hate that like poison. But it's worth it. Then it'll just be me and Sam."

"How can you be so sure it's going to be a boy?"

Judy looked surprised. "A boy? Hell no. It's going to be a girl. Samantha. I can feel it." She rested her hand on her flat belly. "Samantha Dina McCarthy."

Tears sprang to Dina's eyes. "You don't have to do that."

"I don't? Jesus, I didn't know that. I thought it was written in some law book somewhere." Judy reached across the table and put her hand over Dina's. "Give over, will you, Lieutenant? It's okay just to be pleased, you know."

Dina nodded, unable to say anything.

"And do me a favor, will you? Have the goddamn piece of mocha cake."

Dina laughed. "I think I will."

"Way to go," Judy said.

"Judy?"

"Yeah?"

"Congratulations. I love you."

"Thanks, Lieut. I love you, too."

Liam and Cal were sitting at the kitchen table when Dina came home. For a moment, she felt as if she'd gone back in time and wished she could re-engage, somehow make it work.

"Hi, Mom. Want some ice cream?"

She leaned over, kissed him on the cheek, brushed a hand over his blond hair. The love she felt for her child sometimes overwhelmed her. Having Cal made her fully understand her parents' loss. She wasn't sure she'd be able to survive as well as they had if something happened to Cal.

She greeted Liam coolly. They had not, like so many divorced couples she knew, become friends, although they were civil to one another, especially in front of their son. The trouble, she thought, was that she was still attracted to Liam.

He was a gorgeous man, over six feet, lean but muscled. His tight, curly hair looked like a crop of freshly washed blackberries, and his face seemed sculpted, cheekbones high, chin squared like a building block.

"Want some ice cream, Mom?" Cal repeated.

The mocha cake was still with her. "I think I'll give it a pass, honey."

"You don't know what you're missing, Mom."

"Next time," she said. "What'd you do today?"

"We went to a magic show."

"There's this place on Carmine," Liam explained. "They give shows on weekends."

"It was neat, Mom. You should've been there."

Yes, she thought, I should have. But even when they were a family, it was rare that she was able to accompany them. At the last minute, an emergency would occur, and she'd be called away, leaving husband and child to fend for themselves. Who the hell said you could have it all?

At first, it had seemed so right between them. Liam thought being married to a cop wouldn't bother him, and she believed supporting him while he tried to write would be fine. They'd both been wrong: she resented being the sole breadwinner, and Liam couldn't live with the possibility of her being blown away every time she went to work. Their last argument echoed so many others that had gone before, except it had been more cutting, crueler.

"I never know if you'll walk through that door again," he'd said. "You have no idea what that feels like."

It wasn't true. Growing up, she'd felt that way every time her father kissed her good-bye. And watching her mother's effort to make things appear normal, she'd registered the fear in *her* eyes.

"No," Liam said. "I'm sorry. You *do* know. You've just chosen to forget it, like so many other things."

She didn't ask what he meant. He'd always accused her of ducking feelings, and maybe he was right. Why should she be different from every other cop she knew?

"Dina, I've talked to Renata about this," Liam went on. "I know what she's gone through all these years. She's told me how you'd cry sometimes when Mike didn't come home, sure he was dead, even though she tried to reassure you."

She *had* forgotten that. "She shouldn't have told you."

"Why not? Aren't I part of the family? Don't I count? Look, we've been over this thousands of times, and the point is, I can't take it anymore."

He was asking her to give up her career. Frightened she'd lose him, she attacked.

"If I leave the force, who the hell do you think is going to support the three of us?"

"We'll get other jobs."

"*We?*" she said acidly. "Since when do *we* have jobs?"

The pain of her words crossed his face, like a visible wound. "You may not understand this, Dina, but I've been working every day except Sundays since we've been married."

"I do understand that. I also understand that you've written three unpublished novels and a fourth one is in the works."

"Thanks."

"Liam, how about a reality check here? It doesn't look like you're going to make it as a writer. All I'm trying to point out is that if I quit we won't have any money. I mean, you *are* aware, aren't you, that it's *my* paycheck that puts food on the table?"

"Yes, Dina," he said stonily. "I'm aware of who pays the bills. And in case you think this was my idea, let me remind you that it was *you* who wanted to be Lady Bountiful, *you* who said that in the past artists had sponsors and you'd like to be mine, *you* who said you didn't want a traditional marriage, anyway."

"I didn't know then what I know now."

"Which is?"

"That it would be so goddamned hard."

"It doesn't have to be hard. I'm willing to do it differently. I've been offered a teaching job."

"Where?"

"Vermont."

Her expression told him what she was thinking.

"Look, being a cop isn't the only goddamn job in the world."

"It's the only job in the world for me."

"Why? What's so special?"

"I can't explain it."

"Are you staying with the cops because you know it drives your father nuts?" Liam asked.

"I don't give a damn what it does to him."

He laughed. "Come off it, Dina. It sticks in his craw that you're on the cops, and you know it."

"He's long since gotten over that."

"Has he?"

She didn't answer because she wasn't really sure.

"This isn't getting us anywhere." He put his hands on her shoulders. "I love you, Dina. We can work this out. You can find some other job you'd love."

"In Vermont?"

"Why not?"

"Like what?"

"You could practice law."

"Oh, get serious. There's something like one lawyer for every two hundred people in this country. Besides, I'd go nuts being a lawyer. Especially in some one-horse town."

"Dina, listen," he said in measured tones. "Every time you leave to go to work I get sick to my stomach. I mean it. I'm nauseated the whole time you're gone. If you're on duty at night, I don't sleep. I can't do my own work, and I'm no good to Cal."

"I can't quit, Liam. I just can't." She recognized the finality of her statement, but promises would be lies, postponing the inevitable.

"I want a divorce," he said simply.

Relief swept over her as though she'd been waiting all her life for these words.

"And I want Cal," he added.

"You've got to be joking! How do you expect to support him? You can't take him to Vermont, you know."

"Who'll take care of him if I'm not here?" he rebutted.

"I'll hire someone. Without you to support, I'll be able to afford it."

"You're a bitch," he said quietly.

"And you're a bastard," she returned.

Reduced to name-calling, the argument ended. Liam packed a bag and left. He hadn't taken the teaching job. Instead, he'd stayed with his sister in Tribeca for the first six months, then worked as a waiter while he continued to write. A year after he left her, he sold a novel. It was about them. She hadn't read it.

In the beginning, they barely spoke when he came for Cal, but little by little, they'd become friendlier. Neither of them had found anyone else. Some days she imagined their getting back together. But when she was being sensible she knew it could never be; she wasn't going to change.

Being a cop was like nothing else. It was making order out of chaos. And not knowing what would happen next: the excitement, the variety, living on the edge. The very things that Liam couldn't live with were what made the job so seductive to her. But it wasn't all good. There were the horrors, like killing Buddy Green.

Cal said, "Want me to show you a trick the guy taught me?"

"After you get on your pj's."

"Ah, Mom, it's early."

"Do what your mother tells you, Cal."

"O-kay," he said reluctantly.

"I'll come in and say good-night when you're ready."

"Will you, too, Dad?"

Quickly, she said, "Say good-night to Dad now; he'll be gone by the time you get in bed."

Liam hugged his son. "Don't let the bedbugs bite." When Cal

was gone, he turned to Dina. "You have a date or something? You seem to want to get me out of here in a helluva hurry."

"It never goes well if you stay too long, Liam."

She picked up the ice cream bowls and took them to the sink. He followed, putting his arms around her from behind.

"Don't," she said and wriggled out of his grasp.

"Why not? You're still attracted to me, I can tell. And God knows I still want you."

"It's pointless."

"Why can't we have an affair?"

"Oh, Liam, give me a break." She walked past him into the living room.

"I'm serious," he said.

"I know you are; that's the trouble." She lit a cigarette.

"You don't think we could handle it?"

"I know *I* couldn't. Let's not get into this, Liam, okay? I've had very little sleep."

His face hardened. "You working on this nun thing?"

"Yes."

He grabbed his blue windbreaker. "I should've known," he said bitterly. "Murder was always more interesting to you than sex."

"That's a rotten thing to say, Liam."

"I'm a rotten guy." He pulled on the jacket and opened the door. "All work and no play makes Dina a dull woman."

"Don't make assumptions," she said.

"What's that mean?"

"It means you don't know anything about my life."

For a moment he looked hurt, as though she'd betrayed him; then he was gone.

She felt terrible. She'd wanted him to believe there was a man in her life, wanted to hurt him, but now she was sorry she had. Liam didn't deserve her anger because she was nowhere on a major case. Every moment that ticked by pushed her farther away from a solution.

How many more nuns would be raped and murdered before they found the killer? And what if they never did? What if he kept on killing one nun after another? But the grisly truth was, the more he killed, the better their chance of catching him. The multiple murderer was more likely to make a mistake than the killer who struck just once. Still, she didn't want him to kill any more nuns. She wanted to get him *now*.

"Hey, Mom," Cal called from his room, "I'm ready."

"I'll be right there," she answered.

Stubbing out her cigarette, she realized she'd begun thinking about Liam and ended up speculating about the killings. Maybe Liam was right. Maybe murder interested her more than anything else. God help her if it was true.

On Monday morning, the task force moved to the main office in the Thirteenth Precinct. The new room was much bigger than the one they'd been in. It was painted blue and had large windows overlooking Twenty-first Street. Two computers and printers were at one end of the room, and against a wall were filing cabinets with small drawers. The information they'd feed into the computers would be transferred to hard copy on index cards, then stored in the cabinets. They'd compile recorded telephone messages, statements from informants and witnesses, forensic data, medical reports, weapon classification, motor vehicle identification, addresses and phone numbers and other details that would be labeled later. Everything would be cross-referenced. Larger gray cabinets stored exhibits.

A group of desks, each with a telephone, was set against another wall. Nearby was a photocopying machine. Two detailed maps showed the areas of the murders.

In the center of the room, the task force sat on mismatched wooden chairs around a large conference table. Fluorescent lighting made everyone look sick. The air was layered with smoke and the smell of coffee. All but Donato had a danish or roll in front of them.

Dina opened a file. "We have the second forensic report. Our perp is a secretor, so we were able to get a pretty conclusive make on his blood type. Sister Honora was type A and Sister Angelica type B. A vaginal smear and a saliva test from Sister Honora's breast tested type B. The vaginal smear from Sister Angelica only tested B, so that's inconclusive. But the saliva test from her breast tested B."

They all knew that this information only helped to eliminate suspects. The killer was type B, so a suspect who was A and not a secretor could be excluded on that basis.

"A vegetable fiber was found on Sister Angelica's habit," Dina continued. "It's green cotton. Maybe we'll be able to match the fiber to a shirt or pants of a suspect. Of course the fiber may not have come from the killer. Forensic is checking the convent today for fibers. The best news is we have a head hair sample."

"All riiight," Bobbin said.

"It'll also help later with elimination. The hair sample has sheath cells present, which means it was pulled from the killer's head. They were found in Sister Angelica's fist."

"Good for her," said Alma Delgado.

"The PGM also showed he's a type B. And something better. He uses a hair spray." Narrowing down a suspect by hair spray was like looking for a black man in Harlem. Still, it was something. "They're testing for type. The stab wounds were made with a sharp boning-type knife, and the fingers severed by a cleaver." She closed the folder, got up and wheeled over a portable bulletin board.

The time, date and address were listed below the words SISTER HONORA. Under this were photographs of the nun's apartment. Most of the pictures were of the bedroom. The body was shown from many angles.

Donato moved a second bulletin board into place. It had the same type of information about Sister Angelica.

Dina opened another folder and read the property vouchers, first for Sister Angelica and then for Sister Honora. When she was finished, she said, "And that's all, folks."

Lachman said, "I got something, Lieut." The young detective opened a folder and took out a newspaper clipping. "It's about Sister Honora. Seems she got hit by a cab. There's a picture of her on crutches and a story about HAFH."

Dina glanced at McCarthy.

"I have Dceck checking cab companies," she said.

"Don't have to," Lachman said, tapping the clipping. "Name's right here. The driver's, too."

"Good work, Lachman."

He passed the clipping down to Dina. "You really should thank the sarge," he said, indicating Donato. "He was the one told me about the crutches, so I asked Sister Margaret why Sister Honora woulda had 'em."

Dina gave Donato a nod, which he acknowledged with the slightest tilt of his head.

"This is dated January twenty-third," Dina said. "My guess is that our guy got onto her then."

"It even tells where she lives," Lachman said.

"Thanks a bunch," Bobbin said to the absent *Post* reporter.

Dina handed the clipping to McCarthy. "Interview the cabbie as soon as possible. Lachman, I want you to find out if there's been anything in print on Sister Angelica in the last year. Try Sister Zita at St. Paul's Convent."

"Will do."

Dina put the clipping in a folder and when she raised her eyes saw that Keenan was looking at her, his head cocked to one side, elbow on the table, fist propping up his chin. She quickly looked away. The arrogance she detected in him made her feel as though he were constantly challenging her.

She returned to Lachman. "Did you turn up any witnesses?"

Lachman flipped open his note pad. "Nobody in Sister Honora's building heard nothing. According to them, one and all, they was either not home at the time of the murder or they was watching television and eating apple pie a la mode like Mr. and Mrs. Average Joe in suburbia. More healthy, normal apartment dwellers you wouldn't never meet." He closed the pad with a flip of his wrist. "And this is said, mind you, with their noses running, them scratching like chimps, the track marks up the wazoo, ya know what I mean? I thought I was in a rehab or something. What a place." He ran two fingers over his reddish mustache and shook his head in disbelief.

"Bobbin?"

"Checked out three apartment houses on Fifty-fifth Street, but like Marv, nobody knows nothing. I mean, why the hell should they? They're home snug in their beds while a nun is out running round after midnight. That makes sense, right? Right. It's like Jo Ann, my second oldest daughter. To her it makes sense she should go away to college so she could find herself. Going to City's not good enough. She needs freedom, needs to find out who she is. I told her, I said, *I* know who you are, you're Jo Ann Bobbin, seventeen years old who's my daughter who is going to City like your brother and sister before you or you're going nowhere, that's who you are."

"Spare us the Bobbin Roster today," Pesetsky said, kidding. "We don't need to know from Jo Ann and Marie and Thomas and Peter and Saul."

"Paul," Bobbin corrected.

"Huh?"

"Paul, not Saul. Why would I name a kid a mine Saul? Saul's a Jewish name."

"Watch it," Lachman said. "We don't need no anti-Semitic stuff at eight-thirty in the morning."

"That's right," Judy McCarthy put in. "Wait 'til quarter to nine for the anti-Semitic remarks."

Everybody laughed.

"I thought you were a black Jew like Sammy Davis," Pesetsky added.

"Very funny, very funny," Bobbin grinned.

"Okay, okay," Dina said. "Is that all, Bobbin?"

"Yeah, pretty much. I got a lot more work to do on that block." He consulted his notebook. "A Steve Stilwell of 110 East Fifty-fifth says there's a dude who hangs out round there sometimes. Carries his bedroll in a shopping cart. I'll check him out. And some more apartment houses."

"Pesetsky?"

"I spent about five hours with Father Briney, and Delgado talked to Sister Margaret. We got a list of names of people who've passed through there. Most of them just first names and no addresses. I think that's a dead end, Lieutenant. Then we talked to all the kids who are around there now. That was real helpful," he said sarcastically. "It's like they think they're protecting the Sister or something. They got it ass backwards."

"Keep on it for a while." She turned to Delgado. "What did you think of Sister Margaret?"

Pesetsky answered. "She's a dip. They all are there."

Dina was surprised Pesetsky had answered for his partner. It wasn't like him. "Delgado?" she tried again.

Her black eyes glistened with anger. "Sister Margaret's a nice woman, but she didn't shed any light on the situation. I'll tell ya though, I think she's hidin' somethin'."

Pesetsky's head snapped around to look at Delgado. It was obvious that this was the first he'd heard of this suspicion.

"Why do you say that, Delgado?" Dina asked.

She shrugged. "I don't know. Just a hunch."

"Fucking women's intuition," Lachman said.

Delgado ignored him. "Somethin' about the way she couldn't look me in the eye sometimes. I mean, wouldn't ya think a nun wouldn't have any secrets, nothin' to hide and all that?"

"Maybe she's gettin' off with the priest," Lachman said.

"Nah. I don't think that's it," Delgado said.

"Hey," Lachman added, "them nuns and priests are always fucking their brains out." He laughed and looked at the others for approval, trying hard to be one of the gang.

It didn't work.

"Pursue your hunch about Sister Margaret, Delgado. Today I want you and Pesetsky to interview Sister Honora's Mother Superior at Sacred Heart."

When Dina had gone to Sacred Heart, from first to third grades, the Mother Superior had been a tyrant, wielding a ruler like a nightstick. Those years had been so unpleasant she'd chosen not to do the interview herself. Walking into the place would have depressed her. Also, Dina associated that time with unhappiness at home. Her mother had wanted to move uptown, but Donato held out for his independence, unwilling to give in to the Fiorentini money. Eventually, he'd capitulated, and they'd left Little Italy for the Upper East Side. They stayed there two years until compromising by moving to the apartment they had today.

"Delgado can do that alone, can't she?" Pesetsky asked. "I want to keep on what I've been doing, like you said."

Delgado squared her bony shoulders. "Sure, no problem. I can do it alone. No problem," she said again defensively.

Something was going on here, Dina thought. "No. I want you to interview her together. It goes better that way, you know that."

Pesetsky opened his mouth, but Dina cut him off before he could protest. "McCarthy?"

"I've interviewed so many blond sex offenders," she said, "they're coming out of my ears."

"Better there than some place else," Bobbin said.

"You're right there," McCarthy replied.

Dina knew that Judy went along with the joke because she didn't want to act like a stiff. It was easy for Dina to refuse to join in the dirty talk now that she was a lieutenant. But Judy still had to work with these men in a peer position. Still, it was a no-win situation. If you objected to the jokes, you were a prude, but if you went along, they thought you were trashy. Trashy was better, of course. At least you didn't feel all alone all day, every day.

"I'd like you and Keenan to interview the two priests who say mass at St. Paul's convent." Dina handed her a sheet of paper with their names and address. "Keenan?" Dina was aware she'd saved him for last, but she wasn't sure why.

Bobby Keenan was wearing a light green Lacoste shirt, the collar turned up. His gray pants had elastic at the waist. The jacket was a dark green windbreaker.

"I've been interviewing, too. Nothing so far. Well, a maybe, I guess, but nothing to make my heart beat fast." He smiled at her, and their eyes met.

She felt heat in her chest and neck. It made her angry. "Keep on it," she said quickly and turned her gaze away from him. "Donato and I are going to interview Sister Angelica's brother this morning.

Maybe we can find out what she was doing on the streets after midnight. That's all."

They finished off their coffees and cakes, threw garbage in the green cans and started for the door.

"Pesetsky and Delgado stay for a minute," Dina said. "Donato, I'll catch up with you at the car." When the others had gone, she sat on the edge of the table. "So what's up with you two?"

"What d'you mean?" Pesetsky asked.

Delgado's lips were pressed tightly together, a white aureole around them.

"Look, John, I wasn't born yesterday. Something's going on between you and Alma. I want to know what it is."

Pesetsky ran a hand through his brown hair, a forelock falling over his eyes. "I don't know what you're talking about, Lieutenant."

"You answered for Delgado earlier. I've never seen you do that. And you're mad, Delgado. I think you're mad at Pesetsky."

"It's nothing," Delgado assured her.

"I don't think it's nothing. You didn't want to go on the interview with Delgado, Pesetsky. What's that about?"

"I thought we'd do better, get more done, if we split up."

Dina didn't believe him, but she knew she wasn't going to get anything more from them. "Okay. But if there's anything wrong between you, come to me so we can talk it over. I don't want either one of you jeopardizing this case for personal reasons. Okay?"

They agreed, and she told them they could go. She picked up her folder, bag and jacket and turned out the lights. Outside, she ran smack into Keenan.

"Sorry," he said. "I left my notebook on the table."

She felt flustered, unable to think of anything to say. What the hell was this? She refused to be the competent woman with power who goes all soft at the sight of a good-looking man. Nobody wanted to be a cliché.

"Turn the lights off when you leave," she said, walking toward the stairs.

"Hold on a second, and I'll go down with you."

"Sorry," she called over her shoulder. "I've kept my partner waiting long enough." That ought to do it, she thought. Do what? She might not *want* to be a cliché, she told herself, but she *was* one.

Eight

Sister Angelica's brother, Bert Harris, lived in Chelsea. The neighborhood had been slowly changing over the past decade. Restored brownstones were now in the million-dollar range. There were trees on some blocks, and new restaurants and boutiques sprung up on a weekly basis. Still, it wasn't an area where out-of-towners went on weekends to have brunch, look around. It didn't have the art galleries of SoHo, the mythical decadence of Greenwich Village or the yuppie crowd of Columbus Avenue on the Upper West Side. Chelsea was still a neighborhood where most of the people on the streets were the people who lived there.

Donato and Dina were surprised when they picked up Harris's address; they'd assumed his apartment would be near the murder site. Now Sister Angelica's presence in the East Fifties, after midnight, was even more puzzling.

Walking alongside Dina, toward Harris's building on Twenty-fourth Street, Donato felt her silence as though it were a third person. When she'd joined him at the car, she'd seemed disturbed, distracted. When he'd asked her about it, she'd challenged him.

"Nothing's the matter. What do you mean?"

"You look upset."

"You're imagining it."

A few minutes later he'd tried again. "Is it the case or something else?"

"Look, Donato, I told you, there's nothing wrong."

"Is it me? Us?"

"No, but it's going to be if you don't get off my back."

Today she'd asked him to drive, so he'd concentrated on that, telling himself not to take things personally, that his daughter had her own life and it had nothing to do with him.

They parked, walked along in silence, then turned in at a refurbished brownstone. Green window boxes with pink geraniums graced two first-floor windows. Set in the center of a red door was a brass knocker in the shape of a lion's head. Harris's apartment was on the second floor. He rang them in, and they climbed red-carpeted stairs to the first landing.

Harris stood in front of his door. In his early forties, he was balding and heavy. His belly hung over his pants like an uncooked doughnut. He wore a white shirt, frayed at the collar, but his striped tie seemed new and clean. A gray cardigan showed stains, his elbow through the right sleeve. Tan trousers were too long, the cuffs loitering over worn maroon slippers.

He was not a suspect. He worked as a Linotyper from ten-forty-five at night until seven-forty-five in the morning. On the night in question, he was at his machine and took his forty-five-minute lunch break in the employee dining room.

After they showed their shields, Harris ushered them inside. In a medium-sized room, a tired, flowered couch and two sagging club chairs were grouped around a dirty, white brick fireplace. Ash coated the hearth, and dustballs rolled across the lean nap of a brown carpet. A makeshift coffee table was laden with copies of *The Daily Worker*, *Popular Science* and *Byte*. Everything in the room looked dull, as though it were covered in a fine gray film.

Harris, his back to the fireplace, stood facing them.

"Why don't we all sit down?" Donato began.

Hesitantly, Harris chose a corner of the couch. Dina sat at the opposite end and Donato took one of the chairs.

"We appreciate your seeing us, Mr. Harris. We know this must be a difficult time for you," Donato said.

"Yes," he answered in a strangled voice.

"Could you tell us about your sister's visit on Wednesday?" Dina asked.

"Like what? What do you want to know?"

"What time did she arrive?"

His gaze shifted around the room in quick short darts. "I don't know. No. Wait a minute. I think I *do* know. About four. Yes, I'm sure of it because I was just finishing my peanut butter on rice cakes. I always eat at the same time. Three-thirty. I read a magazine and eat. It takes me about half an hour. So that's why I remember the time. Sometimes I have an apple," he added.

"How did your sister seem?" Donato asked.

"How did she seem?" He toyed with a loose button on his sweater.

"Was she troubled, happy, angry, what?"

"She was all right. Maybe she was a little nervous, jumpy. No. Not jumpy. Nervous."

"Did you ask her why?"

"Ask her why what?"

Donato marshaled his patience. "Why she was nervous."

"Why would I do that?" He looked genuinely bewildered.

Dina asked, "Weren't you concerned?"

"Concerned?"

"Didn't it worry you that she seemed nervous?"

"Do you want something?" he said suddenly. "I don't have any soda, but I have juice. I know you can't drink on duty. But this is just plain apple juice. Do you want some?"

They both politely refused.

Harris jumped up, crossed to the empty chair, sat there.

It was a good thing this guy had an airtight alibi, Donato thought, because he'd be number one suspect if he didn't.

"Mr. Harris," Dina said, "let's get back to your sister." She smiled, but he looked away, down at the filthy hearth as if something important were there. "Had you seen her nervous like that before?"

"Like that before?"

Donato thought he'd go crazy if this guy didn't stop repeating everything. "Was she often nervous?"

"Gretchen was always high-strung," Harris said.

"Gretchen?"

"My sister. That was her real name. She couldn't become Sister

Gretchen, I don't know why, so she chose the name Angelica." He screwed up his face as if he were smelling something bad. "Angelica. Who could live up to that name?"

"She was always high-strung?" Donato prompted.

"When she was a kid, she'd get hives from the slightest thing. Once when our parents were going out, she cried and cried and tried to make them stay home. They told her they were going out to see a man about a dog. The next day when they didn't have a dog for her she got hives and vomited. That's the way she was." He nodded once for emphasis.

"Okay, Bert, let's get back to Wednesday." Donato decided it was time to start calling him by his first name. "What happened after your sister arrived?"

"Happened?"

"How did you spend the afternoon?" Dina asked.

"We went for a walk. Personally, I didn't want to go, but she wanted to walk around the neighborhood, so I went."

"How long was the walk?"

"How long?"

Neither Donato nor Dina answered him.

He looked frightened, as if he'd lost his place in a play. "You want to know how long the walk was?"

"Yes," Donato answered, feeling outwitted.

"I don't know. About an hour. No. More like two hours. Maybe. I don't know. An hour and a half?"

"Only you know, Bert," Dina said.

Harris's skin appeared damp. "I think it was about an hour and a half."

"What did you do after the walk?"

"What did we do after?"

"Yes," Dina said.

Donato was grateful to hear annoyance in her voice.

"We came back here, I think. No. We went to the movies. We took the subway to Forty-second Street, and we went to the movies."

"You went to the movies on Forty-second Street?" Donato couldn't imagine a nun in those sleazy movie houses.

"Well, not exactly. We got off the subway there, but we walked to Broadway and Forty-fifth. We went to the movie there."

"What did you see?" Dina asked.

Harris stared past her, his fingers splayed across his knees.

"Bert?"

He refocused on her. "What did I see?"

Donato gave in. "What did you and your sister see? What movie?"

"We saw . . . I think we saw *Death Wish Four.* Yes, that's what we saw. *Death Wish Four.* "

Donato wondered why a nun would see a violent film like that. "Did you and your sister go to the movies often?"

"Did we go to the movies often?"

Impatient, Donato said, "Please answer the question."

Harris looked at Donato. Unruffled, he answered, "Yes, we always went to the movies."

"And did you always see films like that?"

"Like what?"

"Violent films," Dina said.

"Violent films," Harris stated, as if he'd never thought about it before. "I guess we did. That's all there is, anyway."

"Did Sister Angelica like violent films?" Donato asked.

"She never complained."

"Then *you* chose what you'd see?"

"Yes. Well, no. Sometimes she did. I chose it on Wednesday."

Dina said, "What did you do after the movie?"

"After the movie?"

"Yes."

"I went home."

Donato and Dina looked at each other.

"Do you mean that you went home alone?" Donato asked carefully.

"Yes."

"And your sister?"

"Gretchen? She went about her business, I guess."

Dina said, "You mean you don't know where she went?"

"That's right. I'm not my sister's keeper, you know." He gave a small dry laugh.

"What would you say, Bert, if I told you that your sister said she was spending the night with you?" Donato said.

"Spending the night with me?" He appeared shocked. "She couldn't spend the night with me. I only have one bed."

"You mean she never spent the night here?"

"No. Never. There's just the one bed. Well, there's the couch," he gestured toward it. "But it's not comfortable, and it doesn't open up. It's not a convertible."

"So you went home and your sister went . . . did you see her to a subway?"

"See her to a subway? No. *I* went to the subway. To come home."

"And where did she go?"

"Where did she go?"

Donato chewed on a finger of his balled fist, then dropped his hand and said harshly, "I'm fed up with you repeating everything we say, Harris. Answer the goddamned question. We want to know the very last time you saw her. When you said good-bye, where was she?"

Harris seemed unaffected by Donato's outburst. "She was waving good-bye from the window of the cab."

"The window of the cab?" Christ, he thought, now I'm doing it.

"Did you hear her tell the driver where she was going?" Dina asked.

"No."

"Which way was the cab headed?"

"I think it went downtown. Yes, downtown. We were on Broadway."

"What kind of a cab was it? Did you notice the name of the company?"

"It was a yellow cab."

"Great," Donato muttered.

"Was the driver a man or a woman?" Dina asked.

"A man or a woman? I didn't notice."

"Weren't you curious as to where she was going?"

His mouth was slack, the lips pallid. "No, I wasn't curious. Why should I be? What did it have to do with me?"

Dina stood up; Donato followed suit. "All right, Bert, thanks very much. Don't leave town without letting us know."

"Leave town?"

"Tomorrow come down to the Thirteenth Precinct to make your statement."

"Where would I go?" he asked.

"Go to the second floor and . . ."

"No, not that. You said, 'Don't leave town.' Where would I go?"

How about hell, Bert? Donato thought. Why don't you go to hell?

Back on the street, they looked at each other and burst into laughter.

"Good Christ," Donato said through guffaws. "I thought I'd go nuts."

"Me, too," she said, still laughing.

As they made their way down the street, they went from giggling to roaring. Tears ran down Donato's cheeks. Dina was holding her side. Whenever one of them seemed to be gaining control, the other would initiate a new round. After a few minutes, Dina put her hand on his arm.

"Stop," she said breathlessly, "we have to stop."

They were off again.

Donato gently grasped her shoulders, faced her. "Listen, kiddo, we're not . . . we're not being professional," he said. This made them howl louder than before, and Dina fell helplessly against him, her forehead on his chest. He wrapped an arm around her.

When they realized what had happened, they pulled away from each other, retreating to their entrenched positions, the laughter tasting stale on their tongues, like old birthday cake.

Walking to the car, Donato wiped his eyes with his linen handkerchief, stuffed it back in his pocket. He wanted to call a truce, tell her he loved her, for God's sake. But he couldn't. A reconciliation would have to come from her. He unlocked the passenger door and went around to the driver's side.

It was so damned hard. Getting in, he recalled the end of an old rhyme: *Here comes the chopper to chop off your head.* It was the perfect sentiment. Any misstep on his part made him feel she was ready and waiting to chop off his head. The hell with that.

Pesetsky and Delgado hadn't been able to interview the Mother Superior at Sacred Heart, but had set up an appointment with her. Delgado's gut feeling, that Sister Margaret was hiding something, hadn't been confirmed, but she planned to keep on her.

Keenan and McCarthy had questioned the two priests who said mass for the Sisters of St. Paul. Neither shed any light on the dead nun's personality. McCarthy had set up an appointment for four o'clock with the cab driver who'd hit Sister Honora.

Lachman reported that there'd been nothing in print about Sister Angelica. He and Bobbin had continued their inquiries in the East Fifties, but every lead they followed turned sour.

Dina read and reread Sister Angelica's letters, finding nothing. And after going over the papers taken from Sister Honora's apartment, Dina believed that the nun was exactly who she seemed to be. No new names were introduced; no secret codes revealed.

Hour after hour, Donato poured over everyone's reports, searching for missed links. There was nothing to discover.

The word had gone out to cab companies asking if any driver had picked up a nun in the Times Square area on Wednesday evening. Now all they had to do was wait until a cabbie came forward.

A number of sex offenders had been interrogated but none of them panned out. This could mean that the killer was from another state or that this was something new for him. Either way, without a motive, the task force was nowhere.

The green fiber found on Sister Angelica's habit turned out to be from Bert Harris's flowered couch.

Final Net was the hair spray the killer used, narrowing the field to millions.

And every member of the task force knew that if the killer didn't strike again, the chances of finding him grew slimmer and slimmer.

Donato was anxious. That morning Renata had asked him to have dinner with her. On occasion they were both home at the dinner hour, but usually Renata took hers to the bedroom to watch the news, while he read with his in the dining room. This felt like a date. And it made him uneasy.

Walking through the streets of SoHo, thinking about Renata and the case, he automatically processed what he saw. These streets had changed drastically in the last ten years, going from factories and luncheonettes to glamorous loft living spaces, galleries, boutiques and over-priced restaurants. The late sixties had brought in the artists, but now only the successful ones could afford to live here. Most of the lofts were occupied by business people with money. Still, the place attracted tourists who dressed in outlandish costumes and didn't realize that most of the time they were ogling each other instead of the neighborhood's artists.

It was here, on Prince Street, in 1976 that he'd met Tom Blackwell, the photorealist. There'd been a murder and the MO matched a case he'd been working on in the One-Nine.

Blackwell, a man in his early thirties, with a curly head of reddish hair, a mustache and full beard, had been a witness to the murder, and Donato spent a great deal of time with him. At first he'd been wary; he'd never known a successful painter before. For him painting was like a dirty secret; he'd always wanted to do it himself but was too afraid to take the risk, try the unknown.

But as he got to know this soft-spoken, gentle man, Donato admitted his lifelong interest in art and, after much coaxing, showed Blackwell his drawings. Impressed, Blackwell offered to give Donato instruction.

For almost five months, fearful of failure, Donato resisted, but Blackwell wore him down, and they began the lessons. Donato studied with Blackwell for three years, then went off on his own. Blackwell urged Donato to show, even brought his dealer to see Donato's work, but Donato refused.

He'd never been sure if he feared rejection by critics or the ridicule of his co-workers. What he told himself was that he was a cop and that came first; art was a sideline, a hobby. Now he painted when he could grab the time and never during a major case. But as he walked the streets, his eyes recorded what he saw and stored the images.

At the corner of Prince and West Broadway, a sidewalk salesman had set up a table displaying boxes of colorful socks. A young woman, her hair spikey and purple, dressed in a man's madras jacket, the sleeves rolled up to midarm, tight black pants, and black high-top sneakers, haggled over a price with the vendor. By her accent, Donato figured the Bronx. He was good at placing New Yorkers by their speech.

He turned up West Broadway. Expensive stores, including Rizzoli's, lined both sides of the street. People sipped drinks at several of the outdoor cafés even though the day was nippy. A boy on a skate board whizzed around him. Two preppie girls in crewneck sweaters, their polo collars turned up, gave him flirtatious glances. Disgusted, he wanted to say something to them, but their backs were to him by the time he turned around. And what could he have said, anyway? At the corner, in the empty lot where vendors set up on weekends, a woman, covered in street filth, looking sixty or more but probably in her forties, sat on the ground, filled paper bags surrounding her.

"Hungry," she said, looking up at Donato.

He walked past. Stopped. Came back. Reaching in his pocket, he pulled out a dollar, leaned down and gave it to her. Her hand touched his, and he pulled away as if it might contaminate him. She shook her head, hurt, understanding his gesture. He wanted to apologize, give her more money. Instead he turned away, kept going. You can't care about them all, he told himself. But it didn't wash.

After crossing Houston Street, he was technically in the Village. West Broadway became La Guardia Place. At Bleecker he entered New York University country. The students he passed looked like twelve-year-olds, but Donato knew it was he growing older, not pupils growing younger.

As he walked through Washington Square Park, ignoring the dope dealers, he wondered again why Renata wanted to have dinner.

Five years ago, he would've been sure the topic was Sara Nieminski. Thinking of her now, he experienced an unexpected wave of sadness, longing.

Most cops had affairs. If not affairs, then quickies with witnesses, victims, other cops. Donato had always prided himself on being different, uninterested in anyone but his wife. There were other, beautiful women in the world—he'd even admired some of them—but he'd never needed anyone but Renata, never desired another woman . . . until he met Sara.

And it wasn't that Sara was so gorgeous, brilliant, irresistible either. It was the timing. Rich had been dead almost three years, and things had not gotten better between him and Renata. Nor had they gotten worse. They simply hadn't changed. From the day Rich died, the two of them had pulled apart. Sometimes he wondered if it would have been different had he confided in her, shared the truth, the overwhelming disappointment he harbored about his son, but that kind of speculation was useless.

Sara had been the victim of a crime—a burglary and attempted rape—and that was how he'd met her. She'd fought off her attacker with words; still she was scarred. She needed someone, and he was there, needing someone, too.

Sara wasn't even thirty. She was blonde, tall and slender, her almond-shaped, brown eyes defenseless, like a baby bird's. A melancholy smile creased a fragile face, skin almost translucent.

And he, lonely, snared in a trap of his own design, kept coming back to interview her long after it was necessary. Deep in denial, he manufactured reasons, bought his own inventions until it was too late.

He'd sat across from her in her small, neat living room, memo pad on his knee, once again reviewing the description of the perpetrator. And then he couldn't go on with it any longer, dropped the pad in his pocket, abruptly rose.

"What is it?" she asked.

"I have to go."

She stood. "All right. I understand."

"Do you?" He knew he shouldn't have asked, couldn't stop himself.

"Yes."

They stayed in place, staring at one another, afraid to move.

"Sara," he finally said, like a prayer.

"If we do," she said, "it will change everything . . . forever. There won't be any turning back."

"I know."

"I've enjoyed your friendship, needed it. You've made a difference in my life."

"We'll always be friends," he said.

She shook her head. "No. Not unless you leave now."

"Then what about tomorrow? The next time I see you?"

"We shouldn't see each other for a while."

"I don't think I can do that."

"Neither do I," she said.

"I'm too old for you," he said.

"I'm too young for you."

He took a step toward her, and she raised both hands, palms out. He stopped.

"We have to know," she said, "that it'll come to an end and eventually we'll lose each other completely."

"We can't *know* that," he insisted.

"And we have to *know*," she continued, "that one of us will be hurt." She smiled ruefully. "Probably me."

He couldn't imagine hurting her but recognized that she was almost certainly right. "I'll go," he said, but didn't move.

They stayed motionless, looking into one another's eyes.

After a time she said, "I'll try not to make demands."

"I'll try to be fair," he said.

She lifted her arms and held them out to him. Moving slowly, he entered her embrace, then picked her up. She seemed weightless, like lace. He carried her to the bedroom, where he'd only been once, the day of her attack, and set her gently on the bed.

He removed her clothes carefully, as if she might renege should she notice. Then he undressed himself and lay down next to her. Naked, they didn't touch, didn't maneuver that last inch, trying to fool themselves that there was still a choice. Finally, resigned, they moved, the length of their bodies meeting, joining surface to surface, then sighed, as though all their lives they'd waited for this moment.

She'd been right, of course. Sex changed everything. As wonderful as it was, now there were lies, broken promises, recriminations, guilt. Still, they'd gone on for five years. He kept expecting Renata to know, to confront him, threaten to leave him, but she never did. Often he wondered if it was his skill at covering or if she knew and didn't care.

Never did he entertain the idea of leaving Renata. He loved her and she was his wife, the mother of his children . . . his child. He loved Sara, too. But it was different.

Sara kept him alive, kept him from doing what Rich had done. And she filled the time when he might have been thinking, going over things again and again.

Eventually, Sara left him.

"I have to, Mike. I want a real life. A marriage, children."

He'd known this would come, but he hadn't known how much it would hurt.

"We knew what the risks were from the beginning," she said. "Remember?"

"Yes. But you said you'd be the one to be hurt."

"Oh, Mike," she said, "I am."

For the next six months, he'd grieved, and it brought back all he'd felt about Rich. Then came the Peak case, and everything collapsed, pushing Sara to a new place, a dark corner he almost never visited unless something reminded him.

Like today, wondering why Renata wanted to have dinner. At Twenty-first Street, he crossed Fifth and headed east toward the One-Three to pick up his car. Obviously, Renata had something weighty to talk over, something that required time, some civility. It had been so long since anything important had mattered to both of them at the same time that he was at a loss. But as with every good mystery, he mused, patience would get results and soon all would be revealed. The thought alarmed him and he shoved it to the back of his mind.

At the corner of Eighty-first and Broadway, Donato went into the bookstore. He loved Shakespeare's and often spent time browsing there. But after five minutes, he found he was looking at titles without registering them and left. In front of Zabar's, he debated whether to get a gooey dessert, then decided Renata would accuse him of being hostile, trying to fatten her up, so instead he went to Rudolph's on Eighty-second.

The small store was in a basement, and almost every available space was furnished with food. There were barrels of pickles, sour tomatoes, green and red peppers. Vats were filled with hummus, baba ghanoush, green and black olives. Cheeses of every kind lined the shelves; salamis and sausages hung from the ceiling. Large glass jars held pistachios, cashews, peanuts. Chunks of halvah sat next to pounds of peanut brittle. Maneuvering around the tiny store was impossible for anyone except the owners, Rudolph and his wife, Lena, who operated like ballet dancers.

Only Rudolph was there now. He had a long sad face and melancholy eyes. Even at his happiest the man looked gloomy.

"Ah, it's the sergeant," Rudolph said as if he were telling someone.

"How are you, Rudolph?"

"Well, you know," he answered, turning his hand back and forth. "Up, down."

"How's Lena?"

He rolled his eyes skyward. "It's the feet this time. She needs an operation."

"Not serious, I hope."

Shrugging, he said, "Who knows? But, look, who could complain? We got our lives, right? And we ain't out on the streets like some."

A picture of the homeless, dirty woman he'd insulted flashed across Donato's mind.

Rudolph went on. "We got food to eat, clothes on our backs and a roof over our heads. We could go blind, we could have C, we could be killed in our beds, but we ain't, so who could complain, right?"

"Right. You have some good dills today?"

"Don't I always? How many?"

"Two." Renata loved dill pickles. He'd known her to make a meal of them.

"Two dills coming up."

Rudolph opened a barrel and reached in with a set of tongs, pulled one out, shook his head, tossed it back. He repeated the procedure three times before he found two he deemed suitable for Donato. Then he wrapped them in wax paper and dropped them in a brown bag.

"For the missus?" he asked rhetorically. "That's nice." Rudolph smiled, but he still looked sad. Then he moved closer and whispered. "Sergeant, you working on the sisters?"

For a moment, Donato didn't know what he meant. "Oh . . . yeah, yeah, I'm on that. Why?"

"There's one comes in here time to time. You think she's safe?"

"I don't know, Rudolph."

"This one's a little . . . you know." He pursed his thick lips, shrugged.

"What do you mean?"

"Wish I could find words. Something . . . something funny."

"Like what?" Donato's interest was piqued.

"I can't say. It's a feeling. Lena had it, too."

"What does she look like, this nun?"

"Like a nun. You know how they look, plain face, round glasses."

Donato did not bother to tell Rudolph that neither Sister Honora nor Sister Angelica had worn glasses. "How did you know she was a nun?"

"How did I know? What? I don't got eyes?"

"Was she wearing a habit?"

"The black with the white around the face. Black shoes and the beads hanging." He made a sweeping gesture around his hip.

"So what gave you a funny feeling?"

"I don't know—that's what I'm saying. I only know after she leaves the first time, me and Lena, we look at each other. Lena says, meshuge. I agree." He shrugged again.

"Lena didn't say why she felt that way?"

"Like me, she couldn't put the finger on it."

"When's Lena going to be here?"

"Maybe tomorrow if the feet feel better."

"I'd like to talk to her."

"You can talk all you want, she won't tell you nothing more than me."

"I'd like to talk to her just the same, Rudolph." Donato knew women frequently picked up on things men failed to notice.

"I'll tell her."

Donato started for the door.

"You got any . . . what d'you call it . . . leads?"

"A few."

"You'll get him. I'm not worried."

Donato smiled and waved good-bye. "I hope you're right, Rudolph. I sure hope you're right."

Renata Donato was four years older than her husband. Her blonde hair had turned gray years before, but she had it dyed a flattering golden color every month at Kenneth's. She had slightly slanting brown eyes and a high-bridged nose. If it hadn't been for her uncompromising mouth, she would have been a beautiful woman. She had been until the death of her son. But then she'd changed; anger and bitterness became the staples of her life.

Across the table from her, in the Metropolis restaurant, Donato tried to remember what she'd looked like when they'd met. He'd been eighteen, she twenty-two: seductive and dangerous, a seasoned woman. He'd appeared older than his years, but he'd had no real experience with women, only the frantic fumblings on rooftops or in darkened hallways with frightened younger girls. His brother's offer of a whore had not appealed to him. But Renata Fiorentini had.

Working as a carpenter's assistant, he'd been on the Fiorentini job two days before he met her. The instant attraction was mutual. He told her he was twenty-three. Knowing she was out of his class, he hesitated to start anything, but she made it clear she didn't care, so the affair began. In secret. And then, almost immediately, she'd gotten pregnant with Richard.

Francesco Fiorentini was enraged. To him Donato was a peasant, scum (an opinion he still held), but since the Fiorentinis were Catholics, there was no possibility of abortion, so Fiorentini insisted Donato marry his daughter. That was no hardship for either of them because they were totally in love. When they took out the marriage license, Renata learned his age.

Fiorentini also insisted that Donato come in to his maraschino cherry business, and Donato obeyed. Renata hoped her father, getting to understand Mike, would soften toward him. But he never did. Instead, he tried to destroy Donato on a daily basis. Still, for Renata's sake, Donato stayed with it almost four years.

During the last one, he applied to and was accepted by the NYPD. Renata knew Donato had given his best to the Fiorentini job, so even though she hated the idea of his becoming a cop, was fearful for him, when he announced his decision to her father, she backed him up. Just as she'd backed him up all through their marriage, until Rich died. Even then she hadn't turned against him—she'd just withdrawn, walling herself off from everyone. It was later, when she'd learned Rich had killed himself and why, that she'd turned on him.

Now he watched her sip a vodka martini. She'd made reservations at this restaurant, and he was smart enough to know that eating out was meant to put them on neutral ground. But why? He didn't delude himself that she wanted to straighten out their lives, reconcile. More likely it was something too toxic to discuss within the confines of their home.

Donato had had enough suspense. "So what is it, Renata? What do you want to talk about?"

She smiled sadly. "There's no subtlety about you, is there?"

He took a swallow of beer. "I don't see much point in playing games after all these years."

"You're right," she said. She took a long thin cigarette from her gold case and waited for Donato to light it.

"I don't have any matches," he said, wondering if she'd noticed that he no longer smoked.

She foraged in her bag again, coming up with a Bic. "That's right," she said, blowing smoke through her nostrils, "you don't indulge anymore."

He didn't know why, but it pleased him that she had noticed. A coil of feeling for her unsprung in his chest, surprising him.

"I thought this would be easy," she said. "But it's not." She took another sip of her drink. "I'm sure you know why I asked you to have dinner tonight."

"No, I don't."

She laughed. "You're supposed to be a detective."

He gave her a tired smile.

"I want to separate," she said flatly. "I can't go on living the way we've been."

Donato felt shocked. "What's a separation going to do for us?" He gnawed on his finger.

"We won't be living in the same house like two zombies. And then later, after Papa dies, we'll get a divorce."

It had never occurred to him that they might divorce. He would have gone on, sharing the same quarters as though they'd been relegated, by an unseen hand, to a dry, sterile life forever.

Renata said, "I can't get a divorce while he's alive. It would hurt him too much."

He nodded. Even though he hated the son-of-a-bitch, he knew a divorce might kill him, and he didn't want that on his conscience. And then it occurred to him that he would have to move. "When were you thinking about doing this?"

"As soon as possible."

"You make it sound urgent."

"It is."

"How so?"

"I don't think I can stand another night sleeping in bed with a stranger," she said stridently.

"You've made us strangers, Renata."

"Oh, no, you don't. Don't try and blame this thing on me. You did it. You and your protection." She spat out the word.

"Why can't you understand that was all I was trying to do?"

"Protect me from what?"

"From the kind of pain I had to suffer. It was bad enough that he was dead. What purpose would it have served for you to know he'd killed himself?" he said in a hushed tone.

"I still think there was something more to it. I feel it here." She hit her chest with a clenched fist.

"I didn't want you to feel responsible, to live every day like I do, wondering what it was you'd done, or not done, that turned your son into a junkie who killed himself. I've told you this, and I've told you that I'm sorry, that maybe I made a mistake. But you've hung on to it, nursed it and fed it and made it grow."

She stared at him, her eyes ruminative; then they dimmed like two fading stars. "Look, it doesn't matter anymore who did what. The marriage is dead and has been for years. Surely this doesn't come as a surprise to you, Michael."

"No. But what do we need to separate for? I'll sleep in another room, if that's the problem."

"That's not the problem. It's your presence. I feel alone, but there's this person living with me, so I'm not really alone. Do you understand?"

"No."

She finished her drink and signaled the waiter for another. "It honestly doesn't matter whether you understand or not. The point is, I don't want to go on the way we've been. It's over."

"Just like that."

"Yes."

He wondered if he was afraid to be alone. First, he'd lived with his family and then with Renata. He'd never been on his own. "I'll have to find a place," he said.

"Of course."

"It might take time. Apartments aren't easy to find."

"I'd like you out by the first of June."

Six weeks. "What'll we tell Dina?"

"The truth. Or would you like to *protect* your thirty-four year-old daughter from that? Anyway, do you think for a moment she's been fooled by this stupid charade we've been living for the last four years?"

No, Donato thought; only he had been fooled. Why else would he feel so shocked, so numb?

The waiter put the new martini in front of Renata. "Would you like to order now?" he asked.

"No," she said quickly. "Not now."

Donato had lost his appetite. "I'll move into Rich's room until I find a place," he offered, realizing it was the only place he'd be comfortable. Dina's room felt alien to him, like a foreign country.

"Good," Renata said.

"How long have you been thinking about this?"

"Years. I don't know why, but I've been afraid to leave you."

"And now?"

"I'm afraid, but I don't care."

He choked out a small dead laugh. "Anything's better than living with me, huh?"

"Yes."

It stung. He didn't want to sit there anymore. He couldn't take the hatred, the contempt she had for him. "I have to leave," he said softly.

"I thought you would," she said.

Donato didn't bother to ask her what she meant. He stood up and headed toward the door. The only thing he could think about was getting out of there, away from Renata, her eyes cold and accusing.

Outside the night air was damp, as if someone were watering a lawn nearby. All he wanted to do now was to get drunk. He hadn't had that desire for a long time. Not since after the Peak case. Then, as now, he'd wanted to forget everything, just blot it all out.

Nine

He sprayed his hair and returned the can of Final Net to the shelf. In the bedroom, he put on his dress shirt, then carried his tuxedo jacket and tie into the living room. He'd been eager to get out of there before his wife came out of her bathroom and started talking. She was always talking. That was one of the nice things about his mother; she knew when to shut up.

At the bar he opened a bottle of La Louviere Blanc, poured himself a glass, walked to the floor-to-ceiling windows and looked out at the East River. Glancing to his right, he could see the glow of the Fifty-ninth Street bridge, the sweep of the river, boat lights, the moon like a lemon rind, and he was filled with gratitude. And then *she* popped up in his mind like ready toast, spoiling his good feeling.

He'd been watching Sister Bambi (he called her that because she moved like a graceful deer) for six weeks. The plan had been to make her his second, but then Sister Angelica presented him with an opportunity he couldn't pass up.

He took a long swallow of wine. That night it was almost as if he'd been divinely guided. Being in that neighborhood at that hour was a stroke of fate. After the experience with Sister Honora, he couldn't sleep. It hadn't occurred to him that he'd have that reaction. After all, it wasn't as if the incident were *his* fault.

Was it he driving the cab that hit her? Did he ask to have her picture in the paper? Should he be blamed because that asshole in his office read the *Post* and left it lying around?

Anyway, that night, the whole deal with Sister Honora had thrown him, so he found himself walking. He must have covered hundreds of blocks, and then suddenly he was in the East Fifties, where Sister Angelica visited once a week, on Wednesday nights. And this was a Wednesday night, or, rather, Thursday morning.

He had resigned himself to the fact that he'd never get at her. The only time she was alone was when she went to the man's house in Chelsea or took a cab to the house on Fifty-fourth.

But for the hell of it, since he was practically there, he walked to that block on Fifty-fourth and for about fifteen minutes stood across the street from the house. Then, just as he was about to leave, there she was, out on the street, by herself, at quarter to one in the morning. Now was that fate or not? Whatever it was, nobody could say the onus was on him.

He walked over to the mirror, put down his drink and began working on his black tie, trying to get it perfect. He hated parties, but he wouldn't mind this one because he knew he looked good in a tuxedo. Women would be swarming around him.

Sister Honora was another matter. With her, he was able to pick and choose his time since she didn't live in a convent. But he certainly hadn't expected to do two in such a short period of time, and he would have preferred spacing them. Still, when the iron's hot you have to strike.

Looking down at his watch, he noted that six days ago at this time he'd already finished with Sister Honora. By now he'd been sitting in Teresa's, on First Avenue and Sixth, having his dinner. He could never get his wife to go there with him. She thought the place was tacky. She didn't understand the beauty in having half a roast chicken with carrots and boiled potatoes for $3.95. She just didn't get it.

How would he have felt then, if he'd known the night was just beginning for him? He laughed out loud.

"What's so funny?" she asked, coming into the living room.

"You had to be there," he answered lightly.

"I'll bet," she said sourly. Squeezing between him and the mirror, she turned her back to him. "Zip me."

His face showed nothing. He knew she was looking at him in the mirror, trying to figure out what he'd been laughing about, spying on his mind. Finished with the zipper, he leaned down and kissed her neck. She shivered and turned, facing him, and pushed her body up against his.

"How can you be so sweet sometimes and then other times . . . I don't know, be so . . . awful. I feel like I'm married to a Dr. Jekyll and Mr. Hyde."

He smiled at her, one of his best "I'm just a naughty boy" looks, like Gary Cooper.

She ran a hand over his face. "Why do you have to be so gorgeous?" She kissed him, shoved her tongue in his mouth, rubbed her breasts against his chest.

He moaned, pretending he liked it, then gently pushed her away. "We don't have time."

She reached for his crotch. "You're not even hard."

"I would be in another second."

"Really?" she said sarcastically.

He wanted to slap her then, knock the stupid cunt across the room. "Think what you want." It wouldn't have been like this with Dorothy. She would've been his slave. Goddamn Dorothy.

"You talk a good game, mister, but when it gets down to the nitty-gritty, you're a washout." She walked away from him, out of the room.

Tears sprang to his eyes, surprising him. It was the memory of Dorothy that moved him. He'd done his best to bury the past. But then last January, through no fault of his own, there she was again, and all the memories had come tumbling back like change cascading from a slot machine. Finishing with his tie, he poured himself more wine and went to the window again. Dorothy would have loved this view.

They'd met in chemistry class their senior year. At first they'd ignored each other, but then she saw that he was having trouble with the work and offered to help him. They went to her house after school and studied at the dining room table. Dorothy's mother brought them milk and cookies.

Three times a week, he went to her house to be tutored. He liked being there, liked being with Dorothy. After about a month, he screwed up all his courage and asked her to go to the movies with him on Saturday night. She said yes.

His mother had helped him decide what to wear. She was happy for him. But his father razzed him, saying whoever this Dorothy was, she was probably a dog's dinner. He'd hated him then, almost more than he ever had. The truth was, Dorothy wasn't very attractive, but he didn't care.

That first date with her had filled him with anxiety. After a big fight, his mother had finally convinced his father to let him have the car, and he remembered pulling up in front of Dorothy's house, sitting there, thinking about leaving. He worried that he'd do something stupid and she wouldn't go out with him again, or help him with chemistry. But then he forced himself to get out, ring her doorbell.

For the first time, he met Dorothy's father. He could tell right away that the man didn't like him, but he didn't give a damn, as long as Dorothy did.

And she did. She let him hold her hand in the movies, and when he took her home, she let him kiss her good-night. Driving back to his house, he felt as if he were floating on a cloud. He couldn't remember ever being that happy.

There were more dates, and one day he'd overheard a girl from the top crowd say to another one: "Isn't it great that the troll [that was he] found the anteater [that was Dorothy because of her long nose]. I guess that proves there's somebody for everyone." And then they'd laughed.

But he didn't care what they thought or how much they laughed. Having a girlfriend made him feel right. He'd never, in all his life, felt right, normal.

"I'm ready," his wife said.

He whirled around as if he'd been caught at something.

"My, my," she said, "we got *noives* tonight."

Ignoring her, he asked, "Where are the girls?"

"In their room doing homework."

"I'll just say good-night to them." He put down his glass and brushed past her.

Rebecca and Stephanie were lying on their beds, headphones firmly in place. He stood in the doorway, watching them; it was hard to believe he'd created them. Fathers were supposed to adore their daughters, and although he didn't mind their being around, he didn't have any particular feeling for them.

"Hi, Dad," Rebecca said, sliding the earphones back. "You look hot."

"I do? Well, I'm not hot; it's cool tonight."

They laughed.

"Oh, Daddy, you're so cute," Stephanie said. "She didn't mean hot hot. She meant sexy."

This kind of talk offended him, but he knew it was the way fathers and daughters related these days. "Oh, sexy," he said, feigning amusement. "Well, that's different. C'mon, give your old dad a kiss good-bye."

They jumped up, and each one gave him a hug and kissed him on the lips.

"Mmmm, you smell good, too, Dad," Stephanie said.

"You know who Carol said you looked like?"

"Who's Carol?"

"Oh, Daddy, you're so crazy."

His gut tightened.

Rebecca went on. "You don't remember anything. Sometimes I wonder about you. Carol is Stephanie's very best friend, and she says you look like Don Johnson from *Miami Vice.*"

He knew who Johnson was and had noticed the resemblance himself. "Well, tell Carol thanks for the compliment, but she's way off base."

"That's what I think," Rebecca said.

He wanted to slap her. "Smart girl. Okay, got to go now. We won't be late. The number's on the blackboard."

"We'll be fine," Stephanie said.

"I know you will. You're my two big girls, aren't you? C'mon, plant another one," he said, pointing to his cheek.

Walking down the hall, he realized he was shaking. The memory of Dorothy had made him anxious, and he was starting to feel *that way* again. It was too soon. He wasn't ready for Sister Bambi. Anyway, it was night. Getting Sister Angelica at night was just luck. And he hadn't been properly prepared. It was a wonder that he hadn't blown it.

The pressure was building inside him. Goddammit, why the hell had he let himself think about Dorothy? He had to have more control because once the feeling started it couldn't be stopped; it had a life of its own. Quickly, he ran down his appointments for the next day. He was free after three. He hoped he could hold out and he hoped Sister Bambi would be ready because by then he'd be more than ready. He'd be bursting.

Ten

When Dina entered the task force room at the One-Three, Bobby Keenan was sitting at the conference table eating cookies and drinking milk. She thought the choice fitting for an adult who called himself Bobby, then chastised herself for being mean. They said good morning, and Dina put her files on the table and pulled out a chair. Lifting the lid off her coffee, she inhaled deeply, enjoying the aroma. There was something about drinking coffee in a cardboard container that she liked better than drinking it from a cup. Besides, precinct coffee was always awful.

"Would you like a cookie, Lieutenant?"

"No thanks. It's a little too early for me."

He smiled crookedly. "I'll bet you're one of those people who eats dessert last."

"Most of the time I don't eat it at all," she said. And then worried that she'd sounded prissy.

"Have to watch your weight, huh?"

"That's not the reason," she snapped.

"Yeah, that's what I said, couldn't be because you had to watch your weight, a woman like you."

She ignored him.

"So why don't you eat desserts, Lieutenant?" He popped a piece of cookie in his mouth, smiling while he chewed.

"It's none of your business, Keenan, but I'll tell you, anyway. Maybe you'll learn something. Sugar isn't good for you." All she could think about was the chocolate cake she'd had with Judy a few days before.

"I know. I never eat sugar." He held up a chocolate cookie. "Made with fructose and corn syrup. And there's no dairy in it either. It's a Tofutti cookie. Made out of tofu."

"Sounds delicious," she said facetiously.

"It is. No kidding." Picking up a cookie, he walked over to her. "C'mon, try one."

"I don't want a cookie." She leaned back as if he might stuff it in her mouth.

"Take a risk. It's a new taste thrill. Don't you like thrills, Lieutenant?" His smile gone, he pretended to be serious.

"Drop this, Keenan." Furious that he'd made her look priggish and stiff, she opened one of the folders and began going through papers.

"Okay, it's your loss." He sauntered back to his chair. "I'm obsessed with these cookies, I admit it. I drove all the way up to Seventy-sixth and Broadway last night to get them." He drained the container of milk, pulled a handkerchief from his back pocket and wiped his mouth. "I'll tell you what's bad for you if you want to talk bad. Coffee. That stuff is poison. How many cups do you drink a day? Six, eight?"

"Look, Keenan, I'm not interested in a health lecture. If I decide to go for seaweed, I'll subscribe to *Prevention* magazine."

"Just trying to make conversation, Lieutenant."

"Don't bother; this isn't a social occasion."

He fell back in his chair, both hands up as if he were being arrested. "Hey, listen, you don't have to tell me twice." Not missing a beat, he said, "You have beautiful hair, Lieutenant."

Astonished, she looked up.

He gazed back, completely guileless.

After a few moments, this made her smile. Then slowly, he

smiled. Dina felt it to her toes. She said, "You're incorrigible, Keenan."

"Is that what I am?" he asked huskily.

"Yes. I think you are." She was lightheaded, undone.

"You're probably right."

Had Delgado not opened the door just then, Dina wasn't certain how long she might have continued looking into his blue eyes, feeling she might drown.

Keenan went back to his cookies.

Dina returned to her papers, but she couldn't concentrate. From the time she and Liam had split, she'd carefully constructed a wall between herself and men. She'd had a date here and there but no interest in falling in love again. So why couldn't she have an affair like other people did? Why did it have to be serious? Oh, get a grip, she said to herself; what am I thinking about? The man said I had pretty hair. Obediently, she put aside any feelings for Keenan as the others filed in. Then she started the session with Bobbin.

Dwarfing the wooden chair, he tried to get comfortable as he opened his notebook. "I made contact with this dude who lives out of a shopping cart on Fifty-fourth Street. Says his name is Nick. Plays the guitar and sings."

"A fucking Elvis," Lachman added.

"Yeah, an Elvis who hasn't taken a bath for maybe eight, nine months. Anyway, this dude says on the night in question he was in his usual spot on Fifty-fourth, having some light refreshment . . ."

The others laughed.

"Thunderbird perchance?" McCarthy asked.

Bobbin passed a hand over his chocolate face. "I don't think it was Vat Sixty-nine. Anyway, the dude says he saw a nun come flyin' down the street, looking wild-eyed."

"Maybe it was Sally Field," Pesetsky said.

"Yeah, the fucking flying nun," Lachman added.

Bobbin went on. "He says he couldn't believe what he's seein', thought he was havin' the goddamn dt's."

"I bet he took the pledge right then," Keenan said.

"You got it, brother. The dude falls to his knees and starts prayin'."

"Come on," Delgado protested.

"Serious," Bobbin said. "Anyway, the sister, she just goes right past, pays him no mind."

"Anyone following her?" Dina asked.

"Said he didn't see anybody else."

"What time was it?"

"You got to be kidding. Think this dude's wearin' a watch?" Bobbin sighed. "But I ask, just the same as you. Night, he says. Then, he says, she turned the corner at Fifty-fourth and disappeared. That's it."

"Lachman?"

"I came up fucking empty, Lieutenant. After Roy got the info from Nick, I canvassed all of Fifty-third and Fifty-fourth from First Avenue to Park. Zip."

"Keep on it. And try this Nick again; see if you can pin down a time." She held up a hand to interrupt the protest before it began. "I know who you're dealing with and I don't expect miracles, but you never know—there might be a way to get a time frame from him. Be creative."

"Thanks a bunch," Bobbin said good-naturedly.

"Delgado?"

Seated next to the bulky Bobbin, she seemed more diminutive than ever. "We interviewed the Mother Superior of Sacred Heart. She's a tough old broad, I gotta tell ya. Whew!"

Keenan said, "The Mother Superior in my school ate nails for breakfast, bolts for lunch and—"

"Screwed for dinner," Lachman interrupted, laughing so hard his chair almost toppled over.

Only Bobbin laughed, probably out of pity for his partner, Dina thought.

Delgado went on. "She said Sister Honora was always a good nun and the reason she'd picked her to live outside the convent was because she was," she looked down at her notes, "level-headed, mature and very intelligent." Delgado shut the pad. "When we asked if maybe she'd gotten involved with someone, you know, like a guy, that lady lit into us like there was no tomorrow. I mean, she went the whole nine yards. I felt like I was eight years old or somethin', right, Pesetsky?"

Pesetsky still had a sour look, as if he'd eaten spoiled food. "Yeah, right," he said, apathetically.

Something was definitely wrong between these two. She'd have to speak to them again after the session was over. "Anything else?"

"We went back to the center after we spoke to the Mother Superior. Sister Margaret's definitely hidin' somethin', Lieutenant. You think so, too, don't you Pesetsky?"

Before he spoke he ran a hand over his face as if he were washing it. "Yeah, I think so."

"Like maybe there *was* a boyfriend?" McCarthy asked.

"That doesn't make sense," Keenan put in. "You mean there's some guy out there having affairs with two nuns, killing both of them?"

Pesetsky said, "Nobody said the boyfriend's the killer."

"I don't buy Sister Honora having a boyfriend," Donato said.

"Voice from the dead," Bobbin commented.

Donato gave him a thin smile. "I didn't think it showed."

"I don't have anythin' else, Lieutenant. We couldn't crack her," Delgado said.

It was time to bring in McCarthy to interrogate Sister Margaret. It was what McCarthy did best. "Okay. I'm going to take you and Pesetsky off HAFH. Exchange notes with McCarthy and Keenan, and you two give Sister Margaret a try. McCarthy, how did it go with the cabdriver who hit Sister Honora?"

"He remembered it, naturally. Said he had a passenger who left the scene. Guy going to work. The driver didn't have anything more than we already know."

"How about him? Alibis for the night the nuns were killed?"

"Airtight," McCarthy said.

"Anybody ever find the passenger who skipped?"

"Don't know. Sister Honora walked in front of the cab from between two parked cars, so there wasn't a suit. Probably nobody ever looked for him. No need."

"I guess. Did you get a description of the passenger?"

"I didn't think it was . . ."

"Get one. You never know," Dina said. "Both nuns' funerals are today. Bobbin and Lachman go to Sister Honora's, and Pesetsky and Delgado go to Sister Angelica's. We have to find out how our guy gets to these nuns."

"Could be he's a priest," Bobbin said.

"That's a possibility, but we can't interview every priest in New York."

The phone buzzed. Dina picked it up, listened for a moment, hung up. "Donato, the cabbie who picked up Sister Angelica on Wednesday is here. Go talk to him. Pesetsky and Delgado stay. The rest of you can go."

As he left, Keenan gave her a smile she didn't return.

"I'm not satisfied you told me the truth when we talked before. What's going on between you two?" Dina asked.

"Nothin'," Delgado answered quickly.

"I don't believe that. Pesetsky?"

"Nothing." He studied his nails.

"Don't give me this crap. I want to know what's wrong."

Alma Delgado looked down at her gray leather boots, clicked the toes against each other.

"Pesetsky," Dina said, "you seem disgruntled, unhappy."

"How come you put Lachman and Bobbin together?" he said abruptly, as though he'd just heard her.

"I thought putting the newest detective with the oldest might be good."

"You think Bobbin's better than me?"

"I didn't say that. Did you want to be partnered with Lachman?"

"Lachman, Bobbin, Keenan, I don't care."

"Just not Delgado or McCarthy, right?"

"You got it," he said defiantly.

Delgado was nodding, glad the truth was finally out in the open.

"And me, Pesetsky?"

"What about you?"

"Have you felt this way working with me?"

"Look, I have nothing against women being on the force," he said, evading her question, "but sometimes, some places, they don't belong, you know what I mean?"

"No," Dina said, checking her anger.

"Well, naturally, you wouldn't. I must be a jerk for expecting you to understand." He lit a cigarette, flipped the match in a red metal ashtray.

"I'm not changing partners now, Pesetsky. If you want off the team just say so."

Pesetsky stood up. "I'll stick."

"Good. Then I expect you to treat Delgado as an equal. I want you to work together, not against each other. Do you understand?"

They said they did, and Dina excused them. Sitting on the edge of the table, she found herself shaking. From the outset, she'd had to contend with chauvinistic treatment on the Force. Her first partner wouldn't let her drive the patrol car, making it clear what he thought of women drivers. Then they'd interrupted a liquor store holdup, and she'd kept him from being killed. After that he decided she was fit to drive. But his attitude never really changed, and when she advanced before he did, he implied she was sleeping with the lieutenant.

Each step of her career had been the same. Always, she had had to prove herself exceptional. She had to make an extra effort, push harder, work longer hours. And the final bind was, if she showed emotion, she was labeled unprofessional; if she showed none, she was unfeminine.

As she started for the door, the phone rang. It was Keenan.

"What is it?" she asked, feeling out of kilter.

"I wanted to know if you'd have dinner with me tonight?"

She didn't answer.

"I think you should," he persevered.

"Why?" she asked.

"Because I think something important is happening between us."

Dina felt his words as if he were touching her. It made her mad. "I don't know how late I'll be working."

"There's this place on Third Street I like a lot. It's a vegetarian restaurant but not what you think. I mean, it's not the usual bean sprouts with a couple of celery stalks thrown in. It's good, no joke. Quantum Leap. Third between Sullivan and Thompson. Since we both live downtown, I thought it would be convenient."

"How do you know I live downtown?" she asked, annoyed.

"Don't go crazy, okay?"

"I'm not going crazy, Keenan," she said, thinking about hanging up on him. "I simply want to know how you know where I live."

"I'm a detective," he said.

Was he laughing at her? "Look, I don't think I'll be able to make it."

"How about this?" he said quickly. "I'll be at the Quantum Leap at eight-thirty. If you can make it, swell; if not I'll catch you another time. I got work to do now. So long, Lieutenant."

She slammed the receiver back in the cradle. Who the hell did he think he was, saying something important was going on between them? And what the hell was he doing asking her out in the first place? She was his superior.

Slinging her leather bag across her right shoulder so she would have access to her gun if she needed it, she thought, if it isn't Pesetsky resenting me, or Donato playing papa, it's Keenan trying to . . . to what? All he'd done was ask her to have dinner with him. So what if he was a little cocky? Smiling, she recalled his response to her question of how he knew where she lived. Then she felt angry all over again at his arrogance and assumptions. Well, he could presume all he wanted; there was no way she was going to meet this guy for anything, let alone dinner in a vegetarian restaurant. No way.

Donato had talked to the cabdriver who remembered taking Sister Angelica to the brownstone on East Fifty-fourth on Wednesday evening.

Standing on the steps, Dina and Donato stood staring at the names. There were two apartments. Donato's hand shook as he reached out and rang the bottom bell.

Dina noticed the tremor but said nothing. Maybe he was sick, trying to hide an illness from her, the department. She knew Donato, unable to abide pity, would keep it to himself if he were ill.

There was no response. Donato tried the second bell.

Glancing at him surreptitiously, Dina thought his face looked ragged, as if he'd drunk too much the night before, hadn't gotten enough sleep. But he'd told her he'd cut down on his drinking.

A woman's voice came over the intercom. They told her who they were, and she rang them in.

Climbing the stairs, Dina noticed at each landing the deep indentations called coffin corners, built so that a casket could be maneuvered up and down the narrow staircase. As always, the thought of death, particularly her own, chilled her.

A woman stood at the top of the stairs. Donato showed his shield.

"What's this about?"

"What's your name, please?" Dina asked.

"Mrs. Curran," she answered uneasily.

"May we come in?"

Reluctantly, she agreed.

The large room was painted a linen white. Ceiling moldings were elaborately carved, and the furniture was mostly Louis XVI. The chairs looked fragile, and table surfaces held objets d'art, photographs in gold and silver frames.

"Please sit down," Mrs. Curran said.

Dina chose a chair with fluted legs. She watched Donato glance from one piece to another, trying to decide what would hold him best. He eased himself down on a rose-colored love seat as if the piece might splinter.

Mrs. Curran was in her middle fifties. Her hair was an ash blonde, no trace of gray. She had brown, despondent eyes and a heart-shaped face with skin the off-white color of skimmed milk. She wore a long blue velvet dressing gown that zipped up the front. Dina thought she'd had a face lift, the line of her chin too definite for someone her age.

"We're here to ask you about Sister Angelica," Dina said bluntly.

It worked. Two spots of color stained the woman's cheeks. "Who?"

Donato said, "Mrs. Curran, we know that Sister Angelica came to see you on Wednesday evening about eight, eight-thirty."

"I don't know what you're talking about," she said lamely.

"I think you do, Mrs. Curran," Dina said.

She moved away from them to the far end of the room, her back rigid. "You must have me confused with someone else." She blew a wreath of smoke above her head.

Donato and Dina exchanged a look that said they were right on the money. Dina signaled him with the tilt of her chin. He rose and walked to Mrs. Curran.

"We can talk here, or we can talk at the station house. It's up to you."

She looked at him, a luster to her eyes, as if she had a fever. "I don't know what you're talking about," she said again, but with less conviction.

"All right," Donato said, "please get dressed. We'll have to go downtown."

"You can't do that," she protested.

"Yes, we can. Now get dressed," he ordered.

Mrs. Curran whirled around, looking at Dina beseechingly. It was what she'd been waiting for. She joined the two of them and gently laid a hand on the woman's shoulder.

"He's right," she said, "but I don't want to do that, Mrs. Curran. So why don't you sit down and talk it over with us here." Dina guided her back to the couch and sat next to her. Donato stood nearby.

"Oh, God," Mrs. Curran said, "I can't get involved in this, I really can't. You have no idea what it would cost me."

"Tell me about it," Dina urged.

"How did you know?" She looked at each of them. "How did you find out? Oh, it must've been the cabdriver. She told me she took a cab. Usually she didn't. She came by subway." She laughed suddenly. "It was *I* who told her to take cabs. I said I'd pay for them. I didn't like the idea of her riding subways. They're so dangerous, don't you think?"

"Did you kill her?" Donato asked.

"Oh, God no, I . . ."

They waited.

"Of course I didn't. Is this going to come out? That she was here."

"That depends," Donato said.

"On what?"

"On how cooperative you are."

A small, insolent smile played around her lips. "I don't like you," she said.

Dina felt hurt for Donato. It was ridiculous.

Mrs. Curran turned to Dina. "Does he have to be here?"

"Yes. Don't worry about him," she added, trying to sound as if she were Mrs. Curran's conspirator. "Why don't you tell me what happened." She purposely didn't say us.

"Will Craydon have to know? Because if he does it'll all be over. His mother will be right there urging him on." Shrill laughter spilled from her mouth. "Oh, she'll be the first in line. And I wouldn't care, actually, but it would be very hard on Jason and Linda."

Mrs. Curran, Dina noted, was one of those people whose focus was so narrow she spoke to strangers of her intimates as though they should know who they were. She had to make an effort to hide her irritation. "Who's Craydon?" she asked.

"My husband. Craydon doesn't have any idea . . . you won't be giving this information to reporters, will you?"

"No," Dina answered truthfully. "How did you know Sister Angelica?"

"We were friends of the family. In Rhode Island. When Angelica was assigned to the order in New York, Rita asked me to look her up, keep an eye on her."

"Rita?"

"Her mother."

"Then you know Bert, her brother?" Donato asked.

She rolled her eyes heavenward. "Isn't he something? Yes, I know Bert. Haven't seen him in years, but Angelica told me he hadn't changed." She leaned toward Dina. "Have you considered him as a suspect? I mean, I think he's capable of anything. Especially where Angelica is concerned. I think you should check him out."

"He has an alibi," Dina said. "Who are Jason and Linda, Mrs. Curran?"

She looked stricken. "How do you know about them?"

"You just mentioned them," Donato said.

She glanced at him, rankled by his presence. "They're my youngest children. The other two are gone," she said, as if they'd disappeared, rather than grown up. "Linda's fifteen. She goes to Brearley. Jason's seventeen. He's at Trinity. It's a good thing you came this morning while everyone's out. You won't be coming back will you?" She seemed panicky.

"If you cooperate now and tell us everything, there probably won't be any reason for us to return," Dina explained, wondering what chance they'd have of getting the truth out of this woman.

Mrs. Curran jumped up, paced, lit another cigarette. "I don't know where to start."

"Why was Sister Angelica here last Wednesday night?" Dina asked.

"She came to visit, of course."

Dina noticed that the woman was no longer looking in her eyes. "How often did she visit you?"

"Once a week. When Craydon is out of town and the children are with their grandparents. It isn't that Craydon didn't like her. He didn't even know her. I mean they'd met, but, well, being around a nun made him uncomfortable. So we had our visits when he was away."

"Do you know why she told the people at the convent that she was staying overnight with her brother?" Dina asked.

"No."

It was a lie. Donato picked up his cue. "I think you do know."

Mrs. Curran refused to look at him. "It was just simpler, that's all. You know how mother superiors can be. It was easier; that's the only reason."

"All right," Dina said, believing her. "What did you do when she visited?"

"What do you mean by that?" she asked defensively.

There was something to learn here, and Dina felt excited, as if she were about to win at roulette. "How did you and Sister Angelica spend your time together?"

Mrs. Curran crossed her arms over her chest protectively. "We talked, had dinner, listened to music."

"What kind of music?"

"What difference could that possibly make?"

"It will give me a picture. Tell me what happened on Wednesday night, Mrs. Curran," Dina said mildly.

"Oh, God. All right. At first everything was fine, as usual. I'd made a lovely cheese soufflé, a watercress and endive salad, asparagus vinaigrette. We drank some wine, talked. We had dessert, chocolate mousse, her favorite. Then we came in here. I made a fire. It was chilly and fires are so cozy."

And romantic, Dina thought.

"We talked some more, drank more wine, at least I did. Perhaps I drank too much. Oh, I don't know how to explain this."

"You're doing fine," Dina encouraged.

"You see, Angelica and I have . . . had a special relationship. Do you know what I mean?"

"Why don't you explain it to me."

"We were listening to music, Brahms. She was sitting where you are. I was sitting there." She gestured over her shoulder toward Donato. "And then . . . I don't know why I did it. As I said, perhaps I'd had too much to drink." She looked down at the rug, her cheeks coloring. "I got up and went to sit next to Angelica. And then I took her hand. Oh, we'd always been affectionate with each other. She thought nothing of giving me a hug. But this was different."

They waited for her to go on.

She began to cry silently, tears streaking her powdered cheeks. "She let me hold her hand—in fact, she held mine back, if you know what I mean. When you hold someone's hand and they're not interested, their hand just lies in yours like a dead thing. But she didn't do that. So I thought . . . I thought she felt the same. Oh, God, what a fool I made of myself." She looked up at Dina, her eyes red, haunted. "Please. Don't make me go on. I think you know what happened."

"I know this is difficult, Mrs. Curran, but we need to know. What did you do then?"

She closed her eyes as if being in the dark would make it easier. "I kissed her . . . on the lips." Her hands flew to her face as she began to sob.

"And then?" Dina cut through her crying. "What happened then, Mrs. Curran?"

"She . . . she was horrified. She pushed me away and jumped up. I ran after her, trying to apologize. She insisted on leaving. It was late, almost midnight. I begged her to stay. I mean, where was she going to go at that hour? I promised her I wouldn't come near her again, that she could leave first thing in the morning. Finally she agreed."

"She stayed?"

"Yes. She went to her room and I to mine. When I woke in the morning she was gone, of course. It was about ten. I assumed she'd spent the night and left early. But now I know that isn't what happened. I can't believe she's dead. I loved her so. And I killed her. It was my fault. She never would have left if I hadn't . . ." She shook her head violently as though she might rid herself of the responsibility.

Dina opened her bag and got out some tissues. She handed them to Mrs. Curran as she slumped like a puppet with cut strings.

"Where do you suppose she was headed when she left?" Donato asked gently.

"I don't know, her brother's perhaps." She looked up, her eyes pleading. "I thought she felt the same as I. I should have known better . . . I really should have known."

"Maybe you didn't want to know," Dina suggested.

"Yes. I suppose that's right. It's not as if I'm . . . an innocent. Will this have to come out?" Mrs. Curran asked.

"I don't see why. But we may want to talk with you again."

"You won't come when Craydon's here, or the children?"

"We'll call first," Dina assured her.

At the door, Mrs. Curran said, "You must think I'm vile."

"We're not here to judge you, Mrs. Curran," Dina said.

"In my day, you got married right after college. That's what you did. Today it's different. Look at you. A lieutenant on the police force. That would never have happened in my time. Are you married?"

"Divorced."

She nodded. "That's the other thing. My generation didn't get divorced. There's never been a divorce in my family. I'd like to leave Craydon. I mean, we don't have a marriage anymore, not really. But where would I go? What would I do? Could I be a police lieutenant? It's too late for me." She began to cry again. "And it's too late for Angelica."

Dina reached out, touched her hand. "Try not to be too hard on yourself."

At the bottom of the stairs, they could still hear her sobs, deep from within her, as though she were trying to dredge up the last vestiges of her guilt.

They hit a deli on Lexington Avenue where Dina got coffee and Donato bought a corned beef on rye and a Dr. Pepper. Sitting in the car, Donato wolfed down the sandwich. Now Dina was sure he had a hangover.

"Is this part of your new, healthy life?" she asked. "If I didn't know that you'd cut down on your drinking, I'd think . . ."

"Don't be a smart ass, kiddo. I feel like hell."

"How come?"

"Because I tied one on last night, that's how come," he said.

"Want to tell me about it?"

"Not particularly. Well, hell. You're going to know soon enough. Your mother's kicking me out."

Dina felt stunned and hurt, as if she were a small child. She knew things had gotten worse between them since the truth had come out about Rich's death, but she hadn't expected this.

"Are you going to get a divorce?"

"I don't know. It's up to Renata, I guess."

"Don't you have anything to say about it?"

"Hey, come on, Lieutenant, give me a break here."

"Well, I mean it, Donato. Is it all Mom's show?"

"I don't stay where I'm not wanted. She said something about divorcing after the old man dies."

For a moment, the only sound in the car was the crunching of Donato's dill pickle.

"Do you *want* a divorce? Can you at least tell me that?" God, he could be irritating.

"Let's just drop it, okay?"

"No, it's not okay." He did that with everything unpleasant, and it infuriated her. "Look, Donato, despite what's happened between us, you're my father, and I think I have a right to discuss this with you."

"You know something, Dina? You don't. What happens between your mother and me is our business. I'm sorry I brought it up at all." He took a handkerchief from his jacket pocket and wiped his mouth, a smear of mustard staining the cloth.

She had to concede that he had a point. Still, there were some things she felt she was entitled to know. "Could you just tell me if *you* want a divorce?"

"I don't know. I'm not sure. Maybe it would be the best thing. What did you think about the Curran woman?"

Terrific, Donato, she thought, just slide around it. What the hell. "I think she's telling the truth."

"I didn't mean that. I meant, you know." He shrugged help-lessly.

"You mean was I shocked at her being a lesbian or a bisexual?"

"Well, no, not that. I'm not such an old geezer I don't know what's going on these days. But with a nun? Come on."

"There's a book called *Lesbian Nuns*," she said matter-of-factly. "It's not fiction."

"Maybe I *am* an old geezer."

Dina laughed. "Do you think she was telling the truth?"

"Yeah. So that leaves us nowhere."

"Not quite. At least we know what the nun was doing out on the streets at that hour."

"I guess that's something. But how the hell did he know he was going to run into a nun in the middle of the night in the East Fifties? I can't buy coincidence, can you?"

"No. I'd say he was waiting for her."

"Why would he think she was going to come out? According to Mrs. Curran, they always stayed in."

"I think maybe he hoped. What he knew was that there was a nun at that address, and Curran said Sister Angelica spent the night every Wednesday. If you're watching somebody, you know those things. Maybe he waited there every Wednesday night."

The two-way radio crackled to life, the operator telling them that Keenan wanted them to meet him at a restaurant on St. Mark's Place. He had some new information.

Dina started the car. There was no mention of McCarthy, but that didn't mean she wouldn't be there. Anyway, Keenan would surely behave himself while she was with her father. She almost laughed, realizing he made her feel protected, safe. Funny thing was . . . it didn't feel bad at all.

Eleven

Donato had often been to the St. Mark's restaurant called EAT, but not since it had been enlarged, spruced up. For years it was a kind of hole-in-the-wall with bare tables and spare lighting. Now there were tablecloths and metal overhead lights, as if the owners were trying for the popular hi-tech look.

He hoped they hadn't changed the food and prices to fit the decor. Donato especially liked the fries, which were cooked long enough to get dark.

He and Dina walked through the narrow front room into the back where Keenan and McCarthy were. In front of Keenan was a plate of stir-fried vegetables and brown rice. He was using chopsticks. Donato noted the bruise under his eye, wondered what it was from. McCarthy was eating a bowl of chili. A shared bottle of seltzer sat on the table between them.

As they sat down, McCarthy, grinning, said, "We cracked Sister Margaret."

"*You* did," Keenan said. "She's really something. It took McCarthy all of about ten minutes to break her."

Pushing a lock of hair off her forehead, she smiled modestly. Judy was almost like a second daughter to Donato. For the last few years, his *only* daughter. She still came around when she could. They never talked about Dina, just shot the breeze, kidded, the way they used to when she'd spent so much time at their house.

Donato said, "McCarthy could charm Hitler."

"Yeah," McCarthy agreed, "but why would I want to?"

The waitress came for their order, and when she left, McCarthy filled them in. "Sister Margaret was shielding a kid who'd threatened Sister Honora."

"Why didn't she say so sooner?" Dina asked.

"She didn't think it meant anything, said at first she forgot it, then when she remembered she thought it was an idle threat and didn't want to get the kid in trouble."

"And now?"

"She realized that she didn't have the right to hold it back."

"McCarthy helped her along in this realization," Keenan said, smiling. "Rubber hose."

"Just a couple of swings, Lieutenant," McCarthy said.

They all laughed. Except for Donato. And then Dina and McCarthy stopped abruptly. Keenan didn't know what had happened, but took his cue from the others and cut the kidding.

Donato's insides felt like gears stripping. The women looked away from him. Keenan went back to his food. Donato wondered if the Peak case were going to follow him forever.

Breaking the tension, the waitress arrived with Dina's coffee and Donato's juice.

"So where's this kid now?" Dina asked.

"She didn't know. He left the center a few months ago."

"Name?"

"Posie."

"Great."

Keenan said, "The kid likes flowers."

"Did you get a description of him?"

McCarthy took her pocket memo from her handbag, began to read. "About six feet, skinny, light brown complexion, modified afro, long scar on his right cheek. Probably sixteen or seventeen. Drug user."

Donato said, "How did he threaten Sister Honora and why?"

"He came to the center stoned. That's not allowed. You have to be straight to get any help from them, any food," McCarthy explained. "Apparently, he'd done this a couple of times, and Sister Honora warned him. He admitted to chipping once or twice, but the last time they saw him he was nodding out and Sister Honora told him he couldn't stay. He swore he was straight and wouldn't leave. So the nun got a few of the other boys to take him out bodily. As he was being evicted, he yelled that he was going to get Sister Honora."

"That was it?" Dina asked.

"That was it."

"What do you think?" She turned to Donato.

"I think it should be followed up."

McCarthy said, "Another boy at the center told me he thought he lived somewhere on Fifth Street between C and D."

"Around the block from Sister Honora," Dina said.

"I think I can probably zero in on the building," Keenan said. "I need to make a phone call." He popped the last piece of carrot into his mouth, put down his chopsticks and washed his food down with a slug of seltzer. Then he shoved his hands in his jeans pockets, came up with a nickel and three pennies. "Anybody got a quarter?"

Donato gave him one.

"You should carry your own quarters, Keenan," Dina said.

"Yes, Lieutenant," he answered, a mocking tone to his voice.

Donato could see that Dina was angered. He didn't blame her. Being a woman, she took a lot of flack. Keenan wouldn't have spoken that way to a male lieutenant he didn't know well. But she seemed particularly tense today, hadn't said a word the whole way downtown.

Looking at the two women seated next to each other, he suddenly remembered their graduation day.

Despite his feelings about Dina becoming a cop, he was proud as hell at graduation. And he was proud of Judy, too. None of her family had come, so he and Renata had taken them to Il Cortile, in Little Italy. Recalling that day, he ached. Everything had seemed right for the first time since Rich's death, as if they were a family again. Judy, too.

"We want you to know that we love you as much as if you were one of our own," he'd told her.

"Michael's right," Renata added. "You're our second daughter."

Judy's green eyes filled. "You don't know how much you mean

to me. I don't know what I would have done without you or how to thank you."

"Just be a good cop," Donato had said.

And she had been. Although this was the first time Donato had worked with her, he'd kept tabs on her, just the way he'd monitored Dina's career up until the Peak case. After that he hadn't the heart, the interest. Something inside of him had died.

"Did you get a description of that passenger from the cab-driver?" Dina asked.

"Not yet. Why do you want it?"

"I'm not sure."

Keenan returned. He stood behind his chair, his large hands gripping the back. "I've got the address."

Donato could see that Dina was pleased and that she didn't want to let Keenan know it. Christ, he hoped she wouldn't get involved with a cop. Well, it was none of his business. Nothing about his family was his business anymore.

"Let's get going," Dina said.

A man on the first floor directed them to Posie's apartment. Keenan was stationed on the roof, McCarthy in the back alley. Donato and Dina stood on either side of Posie's door.

This was the part of police procedure Donato hated most: those tense moments before gaining entrance to a suspect's hiding place. As a young cop, he'd lost a partner in this kind of operation. Even now he could see Bianchi opening the door, flying backward as a rain of bullets hit him.

Donato, on one side of the door, his back to the wall, held his gun upright, while watching Dina on the other side in the same position. She reached out and banged on the door with the barrel of her gun, then nodded to Donato.

"This is the police, Posie," he yelled. "We know you're in there. Open up." He could feel his pulse racing, the thump of his heart, and idly wondered if he could have a heart attack under these circumstances, something he'd never considered until recently.

Dina rapped on the door again while Donato made another effort to get Posie to open up. They waited, listening. Except for a faint flushing sound somewhere in the building, it was still. And then, from inside the apartment, they heard a window being raised.

"Break it open," Dina said.

With a flat-footed kick, Donato smashed the lock. Wood splintered. The door flew open and they entered, both hands on their guns in combat stances. The room was empty.

While Donato checked the other closed doors, Dina ran to the open window. A black man was dashing down the fire escape, a gun in his hand. "Freeze," Dina yelled, "police."

The man kept going. Dina took a shot at him and missed. It was hard to hit a running man. She stepped through the window on to the fire escape, and Donato followed.

McCarthy appeared from behind the building below. She held her gun in front of her in a two-handed grip. "Freeze!"

The man, who'd reached the last step, jumped to the ground, fired at McCarthy and kept running, disappearing around the side of the building.

McCarthy flipped backward, her gun falling from her hand.

When Dina and Donato reached her, her eyes were open and she was still breathing. Donato didn't stop, but kept chasing the man. From the glimpse he'd gotten of the hole in McCarthy's stomach, he knew the man had been carrying a magnum. McCarthy's chances were slim. He reached the street. The man had disappeared. Now Donato's priority was McCarthy. At the car, he radioed for an ambulance. Then he saw Keenan coming toward him with the handcuffed shooter, pushing him along with the heel of his hand, the man's big gun tucked into Keenan's belt.

People had stopped along the sidewalk, watching the show, and Donato heard a woman say, "They making a movie or something?"

"Good work, Keenan," he said.

"Where's the lieutenant and McCarthy?"

"In back. This fucker shot McCarthy."

Keenan grabbed the shooter by the back of his collar and yanked it tight. "Let's go, scumbag."

"Take it easy," Donato cautioned. "We don't want to blow it."

Keenan loosened his hold as they returned to the back alley.

Dina had taken off her coat and put it over McCarthy, covering the wound. Blood had collected in a puddle on the cement. McCarthy's face had drained of color.

Keenan threw the shooter against the wall, his gun shoved into the man's back. "How bad is it?" he asked Donato.

"Stomach."

"Shit."

"I called the ambulance," Donato said.

Dina was stroking McCarthy's hair. "Good. She'll be okay," she said automatically.

"Sure," Donato said, selling himself as well as Dina. But when he looked back at McCarthy, he saw that her eyes were closed and that she was suspiciously still.

Dina saw it, too. "Judy . . . Judy . . . come on," she pleaded.

A numbness invaded Donato, as if he'd been shot full of novocaine.

Dina continued to beg. "McCarthy, don't quit now . . . Judy, please . . . ah, don't . . . come on . . ."

Donato could see that she was dead. He knelt down and put his arm around Dina. "She's gone," he said softly.

Dina's eyes petitioned him to say it wasn't true. He wished he could tell her what she wanted to hear. She seemed so young at that moment, innocent and guileless, the loving child she'd once been. A sob caught in his chest for the past, for Dina, for McCarthy, for himself.

"No," Dina protested weakly.

Even though he was sure, Donato reached out, touched McCarthy's neck. "She's gone," he said again.

Behind him he heard Keenan say to the shooter, "You fucking cocksucker."

Donato said, "Did you read him his rights, Keenan?"

"Not yet."

"Do it."

As Keenan recited the Miranda warning, Donato helped Dina to her feet. Filled with love for her, he folded her inside his arms. But she didn't cry; her head rested against his chest for just a moment. When she pulled away, she was Lieutenant Donato again.

"Are you Posie?" she said, walking over to the black man who stood against the wall.

"I'm not sayin' nothin' 'till I got me my lawyer," he answered defiantly. "So don't you be axin' me no questions."

"Your lawyer isn't going to get you out of this one," she said, her voice low and husky from holding back tears. "You're finished, buster."

In the distance, the wail of the ambulance siren sounded like a keening prayer for the dead. Dina returned to McCarthy and sat on the cement next to her, taking her lifeless hand in her own.

Suffering the anger he always felt when an officer was killed, plus the fury over the death of a friend, Donato became aware of another emotion edging out his rage. Ashamed, he tried to deny it. But nothing he told himself changed the selfish sentiment: he was relieved that the shooter had killed Judy McCarthy instead of his daughter.

Dina had gone to tell Judy's family. Donato and Keenan were in the interrogation room with Clinton "Posie" Johnson. There were no windows in the room, just the mirror, a one-way window from the other side. The only piece of furniture was a wooden chair, which Johnson sat on, his legs spread out in front of him forming a V.

Johnson had decided to talk without a lawyer after all. Sister Margaret's description was fairly accurate. He was tall and skinny, with big hands and feet, but his afro needed a trim. A new narrow mustache rimmed his upper lip. There *was* a scar on his right cheek. His face was long and his eyes hated.

Around his neck was a flat gold chain, and on his right wrist a black digital watch. He wore a pair of faded, torn Levi's and a red T-shirt that said HONK IF YOU SEE A HONKIE. He was fifteen years old.

Donato was in his shirt sleeves, his tie loosened. "Okay, Johnson, tell us about Sister Honora."

"Who?"

"Sister Honora," Keenan said. "And don't fuck around. We know you knew her."

"Sister who?"

Donato whirled on Johnson, leaned over, his face an inch away from the boy's. "Listen, motherfucker, you're done. You killed a police officer, and it doesn't mean dick that you're fifteen. This case is a grounder. You know what that is? Open and shut. So you might as well tell us about Sister Honora, how you iced her."

Johnson pulled his head back. "I never iced no nun. Don't you be pinnin' shit like that on me."

"We know about your fight with her, Johnson," Keenan said. "We know she threw you out of HAFH. We know you threatened her."

"So what? What that say?"

"It says that you went to her apartment and stabbed and raped her."

A defiant look crossed his face. "I don't fuck no honkies."

Donato wanted to kick the bastard in his groin so hard he'd never fuck *anybody* again.

"We're not talking about fucking, Johnson," Keenan snapped. "We're talking rape."

"Not me. No way." He shook his head.

"What about Sister Angelica?" Donato asked. He had a sinking feeling that Johnson was the wrong man. He'd been running, had shot McCarthy, for some other reason.

"Who?"

"Knock it off, pigshit," Keenan said. "She's the nun you burned on Fifty-fifth Street."

"Hey, man, what the hell this? I ain't takin' no fall for nobody." Johnson dug in his back pocket. He pulled out a dirty handkerchief and wiped his face with it. "I don't know nothin' about no nuns gettin' their tickets punched."

Donato leaned against the wall. "You saying you haven't heard word one about it?"

"I didn't say that, man. I say I didn't kill 'em and I ain't takin' the fall. Sure, I heard somethin', seen somethin' in the headlines. I don't read no paper."

"How about TV?" Keenan asked. "You watch TV, don't you, Posie?"

"I don't have no TV, man."

"Why'd you run when we knocked on your door?"

"You say you the po-lice." He grinned, showing a missing top front tooth. "I don't like socializin' with no po-lice."

Keenan said, "Why'd you shoot Detective McCarthy."

"Hell, I was protectin' myself. I didn't know she was po-lice. She be pointin' this motherfuckin' piece at me, what I gonna do? I thought she some crazy pussy tryin' to off me."

"The hell you did," Keenan said. "She told you to freeze. You knew she was a cop."

"I swear I didn'." He crossed his heart.

There was a knock on the door, and Bobbin stuck his head in. "Can I see you?"

Donato told Keenan to go on with the interrogation and went outside. Bobbin and Lachman had been sent to toss Johnson's apartment.

"What'd you find?"

"The guy's got a fucking arsenal." Bobbin read from his pocket memo. "A Beretta 9mm parabellum, one Colt-made M1911A1.45 ACP, an M21 sniper rifle and a Steyr model 69 9mm parabellum submachine gun."

"Jesus," Donato said.

"That ain't all. In the back of the toilet in the tank was a waterproof bag with at least two pounds of coke."

"Pure," Lachman said.

"So that's why the scumbag ran," Donato said, more to himself than to them. "Okay, thanks."

Keenan came out. "This fucker says he was in jail on that Wednesday night."

"Check on it." Donato went back into the interrogation room. "What's this shit, Posie? How come you didn't tell us right away you were in jail?"

"You didn' ax me." Johnson was leaning back in the chair, the two front legs off the ground.

Donato wanted to push him over. They should have checked his alibi first. Maybe it was the hangover fuzzing his mind. Maybe he was getting too old. Or maybe it was simply Judy's death. But after what Johnson had done, he'd been so sure of his culpability. It hadn't occurred to him, until just a few minutes ago, that he might have shot McCarthy because he was guilty of something else. That was sloppy. He had no excuse.

"What were you arrested for?"

"The po-lice say I be in on a A&R but no way, man. Not me. I don' go for that shit."

"You just go for coke and guns, huh?"

"Who, me?"

"And murder," Donato said wearily. "You go for murder, too, don't you, Johnson? I bet Detective McCarthy isn't the first you've killed."

Johnson stopped smiling, his eyes like two slate splinters.

Keenan came in and nodded once to Donato.

"Jesus," Donato said. They'd gone after the wrong guy; Judy had died for no reason. Picking up his jacket, he walked to the door. He had to get out of here before he blew it. "Give the narcs a call, Keenan. This motherfucker was sitting on two pounds of coke."

"I ain't got no coke, man. It a plant."

"How about the weapons, asshole? We plant those too?" Donato said.

"I don' know nothin' about no weapons."

Donato stepped in front of him, his fists clenched. "Shut up, Johnson. Just shut the fuck up. You're lucky we didn't blow you away when McCarthy died. But it's not too late. Your death can be arranged as easy as that." He snapped his fingers.

Johnson blinked.

Donato left.

He didn't feel like drinking again, but he didn't know what else to do, where to go. The bar where he'd been the night before held no appeal for him. Eventually, he chose Barney's on Sullivan Street.

It was almost the only place left in SoHo that wasn't chic and didn't cost five bucks for a bourbon and soda. Barney owned the building, so he was safe from developers. None of his patrons were fashionable. A few unsuccessful painters and writers drank there, but mostly it was frequented by people who'd lived in the area all their lives.

Sawdust covered the floor like kitty litter, and a few stained-glass windows almost gave it a hallowed atmosphere. There was a lengthy mahogany bar, and the stools were red vinyl patched with electrical tape. Four booths lined one wall. Above the bar, a black-and-white television was playing *Gilda*. Donato recognized a scene with Rita Hayworth and Glenn Ford.

Most nights Barney tended bar himself because he couldn't bear to miss anything. He was in his sixties but looked much younger, no lines or wrinkles. There wasn't a hair on his head, and to compensate he'd grown a mustache.

"Hey, Mike, long time no see." Barney held out his hand and Donato shook it. "Where ya been keepin' yourself?"

"Well, you know, I live up on the West Side," he said lamely, feeling disloyal.

"West Side, East Side, who gives a fuck? This is where you was born, and this is where you belong."

"Matter of fact, I'm looking for a place. If you hear of anything, let me know."

"Yeah? You movin' back?" he asked, grinning.

"I might be if I find a place."

"That's good, Mike. You'd be closer to your mama that way. How is she, anyways?"

"She's okay. The same."

Barney nodded knowingly. "So what can I do ya?"

"A beer."

Barney pulled the wooden lever and shot beer into a pilsner glass.

Donato pushed a five across the bar.

Smacking his head with the palm of his hand, Barney said, "Hey, what a stupe I am. Vinnie Sellito was looking for you."

"When?"

"Earlier, about five, six."

"I'm going to take this in the back," Donato said. "If he comes in tell him where I am."

"Will do." Barney handed Donato his change.

He started for the back room just as a man got up from the bar and almost bumped into him.

"Hey, Fanelli," Donato said.

"Mike."

In his early forties, he reminded Donato of Alan Alda. Fanelli had been a cop, now he was a PI. But Donato knew him from further back. In high school, he'd dated Fanelli's sister, Yolanda. She'd turned into a lush.

"How's Yolanda?" Donato asked.

"Right now she's okay. Tomorrow who knows? You working on the nun murders?"

"Yeah. Know anything?"

"Nothing."

"If you hear anything . . ."

"Don't worry, I'll get in touch. This one's not for me. Who'd pay my fee, the Pope?"

Donato smiled. "Say hello to Yolanda for me." He clapped Fanelli on the shoulder, and they said good-bye.

The back room needed a paint job, and the linoleum was cracked and buckling. There were three unoccupied tables. Donato chose one where there was no spill from the cool fluorescent lighting. He took off his jacket, hung it over the chair, sat down and sipped the beer, craving a cigarette.

It was Judy. He was sitting here drinking, thinking of a smoke, because Judy McCarthy was dead. As though if he drank his brains out and lit up, she'd live again. After all these years, he was still trying to make bargains, trade-offs. When he was a boy he'd promised God various things if God would just . . . whatever. If You let me pitch a no-hitter, I'll never masturbate again. Hey, God, Let's Make a Deal!

But there was no bargain to make. It was done. Judy was dead. Now he began to run through the *if onlys*. If only what? If only it had been Keenan instead? Or Lachman, Bobbin, Pesetsky, Delgado? Himself? Whom was he willing to sacrifice?

[137]

The last time he'd played his sacrifice, trade-off game had been with the Peak case. Here he was again. The goddamn Peak case. His mind went back to it like a homing pigeon.

When Rich died, he thought that he'd lost everything, that nothing else could ever make him feel so bad. He'd been right. Losing the love and respect of Renata and Dina and being dumped into the Ninth Precinct were devastating, but none of it equaled the loss of his son. Nothing was worse than having your child die. It was against the laws of nature.

When Rich, driven by drugs, killed himself, Donato's world crumbled. Why the hell hadn't he known, detected something in the son he thought he knew so well? As it turned out, it was Rich's best friend, Jeff Meyerson, who really knew him.

"Why didn't you tell me?" Donato had asked him.

"How could I? Be reasonable, Mike. I couldn't betray Rich. But here's the thing: Rich had quit. I swear it. He'd been clean for about two weeks."

The autopsy had shown a high level of heroin in Rich's body. "What the fuck are you telling me?" Anger rose up in him like a rumbling volcano, and he grabbed Jeff by the front of his shirt.

"Hey, Mike, come on, man."

He wouldn't let go. "I want to know what you're saying."

"Rich had quit. That's the truth."

He hung on. "Then he started again—is that it?"

Jeff twisted out of Mike's slackening grip. "Rich went cold turkey and swore he'd never go through that again. It's tough to believe he'd start up only two weeks later. But maybe that's why he . . ." Jeff let the sentence trail off, unwilling to say out loud that Rich had eaten his gun. "Who knows with addicts? They aren't your most trustworthy types."

The word *addict* was like a blow to Donato. And he knew Jeff was right: you couldn't trust junkies. That was why he never used them as snitches. A B&E man you could rap with a felony charge was a much safer bet.

"Even so," Donato said, "something stinks about the whole thing."

"Look, Mike, I don't *know* anything, but I got a funny feeling, okay? Rich knew a lot about the drug scene. Deals that were going down. Stuff like that. Maybe he knew too much."

"Are you saying somebody set him up, killed him?"

"Maybe."

"Who was his pusher?"

"I don't know. He didn't tell me stuff like that."

It was a dead end before it began. Donato had tried all his contacts and come up without a clue as to whether Rich had shot up and killed himself or someone did him. The autopsy hadn't revealed a struggle, but that wasn't conclusive. There were ways to force a man without leaving marks.

Eventually, the word on the street came down that Rich *had* been murdered, but no one had anything to say about who the killer was. On his own time, Donato chased down leads but they always came to nothing.

And then he'd busted Leroy Brown and Hubie Peak.

Brown was a black man with narrow eyes and pockmarked skin. He dressed in three-piece suits and looked more like a Wall Street broker than the dealer he was. Brown had gone to Princeton for two years, then got kicked out for cheating. Still, he had certain ethics, loyalties, but he wasn't above being turned around. Especially when the subject was Hubie Peak.

Peak was white, thirty-five years old, five-ten, one hundred and sixty pounds. His skin was pale, as though he'd had a shock. Blond hair was combed forward into short bangs, and his eyes were a bright blue. He sported gold chains around his neck. Hubie Peak was handsome, rich and powerful and the scum of the earth.

The narcs had wanted Peak and Brown for years but couldn't get near them. And now cops from Donato's precinct had busted them for a hit and run. Brown had never done time and knew if he went up he'd never make it. During the interrogation he indicated he had something good to trade.

"Like what?" Donato asked.

"What'll you give *me*?"

"You weren't driving, were you?"

"No. Peak was behind the wheel. That motherfucker's crazy. I told him to slow down, but he listens only to the sounds in his own head." He blew smoke through both nostrils.

"Okay, we can deal. Tell me what you have."

"Are you sure?" Brown wiped sweat from his face with a white silk handkerchief.

"You have my word," Donato said.

Donato's word was always good, and Brown knew it. "Okay. You've been looking for the person who killed your son, haven't you?"

Donato was stunned. It had been a year since he'd followed down a lead on Rich's death. He'd been trying to let go, trying to make some sort of peace with it. Now here was this piece of filth about to tell him something he'd been trying to find out for years, and he wasn't sure he wanted to hear it.

"What do you know about that?"

"I know plenty." Brown smiled jaggedly.

"What?"

"If I give you who iced him, will you get me out of this one?" No part of Brown moved; he was as still as fallen snow.

"I told you, you have my word." Donato was dizzy, thought he might faint. He wished he'd never busted Brown, wished to hell he'd never heard of him, because what was he going to do when he learned who Rich's killer was? "Tell me."

"It was a man named Walter Albert, better known as Cookie. He forced your kid to shoot up, then, when he was nodding out, stuck the gun in his hand, put it in your kid's mouth, and pulled the trigger. But Cookie Albert's dead now."

Donato moved in on him. "What the fuck kind of information is that, you slimeball? You giving me a fucking dead guy. Am I supposed to believe you, maybe get down on my knees and kiss your feet for this? You got to be kidding."

"Wait a minute, wait a minute," Brown said, bobbing his large hands as if he were dribbling two basketballs. "Albert was just the enforcer. The important dude's the one who gives the order. You know that."

"Okay. Who gave the order?"

"You have to give me protection, money, change my face, that kind of thing."

There was no way Brown was going to get anything like that. "Don't worry about it, we'll protect you."

"Your word?"

Donato didn't care what lies he told now. "My word."

Brown stared into Donato's eyes, trying to see the truth. Finally, he took a deep breath. "Okay. It was Peak. Hubie Peak, who's in the room next-door. He ordered Albert to take your kid out. I swear."

Donato believed him. It was an instinct, nothing he could explain, write a report about. After all these years, he'd come to trust his feelings, have faith in his gut reaction. Rich's killer was Hubie Peak and they had him.

He joined the two detectives interrogating Peak. The look of frustration on their faces was familiar. Donato could tell they weren't getting anywhere.

Peak was sitting on a wooden chair. Large sweaty half-moons stained his pink silk shirt. The room stank.

"Hubie don't want to tell us nothing," Al Baron said.

"Yeah," Tim Finley added, "cat's got his tongue."

"Is that right?" Donato said. He pulled up a chair and turned it so that the back was to Peak when he sat down. It was a safer way to sit in case Hubie got any ideas about kicking him in the groin. "So you don't want to talk about killing a ten-year-old girl, is that right, Hubie?"

"I don't know nothin' about what you're sayin'."

"No?" Donato hoped the others couldn't see he was shaking, especially Peak. "You don't remember driving your new slate blue BMW around seven o'clock on Saturday? You don't remember being on Sixty-first Street doing seventy-five? You don't remember a little girl crossing the street just as you were speeding along? You don't remember dragging her body seventeen feet before she dropped off your bumper, a pulpy, bloody mess? You don't remember that you kept on going like the coward that you are? You don't remember any of that, is that right, Hubie?"

"I don't know what you're talkin' about," he said stubbornly.

"Well, maybe you remember a cop named Rich Donato. You remember him?"

Finley and Baron exchanged a look of confusion.

"I don't know what you're talkin' about." Peak showed no surprise at the abrupt change in Donato's questions.

"Well, true, it was a long time ago. Nine years. Nine years ago when you gave the order to take out the junkie cop. But maybe you don't remember. Maybe you give those kinds of orders so often you can't remember one from another. Is that it, Hubie?" Donato was sweating. He wanted to bash Peak's face in.

"I don't know what yo—"

"Don't say it, Peak," Donato yelled, "just don't say it." He stood up, walked around the chair and leaned over, his mouth against Peak's ear. "Nine years ago you ordered Richard Donato, a police officer, killed. And it doesn't make a fucking bit of difference that you weren't there when he died. It doesn't make a fucking bit of difference that Cookie Albert actually shoved the gun in the police officer's mouth and pulled the trigger. You killed Richard Donato, Peak, just as if you'd done it yourself. That's the conspiracy law and it's a beaut."

Peak turned his head, a defiant smile on his lips. "Prove it," he said.

And that was when Donato knew for sure that Hubie Peak had killed his son. "Thanks, Peak, now I know you did it." He turned to the two detectives. "Take care of this scum," he said and left.

That was it. That was all. *Take care of this scum.* At the hearing, Finley and Baron had used those words as their defense. They'd beaten Peak so badly that he'd died from internal injuries, and under questioning both men said that Donato had ordered the beating. He'd pleaded innocent. That wasn't what he'd meant. Was it?

Finley and Baron were found guilty, dismissed from the Force, sent to jail. The case against Donato was inconclusive. But Halliday had transferred him to the Ninth, where the the dregs of the earth plied their trade. And then kept him, until now, from ever getting a case that might restore his good reputation.

Donato had played back the scene hundreds of times. He'd known that he couldn't prove Peak's part in Rich's death and that Peak would probably walk in the hit-and-run case. But he hadn't meant that Finley and Baron should beat Peak senseless, kill him. Then what *had* he meant?

Halliday pointed out to him that Finley and Baron were known to be quick with their fists. Surely with a statement like *Take care of this scum,* he knew what he was suggesting. Donato denied it. Halliday just laughed.

Had he known? The truth was he couldn't be sure. And that's what plagued him. That woke him in the middle of the night or caught him by surprise as he was ordering a meal, reading a book, shaving. It was a question he couldn't answer.

"Hey, Mike, *paesan,* how you doin'?" Vinnie Sellito had been Donato's snitch for twenty years. Sitting heavily in the chair across from him, he held out a meaty hand.

Time hadn't been kind to Sellito. He was sixty but looked seventy. Two long jail terms had taken their toll. A scar, earned in a knife fight, ran from just under his right eye to below his lip. His big body was soft and lumpy, his hair white, and the dark eyes were underscored by heavy pouches, like miniature mailbags. Sellito had the look of a man who'd failed the life test.

Donato said, "I hear you were looking for me."

"Yeah." He lit a cigarette. "It's a terrible thing, that nun thing.

Who could ice a nun, huh? Hey, ya remember when Joey Loprete hid under Sister Regina's bed?" Sellito's face cracked into a lopsided smile. "And then Joey sneezed and Sister Regina almost shit a brick, ya remember that, Mike, huh?"

"Yeah, I remember." Sellito always needed foreplay before he sold his information. Donato had learned to wait.

"Ah, hell. Those were the good times." Sellito looked over Donato's shoulder as if scenes of the past were playing on the wall. "It's all different now, Mike. It's shit now."

"You're doing all right, Vinnie. You've been out of jail, what . . . three, four years now?"

"Yeah." He looked back at Donato, downed his shot, shivered. "Jesus, Barney's got the worst fuckin' rotgut."

Donato opened his wallet and took out a twenty. He slid it across the table but kept his hand on it. "You have something for me, Vinnie?"

"Yeah, sure. You know you can count on me, Mike."

But Donato wasn't sure. Since Sellito had come out from his last jolt, he'd stepped up his drinking. Juicers weren't any more trust-worthy than junkies. "So what do you have?" he prodded.

"You know Jellinek, the junkie who lives over in Alphabet City?"

"No. What about him?"

"He said, 'bout two hours before the nun was iced another nun went into the building. He figured she was gonna see the other one, ya know what I mean?"

"How'd he know she was a nun?"

"I dunno." Sellito shrugged, then raised his eyebrows, looking like he'd just figured out who was buried in Grant's Tomb. "Hey, why wouldn't he, Mike? I mean, it ain't hard to spot a nun, right?"

"That depends. Was she wearing a habit?"

"Yeah, I guess, or how else would he know?"

"Where can I find Jellinek?"

"Maybe at a shooting gallery, maybe in the park. He'll turn up some place." He moved his hand toward the twenty.

"Don't spend it all on booze, Vinnie."

"Nah, hell, not me, Mike. I got a wife in case you forgot."

He had forgotten. Sellito had a wife and two sons. *His* sons had lived. It was funny how things turned out. Here he was, a cop, with Sellito as his snitch. What would Sellito think if he told him he was a cop because of *him,* because of the botched Weiser Brassiere job? Donato took his hand off the bill.

Sellito scrunched up the twenty in his massive hand.

Donato put on his jacket and walked around the table. "Thanks, Vinnie." He patted him on the shoulder.

"I tole ya somethin' good, huh?"

"Yeah. You told me something good." Donato reached into his wallet again and put a ten in Vinnie's hand.

"Thanks, Mike. You're good people, you always was."

Donato walked quickly through the bar to the phone booth. He dialed Dina. There was no answer. Where was Cal? Then he remembered Dina had said he was spending the night with Renata. He checked the time. Seven-thirty. Could Dina still be with the McCarthys? He called the precinct and learned she wasn't there either. Wherever she was, he hoped she wasn't alone.

Sitting in the booth, he thought about what Sellito had told him. Why hadn't anyone else mentioned seeing a nun going into Sister Honora's building? What he knew he should do now was go home, spend some time with Cal, help Renata with her grief for Judy. But he couldn't. The case was reaching the point where duty bled into obsession. You tried not to get personally involved, but sometimes it was hard. This was one of those cases. Even though he hated dealing with junkies, he had to look for Jellinek.

Passing by the bar, he waved at Barney.

"Don't be such a stranger," he called.

"I won't."

Outside, the weather had changed from the balminess of the afternoon into a soupy, muggy evening. Looking downtown, Donato saw that the lighted tops of the Twin Towers were obscured by fog, as if they'd been cut off at the knees.

His car was parked a few buildings away. He stood staring at it. What a heap, he thought. When the case was over, he'd have to remember to ask for a new one. He unlocked the door, got behind the wheel and turned the key. He felt better than he had in hours. At least now he was doing something rather than pissing and moaning over his beer, feeling sorry for himself. Now he was working. It wouldn't mitigate the pointless tragedy of Judy's death, but it might get them closer to a solution. That had to count for something. Pulling out, he started toward Alphabet City and the junkie, Jellinek.

Twelve

Ellen McCarthy had cried while Dina held her. Sean McCarthy had remained dry-eyed, his lips pressed together in a straight line, a muscle twitching in his cheek. Ellen said over and over again that this was what she'd envisioned from the beginning. Sean said nothing.

Dina had stayed with them for three hours, then driven back to Manhattan in time to pick up Cal and take him to her mother's.

Judy's death had shaken Renata badly, and for the first time, she looked old to Dina. When Cal went to watch television, they drifted into the living room, sat opposite each other in upholstered wing chairs, drinking vodka and tonic.

"Her parents," Renata said hesitantly, "how . . . how did they take it?" Before Dina could answer, she went on. "Am I crazy? How did they take it?" she repeated disgustedly. "They sang and danced, of course." She took a long swallow of her drink.

Dina said, "They were devastated."

Renata nodded, over and over, as if each movement added up the McCarthys' pain.

"You remember; they never wanted her to be a cop."

Renata slammed her glass down, liquid spilling, spreading across the mauve lacquered finish of the coffee table. "And do you think I did?" she said. "Do you think I wanted your brother and you to be goddamned cops? What mother would want it? It's so selfish . . . self-centered. You're spoiled, Dina. Daddy's little girl. Well, I'm telling you, I've had it. I've had it up to here." She drew a line across her throat with her finger.

"Daddy didn't want me to be a cop either," Dina said, as if somehow that would exonerate her in Renata's eyes.

"You're so naïve sometimes. He may have pretended he didn't want it, but he did." Renata lit a cigarette. "You've never understood what it meant for me to marry Mike." She shook her head, as if the meaning was there for Dina to see if only she'd bother to look. "I gave up a whole way of life. Friends, style, travel, everything."

"Nobody forced you to marry him."

Renata stared at her silently, smoke dribbling from her mouth. "You know that I was pregnant with Rich," she said finally, "but don't think that's why I married Mike. I wanted to marry him." She sipped her drink. "My father warned me what my life would be like, but I wouldn't listen. Like you. Like Rich. None of us ever listens to our parents. You'll find out what it's like."

Dina imagined herself estranged from Cal, but refused to show her mother she'd hit her mark.

Renata went on, sardonically. "I thought that Mike and Papa would eventually see the good in each other and that Mike would make something of himself."

"He did," Dina said.

"Oh, Dina, don't defend him. The man couldn't go past sergeant. You know why? Not because he's dumb. God knows, Mike Donato is no dummy. He never went farther because he didn't want to. He didn't want the responsibility.

"Years ago, when Mike was a third-grade detective, we were at a party, and Bill Valden, the CD, told me that Mike was one of half a dozen bright stars on the Force. That's what he called him, one of the bright stars. He said there would be no stopping Mike—he could go all the way if he wanted to. But he didn't want to." Disgust coated her words. "He preferred taking the risks, riding around, following down leads, going on stakeouts, anything except success." She finished her drink, pushed herself off the couch and went to the bar cart to make herself another.

Controlling her anger, Dina said, "Maybe being a first-grade detective/sergeant *is* success to him. Did you ever think of that?"

"That's the point, it is. Oh, not now. Not over there at the Ninth. But before." Renata sat back in her chair with a sigh. "I don't want to get started on Mike. Judy. Poor Judy." She took a swallow of her drink. "You know, I never thought Rich would become a cop. I was so sure. Over the years, he often told me that he wanted to be a doctor, a surgeon."

"He wanted Daddy's approval."

Renata nodded. "And you, too. You wanted Daddy's approval too. But you never cared what I wanted, did you, Dina?"

The truth in her mother's words stung. "I didn't think about it," she said, hoping to soften reality.

Renata smiled morosely. "No, I'm sure you didn't. And neither did Rich. Neither did your father. But I can't blame him entirely. I knew when I married him that's what he wanted. He gave the business a fair shake, I'll say that for him. If he'd just gone on, become the CD, an inspector, stayed inside. Oh, God, Dina. You can't know what it was like every time the man went out that door."

Dina heard echoes of Liam's words. "I know," she said softly.

"How can you? *You're* the one who goes out there, goddammit. You and Rich and Mike. You're the ones who go *out* the door. *I'm* the one who stays behind." She put her head back and closed her eyes as if she were tired from years of waiting for bad news. "So now it's Judy. Are you going to be next, Dina?"

She wanted to comfort her mother, but there was no response to her question, no way to reassure her.

Renata put out her cigarette. "And now what's going on? You and Mike are out there looking for some insane killer. And if you catch him, then what? If he doesn't kill you, there'll be another insane killer to go after. And another and another. And some day, some day the bell will ring, and two detectives will be standing there looking like they'd rather be in hell. But *you* don't care. *He* doesn't care. What the hell."

"I know it's hard for you, Mom, but we have to do what—"

"Go do it, then," she interrupted, waving a dismissive hand.

"You're just upset because—"

"I don't want to look at you now, Dina. I don't want to be around a cop right now. Don't worry about Cal. He'll be fine. You can leave him with me as long as you want." Renata stared into her almost empty glass.

After a few moments, pain wrapping around her like a shroud, Dina picked up her jacket, found Cal, said good-night and, without another word, left her mother's apartment.

Moving aimlessly through the Village, Dina wondered if she were becoming like her father, trying to walk off her feelings rather than facing them.

Judy was dead. It sounded impossible, the words seeming strange, as if they were in a foreign language she couldn't understand. Despite that, the meaning penetrated, leaving her desolate. How could it be true? Renata had turned Judy's death into *her* tragedy, as though Dina were unaffected, untouched in any way. She looked at her watch. Seven hours ago Judy'd been alive, eating lunch, joking around. Six hours ago Dina'd watched her walking into the alley behind Posie Johnson's building.

Dina crossed to the east side of Seventh Avenue and started down Fourth. Two street musicians were playing "Everyone's Gone to the Moon." A small crowd had gathered, and Dina joined them. The music washed over her and held her in place.

Growing up she'd had various best friends, but no relationship equaled the one with her brother. And when he died, he'd left a void she felt sure she'd never fill. Although Judy hadn't replaced Rich, she'd answered Dina's desperate need to love and be loved by a peer.

When the song ended, the crowd clapped in a desultory way, some throwing coins into an open sax case. Dina forced herself to leave, though she didn't know where she was going. It was Judy she'd call feeling like this. And before that, Rich. And before that, her father. Now none of them was available to her. Liam had never been someone she could turn to; that had been part of the problem.

At Sixth Avenue, she crossed and walked up toward Eighth Street. Along the avenue, men and women were hawking used books, fourth-rate art, sunglasses, beads, batteries, old clothes. Dina tried to remember when this kind of enterprise had begun, crowding the sidewalk, turning the whole Village into a giant yard sale. She hated it.

On the corner of Eighth, she looked into the windows of B. Dalton's. There were new books by Anne Tyler and Lee Smith, but she didn't care. Turning the corner, she started down Eighth. It was a junky street now. One shoe store after another, discount clothing shops, fast-food joints. When she and Judy had first come to the Village, Eighth Street had quality stores, good bookshops, a few proper restaurants. Everything changed, everybody died.

Halfway down MacDougal Street, a man stepped in front of her. "Got good smoke, sister. Ludes, blow, anything you want."

She didn't have the energy or inclination to pull out her shield. "No thanks," she said and moved around him. As she continued down the street, she thought of Posie, Judy's murderer. At least there was no way he'd walk. Still, she couldn't imagine his life going on while Judy's was over.

Judy's was over. It couldn't be true. But it was. How can she be dead? She is. And then Dina remembered the baby. How could she have forgotten? Posie killed two of them. She wished he could die twice. And the bastard wasn't even the man they'd been after. If he'd been the nun killer, would it have made Judy's death any easier to accept? Dead was dead. But at least she might have felt some sort of compensation. Not much, but still something other than the solitary dark fact of death.

She thought of the scum she dealt with every day who went on living, who were of no use to themselves or anyone else. *Nobody ever said life was fair.* Donato had told her that for the first time when she was ten. The fifth-grade class had practiced singing carols for weeks, and on the night they were going out to sing, Dina had come down with chicken pox.

"I want to go anyway. I feel fine."

"You can't go, Dina. You have a fever."

"It's not fair, Daddy."

"Nobody ever said life was fair, kiddo."

No, nobody ever did.

Dina stopped at a light and realized she was at the corner of Third Street and Sullivan. She looked at her watch. Twenty-five after eight. Had she come this way purposely? She hadn't consciously planned to meet Bobby Keenan. Crossing the street, she walked slowly down the block toward Quantum Leap. When she was abreast of it, she heard a clicking sound. It was Keenan, tapping on the glass with his ring, smiling at her. Now that he'd seen her, she had to go in.

The restaurant was one good-sized, rectangular room painted white. Large green plants were placed strategically, separating tables, while smaller flora hung from the ceiling. Soft music emanated from two modest speakers in the corners. At the back was a blackboard with the daily specials.

"Hi," Keenan said. "Glad you could make it."

"I didn't feel like being alone," she heard herself saying. And then she knew it wasn't an accident that she was here. "I'm sorry, I didn't mean it that way."

"Forget it. I understand."

Though Judy had been his partner, he'd only known her for a few days; he couldn't possibly be feeling what she was. Still, she had no right to rate his grief. She removed her jacket, placed it over the back of her chair and sat down.

An orange-colored drink sat on the table in front of Keenan.

"Carrot juice," he said. "Great stuff. Want some?"

"No thanks."

"Ever try it?"

"No."

"So give it a whirl." He pushed the glass across the table.

She started to protest, then decided it would be easier to taste it. "It's not bad. Sweet."

"Want one of your own?"

"Okay."

Keenan signaled the waitress and ordered the drink. Turning back to Dina, he said, "How're you doing?"

"Lousy." She felt her eyes filling and looked down at the table.

"You can cry," he said.

"I don't need your permission."

"Sorry. I didn't mean . . ."

"This was a mistake." She reached for her jacket.

"No. I don't want you to go. I don't feel like being alone either."

Touched by his admission, she stayed. "You didn't know Judy before this job, did you?"

"We'd run into each other here and there. I liked her. I didn't know her well. Not like you did."

"She was my dearest friend."

"I know. She told me. She said you were the smartest and most trustworthy person she knew."

Tears threatened again. She didn't want to cry here. It had been the same with Rich. She only allowed her tears to surface in public places, and then she'd cut them off, telling herself it was inappropriate, postponing them until she was alone, but not crying then either. It was six years after his death when she'd finally broken down, mourned him. She didn't want to make the same mistake with Judy.

The waitress set the carrot juice in front of Dina. "You want to order now?"

"Give us a few minutes." When the waitress left, Keenan said, "Judy loved you a lot."

"And I her. I can't believe that pig wasn't even who we were looking for. If we hadn't gone there . . ."

"Are you blaming me?"

"No, of course not." Keenan had acted on information that Judy herself had obtained. And Dina had told him to follow it up, get the address. "I *want* to blame you. Or myself."

"It's no one's fault. If McCarthy had been in charge, she'd have done the same."

"I know. Still, I keep going back over it, trying to rewrite history. Do you know what I mean?"

"I've been doing it all afternoon. If I'd been on the ground instead of on the roof."

"Who decided?" she asked.

"I did. I thought she'd be safer on the ground."

"Would you have done that with a male partner?"

After a few moments, he said, "I don't know."

"And what would have happened if you'd been on the ground?"

"Either I'd be dead or Posie would."

"How would you feel if you'd killed him?"

"Sitting here like this, knowing he killed McCarthy, I think I'd feel great, but who knows? I've never killed anyone."

She was silent, remembering.

"Have you?" he asked.

"Yes." She could tell he was surprised, though he tried not to show it. So few police officers ever fired their guns. "I was a rookie."

The waitress returned. Dina still hadn't looked at the menu.

Keenan said, "Why don't I just order?"

"Yes, please." Normally, this would have annoyed her, but to-night it was a relief.

When the waitress left, Bobby said, "How did it happen?"

"In a shootout. My partner and I got a 10-30. We got there before anyone else. Two perps were coming out of the store as we drove up. When I jumped out, one of them shot at me. I fired back. I ended up with a shoulder wound, and he ended up dead." She took a pack of cigarettes from her bag.

"You can't smoke here."

"You're kidding?"

He shook his head and pointed to a sign on the table that said THANK YOU FOR NOT SMOKING.

Irritated, she put the cigarettes away.

"How did you feel about it? Shooting the perp?"

"At first I was elated. Because *I* wasn't dead. I mean, I knew that I'd done the right thing, that I hadn't had a choice. But afterward, I got depressed. His name was Buddy Green. He was nineteen. It was his first crime."

"There would have been others," Keenan said reassuringly.

"Yes, I know. Still, it was hard. It took me a while to get over it. The press and the public tried to make me look bad, but it was an open-and-shut case. I had no choice."

"A helluva thing to happen in your first year."

"A helluva thing to happen any time."

"Yeah." He smiled sympathetically.

She met his eyes, and something stirred that she hadn't felt for a very long time. It frightened her. And it made her feel guilty. How could she feel sexual attraction when her best friend was lying in the morgue?

"Buddy Green's mother," she went on, purposely breaking the moment between them, "wrote me a hate letter. So did a lot of other people, but I didn't care about them."

"What did the mother say?"

"She said I was a monster, abnormal. She said that any woman who was out there carrying a gun and killing people should be given a compulsory hysterectomy."

"Nice," he said.

"And then she said, she'd like to be the one to give it to me."

"Really nice."

She felt like crying again but fought it back. Their silence was interrupted by the arrival of the food. He'd ordered them each the fish and cheese casserole. Keenan asked for chopsticks.

As they started to eat, Keenan said, "About the desserts. They're great here, all made with honey."

"You really stay in the moment, don't you?"

"Hey, eating dessert is a dirty job, but somebody's got to do it."

"And it might as well be you," she said, smiling.

"And it might as well be me," he agreed, returning her smile.

Neither of them ate much. Keenan had tried the blueberry pie, but he'd quit halfway through. They'd talked about the case, then decided to go back to their headquarters to look at the pictures again. The body of a victim almost always held valuable clues if you could read it correctly. It was Keenan who suggested another viewing.

The pictures of Sister Honora were on one bulletin board and of Sister Angelica on another. Keenan leaned against the table, his hands stuffed in his jeans pockets, staring at the grotesque shots of Sister Honora.

Lighting a cigarette, Dina said, "So we know our killer hates Catholicism, especially nuns. What about the MO? He stabs and then he strangles. The strangling's beside the point. He does it for effect."

"Because of the beads, the rosary."

"Right. And the rape came first. She fought."

"The attack is vicious. Seventeen wounds," Keenan said.

"The same is true of Sister Angelica. Why did he rip open her habit? And Sister Honora's blouse? Why didn't he just stab them through the cloth?"

"Maybe so the wounds would show up better, on the flesh."

"Show up to whom?"

"Us? The photographers? Anybody who saw her," Keenan said.

The door to the office opened. It was Donato. He was surprised. "Sorry. I didn't think anyone would be here."

For a moment, she felt awkward, as though she'd been caught doing something naughty. "It's not a private meeting. We're looking at the pictures again."

Donato checked a smile, and Dina knew it was because he had taught her the value of the photographs, to read the bodies as if they were books.

"Find anything new?" he asked, lighting a cigarette and blowing a stream of smoke above his head.

"I thought you'd quit," Dina said.

"I did. But now I've started."

"Like father, like daughter, huh?" Keenan said.

They both glared at him.

"Hey, I'm sorry, gang. It was just a little . . . sorry."

Dina tried to take him off the hook. "Don't worry about it, Keenan—it's been said before."

Donato said, "How did it go with Judy's parents?"

"They were hurt and angry."

Dina knew he was thinking about Rich. For the first time, she wondered what his lies to her, to her mother, had cost him.

"So what else have we got?" Donato asked.

"Not a helluva lot. I think in this case," Keenan said, pointing at the photographs, "what you see is what you got."

"I hit a dead end tonight, too." He told them about the junkie supposedly seeing a nun going into Sister Honora's building. "I couldn't find this guy anyplace. I'll try later."

"Why don't you get some sleep, Donato? Try tomorrow."

They left the task force room and, once outside, stood awkwardly in front of the Thirteenth. Dina felt uncomfortable about walking away with Keenan, but they'd come uptown in his car. She didn't want Donato to think there was anything between them. Even if there was.

"I'm driving downtown," Donato said, looking at her.

"That's okay. I'll take her," Keenan said. "We both live downtown."

Dina wasn't sure if she was pleased or angry at Keenan. Then she said, "Why don't you just go home, Donato? You look like hell."

"Thanks, kiddo. Sweet, isn't she?" he said to Keenan.

Keenan grinned.

Donato said, "I'm staying on Mulberry for a while. Well, guess I'll take off." He gave them a quick wave of his hand and turned down Twenty-first, walking swiftly.

Both she and Keenan watched him for a moment before they turned away. Donato was staying with her grandmother, and that made Dina sad. She wondered why he didn't go to a hotel. It would be expensive, but surely more comfortable. Maybe, she thought, Donato didn't want to be alone tonight either.

Keenan grabbed a parking spot on Thompson Street. "I'll walk you home," he said.

"You don't have to."

"I want to."

The truth was, she didn't want to go home yet—she wasn't ready to be alone. "Want to have a drink somewhere?" she asked.

"Sure. How about my place?"

"Where do you live?"

"On Bleecker, across from the Little Red School House."

The idea of going to his place made her uneasy. Well, hell, she thought, he's not going to rape me. "All right."

Keenan's building was old, but clean and well-kept. His apartment was a fourth-floor walkup. The door opened into the kitchen. He snapped on a light. A golden retriever sat keening in the middle of the room.

[154]

"Okay, Murphy, come."

The dog, tail wagging, ran to Keenan and jumped up, putting his large front paws on Keenan's chest. He patted his head.

"Okay, good boy. Down. Sit. I want you to meet my boss, Murph. This is the lieutenant I've been telling you about."

Murphy cocked his head.

"What do you think, boy?"

The dog barked twice.

"Me, too." Keenan turned to Dina. "He likes you."

"He doesn't even know me."

Keenan laughed.

"How'd you get him to bark?"

"Secret. So. I've got white wine, beer and vodka."

"Wine."

He took a bottle from the refrigerator, two glasses from the cupboard and poured them each a drink, then led the way into the living room. It was small and neat. A couch was built into one wall; an easy chair sat across from it. Full bookshelves lined another wall and housed a stereo and records. Keenan put one on. It was Chris Connor singing "All About Ronnie."

"I like jazz," he said. "You?"

"I guess. I like *her.*" She sat on the couch. "How long have you lived here?"

He flopped down in the chair, Murphy at his feet. "A year and a half. My brother had it before me. Then he got married and moved to the suburbs. I pay two-fifty."

"You've got to be kidding."

"I never kid," he said, smiling. "It was one twenty-five when John first had it, ten years ago. Of course, there are some drawbacks."

"Like what?"

"It's pretty small. There are two rooms on the other side of the kitchen smaller than this. And the shower's on the second floor."

I'm not going to like that, Dina thought, quickly stunned by her presumption. "That *would* be inconvenient."

"I don't mind. I'm used to it. But other people . . . I mean, you know, guests . . . aren't too crazy for it." He looked embarrassed.

Dina wondered about the women in his life. "Have you been married?"

"Five years. I still am. We just haven't gotten around to getting a divorce."

"What happened?"

"What is this, some kind of interrogation?" he asked good-naturedly.

"I'm sorry. I was just—"

"Curious," he supplied. "Naturally. I can understand that. I'm curious, too. You're divorced. His name is Liam Sullivan, and he's a writer. And you have a kid named Cal."

"Have you been reading my file?" she joked.

"Yeah." He grinned at her.

She was shocked. "Really?"

"Yeah, really. Gonna give me some demerits, Lieut?"

"God, Keenan, you're arrogant."

"You think so? I mean, what's the big deal? I have a friend in Records, and I wanted to know more about you. I mean, it's only smart to know as much as you can about your boss. After all, you've got my life in your . . . holy shit. Christ, I didn't mean that, I . . ."

Keenan was right. Judy was dead. And she *was* responsible. She had all of the squad's lives in her hands, including her father's.

Keenan came over to her, sat down. "Are you okay? You look lousy."

"Thanks, pal," she said.

He took her hand between both of his. "Listen, I'm sorry. I didn't mean . . ."

"But you're right, Keenan. I do have your life in my hands. All of you. I'd want to know who I am, too, if I were you."

"I like who you are," he said seriously.

"Do you? I don't always."

"Who does? You're beautiful, you know."

She was startled and broke into a smile. "I don't think of myself that way."

"You should." He brushed her cheek with his fingertips. "I knew your skin would feel like this."

"Maybe I'd better go," she said.

"If you want to. I wish you wouldn't, but if you want to go now, Murphy and I'll walk you home."

"I don't want to be alone. That's not much of a reason to stay."

"It's a great reason. I can't think of a better one."

"Wouldn't it be better if I wanted you?"

"You do," he said. "You just don't know it yet."

Angry, she started to get up, but he pushed her back gently.

"Don't get mad. I want you, too. The problem is we don't think it's right because of Judy."

"And the fact that I've known you less than a week," she pointed out crisply.

"It's funny, but I feel I've known you longer."

Looking in his blue eyes, the green flecks like bits of spring leaves, she felt as if he'd always been part of her life. "I feel drawn to you, or I wouldn't be here."

"I'd like you to stay. Nothing has to happen if you don't want it to. Neither of us wants to be alone, so we can just give each other comfort."

She knew if she stayed they'd make love. And she was his boss. How would it affect the balance of power? Still, Keenan was right— she wanted him. "I'll stay."

Taking both her hands, he stood up, bringing her with him. He put his arms around her and held her for a few moments, then drew back. "I have to take Murphy out."

The dog was wagging his tail, waiting.

Keenan led her through the living room and kitchen. "The bedroom's back there. Snoop around if you want to. I'll be back soon. C'mon, Murph, let's go." He took a leash from a brass hook on the wall.

When he'd gone, Dina made her way toward the back of the apartment. In the first room, she switched on an overhead light. As he'd said, it was small. Three walls were lined with bookshelves. On the fourth was a door, which she opened. Inside, Keenan's clothes hung neatly, his shoes lined up on the floor. She couldn't get over how tidy he was. Next to the closet was a blue metal file cabinet. She thought about looking inside . . . after all, he'd given her permission to *snoop* . . . but she decided against it and went on to the bedroom.

The overhead light didn't work, so she groped in the dark, finally finding a lamp. When she turned it on, she saw that almost the entire room was taken up by a double bed. The only other furniture was the night table that held the lamp and a copy of the Anne Tyler book she'd seen in the Dalton window.

She wanted to be undressed before he came back. There were no closets in this room, so she put her clothes in a folded pile on the floor and climbed onto the bed. On the wall were a number of framed photographs. A man and woman stood in front of a forties car. He was smiling, she was not. Two boys sat with the same woman on a beach. She wasn't smiling in this one either. Dina guessed that one of the boys was Bobby, but they looked so much alike she couldn't tell which one. There were others, many of them with the man and

[157]

woman and the two boys, some with other people. There was one with the woman and another woman. She was smiling in that one.

Dina heard the front door open and the sound of the dog's feet on the kitchen floor. Quickly, she got under the covers, her heart pounding. She wanted to run. This had been a terrible mistake. She thought of Judy and then Donato. What would he think if he knew? Would he be disappointed in her, disgusted? But this was stupid. She was a grown woman who could make her own decisions, run her own life. Besides, she argued with herself, it was a well-known fact that grieving people often consoled themselves with sex. Sex was life-affirming.

Keenan stood in the doorway. "What a wonderful sight," he said. "Lieutenant Donato in my bed." He swallowed hard.

Dina wanted him to hurry. Fearful, she was wishing time away, wishing it was over.

"Do you want a shirt, something to sleep in?"

If she said no, it would be a signal that she wanted to make love. If she said yes, it would imply the opposite. She deliberated only a moment. "No."

He put out the light.

She listened to him undressing, then felt his weight move the mattress as he lay down beside her.

"Are those people in the photo in front of the car your mother and father?" she asked, stalling, but also wanting to know.

"Yes."

"Are they living?"

"My mother is. He was an alcoholic."

"Is that why your mother looks so unhappy?"

"Probably. She used to go and collect him from the drunk tank about once a month. She'd get all dressed up, put on her white gloves and a hat, as if she were going to a tea party, then go bail him out."

"When did he die?" She felt the warmth of his body even though they were being careful not to touch.

"When I was eight. My mother and my aunt, my father's sister, raised me and my brother. My aunt went out to work while my mother stayed home. They were like a married couple. My Aunt Carrie was the father. It was nuts."

"Is that your aunt in the picture, the one where your mother is smiling?"

"That's Aunt Carrie, all right."

"Where's your mother now?"

"In Queens. That's where I grew up. She's still living with Aunt Carrie. Happiest marriage I've ever seen. Hey, why are we talking about my family?"

"Because I don't know anything about you." His leg touched hers, and she jumped.

"You're nice and relaxed, aren't you?"

Dina laughed. "About as relaxed as Richard Nixon."

"Now *that's* relaxed."

"You never answered me," she said quickly. "What happened between you and your wife?"

"She's black. Her family wouldn't accept me. She couldn't take it."

"And your family? Did they accept her?"

"No. But I didn't give a shit." Keenan slid his hand across her ribs. "You want to know anything more about me, go read my file. I have this friend in Records and for a small fee . . ."

"Thanks." She found his lips with hers.

He touched her breasts; her nipples tightened.

Dina felt him grow hard against her side. She ran her hand over his arm, sucked his tongue into her mouth. Everything tingled. Then he pulled away from her lips. She felt bereft.

"We should wait," Keenan whispered, "but I don't know if I can."

"Next time," she said. "Next time we'll wait."

While they made love, the killer raped Sister Anne Marie, whom he called Bambi, in a room he'd rented for that purpose. And then he murdered her.

At five-ten in the morning, Dina's beeper sounded. It was in her pocketbook, which was on Keenan's couch. She slept on.

Thirteen

When Dina arrived at seven-fifteen in the morning, Donato was already there. He'd been at the crime scene since five-thirty, half an hour after the body of Sister Anne Marie had been discovered.

The nun had been propped up in the backseat of a red Toyota parked on West Eighty-ninth Street. They knew who she was because, hours before, her absence had been reported, and at six-thirteen, a Sister Gloria from the dead nun's convent had identified the body.

Donato was more shaken by this murder than the other two because it happened in his neighborhood. Despite recent events, he still considered the Upper West Side his home.

The newspaper people had left, but Dorothy Nathan of ABC and Don Doerrer of CBS were still hanging around.

"Little late, aren't you, Lieutenant?" Doerrer said.

Dina brushed him aside.

"Where've you been?" Donato asked when she reached him, trying to keep the annoyance he felt out of his voice.

"I didn't hear my beeper," she said and turned away.

He could have kicked himself. Still, he couldn't help wondering why she hadn't heard the phone. And then it dawned on him: she hadn't been at home. She'd spent the night somewhere else, and it didn't take a genius to figure out where. He pushed the knowledge to the back of his mind because it bothered him.

Dina said, "Who found her?"

"A guy named Graeme Flanagan. He's over there." Donato pointed to a short man leaning against one of the cruisers. Dressed in running clothes, he appeared to be in his late twenties.

"Did you talk to him?"

"He left his girlfriend's apartment at ten of five. Came down to his car, put his key in the lock, found that it had been broken into, opened the door and saw her in the backseat. Quote: 'I almost lost it.' Unquote."

"Anyone speak to the girlfriend?"

"Bobbin and Lachman. She confirmed Flanagan's story. I sent them and Delgado and Pesetsky to get some breakfast. Told them to meet us back at headquarters."

"When did they remove the body?"

"About half an hour ago."

"Couldn't you have waited for me to get here?"

Donato felt a surge of anger. She was trying to throw her error into his lap. "I'm sorry, Lieutenant, but nobody knew where you were. I didn't see any point in holding things up since I didn't know if you'd get here at all."

"Well, I'm here, aren't I?"

"Yes, you're here," he said through his teeth.

She lit a cigarette. "Same MO?"

"Same."

"What was she doing out in the middle of the night?"

"She'd vanished yesterday afternoon on her way from the dentist's. Had a root canal done. She was reported missing at about five yesterday."

"And what time did she leave the dentist's?"

"Three-thirty."

"Do we know how long she'd been dead?"

"Approximately eight to ten hours. Goode'll know better later."

"He must have stashed her somewhere before putting her in the car."

A battered blue Ford pulled up, and Keenan got out. Donato felt irritated and told himself to stop being an old fart. When he saw that Dina was uncomfortable, it aggravated him more.

They filled Keenan in, then walked over to the red Toyota, Dina a few steps ahead of the men. The area was cordoned off with yellow tape. A young, self-important-looking cop was standing next to the car. When Dina approached, he stepped forward and put out his arm.

"This is a crime scene," he said officiously.

Donato watched Diana check her annoyance as she identified herself.

"Oh, sorry, Lieutenant," the rookie said, chagrined. "I didn't think . . . I mean . . ."

She ducked under the tape.

The door on the driver's side was open, the front seat pushed forward. There was no blood on the backseat. Forensic had given the car the usual on-the-scene once-over, and a residue of black dust clung to the door and window handles like ash. Later, Forensic would do additional testing. Donato wished for something more than a hair sample, but he wasn't too hopeful: the killer had been very careful so far. There was nothing to see here with the naked eye. They walked away from the car.

"I guess I should get down to the morgue," Dina said.

Donato had meant to talk to Lena from the pickle store, but he'd let his personal problems interfere. "I want to talk to Rudolph and Lena first." It was childish, but Donato felt pleased that Dina knew whom he was talking about and Keenan didn't. "The other day he told me about a nun coming into the store, said they thought there was something strange about her. I want to talk to Lena; then I think Rudolph should see this one, tell us if she's the same nun."

"What was strange about her?" Keenan asked.

Donato spoke to Dina as if she'd asked the question. "I don't know. He couldn't put his finger on it. Anyway, I think we should get up there."

Keenan looked at his watch. "It's only seven-thirty-five."

Dina smiled at Donato, then said to Keenan, "Rudolph opens at six. Okay. Keenan, you go over to the convent and see what you can find out."

"Where is it?" He sounded piqued.

"Seventy-fifth between Broadway and Amsterdam." Donato decided he didn't like Keenan.

"What about a partner for me, Lieutenant?" Keenan asked.

"I'll get on it as soon as I can. Art Scott should be back from vacation by now. You know him?"

"Yeah. He's good."

"We'll check with you later." She turned abruptly and started down the street.

Donato said, "The car's on Ninety-first, Lieutenant."

She spun around, avoiding Keenan as she walked uptown.

Dorothy Nathan, still on the scene, stepped in front of them. "You any closer to the identity of the Sister Slasher?"

"No comment," Dina said.

"I'll have to say the police are baffled or something like that," Nathan called after them, provocatively.

"Say anything you want," Dina answered.

Walking in silence, Dina's embarrassment about Keenan was palpable, and Donato thought of saying something. But what? He recalled an incident when Dina was sixteen. They'd allowed her to give a party in front of their beach house, and after the gathering had been in swing about two hours, Donato decided to walk down, see how things were going. What he saw shocked him.

The fire illuminating their faces, Dina was lying on her stomach, kissing a boy. Before he could control his emotions, he yelled that the party was over, sending everybody home.

Dina was mortified. She'd cried all night and wouldn't let either Donato or Renata near her. Around dawn, she allowed Rich in her room. Later, Donato apologized. But he didn't tell her that seeing a boy kissing her in a sexual way made him feel old, an anachronism. For the first time, he'd also been made aware that there was a male more important to her than he.

When they got to the car, two teenage boys were sitting on the hood.

"Okay, guys," Donato said, "let's go."

"Where we goin'?" the dark-haired one said.

"Off the car," Donato said, still keeping an even tone.

"How about you make us, dude." The smaller one, with big teeth, laughed.

Standing by the passenger side, Dina watched, her eyes darting back and forth between the boys and her father. She snapped open her purse, her hand ready to grab her gun.

Donato put his key in the lock. "By the time I get in, I want you off the car."

"Listen, granddad, why don't you take your pussy someplace else, okay?"

Donato whirled around, fists clenched, his face turning pink. He reached for the kid closest to him.

"Donato," Dina warned.

He twisted the kid's shirtfront as if it were his skin. "Listen, punk, we're police officers. You don't want us to collar you, you'd better get the hell off. Right now." He released the boy.

"Show me your badge, asshole."

"How about if I show you this," Dina said and pulled her gun from her bag.

The boys slid down from the car. "Hey, lady, we was only kiddin'."

"I'm not," Dina said.

"Don't get crazy, lady," the dark one said in a squeaky voice, backing away.

"Take off," she ordered.

They ran up Broadway, heads down, not looking back.

Donato was shaking. He got in the car, unlocked the door for her. "Jesus, Dina, you know better than to pull your gun in a situation like that. What if one of them had drawn a weapon? What were you going to do, shoot the little bastard?"

She looked straight ahead, her jaw set. "I wanted to frighten them. And I did. Let's go to Rudolph's."

"Is that how you killed Buddy Green?" he snapped. It was out before he knew it.

"Ah, Donato," she said softly, "that was lousy."

He felt like hell. Wanting to tell her he was sorry, he found his mouth wouldn't form the words. He started the car and headed toward West End Avenue.

Why was he so mad at her? Why had he hurt her that way? Because she'd spent the night with Keenan? He remembered Renata suggesting he was jealous when he'd made the fuss at Dina's long-ago party, but he hadn't bought it then and he didn't now. Maybe it was because he felt so damn guilty that it was Judy lying in the morgue and not Dina. If that were true, he had a helluva way of showing his gratitude.

"Dina, listen, I'm . . ."

"Forget it."

"Don't do that."

"Why not? Why should you get off the hook by apologizing?

You're like a smart-ass lawyer who says things he shouldn't in front of the jury, then takes the objection in stride because he's made his point. So don't apologize, Donato. Just sit there with it and feel as rotten as I do."

There was nothing he could say. They drove the rest of the way in silence. On Eighty-second Donato squeezed into a small space between two trucks. They crossed the street and went down the stairs to the pickle store.

Rudolph was behind the counter doing the crossword, and Lena was knitting.

"Look, Lena, it's the sergeant and the daughter. Dina, I ain't seen you in a dog's age."

Dina greeted them.

"You're looking good," Lena said. "Ain't she looking good?"

"Looking good," Rudolph echoed.

Donato said, "We'd like to talk to you about the nun you mentioned to me the other day."

"Ahh." He rolled his sorrowful eyes heavenward. "The meshuge one. You remember, Lena?"

Lena was a round woman, shaped like a beach ball. Her white hair was cut short, and she wore half-glasses. When she spoke, she peered over them.

"I didn't like her, and I felt bad not to like a nun."

"But why didn't you like her?" Donato asked.

She rested her needles in her lap. "The hands. The nails was buffed. I thought nuns don't do that. But she had long fingers and the nails are shiny."

"Anything else?"

"The eyes. You could tell even behind the glasses. Cold." She shivered.

"What color were her eyes?" Dina asked.

"Gray," she said.

"Blue," Rudolph corrected.

"Wrong," Lena asserted.

"Blue," he said again.

"Gray like gloom," she insisted.

"Blue."

"No, no, no. A thousand times no."

Rudolph turned to Donato. "She's wrong."

"He makes me sick," Lena said flatly. "Always the bigshot. Always he knows it all." She began knitting furiously.

Donato had seen these two in action before, and he wanted to avoid a squabble.

"Lena, was there anything else about her that struck you as odd?"

"There was something else, something I couldn't tell you. I wish I could, but it just don't come to me."

"Were there any distinguishing marks, like a scar or a mole?" Dina asked.

"No. Nothing like that. Something, something," she drifted off, her eyes studying the floor, as if the missing piece might appear there.

"Rudolph, we'd like you to do us a favor," Donato said, choosing his words carefully. "Early this morning another nun was murdered. In this neighborhood."

Lena sucked in her breath and clapped a hand over her mouth.

"We'd like you to come with us to the morgue and see if this nun is the one who came in here recently." Donato wasn't sure what it would prove one way or the other. Still, the idea of a nun who seemed offbeat bothered him, and he felt there was a connection somewhere.

Rudolph glanced at Lena, then back to Donato. "No problem," he said apprehensively, his long face sagging.

"It would be a great help," Dina added.

Lena had stopped knitting and looked at her husband with new eyes, as if he were suddenly a person of great consequence.

"You don't mind being here alone, huh?" he asked.

"Don't worry." She turned to Donato and Dina. "We're good citizens, we vote, we do our duty. Not like some who come here, take things for granted, forget where they came from."

Rudolph got his plaid jacket and battered brown trilby from a hook. "Stay off your feet as much as possible." He bent down and kissed his wife's cheek. Then to Donato and Dina he said, "Okay, I'm ready."

The morgue was on First Avenue and East Thirtieth Street. It was a modern building with a gray and white façade and wide glass doors. In the lobby, chrome and vinyl-upholstered chairs were grouped in clusters of four and five. On a long marble wall was a brass inscription: TACEAT COLLOQUIA. EFFUGIAT RISUS. HIC LOCUS EST UBI MORS GAUDET SUCCURRERE VITAE. It meant: Let conversation cease. Let laughter flee. This is the place where death delights to help the living.

The two detectives and Rudolph took the elevator down. When

they got off in the fluorescent-lit basement, they found the corridors lined with shiny stainless-steel boxes. Gurneys against the wall held bodies under sheets. On some, feet peeked out and identification tags dangled from big toes. Drains dotted the concrete floors, evenly spaced.

"Are you all right?" Dina asked Rudolph. His skin, normally a light shade of pink, looked gray.

"Fine. I'm fine. No problem," he said, his voice quaking.

They pushed through the swinging steel doors and turned right. Then they stopped, surveying the scene. The room was huge, brilliantly lighted. All the walls were tiled, spotless; the stainless steel gleamed, as though it had just been polished.

The sour-sweet disinfectant stung Donato's eyes. Four naked bodies lay on stainless steel tables. The chest cavities of two had incisions, the rib cages pulled apart, exposing the organs inside. Large scales hung over each table. Doctors were working on the cadavers.

Donato led the way toward Greg Goode, garbed in traditional green, bending over the body of a woman. A microphone hung around his neck as he gave his findings to a tape in his pocket.

Goode looked up and held out a bloody, rubber-gloved hand. "I'd shake," he said, "but you wouldn't like it." He grinned, showing uneven teeth.

Donato didn't smile. "Is this the nun?"

"This nun's the one," Goode said, smirking at his rhyme.

Dina said, "Spare us, Greg, will you?"

He looked momentarily hurt, then shrugged.

Donato turned to Rudolph, who stood a few feet behind them, his hat in his hands, looking as if he were going to his own execution. Walking back to him, Donato put a hand on his shoulder. "You don't have to do this if you don't want to."

"You read about it, the morgue, you see it on the TV, but you still ain't prepared."

"You want to leave?"

He hesitated. "I'm needed?"

"You're needed."

"So, okay." He inched forward, Donato keeping a steadying hand on his sleeve.

"This is Dr. Goode. Rudolph . . ." Donato stopped. "I'm sorry, I don't . . ."

"It's Karanewski, with a K."

"Hello," said Goode.

"Nice to meet you, Doctor." Rudolph tried a small sad smile.

Donato gently maneuvered him closer to the table. "What do you think, Rudolph?"

"I don't know . . . maybe."

"Look carefully at her face," Dina instructed.

"Could be. But the one I seen had glasses."

"Rice," Goode called.

A tall, red-headed woman looked Goode's way. "Yo?"

"Get the glasses for 1845, will you."

"Coming up."

"Where's the finger?" Rudolph asked, horrified.

Donato said, "The killer does this. You mustn't mention it to anyone."

He nodded, still looking shaken.

"The nails," Dina said. "They're not buffed."

"Didn't have time," Goode parried, "but I gave her a perm."

Donato and Dina exchanged a look of disgust.

"Lighten up for God's sake. You should be used to this by now. Used to me, anyway."

"I'll *never* get used to you," Donato said. He wondered if Goode's kidding was the only way he could make it through the day. Some cops did the same thing. It had never helped him.

Rice handed Goode the glasses. The frames were tortoise shell, the lenses round. Goode hooked them over the nun's ears and set them on the bridge of her nose.

They all looked at Rudolph.

He shook his head. "Hers were metal."

"You mean wire frames, Rudolph?" Dina asked.

"Wire frames. Yes. This ain't the same one, I don't think. The mouth was different, something."

Donato sighed. "Okay, that's it. Thanks, Greg."

"Anytime."

"Was she raped?" Dina asked.

"Same as the others. So far it looks identical."

"When can I have your report?"

"In the morning."

"How about late this afternoon?"

"So why bother asking, Lieutenant?"

"I keep hoping you'll catch on and realize I want reports yesterday. Try to have it on my desk by five today."

"Yessir, Lieutenant . . . I mean, yes, ma'am."

Donato saw Dina bristle, but she kept walking.

Outside, waiting for the light to change on First Avenue, Rudolph said, "I'm sorry, Sergeant."

"For what?"

"Well, you know . . . you needed me, and I come up with zilch." Rudolph's lugubrious face looked even more so.

"You did fine," Donato said.

The light changed, and they crossed the street, got into the car. All the way uptown, they were silent, except for the occasional long sigh from Rudolph in the back. When they dropped him off, they assured him again that he'd been very helpful, but it was clear he was determined to feel a flop.

They started back downtown. At Broadway and Sixty-sixth, Donato asked Dina, "What are you going to do about Keenan?"

"What do you mean?"

He glanced over at her. A pink hue had colored her cheeks. Dina had always been a blusher. He realized she'd misunderstood his question, and it gave him an unpleasant twinge.

"About a partner," he explained.

She tried to cover. "I thought you . . . I thought you might be blaming him for Judy's death."

"No. I just meant to remind you to try getting Art Scott."

"Yes. Thanks. I'd forgotten."

Her admission surprised him. "How're you doing with Judy's death?"

"I feel like somebody's punched a hole in my stomach. I haven't felt like this since . . ."

"Since Rich. I know."

A minute passed before she said, "When Rich died, I was angry . . . furious . . . first with the guys I thought killed him in the shootout, then with him. I felt so damn mad at him . . . for leaving me, even though I believed it wasn't his fault."

"Me, too."

"But *you* knew the truth. You knew he'd killed himself," she said without bitterness.

"Or thought I did."

"What do you mean?"

He'd never told her about Hubie Peak and Walter "Cookie" Albert. Pulling over, he double-parked.

"What's up?" she asked.

He flipped on the hazard signal. "There's something I want to tell you. Something I should've straightened out four years ago when Crider let it slip that Rich hadn't died in a shootout. But I . . . oh, Christ . . . when I told Baron and Finley to 'take care of' Peak I *was* angry. To this day I don't know what I really meant."

"What are you getting at?"

"This is tough as hell, Dina. I think I'm afraid of you. You're a pretty hard marker, you know."

"Am I?"

Donato watched her surprise turn to hurt, but he felt confused, wary. He didn't trust her. One moment she could be vulnerable and accessible, and the next, remote, hostile.

"Am I really?" she said again. "I thought I was pretty fair with you. How should I have acted under the circumstances?" An icy tone tinted her words.

"I don't want to go into that now. That's ancient history."

"You never want to go into anything." She took out a cigarette, lit it.

His insides began to churn. He wished he hadn't started this. But his secrets covered him like cobwebs, and he needed to cut through, be free of the past once and for all.

"I'd like to tell you about this, but I don't want to be judged for what I say."

"Oh, that's neat, Donato. You're going to tell me some shocker, and I'm supposed to promise not to react."

"I didn't say that."

Dina glanced at her watch. "I think we'd better get back to the precinct."

She'd given him his out, but perversely he barreled on, unable to stop, not knowing why. "Hubie Peak had Rich killed."

Her hand, the cigarette between two fingers, froze halfway to her mouth.

"Maybe Rich was planning to turn over, I don't know. Peak felt threatened by him, I guess. Ordered his murder. A small time creep named Cookie took him out."

She drew on the cigarette, then flipped it out the window. "So that's why Halliday sent you to the Ninth. I could never make sense of it. The idea of you going after a dealer because your son had been a junkie, nine years after the fact, just never made sense to me. But you had a *real* reason." She gave a short laugh. "And once again the department managed to keep its dirty laundry buried. You good old boys, you."

"Do you think I wasn't punished enough?"

"Oh, the hell with that. What I don't understand is why you didn't tell me the rest? The *whole* goddamned truth."

"I thought you'd suffered enough, you and your mother."

"You thought it was easier for me to believe that my brother killed himself because he was a junkie? Easier to think my father, my honest cop father, signaled to have a dealer taken out because his son had been hooked? Is that what you thought, Donato? Jesus!"

"I didn't want you to be hurt any more than you had been."

"All my life you've been trying to shield me from pain, and it's never worked. I'm a very big girl now, Donato. I'm your goddamned boss. Now let's get the hell back to the precinct. On the double."

He wanted to say that he hadn't meant to upset her, that he'd hoped for some understanding. But he didn't say anything. He couldn't. They were right back at square one.

Fourteen

A printout lay on the table in front of Pesetsky. "The MO file is in from Computer. There's only one that's close, and it's in Akron, Ohio, but the victim wasn't a nun. The MO was rape, stabbing and a rope around the victim's neck. No missing finger."

"Anyone apprehended?" Dina asked.

"Still open. No suspects."

This was the first task force meeting since the third murder and Judy's death, and the members were subdued. They'd begun to grieve. For some it was harder than others. Bobbin and Delgado had worked with Judy before. Lachman hadn't known her at all, and Pesetsky had met her on only a few occasions. Keenan, of course, had been closest to her in the last days of her life. And then there was Donato.

Immediately to her left, next to Keenan, was Art Scott, Judy's replacement. In his mid-thirties, he wore his long blond hair in a ponytail, an asset for his usual undercover work. His eyes were a faded blue, like pale denim, and he had a round boyish face. Although he was only five-nine, he was solidly built and could easily take men taller and heavier.

Scott was married and had three children, all adopted. One was an American Indian, another black and the baby was Vietnamese. Dina had been at the Academy with Scott but hadn't seen him much in the last five years. Still, she knew he was smart, a top detective. Pesetsky interrupted her announcement that Scott would partner with Keenan.

"Hold on, Lieutenant. I'd like to partner with Scott."

Dina quickly weighed the problem. The partnership between Pesetsky and Delgado, obviously, wasn't getting any better. She should have realized that insisting they remain together would only reinforce Pesetsky's prejudice against women and possibly jeopardize the investigation.

"How do you feel about it, Delgado?" Dina asked.

"That'd be fine with me, Lieutenant," she said briskly.

"Would you be more comfortable with Keenan?"

"I couldn't be less . . ." Delgado started, then cut herself off. "Better ask him how he feels."

Dina turned to Keenan.

"I have no objections," Keenan said.

"All right." Dina wished she could bump Pesetsky from the squad, but time precluded bringing in yet another member. She'd never work with him again though.

"Pesetsky will fill you in," she told Scott. "Let's go on."

Delgado riffled some computer paper, straightened the edges against the table and picked up the first page. "You aren't gonna believe this, Lieutenant, but there've been a lot of nun killings. Well, much more than you'd expect." She ran down the list for each concerned state. "New York's had three. Different MOs from our guy."

"Check those further," Dina said.

"You want us to interview the convent people and police?"

"See what you can get internally first."

Lachman and Bobbin's report on the latest murder added nothing she didn't already know. Then it was Keenan's turn.

All through the meeting, she'd been averting her eyes when he looked at her. She told herself it was because she didn't want Donato to know. Anyway, this was no place to show her feelings. When she called on Keenan, she kept her eyes on the papers in front of her.

He had interviewed the nuns at Sister Anne Marie's convent, turning up nothing helpful: no known enemies, no special relationships, no possible motive. He closed his notebook and said, "I guess we all know we've got a serial killer on our hands."

"You just figuring that out, Keenan?" Lachman asked.

Keenan ignored him. "He's going to keep doing it until we catch him."

"Or until he wears down," Donato added. "It's possible that he's in a fugue state."

"What's that, Sarge?" Lachman asked.

"It's when a person has a temporary loss of memory, then gets it back, but doesn't remember anything."

"That ain't no fucking fugue state, Donato," Bobbin said. "That's a smart lawyer's defense."

They all laughed, and some of the tension broke.

Scott said, "It's that disease they get on soap operas."

"Hey, Scott," Delgado said, "you been watching the soaps, or what?"

"My wife watches them, tells me the stories. Every day somebody else's got amnesia."

"Go on, Keenan," Dina said, and this time she couldn't avoid his eyes. She felt as though he could see into her soul.

"Every nun in this town should be made aware of what's going on and be advised to use extreme caution when going out. Maybe they should go back to the old days of nuns traveling in twos."

"Good idea. Get the people you need from the various precincts, have some flyers printed." Dina rose, and as some of the others started to get up, she said, "Hang on, we're not finished. I've got a psychiatrist coming in."

There were groans and mutters of protest.

"Okay, okay. But this one's on our side. He's going to give you a profile of our killer."

"You mean the doc got our asshole to pose for him, Lieut?"

"Shut your mouth, Lachman," Bobbin said. "Maybe you'll learn something."

Lachman gave Bobbin the finger, and Dina gave them both a withering glance, then opened the door and invited the doctor in.

He was tall, and his eyes were cavernous in a billowy face. Gray hair sprang from the sides of his head like clumps of weeds on an untended lawn. Wearing a rust-colored, crumpled corduroy suit, an off-white shirt and a green small-knotted tie, he had the look of a man tired of his profession, perhaps of life.

"This is Dr. Stewart. Sit over here, Doctor." Dina indicated her place, then sat in the only available chair, behind Donato and across from Keenan.

Stewart took a piece of paper out of his inside jacket pocket and laid it on the table. From another pocket, he produced a hard black case, snapped it open and withdrew a pair of gold-rimmed glasses, which he carefully looped over his ears. Clearing his throat, he said, "Umm, I believe we're dealing with umm a sociopath."

"Here comes the bullshit," Lachman said in a stage whisper.

"What's that?" Stewart asked.

Dina said, "Nothing, Doctor, go on," and eyed Lachman warningly.

Stewart looked over the group as though he were combing it for spies, then continued. "According to the evidence I've been given, umm, I'd say he's in his late twenties or early thirties, could be married, and is highly intelligent. Umm, the killer is undoubtedly a Catholic, more than likely a lapsed one. Perhaps he suffered some kind of torment from a nun as a youth."

"What about the finger, Doc?" Delgado asked.

"Umm, yes, the finger." Stewart removed his glasses and wiped them with a piece of material he took from his case. "That could be a number of things. For instance, it's, umm, possible that a nun poked him with the fourth finger of the left hand, humiliating him." He held out his ring finger and awkwardly jabbed at the air. "At any rate, the finger might be significant but does not have to be. Sociopaths like to do bizarre things.

"With a sociopath no real reason is necessary for anything he does. He, umm, probably believes the murders are justified, that he, umm, is not responsible, that he has been forced into committing the murders due to something the victims have done. The sociopath tries to project the image that *he* is the victim of a hostile world, and uppermost in his mind is the desire to dupe others before they deceive him. In short, people are out to get him." He returned his glasses to his face.

"Why hasn't anybody noticed this nut before this?" Scott asked.

"Umm, a person like the one we're discussing has been a sociopath from early childhood, probably from birth, but he's never been diagnosed. Naturally, the illness is not flagrant or visible at all times.

Nevertheless, he is always in the sociopathic state, and, umm, I've no doubt that he passes for the average person."

"So why now?" Keenan asked.

Stewart smiled condescendingly. "Because these murders have come to light does not mean there haven't been others. Umm, not necessarily murders of nuns. But he might have killed a childhood friend and gone undetected. Or others. Perhaps in a remote place, in less sensational ways. Umm, killing a nun attracts attention."

"Well, why *nuns* now?" Keenan persisted.

"I understand that there was a newspaper article about the first nun who was murdered. That could be enough to trigger him."

"So then there is a connection . . . between the murderer and the victims?" Delgado asked.

Defensively, Stewart pulled in his neck, like a turtle. "I did not mean to imply that there was no connection. A sociopath's motivation for his actions is very logical to him. Umm, with serial killers, however, after the first one, the one that may have been triggered by something like the newspaper article, that motivation can disappear and the killing itself becomes the purpose because the killer enjoys himself and cannot stop . . . does not *want* to stop."

The room was hushed as Dr. Stewart's last words sank in. Not that it was news to them. They knew about killing for fun. Still, it was a reminder of what they were up against.

After Stewart left, Dina turned back to the group. "The profile Stewart gave us isn't the one I'm going to release to the press. I'm going to tell them that the killer is a loner, has below-average intelligence and holds a menial job of some kind."

"I don't get it, Lieut," Lachman said.

"Part of the thrill of killing is to confound us. Our guy feels superior to most people, especially cops. And he's got an incredible ego."

"So," Donato said, "you're falsifying Stewart's report to insult the killer?"

"That's right."

"Forcing his hand?" Keenan said critically.

"We've got a serial killer on our hands, Keenan," Dina snapped. "You said so yourself. No matter what we do or say he's going to kill again. But if he feels challenged or insulted, he might just make a mistake. So if anybody from the press asks, stick to the false description. And we're still keeping back the missing-finger info."

When the others had left, Keenan and Donato remained behind.

"I'd like to talk to you, Lieutenant," Keenan said.

She couldn't say no. It was her duty to respond to any member of the task force who needed to talk. She turned to Donato. "Wait for me in the car, okay?"

Donato glanced at Keenan, then nodded at Dina and left.

"Well?" she said, feeling apprehensive.

"What the hell does that mean?"

"Look, Keenan, we have a lot of work to do and . . ."

"I don't know about you, Lieutenant, but I'm not used to being treated like a whore."

Her face flushed. "I don't know what you mean."

"I think you do."

"If it's about last night . . . well, it doesn't give you ownership."

"Ownership?" he said, incredulous. "Christ almighty, I'm talking about a little human kindness, acknowledgment that you know me."

"You're being ridiculous, Bobby."

"The hell I am. You've barely looked at me. And when you have, it's as though I'm a stranger. Listen, if you want to consider last night a one-night stand, that's okay by me."

She didn't know what she wanted. No, that wasn't true. She wanted *him.* But it was too complicated, too difficult to deal with now. Still, if she told him this, he'd find a way to convince her otherwise. "I think that's best," she said coolly.

He gave a short scornful laugh. "Oh, you're really something, lady. Now I understand your nickname."

She wanted to know what he meant but wouldn't ask.

He didn't make her wait. "The Ice Maiden," he said, throwing out the words in fast frosty bites. "Yeah, that's what they call you, Dina. I thought they were wrong, that it was just a persona you adopted because it was tough being a woman in charge. Last night I was sure they were wrong. Now I see that's exactly what you are. Ice." He walked out of the room, slamming the door behind him.

She gathered up her papers and began stuffing them into a worn leather briefcase. Any woman in charge gets called something comparable. Look at Margaret Thatcher. Well, too bad. I don't have time for this. Then she stopped. Why had she let him go that way? Since Liam, he was the first man she'd felt anything for. Fear. There was no denying it. She was terrified of getting involved again, and he'd given her a perfect out.

The phone rang, and it was Halliday. He wanted to see her and

Donato forthwith. It was a call she'd been expecting, dreading. But it was a good reminder: with the case getting nowhere, and Halliday on her back, she simply didn't have time for Bobby Keenan. It was as elementary as that.

As she expected, when she stepped outside, the media people were waiting. For the first time in her career, she was glad to see them.

"Lieutenant," David George from the *Times* called, "do you have a statement about this third murder?"

"We have a psychological profile of the murderer," she said, evading his question.

"A psychiatrist's report?"

"Yes."

"Will you give it to us?"

Dina pretended to deliberate. "All right, I don't see why not. Dr. Stewart has been studying the evidence we have and has come up with this profile." She snatched her pad from her jacket pocket, flipped over the pages and began to read: "The killer is probably in his late twenties or early thirties, unmarried, a loner, has below-average intelligence and holds a menial job, if any."

"That's it?"

The *Daily News* reporter said, "Did the good doctor make a diagnosis?"

"He believes the killer is a sociopath."

"The buzzword of the eighties," he complained.

"You asked," Dina said. "That's all I've got now."

Kathi Maio said, "Come on, Lieutenant, Stewart must have given you more than that."

"Sorry, Maio, that's all I can divulge at this time."

"Why is he after nuns?" asked Stan Burns of NBC.

Dina shook her head and started to leave.

"Is it true, Lieutenant, that you're going to be replaced on this case by a man?"

Turning around slowly, she gave Burns a baleful look. "It's as true as the rumor that you're going to be replaced by a woman, Mr. Burns." Walking away from them, she tried not to allow Burns's remark to make her any more disquieted than she already was.

Donato was engrossed in an Elmore Leonard paperback when Dina got to the car. As long as she could remember, he'd carried a book in his jacket pocket.

He looked up as she got in. "How'd you do?"

"Fine."

Marking his place, Donato closed the book and stuffed it into his pocket.

"Halliday wants to see us," she said.

"Surprise!" He turned the key in the ignition.

"So what do you actually have, Lieutenant?" Halliday asked, his eyes an unforgiving blue.

"Truthfully, not much."

Halliday slammed the desk with the flat of his hand. "Dammit, why not?"

Dina was grateful that neither she nor Donato flinched. "He doesn't leave clues," she stated simply.

"Do you have any idea what kind of position you've put me in?"

The only thing Halliday cared about was how he looked. And it was *her* fault, not the killer's.

"I've got the mayor on my back, the PC and the fucking Archbishop, for Christ's sake. The next thing I know I'm going to hear from the Pope. We can't have some fucking maniac out there chopping up nuns while you drag your asses. You know, Lieutenant," he said smoothly, shifting gears, "it's up to you to be creative. We need some imagination here, some original thinking." He ran his thumb and forefinger down the bridge of his long nose.

Should she disclose her plan to Halliday? There was no telling how he'd react, but she had to give him something. She didn't want to be pulled off the case.

"What do *you* have to say, Sergeant?" Halliday asked Donato.

"We both understand how important this case is, and we're doing the best we can, Chief."

"You aren't letting family feuds get in the way, are you?" He raised his bushy eyebrows.

Dina was incensed. Problems between her and Donato hadn't clouded her mind, obstructed the investigation. She was a professional, and Halliday knew that.

"*Nothing* is getting in the way of the investigation," she said. "And we *do* have a plan."

"Good. What is it?"

She glanced at Donato, who gave her an encouraging nod. Then she laid out the scheme.

While she talked, Halliday swiveled in his chair, giving her his profile, his chin resting in the vee of two fingers. When she was finished, he said nothing for a few moments, then whirled back to face her.

"You can't be serious, Lieutenant."

Donato said, "It's not foolproof, but it's worth a try."

"It's worth shit," Halliday shot back. "If you're right, this asshole's going to kill another one to prove how smart he is. I may be wrong, but I don't think we're in the business of promoting murders."

Halliday was smarter than this. He was doing his passive-aggressive act, and Dina wasn't going to fall for it. "He's going to kill again, anyway. But this time he just might let us know more about him. It's not that he wants to get caught, but he'll want to correct our image of him."

"Which means he'll be even smarter, shrewder."

"Not the way you mean," Donato said. "He may prove to us that Stewart's wrong about his intelligence by turning up on the scene, as a witness maybe. Or he'll bring it closer to home, tease the stupid cops, so to speak. But we'll be ready for him because we know the trap we're setting and he doesn't."

"It's about ego," Dina went on. "He's going to have to do something to let us know how smart he is."

"I don't know. It sounds pretty farfetched."

"Well, it's in the works. All we can do now is wait."

"That's not to say we don't have other leads to follow down," Donato said.

"That's right," Dina confirmed.

After a moment, Halliday said, "All right. We'll try it. As you say, he's going to kill again, anyway. What day is this?" He looked at the calendar. "Wednesday. Okay. There'd better be some results by Monday morning. If this case isn't broken by then, I'm going to put somebody else on it. You understand, Lieutenant?"

"Yes, sir."

"And you, Sergeant. If you crack this one, we might just talk turkey. Now get the hell out of here."

Fifteen

Sitting at his desk, he was unable to concentrate. It was getting harder all the time. The day after an . . . incident . . . was particularly difficult. He felt agitated, uneasy. And it made him angry. Angry at *them*. At her. It was Sister Bambi's fault he felt like this today.

God, he was tired. He hadn't slept in over twenty-four hours. Not even a nap. He'd hoped, after dumping her, that he'd catch forty winks at his safe house, but he'd been too restless, drunk too much coffee.

When he thought about how he'd gotten her to come with him, he shivered with a mixture of fear and awe. Fear that he might have been caught, and awe at his ingeniousness. Sometimes he didn't know where his ideas came from. He supposed they were there all the time, locked in some hidden place in his brain, waiting for the right key.

He was sorry he'd have to give up the room on Ninety-sixth. He'd grown quite fond of it. Not that he'd spent much time there. Still, it was his: his alone. There was never any intrusion, no wife, no children to interrupt him. He'd have to get another place. Maybe that's what he should do right now.

The idea made his spirits swell. He grabbed his jacket from the chair and left his office. Nancy Myron, his secretary, looked up at him, her eyes, as usual, filled with adoration. He knew she was in love with him, had been from almost the very first day.

"Going out?"

"Yes. I'm not sure I'll be back, Nancy."

"You haven't forgotten your lunch appointment with Mr. Boyle, have you?"

He had. "What would I do without you?" He smiled boyishly. "I'll have to cancel."

"What should I say?"

He looked deep into her eyes. "You'll come up with something. I know I can count on you."

For a few extra seconds, he held the gaze while she squirmed in her chair. He'd learned to flirt by watching old Rock Hudson / Doris Day films. What a joke that Hudson had turned out to be a fag. As much as he hated queers, he'd enjoyed Hudson's hoax. The stupid public deserved it.

This time he would try the Village. It would be easy down there. People were used to seeing anything. A couple of nuns more or less weren't going to raise any eyebrows.

Hailing a cab, he wondered if the afternoon paper was out. He'd hit a newsstand as soon as possible. After giving the address to the driver, he settled back in the seat and reviewed his work of the night before. Actually, it had been the afternoon when he'd gotten her. Bambi.

She was short and slight, her features delicate, her olive skin unblemished, unlined. If she hadn't been a nun, she would have been beautiful. Even though she'd told him her name was Sister Anne Marie, he still thought of her as Bambi.

It had been so easy. He'd followed her on the opposite side of the street, watched her go into a building on Eighty-seventh. While she was inside, he'd kept walking up and down, watching, waiting. An hour later, she'd come out, and he'd caught up with her at the corner.

"Excuse me, Sister," he'd said, "are you from the Sisters of Mercy convent?"

"Yes, I am."

"And you're Sister . . ." He'd hesitated just long enough for her to supply the answer, then overlapped her name without her realizing he didn't know.

"Anne Marie."

"Anne Marie. You're needed," he'd said.

"What do you mean?" She'd eyed him curiously.

"There's a young girl desperately in need of help. She's asked for you."

"For me? I don't understand."

"Perhaps when you see her you will. Come with me."

"I don't know . . ."

Taking a gamble, he'd said in a confidential tone, "Sister, you *do* have a niece, don't you?"

"Is it Kelly?" she'd asked, alarmed.

"Yes. Hurry."

A piece of cake. He smiled, enjoying the memory. A genius, that's what he was.

Dorothy. He missed her terribly. Lately he was confusing time. He felt as if he hadn't seen her for a few days, the way he did in high school if she was absent, perhaps sick with flu.

And then he was remembering the first time he touched her breasts.

"I don't think you should," she'd said.

"Why not?"

"It's a sin."

"Don't you like the way it feels?"

She'd buried her face in his jacket, wouldn't look at him.

"You do, don't you? You like it." Then, boldly, he'd taken her hand and put it on his erection.

She'd jumped, pulling her hand away as if she'd touched fire. "Oh, no. We mustn't."

But they did. He'd kept talking, cajoling, and little by little she'd given in, letting him touch her, touching him. God, it was good.

"Which side of the street?" the cabbie asked.

Startled, he almost shouted his reply. "Left. I'll get out here," he said as the light changed to red.

The green-painted newspaper stand was next to the subway entrance on Sheridan Square. He saw a headline:

DOC KNOWS SISTER SLASHER

It must be more of the *Post*'s sensationalism, some trumped-up story. Nobody could know who he was. Still, as he bought the paper, he felt a bit queasy. Below the headline was a picture of the car where he'd stashed her, a cop standing in front of it. Tucking the paper under his arm, he looked around, spotted a coffee shop and headed toward it.

Inside Dempsey's, he ordered a cup of coffee but waited to open the paper until the waitress brought him his order. Then, quickly, he turned to page three and started to read. By the time he'd reached the end of the page, he was in a fury. *Below-average intelligence!* What assholes they were. He'd killed three women, that they knew about, and they still didn't have a real clue to go on. Was that the work of someone with *below-average intelligence*? And what was this garbage about his being a loner, unmarried?

Lifting his cup of coffee to his mouth, he saw that his hand was shaking. He hated being out of control, prided himself on always being in command of any situation.

Putting the cup back into the saucer, he looked around to see if anyone had noticed his trembling hand. A woman in a booth near the back was looking at him. Quickly, he turned away. Fucking bitch. They were always giving him the eye. It was impossible for him to go anywhere without women throwing themselves at him. It didn't matter what she'd seen, he told himself. There was no way she could know why.

He looked down at the paper. *Dr. Stewart.* Who the hell was he to judge his intelligence? And this bitch, *Lieutenant Donato,* again. What was wrong with the police, putting a woman in charge of an important case like this? He should rate the best.

An idea began to take shape. Maybe he could observe up close, help them out, as it were. What if he did one right in his own building? Excitement began to ripen inside him. What if he did one and put her body in the elevator of his building?

Let's face it, the others hadn't been *that* imaginative or daring. The latest wasn't bad, but he could do much better. If he could do one in an apartment house with people going in and out all day and night . . . well, the police would have to admit they were dealing with someone *very* clever, someone who couldn't possibly have *below-average intelligence*. Because someone with *below-average intelligence* couldn't conceivably work out something like that. It was going to be an extremely delicate operation requiring genius. But that's what he had. Genius.

And who was going to be the next lucky gal? He almost laughed out loud. He'd find her, follow her, learn her routine and then he'd strike. When everything was ready and not a second before. No need to rush things. This one was going to be his triumph. That goddamn Stewart and that cunt Donato would eat their words.

He picked up his coffee cup and raised it to his mouth. His hand was absolutely steady.

Sixteen

Dina, Florida Bob and Donato sat in a back booth at Augie's with Donald Jellinek. It was obvious to Donato that the man was sick, dying, most likely of AIDS. The look was unmistakable.

In his late twenties, early thirties, he had a large beaklike nose, sharp at the tip like a can opener. His eyes were brown and sunken in his skull-like face, the skin a shade of gray that betrayed his illness. Jellinek's hands never stopped moving: twisting the cellophane from a cigarette pack, dancing across a beer bottle label, tapping to rhythms only he heard. His nose ran continually, and he wiped it across the sleeve of his faded, plaid flannel shirt.

Looking at him, Donato wondered if Rich would have been like this had he lived. But Rich had quit. Still, Donato knew that the percentage of junkies who quit and stayed straight was low, and the shared use of needles was spreading AIDS.

"You guys want me anymore?" Florida Bob had set up the meet.

"No. Thanks," Dina said. She shook his hand.

Donato knew she'd slipped him a bill. Jellinek knew, too, his beady eyes registering the transaction like calculators.

When Florida Bob had gone, Donato asked Jellinek to tell them what he'd seen the day of Sister Honora's murder.

Jellinek sniffed loudly, took a swig of his beer. "There was a lot of action on the street that day, you know what I mean, man? A lot of spics and niggers hangin' out . . . more than usual. I thought maybe somethin' was comin' down, man. I wanted out of there before there's any action, but I'm waitin' on this dude, can't leave. The second the dude shows up I'm out of there, know what I mean, man? But the dude's late so I'm scopin' the scene when I see this nun coming down Sixth Street." He scratched his scrawny neck. "They look like fuckin' penguins, don't they? Fuckin' dude still doesn't show and I'm gettin' strung out, know what I mean, man?"

"The nun," Donato prompted.

"Yeah, the fuckin' nun. I noticed her, 'cause she was fuckin' big, man." He raised his hand above his head to demonstrate the nun's height.

"How tall?" Donato asked.

"I jus' tole you, man. Real fuckin' tall."

"Six feet?" Dina asked.

"Could be."

"Look, Jellinek," Donato said, "this is very important."

"So whaddaya expec' from me, man? Do I look like a human tape measure, or what?" He sniffed again, ran his arm across his nose, then went back to picking the label off the bottle.

Donato slid from the booth and stood up. "Was she as tall as I am?"

Jellinek looked Donato up and down. "Yeah, maybe."

"What do you mean, maybe?"

"Lissen, what the fuck is this? You want it in fuckin' centimeters? I'm tellin' ya, I didn't go up to the fuckin' nun with a yardstick. And I'm fuckin' wasted, man. This fuckin' dude I'm waitin' for is two fuckin' hours late and I'm shittin' blue, you know what I mean, man?"

"So how tall was she?" Donato sat down next to him.

"I don' need this, man. Come on, what's this shit? Florida Bob said this was strictly voluntary, man."

"We're just trying to get an accurate picture," Dina said, "and you may be the only one who can help us."

"Yeah?" He seemed pleased.

"Just tell us what you saw," Donato said.

"That's what the fuck I'm tryin' to do, man."

"What time did you see her?" Dina asked.

"I dunno. About four. Yeah. I was supposed to meet this fuckin' dude at two, so it was four."

"You saw her come down the street," Donato said. "Then what?"

"Then nothin'. I mean, she comes down the fuckin' street and she turns in at 609. I'm across from there, man, waitin' for this fuckin' dude."

"She went into the building?"

"Yeah."

"Did you see her come out?" Donato asked.

"No. This fuckin' dude finally showed up, man. I left the street right after that."

"So that was it?"

"Yeah, that was it. Whaddaya want, a fuckin' book?"

"What I want," Donato said, "is for you to tell me how tall this nun was."

"Jesus fuckin' Christ." He tried to get up and out, but Donato didn't move. "I tole ya. This nun was big for a nun. I can't get no more opinionated than that, man."

"Do you mean big for a woman?" Dina asked.

"Yeah," Jellinek said, brightening. "Big for a woman."

Donato had phoned Lena Karanewski and asked her if the nun had been tall. She'd become excited. Because she was short, she said, everybody looked tall to her, and only when Donato put it into words, had she realized what had bothered her. The nun was very tall for a woman.

After that they'd radioed the information to the Bureau of Criminal Identification, who would relay it to every convent in the city. And then they'd gone to the luncheonette on Sixth Avenue and Waverly Place.

Donato burned his lips on the steaming coffee and almost dropped the cup. He was elated. It was the first time in the case that a piece had fallen into place. Now they knew how the Slasher got close to them, tricked them, led them to their executions. He dressed like a nun.

"We should have known," Dina said.

"I know."

"Sloppy," she said.

"You're right."

"We'd better get it together."

"Couldn't agree more."

"Good. Do you think he's a transvestite?"

"Could be." Then he snapped his fingers. "Hey, you know that guy in the Village? Calls himself Sister Bang or some damn thing?"

"The one who goes around on roller skates?"

He nodded. "What do you think?"

"I think we should go find him."

Donato gulped his coffee, leaving half of it. On the way out, he bought a doughnut from the counter.

"You drive," she said.

"I'm eating."

She looked at him. "What's happened to your healthy diet?"

"It's gone to hell."

"Good. I didn't know who you were."

There were a number of gay men walking along Christopher Street, obviously offering themselves, looking for sexual partners.

Donato didn't hate these men the way some of the other cops did, but he didn't really understand them. He couldn't imagine making love to a man.

Dina pulled the car over to the curb. Donato jumped out, and a young blond man wearing a leather jacket and sporting a neat mustache whirled around, looking frightened.

Donato held up a hand as if to signal the man that he was not in any danger. "I'd like to ask you a question."

The man eyed him warily, then bent down and looked in at Dina. "Not interested," he said.

"No, you don't understand."

He laughed. "Listen, bud, I understand. I just don't dig three-somes, okay?"

Donato pulled out his leather case and flipped it open, showing his shield.

"Look, you can't harass me like this. I know my rights. I can get the National Gay Task Force on this in five seconds."

"Will you hold it a goddamned minute?" Donato said. "I just want to ask you a question. You ever hear of a person called Sister Bang?"

The man smiled, hooking his thumbs into the pockets of his tight jeans. "You mean Sister Bang Bang?"

"Right. You know where I can find him?"

"I might know where you can find *her.*" He smirked, knowing the pronoun made Donato uncomfortable. "Why do you want her?"

"That's none of your business. Look, you can tell me right now or I can take you in and we can talk about it there."

"Take me in on what charge?" he asked smugly.

"Soliciting."

"Just try it. Go ahead and see where you get."

Donato was pissed off. He didn't like being threatened. Still, all he'd need now was a charge that he'd interfered with somebody's civil rights. Halliday would love it. He made himself cool down.

"Listen, I don't want any trouble with you. I'm investigating a murder case, and I need to talk to this Sister Bang Bang." He felt silly saying the name. "If you know where I can find . . . her, I'd appreciate it if you'd tell me."

The man ran a hand through his hair. "You want the truth? I haven't the foggiest. I don't know her any more than you do. You guys think we all know each other, hang out together just because we like to suck cock. Do you hang out with every creep who comes along just because you both dig pussy? No. And neither do we. As far as I'm concerned, Sister Bang Bang is a douche bag. It's guys like him who give guys like me a bad rep. People think we're all like that because that's what the media focuses on. Look at me. Do I look like a fairy? A queer? A pansy? Or do I look like any other guy on the street?"

"Jesus," Donato said.

Tirade over, the man walked away.

Donato stopped the next man who came along, but he said he was from Idaho and had just gotten into town. The man after that suggested they check the bars on Twelfth Avenue.

Twelfth Avenue ran parallel to where the West Side Highway used to be. It wasn't a pretty street. Even when the sun was out, it looked bleak, like somebody had forgotten to wash it. The docks were on one side, and on the other were warehouses and meat-packing plants, the gay bars stuffed in between. They all had names like The Anvil, The Toilet, Hardrocks.

Dina pulled up in front of a place called The Ironman. They agreed that she'd wait in the car.

Inside, the only light came from a few candles at either end of the bar. Donato felt like he was in a cave. When his eyes adjusted, he could see that the place was almost empty. Two men sat at a table and one at the bar. The bartender, dressed in chinos and a red tank top, was wearing a headset and nodding in time with what he was listening to.

Hanging over the bar were chains, handcuffs, armor and two crossed swords. Donato got the idea. As he approached, the bartender said, "Uh-oh, fuzz." He pushed back the earphones.

"Haven't heard that word in years," Donato said. "You're dating yourself."

"No, I'm dating Ben. Who are you dating?"

Unsmiling, he showed his shield. "I'm looking for Sister Bang Bang."

"We don't have any sisters in here, officer, only brothers. You want sisters, you go down two blocks to Mimi's." He put his earphones back in place, picked up a glass and started polishing it with a fresh towel.

"Did you ever *hear* of Sister Bang Bang?"

He raised one earphone. "What?"

Donato heard the tinny sound of horns as he repeated his question.

"I hear of lots of people. I'm giving you good advice. Go down to Mimi's." He let go of the earphone and turned his back.

Donato left. He flopped into the front seat with a sigh. "Down a couple of blocks there's a place called Mimi's."

"He's there?"

"Who the hell knows? Guy in there suggested I try it."

Dina put the car in gear and moved away from the curb. "You sound discouraged."

"Depressed. The scene, as they say, depresses me."

"Don't be a homophobe, Donato."

"Homophobe? They're homophobes," he said, gesturing toward the street. "Nobody wants to claim Sister Bang Bang as their own. He embarrasses them."

"There's a caste system in every society."

"Pull over here," he said.

The lights in Mimi's were brighter. If Donato hadn't known better, he would have thought the place was patronized by women. But the five customers wearing dresses and sporting eyeshadow, lipstick and blush were men. Two were beautiful, the other three grotesque. No one was dressed as a nun.

He went through the routine with the bartender, got nowhere and then approached three of the transvestites sitting at a small table. He asked about Sister Bang Bang.

The youngest and most beautiful put his hand over Donato's. "Why do you want her, honey?"

Donato thought the man looked exactly like Susan Hayward. "I'm investigating a murder, and I need to talk to him . . . her."

"Is it the nun thing?" asked a dead ringer for Telly Sevalas with long brown hair. "You afraid Sister Bang Bang'll get her ticket punched?"

That hadn't occurred to Donato, but he saw it as a good ploy. "Right."

The three men looked at each other; some signals Donato couldn't read passed among them. Then Susan Hayward batted his eyelashes at Donato.

"You sure you're not going to pop Bang Bang?"

"Why would I collar her? Has she done anything?"

"Not our Sister Bang Bang. Pure as the driven snow," said the third one, a cross between Gloria Grahame and Marjorie Main.

"Where can I find her?" Donato said. It was getting easier to use the female pronoun.

"What's your name, sweety?"

"Donato."

"That's your first name?"

"Mike."

Marjorie/Gloria beckoned him with a long finger, the nail scarlet. Donato leaned over.

"Listen, Mike, we'd love to help you, but our throats are too dry. Know what I mean, lover?"

He dug into his wallet and pulled out a twenty. "Maybe this'll help."

"Whaddaya say, girls?"

"He's cute," Susan Hayward said, "let's give him a break."

"I agree," Telly grunted.

"Okay," said Marjorie/Gloria. "Sister Bang Bang lives at Fifty Perry Street. Top floor."

"Thanks," Donato said.

"Anytime, lover." Telly said. "And listen, don't be a stranger. The girls and me, we could give you a good time."

Donato thanked them again and hurried outside, their shrill laughter ringing in his wake.

"Okay," he said to Dina, "I got the address."

Dina started the car. "What's up? You look awful."

"Nothing, let's go." He gave her the address.

"Somebody make a pass at you, Donato?"

"Can it, kiddo." He felt nettled. Where did she come off questioning him like that? But he knew she'd say the same to any partner.

After parking on West Fourth Street, Dina and Donato walked up to Perry, turned the corner at Charlie and Kelly's restaurant, and passed a group of people standing around on the sidewalk, drinking coffee from paper cups. They stopped in front of terra cotta steps flanked by thick newel posts painted the same color. On top of these were black-winged gargoyles, their mouths open as if they were screaming.

"Dees must be da place," Dina said, wiggling her eyebrows.

Donato smiled. "Got to be."

The front door was unlocked, and there were no bells. Mailboxes were set into the left wall. The top floor had two apartments. Number 7 was listed in the name of J. Engelson, and 8 had two names: C. Barba and D. Reheis. They decided on that one because the name card was written in calligraphy. The stairs were narrow but clean, and on the fourth-floor landing they felt their guess was confirmed by a painting of fat little angels in a gold, oval frame, hanging on the door of apartment 8.

The man who opened the door was tall, muscular, and wore jeans and a V-neck blue sweater showing a bush of brown chest hair. "Yeah?"

Beyond him, Donato could see a blonde woman, or someone who looked like a woman. He showed his identification and said whom they were looking for. The man nodded once, indicating they had the right place, and asked them in.

The blonde woman wore a purple velvet robe. She was lounging in an overstuffed chair, reading *W.* When she raised her head, she smiled. Her black eyes were round and heavily made up, the dark lashes long.

Donato felt uncomfortable. The woman looked so real. But she didn't seem very tall. "We're investigating the recent murders of three Catholic nuns, and, as you ah . . . sometimes dress in a nun's garb, we thought . . ."

"Oh, no," she said.

"Sister Bang Bang," Dina began, "we . . ."

"No," the woman said, "you don't understand. *I'm* not Sister Bang Bang. *He* is. I'm his wife, Ceil."

The man wore an amused smile. "A natural mistake. You see, it just shows things are often not what they seem." He offered his hand. "I'm Dan Reheis, better known as Sister Bang Bang."

Donato thought he could hear the shrieking laughter of the three from Mimi's. Reheis was at least six-four. Donato shook his hand. The man's grip was strong.

"Sit down," Reheis said. "Would you like some coffee?"

"No thanks." Dina and Donato sat on a brocaded sofa. "Mr. Reheis, why do you dress like a nun?"

"Why not?"

"Do you like Catholic nuns?"

He shrugged. "They're all right."

Donato said, "Were you raised a Catholic?"

"No."

"What's your religion?"

"Is that any of your business?"

"Everything is our business, Danny," Dina said.

"Dan. Look, what is this? You think I had something to do with the murder of those nuns?"

"Where were you last night between midnight and seven A.M.?"

"He was with me," Ceil said. "First we were in the bars, and then we came home, ah, about three, wasn't it, baby?"

"Three-thirty, I think."

"Then what?"

"Then we went to bed."

"You didn't leave the house again?"

"No."

"Do you agree with that, Ceil?"

"Of course I agree with it. It's the truth."

Dina said, "You're married, but you have different names on the mailbox."

"We're artists. It's important for our careers. And if I were you, honey," Ceil said to Dina, "I'd change my name so it wasn't the same as your husband's. It looks better, know what I mean?"

"I'm not her husband," Donato said. He felt as if he were in a French farce.

"See, names don't always tell the tale. Me and Dan have been married four years. You thought he was a fag, huh?"

Donato was silent.

"Everybody does. But he's not. I can vouch for that." She raised one plucked eyebrow as if daring them to prove otherwise.

"What do *you* do?" Dina asked her.

"I'm an exotic dancer."

"What exactly is it that you want?" Reheis asked, annoyed.

"I'd like to see your . . . outfit," Donato said.

"What for?"

Dina said, "Don't give us a hard time, Danny. Get the nun's outfit."

"Dan."

"Get the outfit," she repeated.

"Dyke city," Ceil muttered.

Reheis stood up slowly, gave Dina a stony look, then disappeared into the next room. When he returned with a black robe and hood with a white wimple, he laid it out over a chair like a billowy corpse.

"Where did you get it?" Dina asked.

"I bought it."

"Where?"

"Unlimited Costumes."

"Where's that?"

"Broadway near Forty-fifth."

"How much was it?"

"A hundred and fifty."

"When did you buy it?"

"Two years ago."

"Why did you buy it?"

"For my act."

"What act?"

"What the hell do ya think Sister Bang Bang is?"

"You tell us."

"It's my act, my gig. I play the clubs."

"You're a female impersonator?"

"That's right."

"Do you ever just walk around the streets in your disguise?"

"It's not a disguise."

"Do you ever walk around the streets dressed in that?"

"If there's a parade or something."

"But not on a daily basis?"

"No."

Dina rose. "I wouldn't, Mr. Reheis. There's a killer out there

[195   ]

who doesn't like nuns. He might think you're a real one."

"Jesus, honey," Ceil said, "maybe you better start dressing at the clubs."

Reheis shot her an angry look.

"So you *do* wear it on the street."

"Not to hang around. To go to work and to come back."

"Why?"

"It gets me in the mood."

"If I recall, you wear roller skates, too."

Reheis smiled. "That's right."

"Well, that ought to keep you safe."

"I don't always wear them. Mostly in parades."

"Maybe you'd better start wearing them all the time."

"I'll think about it."

Dina said, "Don't leave town, Mr. Reheis."

"I can't believe you said that."

"Believe it."

Unlimited Costumes was sandwiched between a Nedick's and an electronics store (Everything Must Go) and one flight up a dirty narrow staircase. At the top of the stairs, a glass door with the name of the company painted on it was locked. Donato pushed the buzzer.

"Who is it?"

"Sergeant and Lieutenant Donato of the New York Police Department," Donato said. Then to Dina, "Jesus, that does sound crazy."

The locking device was released. Inside, mannequins in costumes hung from the ceiling and walls. A witch and a devil dangled over the doorway forming an arch.

A young woman, her hair cupping her brow in orderly bangs and dyed the color of a yellow pad, stood behind a counter. She seemed uneasy, her eyes darting from face to face.

"So what can I do for you, Lieutenant?" she said to Donato.

He felt for Dina. It must piss her off. "She's the lieutenant, I'm the sergeant," he said. "Are you the owner?"

"Who me? You gotta be kidding. Do I look like an owner?"

"We'd like to see the owner."

"Mr. Jaysnovitch is the owner."

"We'd like to see him then."

She picked up a white phone and punched one of the buttons. "Gloria, there're two police . . . people out here, want to see Mr.

Jaysnovitch. Yeah. Okay." She turned toward them and smiled anxiously, showing a large gap between her two front teeth, then back to the phone. "Yeah? Okay." She hung up. "Mr. Jaysnovitch will see you. Gloria'll be out in a second."

"Thanks," Dina said. "Do you rent nun costumes?"

"Sure. We did *Agnes of God* when it was on Broadway."

A door to the left of the counter opened, and a middle-aged woman with a lumpy body like a bag of oranges gave them a sour look. "You the cops?"

"Right."

"Come on."

They followed her past racks of costumes into an office. A desk with a manual typewriter crowded the anteroom. Gloria knocked once on a wooden door.

"Open," a nasal voice came from inside.

She did and motioned them in.

Jaysnovitch, a man in his seventies, sat behind a green metal desk. A pair of reading glasses hung around his neck on a gold chain. His head was bald except for a small gray thatch in front that he wore like a question mark. He was in his shirt sleeves, bisected by white armbands, and a brown suit vest.

"Hallo," he said, standing up and offering his hand to Donato, then nodded at Dina. "What ken I do for you, d'tectiffs? Siddown, siddown."

"We'd like some information about costumes," Dina asked.

"Thet I ken tell you. Vot you vanna know?" he said to Donato.

"Do you keep a record of customers who rent costumes?"

"I vouldn't be in business if I donn. I rent a costume, onless I know who da poisson is, vhere da poisson lives, how'm I gonna get d'costume beck? Ya donn know vot tieves people is!" He laughed suddenly, like a terrier yapping. "Who I'm telling dis to?" He shook his head in disbelief.

"And how about when you sell costumes, Mr. Jaysnovitch? You keep a record of those?"

Slowly, he elevated his shoulders. "Depends. If d'customer donn vant ta gimme a address, vot ken I do? But almost all da time day gimme someting. Vid da renters I get dentification, but if day buy vid kesh," he shrugged again, "vot ken I do?"

"What do you mean, they almost always give you something?"

"Da address. Day gimme a address not to look suspicion, draw attention."

"I don't understand," Dina said.

He addressed Donato. "Da gay boys. Day like to dress up, pent dare faces. But day donn vant to say who day are. Not to look suspicion, day gimme fake name and address. Vot do I care? Day tink I'm gonna put a pink triangle on dem? Lif and let lif, I say."

"But most people give you a name and address, and you keep a copy of the bill?" Dina asked hopefully.

"For fifty years."

Donato and Dina looked at each other. It was going to be a helluva job even though they'd only go back five.

"Are the bills separated in any way? By subject, for instance? Witches together, ghosts, that sort of thing."

"No. Only da rentals and da sales is diff'rent."

"But you do put the type of costume on the receipt?"

"Naturally," he said, with pride.

Donato said, "How many costume houses are there in New York?"

"Goot ones?"

"Good and bad."

Jaysnovitch leaned his head back against the worn nap of his chair, raised his eyes toward the ceiling and began counting on his fingers. "Twelfe."

"We'd like to go through those bills," Dina said.

He said to Donato, "You got any idea da bonch bills I got beck dere?" He thrust his thumb over his shoulder.

"How many?"

"Sales *an'* rentals?"

Dina looked at Donato. "I don't think he'd rent, do you?"

"No."

"Sales," she said. "And just for the last five years."

"Just sales. Lemme tink. Fife years. You got maybe, two, tree tousand."

Donato made a mental calculation. Twelve houses would mean approximately thirty-six thousand receipts to go through. But who said they all kept records? And chances of their guy giving his right name were slim. But they had to do it. You never knew.

"Pardon me, you donn mind me esking, vot kind of costume you looking for?"

"A nun's costume."

Jaysnovitch raised his eyebrows.

"Could you show us where you keep the bills?"

He led them through a door and down a dimly lit corridor into a room approximately twelve by fifteen. Metal shelves ran up all four walls, and green mottled index boxes lined them.

"Dis is it. All dis. Dis year starts here and den goes beckward. Da boxes is labeled 'sales' or 'rentals.' "

"We should take them downtown," Dina said to Donato. "The names will have to be checked against the computer."

"The other houses, too?"

"Yes."

She was right, but the extra hours ahead loomed large and ugly. It wasn't the kind of work Donato wanted to do anymore: sifting through things, sorting, comparing, checking, finding a match. The thrill was gone. He hadn't known it until now. Maybe after this one he'd really consider retiring.

"Okay," Donato said. "I'll go downstairs and radio for a truck."

"Get the team in, too, while you're at it. We'll meet back at the precinct in two hours."

After Donato radioed for a truck and got in touch with the rest of the team, he walked down Forty-sixth Street and found a bar. The Dew Drop Inn.

There were three men at the bar, all of them alone, hunched over their drinks as if someone might try to steal them. The place was dark and smelled of stale beer and cigarette smoke. Music, slow and sultry, sent out a lonely beat. The only light came from behind the bar, the jukebox and the exit sign. Donato took a seat.

The barmaid chewed gum and wore a low-cut blouse, showing deep cleavage. As Donato gave his order, he realized that he was in a topless place. A woman was climbing up to her perch behind the bar.

She was young, middle twenties. Masses of red hair framed an oval face. Her eyes said nothing; she was inured to her surroundings.

The woman removed a short Japanese kimono and put it neatly over a stool. She was wearing black, high-heeled, open-toed shoes and a green bikini bottom. Her nipples were hard and pink, the breasts large and fairly firm. But it was clear that in a few years their weight would drag them down and she'd be out of a job. A new tune started, and she began to undulate her hips. She gazed over the heads of the men at the bar as if she were seeing something only visible to her. Something boring.

Donato wondered if she was stoned. He sipped his drink and

watched her. He didn't find anything erotic in what she was doing. All he could think was that she was somebody's daughter. Did her father know what kind of a job she had? And if he did, did he care?

What if Dina had turned out like this, dancing topless in some sleazy joint, smoking dope, snorting blow, her future a foregone conclusion: used and abused by men, maybe an early death? But she wasn't like this woman. She was capable, competent, intelligent and accomplished. She was a loving mother. And she hated him.

No. She was angry with him for protecting her, for covering up, for lying. Still, sometimes it felt like hate. What would she have done if she'd known that her first year on a beat he'd checked up on her every hour, driven by in different cars, scurried along in the dark on the opposite side of the street, lying in wait should anyone threaten her safety. He couldn't help himself. Was it deep love for his daughter that prodded him to shield her from any possible harm, or his own inability to withstand more pain?

A fine residue of guilt covered him like mist. It was different with a daughter. You expected less. And wanted things *for* them, not *from* them. He loved Dina. But she was his daughter, not his son. The scotch was digging up the truth: he was one of those men, a cliché, who thought it more important to have a boy, a son, an heir to carry his name. He felt disgusted with himself.

When the music ended, the woman stopped as though her plug had been pulled. Nobody stuck money in her bikini. She walked over to the bartender, and he handed her a glass. It looked like orange juice. She swallowed the drink in one long swig. Then she walked back to the center of her small stage and waited. The music started again, and she began her gyrations, the same blank look in her eyes.

He finished his drink and left. Walking back to Unlimited Costumes, he thought maybe it was time to tell Dina the truth: she was right—he was a stereotypical father who thought that having a son was the most important thing in his life and that his world had collapsed when his son died. Maybe they could start over, then, if things were aboveboard, out in the light. Maybe she could forgive him and he could tell her how much he loved her. And they could be friends again. He and his daughter.

Seventeen

It was eight-thirty when the call came in. The man on the phone had asked for the person in charge of the nun case, but when Dina responded, he became reluctant to talk. Fatigue made her impatient, and she was about to hang up when he said, "I know who's icin' them nuns."

"Who?" She motioned to Donato to pick up an extension.

"Forget it. I ain't tellin' *you.*"

"You said you wanted to speak to the officer in charge, and I'm that officer. Either speak to me or *you* forget it."

"Well, I ain't sayin' no more over the phone."

"Where are you?"

"Why?" he asked suspiciously.

"If you won't talk on the phone, then we'll have to meet. Unless you want to come here, I'll have to know where you are."

"I ain't comin' there."

"So where are you?"

There was a long pause, and for a moment Dina thought he'd hung up.

Then he said, "I'll meetcha. There's a pizza joint on Broadway and Eighty-seventh. Called Cozzubbo's."

"I know it." It was one of her favorite pizza places.

"No kiddin'."

"What time?"

"Half an hour."

"How will we know you?"

"Who's *we*?"

"My partner and me."

"Oh. I'm wearin' a leather jacket and I got a beard."

It was hardly a distinctive description, but it would do. She told him they'd be there at nine.

As Dina was getting ready to go, her eyes met Keenan's and she turned away.

The task force had been working on the costume sales slips for two hours. So far they'd pulled fifty-two names. Those, and any others found, would be run through the computer to see if the buyers had sheets. The ones who did would be interviewed first. The rest would be broken down according to area, each team assigned different districts. Some of the names would be phony. If the killer was one of the buyers, he would, almost certainly, have given a false name.

Before leaving, Dina spoke to the squad.

"I know you're all tired, but it's important that we get a handle on this as soon as possible. Once you've worked out what areas you're going to cover, you can break. If any of you wants to run down buyers tonight, that's up to you. If not, we'll start tomorrow morning." She hadn't told them about Halliday's dictum, but they were all aware that time was running out.

"Excuse me, Lieutenant," Delgado said. "Tomorrow morning's Judy's funeral."

Deep in denial, Dina had managed to put Judy's death in the back of her mind.

"Yes, of course," she said, as if she'd known it all along. "After the funeral, we'll get started."

They didn't talk on the ride uptown. A few times Dina thought Donato was going to say something, but he remained silent. She was glad because she felt too depressed for conversation. It no longer seemed impossible that she would never see Judy again, and it hurt terribly.

Then there was Bobby. She thought how different she'd feel if she were going to see him later. Everything was easier to handle when you shared it with someone you cared about.

Ice Maiden. God, she didn't want to be one of those terrible competent women, tremendously successful and achingly lonely. She wanted to have it all, and why not? Because it hadn't worked with Liam didn't mean it couldn't work with Bobby. Maybe she shouldn't have been so hasty.

Donato parked the car. They walked to Broadway and turned uptown. The night was warm for April, the first after a long cold winter, and the street was crowded. People were eating ice cream, chewing on cookies. It reminded Dina that she hadn't eaten since the night before with Bobby.

"God, I'm hungry," she said.

"Me, too."

"How about a pizza?"

"Fine with me."

Dina couldn't remember the last time she'd shared a pizza with her father. When Dina was in her early teens, Renata would often go to her parents' for dinner on Friday night, and if Donato was home, they'd get a pizza from Cozzubbo's. He used to tease her about how much she ate, often packing away five slices to his three. During these meals, he'd tell her fascinating cop stories. Even then she'd wanted to be a cop, but when she'd expressed it once, Donato had hugged her and said it was no work for a woman. She should be a teacher, a nurse, maybe a stewardess.

Recalling that now, she wondered why she'd been surprised at his attitude when she'd made her decision. She should have known how he'd react. Funny the things you didn't choose to remember.

Cozzubbo's had a take-out counter in front and booths and tables in back. The bottom half of the walls was painted red, the rest white, the ceiling and trim green.

"Big or small?" Donato asked.

"Big," she said without hesitation.

Donato smiled. "Why did I ask? You want anything on it?"

"Pepperoni."

He gave their order. It was five to nine. Scanning the room, they saw no one with a beard wearing a leather jacket.

After they were seated in a booth, Donato said, "What do you think the chances are?"

"The usual." There was a better than even chance he'd be a nut. She was facing the front of the restaurant, and when he came in, her expression made Donato turn around.

The man had a full salt-and-pepper beard, was about five-ten and probably weighed close to four hundred pounds. He waddled over to them, ascertained who they were, grabbed an orange plastic chair and placed it at the end of their table. By the time he sat down, he was breathing heavily.

A large head with many chins hid his neck, and his nose resembled a snout. Inky black, gray-streaked hair was combed forward, unparted. Blue overalls and a work shirt were under a cheap, leather jacket. His yellow work boots were the size of footballs. He had huge hands, the fingers like hot dogs, the nails chewed to the quick.

"What's your name?" she asked.

"What difference does that make?" He squinted at them, blue eyes like two quarter-moons.

"You afraid to tell us?" Donato said.

"I ain't afraid. Did I say I was afraid?"

"It would be easier if we knew your name. I'm Lieutenant Donato, and this is Sergeant Donato."

He looked from her to him, then back again. "You related?"

"No," she said. "It's just a coincidence. So what's your name?" She hoped it wasn't Tiny.

"It's Alby. Just Alby."

The counterman yelled, "Donato, pepperoni pizza, large."

Donato stood up, then realized he couldn't get past Alby.

Alby stared at him but didn't move.

"I can't get out," Donato said.

Alby smiled as if he were glad. Then, still sitting, he scraped the chair back a few inches. Donato had to hold in his gut to get past.

Alby said, "You look like him. Sure you ain't related?"

"Why don't you tell me what you know," she said.

"So yer the boss, huh? How does that make him feel?"

"Look, Alby, you said you had information about the killer. Either you do or you don't."

"Hold your water. I got it, I got it. Don't be a ballbreaker."

Ballbreaker. She often heard that when she asserted herself. Alby wouldn't have given Donato a hard time, asked him personal questions.

Donato came back with the pizza. It smelled wonderful, the oil, garlic and tomato blending, the cheese running. Donato pulled two pieces out from the pie, allowing them to cool.

Alby stared at the pizza, saliva at the corners of his mouth.

Dina didn't think she could stand to watch him drool. "You want a piece?"

He looked at her as if she'd told him he'd won the lottery. "Hey, yeah, that would be good. I ain't ate since breakfess."

"Help yourself," Donato said.

Alby moved quickly, expertly folded a wedge in half, then popped it into his mouth as if it were a stick of gum. The slice was gone in two bites.

"Good," Alby said, his gaze returning to the pie.

Donato met Dina's eyes. She got his message, and it broke her heart. As she bit into her own piece, she knew it would be her only slice.

With a mixture of revulsion and awe, they watched as Alby devoured five more pieces in less than eight minutes. When he was finished, his beard was festooned with bits of cheese and tomato, the corners of his mouth red.

"Okay, Alby, tell us what you have," she said.

"You got a smoke?"

Dina pulled a pack from her purse and offered it to him. He tapped out a cigarette, then pocketed the rest and waited for a light. She threw him some matches.

Blowing out a fume of smoke, he belched. "So anyways," he started, as if there'd only been a slight interruption, "I live in the building where the nun was iced."

"What building?" Dina asked.

"On Ninety-sixth between Broadway and Amsterdam. I live on the first floor. I'm a night person or I would've of called youse earlier. But I didn't know what happened 'til later. Then I hadda think it over."

Donato said, "Get to the point, Alby."

"There's this guy, lives on the first floor in the back. Moves in about three, four weeks ago, maybe less. He ain't around much, but I seen him once or twice. Anyways, last night, about five in the morning, I hear some funny noises in the hall. The building's always being broke into so I go to my door, listen good." He turned his head to the side and mimed putting his ear against the door. "I hear like a draggin' noise, and I don't want to open up 'cause, hey, what the hell, who knows what's out there?" He sucked on the cigarette as if it were a straw.

"So anyways, I wait until the sound is past my door, then I open it careful, and what to my wonderin' eyes should appear?"

Dina almost laughed.

"This guy who lives in 1B and . . . a nun. He's draggin' her, like the nun is drunk, which how could that be? I think maybe I should ask him if he needs help, then somethin' tells me don't butt in. So I watch. He gets her through the front door, and then they're gone. That's it. I go back to what I was doin'."

"Which was what?"

"I was makin' a model."

"What was she doing while you were watching the man and the nun?" Donato asked, appalled.

"Huh?" He looked genuinely puzzled.

"The model. What was she doing?"

When it dawned on him what Donato was asking, his face cracked into a grotesque grin, the eyes disappearing, the nose spreading across his face like suet in a hot pan.

They waited.

Alby laughed, a deep roar; his body shuddered and his belly shook the table. It took him almost five minutes to pull himself together. "Not that kind a model," he said. "A airplane model. A B29 from the war. I make 'em. I got two hundredt-seveny-six. The B29 is gonna make two hundredt-seveny-seven."

"An airplane model," Donato said. "Christ almighty. Okay, so you went back to your model, then what?"

"Then nuttin'. I go to bed aroun' six-thirty. When I get up later an' go out for my breakfess, I hear everybody talkin' about this murder. Louie Beller, the guy what works in the dry cleaners, gives me the skinny. So then I put two an' two together. Then I think on it and tha's when I call youse."

"What did the man look like?"

"You mean 1B?"

"Yes."

"Got one of them mustaches goes straight across."

"A toothbrush mustache?"

"Yeah, right."

"What color?"

"Black. Like his hair."

"He has black hair?" she asked, surprised.

"Yeah. Black."

"You sure?" said Donato.

"I'm sure."

Dina looked at Donato and could see they were thinking the same thing. The missing finger told them they didn't have a copycat killer on their hands, and since the hair samples taken from the earlier killings were blond, it had to mean the Slasher was wearing a wig. Knowing he got close to his victims by wearing a nun's habit, the mustache had to be fake as well.

"Will you take us to the apartment?" she asked.

"You gonna make it worth my while?"

"What do you want, Alby?" Donato asked.

"I gotta live," he whined.

"Tell us what you want."

"A hundredt."

"No way," Donato said and stood up, although he knew he wouldn't be able to get out unless Alby let him out.

"Hold your water. How about seventy-five?"

Dina took two tens out of her bag and placed them in front of him. "Take it or leave it."

He stared at it for a moment, then scooped up the bills and shoved them into a pocket. "A person's gotta eat," he said.

It took them twenty minutes to walk at Alby's pace from Cozzubbo's to the apartment on Ninety-sixth.

They pounded on the super's door for nearly a minute before he answered. When he finally opened up, he looked as if he'd been sleeping in a garbage compactor. His breath reeked of alcohol.

Frank Lach was a big man with a slight stoop. He had a flat nose, gray eyes and thin lips like two healed razor cuts. He wore grimy gray cords and a black turtleneck.

"Yeah, whatisit?"

They showed their shields.

"I ain't done nothing."

"We didn't say you had," Dina said, wondering if he were guilty of something. "We'd like to come in, Mr. Lach."

"How'd you know my name?" he asked defensively.

"Alby told us."

"Fat fucker," he mumbled.

"We believe there's been a murder in this building, and we'd like to come in, ask you a few questions, Mr. Lach."

Reluctantly, he opened the door wider and stepped back, allowing them to pass. Dishes were piled in the sink, clothes, coiled and twisted, strewn over the worn furniture, containers of half-eaten food on every surface, bags of garbage spilling over, splattering the floor, and empty liquor bottles, like glass ornaments, everywhere. Lach gave them a look as if daring them to comment on the condition of his place.

"We'd like to know about the tenant in 1B," Dina said.

Lach rubbed both hands over his eyes, then tried to focus. "1B. That'd be Mr. Lockwood. Somebody killed him?"

"What's his first name?"

He tightened his brow, trying to think. Licking his lips, he eyed a bottle that held about a quarter of an inch of whisky. "You mind if I have a little drink?"

"Yeah," Donato said. "We mind. You can have your drink after you answer some questions. What's Lockwood's first name?"

Lach clenched his teeth and gave Donato a lethal look. "I'm thinking. Kevin. Yeah, Kevin is it. What happened to him?"

"What's Mr. Lockwood look like?"

"I dunno. He just looks like a guy." His eyes drifted over to the bottle again.

Dina nodded to Donato.

"Have the drink," Donato said.

"Hey, thanks." He grabbed the bottle and upended it into his mouth, holding it there long after there was anything left inside. Putting down the bottle, he said, "I've had some bad luck lately," as if his need for a drink were circumstantial.

"Lockwood. What does he look like?"

"He's got black hair. Mustache, glasses—like a teacher."

"How old would you say he is?" she asked.

Lach shrugged. "I ain't too good at ages."

"Take a stab at it."

"I dunno. Maybe thirty-five, like that."

"How tall?"

"Six feet, maybe more."

"Weight?"

"No fat on him. Looks like he works out."

"Would you recognize him?"

"Whataya mean? 'Course I'd recognize him."

"What color are his eyes?" Dina asked.

"I dunno. I ain't too particular about guys' eyes, if you get my drift."

"We'd like you to open up Lockwood's apartment for us," Dina said.

"Is the guy dead?" he asked nervously.

"Get the key, Lach."

When the door to 1B opened, they knew they were in the right place. The room held only two pieces of furniture: a straight-backed chair and a single bed, which was sheetless. The mattress was blood-soaked. Behind the bed, the dingy walls were splashed and streaked with blood like a modern painting, and in some places, they weren't quite dry.

On the floor, there were pools of it, and in one place, there appeared to be a print of a right big toe and the next two, as well as the ball of a foot. The print was large, and it would have been surprising if it had belonged to a woman. Especially to Sister Anne Marie, who had been small and delicate. Three lengths of bloody rope lay on the floor near the chair.

Half an hour later the Forensic people were dusting for prints, taking blood samples, photographing the room and the footprint, tagging the ropes. The piece of floor with the bloody print would be removed and sent to the lab.

Dina made it clear that she needed results by morning but knew she'd be lucky if she got them in twenty-four hours.

The name Kevin Lockwood had been run through the computer, but the only one that came up was sixty-five years old. It was no surprise because they were sure the name was an alias.

They questioned the tenants, and the majority described Lockwood the same way Lach had. It was almost certain that the killer had been wearing a disguise, but Lach and three others agreed to come down the next day and go through mug shots. If that didn't pan out, they could work with the police artist to get a composite drawing. The partial footprint was the best piece of evidence so far. It was something concrete, even though it could only be used once they had a suspect.

The apartment felt big and empty without Cal. Dina sat at the kitchen table eating a dish of Ben & Jerry's Heath Bar Crunch, but even that couldn't console her tonight. She felt edgy. When Rich had died, she'd seen a therapist who'd said she was suffering from agitated depression. Perhaps that was her trouble now.

It was midnight. She wondered if any of the squad were still at the precinct, found herself dialing. All gone. Chances of breaking the case through the costume receipts were slim, but by now the Slasher would have read his profile in a newspaper or heard her give it on the evening news. Was he already figuring out how to outwit them, planning an even more daring murder than the one he'd pulled off less than twenty-four hours ago?

Maybe she shouldn't have baited him. Maybe he'd had enough with Sister Anne Marie. If he *was* in a fugue state, Sister Anne Marie might have been his last. But she didn't believe it. Something told her this creep was going to go on until he was caught. She'd done the right thing. Hadn't she?

While she was rinsing out her empty dish, the phone rang.

"I didn't wake you, did I?" Renata asked.

"No. Is something wrong? Is Cal all right?"

"He's fine. I'm calling because . . . because I didn't like the way we parted yesterday."

Dina lit a cigarette. "I didn't like it either."

"It was because of Judy," Renata said. "Judy and . . . Rich."

"I know." Thinking of what Donato had told her that morning about Rich's death, she wondered if she should tell her mother.

"So I called to say I'm sorry."

"Thank you." She hadn't promised Donato not to tell her. If she told, would it be a betrayal?

"Are you all right, Dina?"

"I'm fine."

"What is it? Something's going on. I can tell."

"Nothing's going on."

"I know there was another murder. Is that it?"

"I guess that's what you're hearing."

"You're not a good liar," Renata said.

"It's nothing, Mom, really." Was she doing what Donato had done, shielding her mother from the truth as if she hadn't a right to know or couldn't take it?

"I don't believe you," Renata said.

"Sometimes I think you're a witch."

"What is it?"

"I'm not sure I'll be doing you a favor."

"So now *you're* going to run my life, decide what I should know and what I shouldn't? In two weeks, I'm going to be sixty."

Unsure of her motivation, she decided to take the plunge. "It's about Rich."

There was silence on the other end of the line.

"Mom?"

"Go on."

"He didn't kill himself. He was murdered." Slowly, Dina told her the rest about Donato and the Peak case.

"How long have you known?" Renata asked.

"Just since this morning."

"Goddamn him," Renata said. "He didn't learn. He saw what trouble his lies caused the first time, but he didn't learn a goddamned thing. How could he have thought I'd prefer thinking my son had killed himself?"

Dina surprised herself by coming to Donato's defense. "His motives were good, I think."

"Oh, that bastard," Renata said, as though Dina hadn't spoken.

"Are you going to tell him I told you?" Now she felt frightened, like a child waiting for her daddy to come home and discipline her.

"I suppose you don't want me to."

"Could you at least wait until this case is over?"

There was a long silence. "It's just more of the same, Dina. More collusion between the two of you. I can't promise you. I just can't. Good-night."

Returning the phone to the cradle, she felt as though she'd betrayed Donato and disappointed her mother: failed them both.

In her bedroom, she stripped, went into the bathroom and turned on the shower. When it was as hot as she could stand, she stepped in and let the water rush over her. The shower massage was turned to its hardest setting, and the water beat down on her back, relieving some of her tension.

While she was drying off, the phone rang. She hoped it wasn't her mother again, but she knew she had to answer.

"It's Bob," he said.

A moment passed before it registered. "Oh, Bobby."

"If you insist."

She was so expert at cutting off feelings, denying what was painful, she hadn't thought about him since the meeting. "How are you?" she asked.

"Terrific," he said sarcastically. "How about you?"

She thought of lying, then said, "Lousy."

"Is your son there?"

"No."

"I'd like to come over."

"I just got out of the shower," she said as if that were an excuse.

"Then I guess you won't be available for a week or two."

She laughed. "It's late, Bobby."

"I know what time it is. We need to talk, Dina."

"Why do you want to talk to the Ice Maiden?"

"Because I'm a masochist," he joked.

She wanted to see him, even felt she needed him. But if she said yes, if she let him into her life again, there'd be no turning back. She didn't want to hurt him or herself.

"I don't know, Bobby."

"It's not finished between us. It hasn't even begun."

"I don't think I can handle this."

"Handle what?"

"An affair."

"You won't have to. I'll handle it for both of us. Dina, I know you care. If you didn't, you would have hung up by now."

"I *do* care. But that's exactly why I feel we shouldn't see each other."

"That doesn't make sense. Let me come over. We'll talk, nothing else."

She smiled. "Maybe you can make that promise, but I can't." She knew she was opening a door, but she didn't care. Why the hell should she be alone? What was the worst that could happen?

Softly, he said, "May I come over?"

"All right."

He was there in ten minutes.

She wore a lavender satin robe Liam had given her years before that she'd never worn. Her hair was still damp.

So was his.

They stood near the closed doorway staring at one another.

"You're beautiful," he said.

"So are you," she said. "Except for your black eye."

"It's not a black eye. When I was in high school, I played football. I got kicked there, and the charcoal got inside the cut somehow. I had five stitches."

Gently, she touched the dark place under his eye.

He took her hand, kissed her palm.

She shivered.

He took a step closer to her.

She moved into him and felt him hard against her thigh.

"Is this what you wanted to say?" she whispered.

"Yes."

"I hear you."

"I know you do." He bent his head and gently bit her bottom lip, ran his tongue across her upper one, then pressed his lips to hers, his tongue finding refuge inside her mouth.

Feelings she'd never had before rushed through her, and she kissed him back, her arms slipping around his neck.

He ran his hands over the slippery satin mounds of her breasts, down her sides, over her belly.

She unbuttoned his shirt and pulled it from his pants and over his shoulders. It dropped to the floor.

He untied her belt, and the robe fell open. His hands cruised her waist, her back.

She undid his belt, pulled down his zipper, freeing him.

He ran his hands over the tight roundness of her ass.

She eased his trousers and jockey shorts over his hips, and they shimmied to the floor.

He stepped out of his loafers, then gracefully withdrew his sockless feet from the trousers and jockeys. He peeled back her robe, and it slithered down her body, crumpling around her feet.

They were both naked.

He lifted her up and carried her into the bedroom, where he lowered her onto the bed, then lay next to her, covering her neck and breasts with kisses. He ran his tongue over a nipple, and it grew in his mouth.

She teased his ear with her tongue and ran her nails over his back.

He rubbed her belly and down the inside of her thighs, then slipped his hand between her legs, parting her.

She kissed him, drew his tongue inside her mouth. Her hand slid over his chest, down his body, over his belly until she felt his wiry hair. Slowly, she drifted up the shaft of his cock, then ran her fingers over the silky tip.

He hoisted himself above her.

She spread her legs.

He found her, eased himself in.

She arched toward him, pushing.

Their bodies moved rhythmically, totally in tune with each other.

His thrusts were slow and long.

She wrapped her legs around his back.

When it was time, he moved faster, and she lifted her pelvis to meet him, their rhythms perfect.

And then they cried out . . . over and over.

A long time passed as they lay in each other's arms, breathless, fulfilled.

Finally, he said, "I'll never call you the Ice Maiden again."

She said, "I'll never give you any reason to."

Judy McCarthy's funeral was held at St. Catherine's in Queens at ten in the morning. Police and city officials, including the mayor, were there. Most of the two thousand police people who attended heard the mass through loudspeakers outside the church.

The task force, all in uniform, were inside. Dina stood between Donato and Keenan. Surreptitiously, she touched Keenan's hand through most of the service.

Over the years, Dina had attended a number of funerals for slain police, but this was the first of a friend. And Judy had been so much more than that. As the priest's voice droned on, Dina responded as she should, kneeling, sitting, standing in all the right places, but she found no comfort in the words of the Mass.

When it was over, they drove in a procession to the cemetery. This was the hardest part. The flag-draped coffin rested next to the gaping hole in the ground. After more words, the folded flag was handed to Mrs. McCarthy, looking lifeless herself. And then the casket began to descend.

Dina wanted to stop it, to turn back time, come out of this nightmare, pretend it wasn't true. But she was forced to accept the reality that Judy was dead as the coffin was lowered into the ground . . . forever.

Later, she and Donato made small talk at the funeral lunch held at the McCarthys'. The rest of the squad had returned to work. When a decent interval had passed, they made their excuses and headed back to Manhattan.

"What do you think about at funerals, Donato?" she asked.

"I think of Rich," he said truthfully.

"I thought you did." After a moment, she added, "It would have been so much easier if it had been me, wouldn't it?"

"What does that mean?" he asked.

"That you wished it had been me instead of Rich."

"What the hell are you talking about?"

"He was your son."

"And you're my daughter. I didn't want to lose my son—that's true. It killed me. Sometimes it still does. Like today. But I never wished it had been you instead of him. I swear, kiddo."

She waited, holding her breath, hoping he'd say that he loved her.

But he didn't say anything.

Eighteen

They were waiting for Art Scott and John Pesetsky. Donato sat at the end of the table smoking a cigarette. He was furious with himself for starting again. Working with Dina was getting to him. Still, it was no excuse to begin smoking. The hell with it. He'd quit when the case was over.

The morning's encounter with Dina had left him shaken. How the hell could she believe he would have preferred her death to Rich's? Had she really no idea how much he loved her? Sure, they'd had their differences, locked horns, but that didn't mean he didn't love her. Even when she was so angry at his lying about Rich's death, it had never occurred to him that she didn't love *him*. Maybe he'd been wrong. The idea depressed him.

You thought you gave your kids everything, and then suddenly you were faced with a new accusation, a new revelation alerting you to your failure as a parent. In truth, he hadn't been home much, hadn't given them the attention other fathers gave. But when he was with them, it was quality time. Hell, that's what all the articles were about these days, quality time. He'd known about that years before some shrink invented the term.

Still, his son had turned out to be a junkie. He didn't like thinking about this because it inevitably led to a question: where did Rich get the money for his habit? He'd asked Jeff Meyerson once, but Jeff just shrugged, and they'd looked away from each other, knowing the obvious answer. No young cop could afford a heroin habit on his salary alone.

And this was where he always stopped. Turned off his thoughts, questions about his son. That was why Rich had remained ennobled in his mind, a young man who'd made a mistake, been cut down in his youth. But that wasn't the truth. It wasn't anywhere near the truth.

Rich had been a junkie who either stole or took bribes. A junkie who conned people, who conned *him*. And if Rich were alive today, he'd still love him because he was his son, but he wouldn't like him . . . he was goddamn sure of that.

And Dina? Christ almighty, there was no comparison. She could be the biggest goddamn pain in the ass, but he liked her anyway. Admired her. And God knew, he loved her. Why the hell didn't she know that? Did you have to say the fucking words, for Christ's sake? Why the hell did she think he tried to protect her? Because he loved her, dammit. It was the most obvious thing in the world, and she couldn't see it. What in hell did the woman want?

Scott and Pesetsky arrived, and Dina brought the meeting to order. Scott spoke first.

"There were fifty-six sales of nun costumes in the last five years, fourteen in the last year," he said, absently pulling at his ponytail. "Of the fifty-six, thirty-seven were bought by women, the remaining nineteen by men. Three of the nineteen were bought in the last year." He turned the page of his memo pad. "Those three are: Geoff Bradley, Twenty-three East Twelfth; Jon Winters, Four-thirty-two West Seventy-ninth; Keith Laine, Six-thirty-six East Seventy-fifth." He nodded toward Pesetsky.

"Bradley is fifty-two, lives with his wife and three kids," Pesetsky continued. "Sale made on December twenty-ninth of last year. Winters is gay, lives alone. Sale made last October twenty-seventh. And there's no Keith Laine at the address on Seventy-fifth Street, never has been. The sale was made on March third of this year, exactly one month before the first murder."

"Has anyone checked out the other sixteen men?" Dina asked. No one had.

"Delgado, you and Keenan take eight, and Lachman and Bobbin take the other eight. Scott and Pesetsky, you find out why Bradley and Winters bought their costumes. Donato and I will check further on Keith Laine. Where did he buy from?"

Scott consulted his notes. "Triangle Costumes, two-forty-seven West Forty-fifth."

She wrote it down, then picked up some papers. "The prelim from Forensic says the partial footprint is a man's size nine and a half. He's probably around six feet and weighs one forty-five. That tallies with the description we got from Alby, Lach and the other witnesses. A number of fibers were found but no fingerprints of the killer. Even so, he's getting sloppy. The partial footprint tells us that. He thinks he can get away with anything. He'll make some more mistakes. We've got extra manpower on the streets near the various convents in the city."

"What about the nuns like Sister Honora, who live in apartments?" Bobbin asked. "Who's coverin' their asses?" He was suddenly embarrassed. "I mean . . ."

"We've alerted the convents that we think he's dressing in a nun's habit, and we have to assume they're informing their nuns who live outside.

"We'll start on the makeup houses, check the sales of black toothbrush mustaches and black wigs since the first of the year. Obviously the closer to April third the better. Somebody hand me those yellow pages."

Keenan gave them to her.

Donato noticed a look that passed between them. If they weren't already involved, they soon would be. Maybe it would be all right. Maybe two cops in a relationship fared better than when it was only one. He wondered how he and Renata would have done had he been in some other line of work.

Dina counted the number of theatrical makeup places. There were eighteen. "Donato and I will take the first nine. Scott and Pesetsky, you take the second nine after you've checked out Gorman and Winters."

"You think maybe this dude's an actor?" Bobbin asked.

"If he's not a professional, he's a pretty good amateur. Keenan check Actors Equity; see if there's a Keith Laine listed. Delgado, check out SAG."

"SAG?" Lachman asked.

"Screen Actors Guild," Keenan answered.

"Is there any way to check on amateurs?" Delgado asked.

Scott said, "Nah. If they're not listed with Equity or SAG, then there's no place to check."

"We can keep our eyes on the amateur productions around town," Dina said. "You never know. Anybody have anything else?"

No one did.

"Then let's get on it. We'll reconvene here at eighteen-hundred hours."

The apartment house at 636 East Seventy-fifth Street was typical of the area: white brick with long, double glass doors. The doorman wore a blue uniform with gold trim. His visored cap seemed to rest on his large ears. He had a narrow nose and a small sharp mouth.

"What's your name?" Dina asked.

"Charlie."

"Charlie what?"

"Charlie Sweet, and I don't need no comments."

Donato smiled. "How long you been working here?"

"Since the inception of the building."

"How long is that?" Dina asked.

"Fifteen years."

A woman with a small dog approached. Sweet touched his cap and opened the door for her.

"Afternoon, Mrs. Bard. Hi there, Alexis," he said to the brown-and-white dog.

Mrs. Bard gave Donato and Dina a once-over and clearly decided she didn't like what she saw.

When she was gone, Sweet spoke softly from the corner of his mouth. "Mrs. Bard lives for her dog. She don't have much use for people. The dog's this Jack Russell type. Pretty rare."

"Do you know all the tenants?" Dina asked.

"Naturally."

"By sight or name?" Donato asked.

"Both. You got to. That's an important part of the job."

"Is there a Keith Laine here?"

"No."

"Has there ever been?"

"No."

"You seem very sure of that, Mr. Sweet," Dina said.

"I *am* sure. See, I got one of them minds. Photographic or something. I hear a person's name I never forget it. Face neither. My wife's been wanting me to go down to Atlantic City, play poker, but I tell her, I say, Ethel, I don't think God give me a photographic mind to make money with."

A tall, attractive woman in her late thirties headed toward the door.

"Afternoon, Mrs. Lawrence. Cold any better?"

"Not much, Charlie, thanks."

"Maybe you shouldn't go out today."

"If I don't, I think I'll go crazy. I've been cooped up for four days, and now Mr. Lawrence is home with it. See you later." She smiled noncommittally at Donato and Dina.

Sweet talked out of the side of his mouth again. "Mrs. Lawrence tips better than anybody in the building. They're a real nice couple 'cept she's one of them wears the pants in the family. Goes out to work. Women belong at home, I say." He looked at Dina, suddenly realizing what he'd said. He gave her an apologetic smile.

"How many other doormen are there?" Donato asked.

"Four."

"Could you check with them, ask if they ever heard of Keith Laine?"

"I told you, no Keith Laine ever lived here."

"Who's the super?" Dina asked.

"Well, there's three, but Fred Stubbs is the boss. He's been here since the inception, too."

"Where can we find him?"

"Go to the back, take the elevator to the basement. He's usually around there doing something or other."

They walked through the white-marbled lobby. A profusion of green plants stood next to columns and hung from the ceiling. Several walls held large modern paintings.

When the elevator arrived, several people got off. They stepped in and pushed B. In the basement, they found a man working on a washing machine and asked if he was the super. He wasn't, but directed them around a corner, where they found Stubbs sitting, smoking a cigarette.

A big black man, his hair was cropped close to his head, and he had a patch over one eye. He wore jeans, high-topped black sneakers and a khaki shirt, the sleeves rolled up over muscle-bound arms.

"What you want?" he asked, scowling.

They identified themselves, said they wanted to ask a few questions and went through the routine about Keith Laine. Stubbs insisted he'd never heard of him.

Donato said, "You know the tenants pretty well?"

"I fix their toilets. Can't know people better than that."

"Mr. Stubbs," Dina said, "are there any male tenants who strike you as peculiar in any way?"

"What kind a peculiar you talking?" Stubbs licked his thumb and forefinger, then crushed the lit end of his cigarette between them, dropped the butt on the cement floor.

"We're particularly interested in males between the ages of thirty and forty, six feet or more and weighing between one-forty and one-fifty," Donato added.

"Shit, that could be a lot a guys."

"Can you imagine any of the male tenants dressing up in a costume?"

"What shit you talking about? Hey, now wait a minute. There this one sucker in Penthouse D. Artist type. Do pictures for the front a books, shit like that. He a little weird."

"How?"

"He stay up all night, sleep all day. He got weird shit in there. Like whips and chains and shit."

Donato felt his pulse quicken, the old feelings of the hunt taking over.

"He got costumes up there, too, now I think about it."

"What kind of costumes?" Dina asked.

Stubbs shrugged. "Like capes and shit like that."

Could a habit look like a cape? Donato wondered. "Did you ever see a nun's costume?"

"You mean like one a them sisters wear? Them black things with the white shit around the face?"

"Yes."

"Not 'specially. Not so's I can recall."

"What's this man's name?"

"Kim Lyle."

Donato looked at Dina. They'd both thought the same thing. The man in Penthouse D had the same initials as Keith Laine.

While they were ringing Lyle's bell, a man came out of penthouse C. He wore a blue jacket with the sleeves and collar up, gray pleated pants and black loafers without socks.

"Can I help you?" he asked.

"We're trying to see Mr. Lyle," Donato said.

"Oh, well, he sleeps all day. Works at night."

"Do you know him?" Dina asked.

"We're neighbors." He took out a handkerchief, turned his head and sneezed. "Excuse me. My wife gave me her cold."

"You must be Mr. Lawrence?"

"How did you know that?"

It seemed far too complicated to explain so Donato showed his shield.

"Has Kim done something?" Lawrence asked.

"We just want to ask him a few questions," Dina said.

Lawrence glanced at her for the first time.

Donato saw his eyes change. Suddenly, they seemed unfriendly, remote, and then the expression was gone, replaced by an interested gaze. It all happened very quickly, but after years of processing people, he rarely got such details wrong. Still, he hadn't had much sleep lately; his antennae could be off.

Lawrence said, "If you like, I can go back in and phone Kim."

"That would be helpful," Dina said.

Lawrence unlocked his door and motioned them in. "Has something happened in the building?" he asked.

"No," Donato said flatly. Lawrence went to the white table phone and punched in a number.

The room was immense and done completely in black and white. It was one of those places that seemed unlived-in. Standing there, a hand in his pocket, Lawrence looked as if he were posing for a fashion ad.

"Kim," Lawrence said, "it's Russ Lawrence. Sorry to wake you, but the police are here to see you. No, I don't know what it's about. They've been trying to wake you by the bell but . . . okay, right, I'll tell them." He hung up. "He said to give him five minutes. Why don't you sit down?"

"Thanks, Mr. Lawrence," Dina said, "but we've inconvenienced you enough."

"Don't worry about it. You still haven't told me how you know my name."

Donato related the incident with Lawrence's wife.

"You people are sharp," he said, smiling.

"How long have you known Mr. Lyle?"

"As long as we've lived here, which is, let's see, I guess it's about five or six, no . . . five years."

"Was Mr. Lyle living here before you?"

"Yes."

"How would you describe him?" Dina asked.

"You mean physically?"

"What kind of person would you say he is?"

"Oh, I don't know. A little unusual, I guess. I mean take his working habits, for instance."

"Do you know any of his friends?"

"I've been to a few of his parties. His friends seemed nice. If Kim hasn't done anything, what's this all about?"

Donato ignored the question. "Does he have a girlfriend?"

"I think he has lots of them. I don't believe there's anyone special, if that's what you mean. You know . . . I thought you looked familiar," he said, gazing directly at Dina. "You're on that murder case, aren't you? The nun killings."

"That's right."

Donato noticed Lawrence's cheeks flush. He seemed excited.

"Are you questioning Kim about that? Surely, you don't think that . . . but you can't tell me, can you?"

Neither of them said anything.

"You're barking up the wrong tree if you think Kim Lyle has anything to do with killing nuns." He glanced at his Rolex. "I think he's had his five minutes." He walked them to the door.

"Thanks for your help," Donato said.

"Any time." Lawrence closed the door behind them.

"Thought he was going out," Donato said softly.

"So did I."

They rang Lyle's bell, and he answered immediately. Looking at him, Donato felt the thrill of an impending breakthrough.

Kim Lyle was the right age, thirty-five or so; he was at least six-two and weighed no more than one-fifty. Although his hair wasn't blond, it was a very light brown with touches of gray. Tired brown eyes were topped by darker eyebrows. He had a fairly pleasant face, not handsome, but by no means unattractive. A brown turtleneck hung over paint-stained jeans. On his feet were a pair of yellow moccasins . . . no bigger than a size ten.

Lyle's living room was high-tech: lots of glass and chrome. Built-in banquettes, covered by gray carpeting and matching pillows, were the only seats. At the far end of the room was a drafting table and a chair without a back. Donato thought it was the kind you kneeled on. There were no plants, no animals.

"What's this about?" Lyle asked.

"We'd like to ask you some questions, Mr. Lyle," Donato said. The hair was wrong, but there could be blond ones underneath.

"What about?" he said irritably.

"Do you know anyone by the name of Keith Laine?"

"No."

Donato couldn't tell if the name registered. "How long have you lived here?"

"Eight years."

"And you never met another tenant named Keith Laine?" Dina asked.

"That's right."

"Ever use the name Keith Laine yourself?"

"No. Why would I? Listen, do you want to sit down? I'm dead on my feet."

They declined, but Dina said, "Why don't *you* sit down?"

Lyle sat, then sprawled out, his head against the wall. Donato noted that Lyle didn't mind the disadvantage. "What kind of an artist are you?"

"I do book jackets, record slips, posters, things like that."

"You do very well, it seems," Dina said.

"Is that a crime?"

"An observation."

Lyle turned away from them and took a cigarette from a silver and glass case. He lit it with a sleek, silver table lighter.

"I hear you like to wear costumes, Mr. Lyle," Donato said.

"I don't know what you mean?"

"Costumes," Dina said. "Capes?"

"I have a cape, yes."

"Would you get it, please?"

"Listen, are you allowed to do this without a warrant?"

Donato raised his eyebrows. "You want us to get a warrant?"

"I didn't say that. I just wondered if you were allowed to do this without one."

"You don't have to get the cape if you don't want to, Mr. Lyle. We're asking in a friendly way. But if you want us to get a warrant, we can." They both knew that, with what they had, getting a warrant would be almost impossible.

"Can't you tell me what this is about?" He took a drag of his cigarette and blew a stream of smoke into the air. It circled around his head like a rope.

"The cape?" Dina asked pleasantly.

"Jesus Christ," he muttered, "it's like Nazi Germany."

"I'll go with you," Donato said, as Lyle pushed himself up and started to walk away.

"Well, I'm not *going* anywhere. It's over here in this closet." He pointed to a bank of doors set into a far wall.

"That's fine then," Donato said.

"Thanks," Lyle said sarcastically.

They tried to see what else was in the closet when Lyle opened it, but the maneuver was too swift. The cape was black with green trim. They examined it carefully. There was no way it could double for a habit.

"What kind of name is Kim Lyle?" Donato asked.

"A made-up one," he said defiantly. Lyle folded the cape and laid it gingerly on a banquette. "My real name's Jose Ortiz."

"You're Puerto Rican?"

"No. I'm New Yorikan." He smiled. "You never heard that? When I went to Puerto Rico for my father's funeral, all my cousins said, 'You're not Puerto Rican. You're New Yorikan.' "

"Is it an insult?"

"You bet it is. See, I was born here. I grew up in Spanish Harlem, but back there that doesn't count. My sister's been here forty-three years, still speaks with an accent out of pride."

"But you don't have an accent."

"I studied acting, saw what a rat race it was and went back and studied art. I'm a better artist than I was an actor."

Dina said, "And your mother? Is she also a Puerto Rican?"

"No, my mother's Irish. What the hell difference does it make if I'm Irish or Puerto Rican or aboriginal?"

"We were just curious about your coloring, Mr. Lyle," Dina said.

"I look like my mother."

"Where were you on Tuesday from about three-thirty in the afternoon to about five the next morning?"

"I slept until about five . . . five P.M., that is. Then I went out, had some Chinese, came back about seven. Worked."

"Anyone see you?"

"See me where?"

"The Chinese restaurant?"

"Sure. The waiter saw me."

Having dinner between five and seven didn't eliminate him. He might have eaten out to establish an alibi. "Did you talk to anyone from seven on?"

"I don't know. I don't think I did. I'm on a rush job. I put my machine on, turned it down. No, I didn't talk to anyone."

"How about on April third, Mr. Lyle?"

"I'd have to look at my calendar."

"Fine."

Lyle walked over to the drafting table, turned back the pages of a daily reminder. "Same thing. I was working," he said over his shoulder.

"Are you a Catholic?"

Lyle turned around. "I'm nothing. My mother was a Catholic, but my father ran the show. He didn't believe in anything, so we weren't brought up in any religion."

"Where are your whips and chains?" Dina asked abruptly.

Lyle flushed. "I don't think I have to answer any more of your fucking questions."

Donato stepped in as good cop. "No, you don't. But we'd like your help."

"Can't you tell me what this is about?"

Dina said, "Would you be willing to let us run some tests on you?"

"Tests? What kind of tests?"

"Prints, hair sample."

Absently, he touched his hair. "What the hell for?"

"Just for elimination."

"Elimination from what?"

"From being a suspect," Donato said.

"A suspect for what?"

"Murder."

"Shit. I thought you looked . . . it's these nun murders, isn't it?"

"Yes."

"And you think I . . . well, shit. Me?" He laughed nervously. "Hey, I don't think I'm going to answer any more questions without a lawyer."

Sitting in the car, Dina asked Donato what he thought.

"He looks right, has the right initials, and he doesn't have an alibi, but something doesn't gel."

"I think we should put a tail on him though."

"Definitely."

"What did you think of the neighbor, Lawrence?"

"Don't know. He's got one initial that's the same."

"So does Lachman. Why do you think he didn't go out after we were finished with him?"

"Changed his mind, I guess," he said. So why did it bother him?

She started the car. "When he said he recognized me, what did . . ."

"I thought he knew all along," Donato said, surprising himself.

"Exactly."

"So?"

"If that's true, why did he pretend it just came to him?"

"He strikes me as the kind of guy who finds it important to be . . . cool. You notice his clothes?" Donato asked.

"Very cool. And he seemed to be posing all the time. Well, we can't arrest him for being an asshole."

"If we arrested all the assholes in New York," he said, "we'd be in a helluva mess."

Before hitting the costume house, Dina and Donato picked up a bunch of flyers with the composite drawing of the killer. They told each other that it could be Kim Lyle, but neither was convinced. And now that they knew the mustache and hair were false, they didn't hold out much hope for an identification, but they had to try.

Triangle Costumes was on the ground floor of Forty-fifth Street between Broadway and Seventh Avenue. A woman in her late fifties, hair the color of marmalade in an outdated beehive, was behind the counter.

After introducing themselves, Dina asked the woman her name.

"Ellen Nehr, Ms.," she said, a nod on the Ms.

"You worked here long, Ms. Nehr?" Donato asked.

"Twenty-two years, not counting the six weeks I had to take off five years ago for my operation."

"We're interested in a purchase that occurred on March third of this year. It was a nun's costume bought by a man who said his name was . . ."

"Keith Laine," she interrupted.

"That's right," Donato said, feeling a rush of adrenaline. "How'd you know?"

"How many men do you think buy nun's costumes?" she asked.

"And how many in March of this year? I always remember the weird ones."

"Weird because he bought a nun's costume, or was there something else?"

"He was weird because he was wearing a fake mustache and a wig. I haven't been in this biz for twenty-two years for nothing. I know a phony when I see one."

Donato pulled out one of the flyers. "Was this the man?"

Ms. Nehr gave it a cursory glance. "That's him," she said unequivocally. "I knew he was a rotten apple."

Donato felt excited. Now they really had something. It was Keith Laine they were looking for, even though that wasn't his name. They could forget the others. Was Kim Lyle Keith Laine? "Why do you say he was a rotten apple?"

"A feeling. And the eyes. Even though he was wearing glasses I got a good look at them. Blue ice."

"You're sure they were blue?" Donato asked. No one else had been certain about the color.

"Oh, yeah, no doubt. I don't forget blue eyes. You can't ever tell what blue-eyed people are thinking, ever notice that?"

Donato looked at Dina.

"I know," she said, "Lyle's are brown."

He felt lousy again. But witnesses could be wrong. Who was to say Ellen Nehr had the eye color right? Something told him she did. Dammit.

"Tell us more about Keith Laine. How tall was he?"

"About six feet. Probably a blond, at least light brown. I can tell from the skin color. They can't fool me with their makeup and false noses and things like that."

"Do a lot of people come in here in disguise?"

"Enough. The wackos. Why they think they have to putty their noses and put on false beards beats me. I mean, do they think I care? Do they think I don't have anything better to do than care that they want to dress up like Marie Antoinette or Abe Lincoln? What do I care?" she said, her voice rising, white spittles of foam forming at the corners of her mouth.

"If a guy wants to be an astronaut or a Playboy bunny, who am I to say no? They want to be Captain Marvel, let them be Captain Marvel. Do I care if they get their kicks from being Dracula, Carmen Miranda, Santa Claus, the Lone Ranger, Spiderman, Wonder Woman, a nun? I couldn't care less. I have a life of my own, I don't need to make judgments on theirs. Jerks."

Donato wanted to be careful with his next question so that he didn't set her off again. "Is there anything else you can tell us about Keith Laine?"

"He had nice hands. Buffed nails."

"No," Donato said to Dina. Lyle's nails were ragged, paint-stained. He saw the case against Lyle collapsing.

"Anything else?"

"This guy was a real creep. 'You going to a costume party?' I asked him. See, I sometimes like to bug them."

"What did he say?"

"He was a wiseass. He said, 'No, I'm joining an order.' Then he laughed too long, you know how people do that? They laugh too long and too loud, and you want to say, it ain't funny, McGee, but you find yourself with this stupid smile on your puss because you don't know what else to do."

"Do you think you could pick him out of a lineup?"

"Why not? What'd this baby do, anyway?"

"He might be a killer."

"I'm not surprised."

"Why not?"

"Those eyes. They looked like the eyes in a doll. Fake."

Something stirred in Donato, but he couldn't place it, a connection he couldn't make.

They thanked her and said they'd be in touch. Back on Forty-fifth, they walked north toward the first of the makeup houses. An old woman, her head wrapped in rags, her faded red coat ripped and filthy, stepped in front of them.

"Spare some change?" she said. Her face was streaked with dirt and her hooded eyes leaked at the corners like a dog's.

Dina opened her pocketbook, took out her wallet and handed the woman a dollar.

She thanked and blessed Dina, then gave her a smile that was drowned in sorrow.

They walked on.

"Do you do that for all of them?" Donato asked, proud of her.

"I can't. I'd go broke."

He nodded and quickly changed the subject for fear his emotions would show. "I think we're on to him now."

"But who is he? We still don't know that. It couldn't be Lyle."

"No. The eyes. The nails. Shit."

"Keith Laine, a fake name, a fake face."

"Maybe we can get a real face from one of the makeup houses."

"Maybe," she said.

Donato didn't have much hope of that either. Chances that they'd find another Ms. Nehr with a perfect memory were unlikely.

By three-forty-five, they'd hit all nine places, and no one had remembered anything. False mustaches and wigs were sold much more frequently than nun's costumes.

The squad meeting served to reaffirm that Ellen Nehr was the best lead. But they still had to find out who Keith Laine really was, and for the moment, they couldn't do anything but go backward.

Dina asked Keenan and Delgado to return to HAFH to show the flyer to Sister Margaret and some of the kids. They might have seen this man loitering, might remember something else about him that would help.

Scott and Pesetsky were sent to Sister Angelica's convent and to Sister Anne Marie's. Bobbin and Lachman were to talk to Sister Honora's brother and Father Briney, while Dina and Donato went back to talk with Janet Curran.

At a quarter to eight, Donato, no closer to finding the true identity of Keith Laine, went to his mother's apartment.

She was cleaning up the kitchen after making gnocchi, Donato's favorite. She could have bought them homemade from a number of places in the neighborhood, but, even though it took hours to make, she insisted on doing her own. It was a sign she was feeling well and that pleased him. Lately her *spells* had become more and more frequent, and he worried about her. He sat at the kitchen table drinking a glass of red wine.

Time floated backward, and Donato felt like a child waiting for his supper, warm and safe in the confines of his mother's kitchen. But that feeling had never lasted because his father would come home, angry and demanding, and then everything would turn ugly.

"Mama," Donato said, "come sit down." Sometimes his mother refused to speak English. This was one of those days, so they conversed in Italian. "Have a glass of wine with me."

Ottavia looked at him curiously. Then, smiling, she squeezed out the pink sponge, dried her hands on her apron and brought a clean glass to Donato, who filled it.

"Health," he said.

"Health." She clicked her glass against his and drank.

A surge of love for her, as if all the years of dealing with her delusions were stripped away, left Donato with an unfamiliar sense of intimacy, a feeling they could talk at last.

"Mama, why did we go to Italy when I was three?" If he didn't find out soon, he might never have the chance.

She looked away, tucked a disobedient hair into her bun. "Why talk about the past, Michael?"

"It's always bothered me, Mama. I need to know."

"You don't *need* to know. You're just curious."

"All right, that's true. I still want to know. We stayed for two years. Why? Where were Papa and Steve?"

"They were here."

"Were you trying to leave Papa?"

"No."

"Why did we stay so long?"

"You wouldn't understand."

"Mama, please. Don't insult me. With all I see every day, you think I wouldn't understand something about my own mother?"

She smiled oddly, an expression Donato had never seen before. "Michael, some things are better left unsaid."

"That's not true." He'd never felt more hypocritical. Ottavia still believed the original story about Rich.

Her eyes were somber, grave. "This can only hurt you."

"How can what happened then hurt me now?"

She smiled ruefully. "Everything we do has consequences, Michael. Trust me. This isn't something you need to know."

He'd always been convinced that the two years in Florence were connected to his mother's retreat into religious fantasy. "I do trust you, but I have to know anyway," he implored her.

Ottavia stared past him, as if there were someone else in the room from whom she was seeking council. At last she spoke. "I stayed in Florence for two years because Marius Giuliano was there."

"Who was he?"

She sipped some wine, got up from the table, checked her sauce on the stove, then turned to face him. "Marius was the man I'd been in love with as a young girl. It was arranged that we were to be married, but when my family lost all their money, Marius's family wouldn't let him marry me. I had no dowry. So he married my rich cousin, Carolina, and my father forced me to marry Rosario. But Marius and I never forgot each other.

"When I went home because my mother was dying, taking you, my baby, Marius was waiting at the dock for me. When my mother died, I stayed on so that I could be with Marius. I told Rosario that my father needed me and kept delaying my return. Secretly, Marius and I met many times. They were the two happiest years of my life." Her eyes sparkled as if she were living it again.

"And then his father ordered him to open a branch of their business in Rome. Marius couldn't refuse, and, of course, there was no divorce in Italy. For me to move to Rome would have created a great scandal, so I came back here. It made no difference to me then whom I was with, where I lived. But my soul was in jeopardy. My only salvation was to devote myself to God, to do penance by living with Rosario." She returned to stirring the sauce. In an angry tone she asked, "Are you happy now?"

He wasn't. To think of his mother as having uncontrollable passions was almost unacceptable. But what troubled him more was that he'd humiliated her. Lately, it seemed, he couldn't do anything right.

Going to her, he turned her to face him and put his arms around her. She rested her head against his chest.

"Did Papa know?"

"He knew I'd been in love with Marius before I married him. And he knew I didn't love him. But not the rest. Do you despise me now?" she asked.

"No, Mama."

She closed her eyes, shook her head. "What else can you say?"

"It's true. I understand."

"No. Only God understands."

"Then God must forgive you."

"Not yet, Michael."

There was a thumping sound in the hall, and Donato felt a sense of alarm, the dread he'd experienced as a boy after the war, when his brother came home.

"What are you doing here?" Steve said combatively, staring at Donato.

"Nice to see you, too," Donato replied.

Steve was almost bald, a gray fringe ringed his head in a semicircle. Behind round, metal-framed glasses, his eyes had the offended look of a man who collected inequities. A white mustache fell over his lip like the uneven hem of a skirt. His clothes, a threadbare shirt and wrinkled khaki pants, were clean. Ottavia saw to that.

Steve had never married. Living on his GI pension in a small apartment on Kenmare Street, he spent his days hanging around the social clubs, playing cards, drinking espressos.

"Why aren't you out catching the Sister Slasher?"

"We're doing the best we can."

He laughed, a harsh bark. "That's what you always say. All you cops. 'We're doing the best we can.' Decoded it means, 'We haven't got a clue,' doesn't it?" He sat at the kitchen table and handed his crutches to his mother.

She leaned them against the wall. "Who wants to eat?"

Donato's appetite was gone. He poured himself another glass of wine. "Not yet, Mama."

"You here for dinner?" Steve asked.

"Yeah." He didn't want him to know that he was living here, that Renata had thrown him out. "Want a glass of wine?"

"Sure, why not? So what's the story on these nun murders?"

"There is no story. You know as much as we know."

"Terrific. Makes me feel real secure. By the way, how do you like working for your daughter?" he said, smiling.

Donato felt the old antagonism acutely. "It's fine." He finished his wine and poured another glass.

"I think I'd feel like a fucking fool if my kid was my boss," Steve said.

"Then it's good you never had kids," Donato said.

"If I did, I wouldn't let her give me orders."

"It's easy to quarterback from where you sit." Donato felt like pointing out that his brother had chosen a life with no responsibilities, but he saw that his mother was upset already by their nasty exchange.

Steve smiled condescendingly. "I'm an observer of people, Mike. Want to know what I've observed about you?"

"Not particularly."

"I've observed that you have trouble having interpersonal relationships. You know why? Because you're all shut down, like an old machine that's gotten rusty. When Rich died, you died."

"It's nothing you can understand."

"Don't give me that bullshit. You weren't the only one who suffered, you know."

"I never thought I was."

"At the funeral, you couldn't even support your wife or daughter. You didn't give a damn about anyone else. I'm the one who comforted Renata and Dina."

"How could I comfort anyone?"

"You acted like you were the only person in the world who'd ever lost a kid."

"What's your point, Steve?"

"I spoke to Renata today."

Donato felt as if he'd been conned. He downed his wine. "What's happened between Renata and me is none of your business."

"I didn't say it was. I'm merely pointing out the kind of man you've turned into."

Donato laughed. "You've got a helluva nerve, Steve. What kind of man do you think you've turned into? How about *your* interpersonal relationships?"

"We're talking about you, not me."

Donato stood up. "No, buddy boy, *you're* talking about me. *I'm* on my way out." He grabbed his raincoat from where he'd thrown it earlier and headed for the door.

"Michael, aren't you going to eat?" Ottavia asked.

"Not with him," he said and slammed out.

Donato hurried down the steps. When he hit the street, rain pelted him. He put on the coat and turned up his collar. The air had turned cool. He liked it when it rained. The city seemed fresh and new, as if it had just been invented.

He headed for Barney's. Steve's words were still ringing in his ears and he needed to blot them out. He had enough on his mind without that. It wasn't good to crowd your mind with extraneous stuff when you were on a case. Single-mindedness was the key. From now on, he wasn't going to think about Rich, Dina, Renata, his mother or anything else except the case. Maybe Steve was right. Maybe he didn't know how to have relationships, but he knew how to catch killers. Catching killers was something he was damn good at. And that was what he was going to do.

Nineteen

"What's wrong with you?" Andrea asked. "You look like you lost your best friend."

"Work," he muttered. He'd been shaken by the business with the police that morning, but he hadn't yet told Andrea about their visit. He was waiting for the girls to leave the table.

"Sometimes I wish you'd go into some other line of work," Andrea said. "Something that didn't make you so . . . nervous."

She had never accused him of being anxious before. It worried him. Now he wondered if he should tell her about the cops. He couldn't have her thinking he was nervous about that. "I'm just restless staying home with this damn cold."

Stephanie said, "May I be excused?"

"Me, too," Rebecca asked.

When they were gone, Andrea turned to him. "I hope you're not planning to go out tonight."

"I'm feeling much better," he said. He had an appointment with a kid about an apartment on Jane Street near the river. It would be the perfect place. "The police were here today," he said casually. He told her what had happened. "I recognized the lieutenant. She's the one in charge of those nun murders."

"And they wanted to talk to Kim? That's absurd."

"You never know," he said, spooning up the last of his peach cobbler. "Think of Ted Bundy."

Andrea shivered. "No thanks."

"Everybody thought he was a normal guy."

"So what are you saying, Russ? Kim is killing those nuns?"

He laughed. "I'm saying, who knows? The cops wanted to see him about something."

"I think they work on more than one thing at a time."

"These cops are just working this one for the moment. They have a special task force devoted to it." He felt a certain pride about this.

"Well, Kim Lyle is not a murderer."

"Probably not." It was too great a coincidence for them to be questioning someone in this building. Maybe they wanted to talk to Lyle about him. But that was stupid. There was no way they could connect him. The partial footprint the papers were playing up wasn't his. Somebody else had been in the apartment after he'd left. Some asshole. So what did they want from Lyle? And then he realized it was the initials. When he'd started he hadn't given a thought to Kim's name. Maybe it was because he'd put down his own address when he'd rented the costume. That was dumb.

"*Are* you going out?" Andrea asked.

"I promised Howard I'd go over some accounts with him."

"If you get worse, I'm not staying home to take care of you."

"Never thought you would. I'd better get going so I get home at a decent hour."

In the building garage, Russ removed the TWA bag from the trunk of his Datsun. Compulsively, he unzipped it, checking to see if everything was there. Then he locked the trunk again, pocketed his keys and left.

The rain was just a whisper now. He decided to take the subway instead of a cab. It was best not to draw any attention to himself. Especially now that the police had met him. There they were talking to the killer, and they didn't even know it . . . had no idea. Proof

[236]

positive how superior his mind was to theirs. Below normal intelligence, my ass, he thought.

The platform was empty except for a girl leaning against a pillar, reading a paperback. When the train screeched to a stop, Russ and the girl got on. She sat across from him and then he saw she looked like Dorothy. That terrible night came rushing back to him. He wanted to stop the memory, but he couldn't.

He and Dorothy had arranged to meet at their usual spot by the lake. The season hadn't begun, so they'd had the place to themselves. In the front seat of his Ford, Dorothy faced him, leaning against the passenger door. On the radio, the Beatles were singing "Yesterday." Russ reached out for her, but she shied away.

Lately, he'd noticed a reticence on Dorothy's part when they petted, even though all she'd ever let him do was touch her breasts. Still, she'd never pulled away from him like that.

"What's wrong?" he asked.

"I . . . nothing," she answered.

"Something."

"Yes," she said softly. "Something."

He felt angry. "What?"

"I have something to tell you."

His fists clenched in his lap. "What?"

"You're going to be mad."

"No, I won't," he lied. He was certain that she was going to tell him that she loved someone else. As far as his loving her, he wasn't sure that that was what he felt.

He was positive he hadn't ever loved his father. His mother was another story. He knew he could make her do anything he wanted, but he didn't think that was love. Still, he understood that it was good to act like Beaver so his mother would believe he loved her. And that was how he was with Dorothy, too. He did all the things he knew were expected of him.

"Tell me," he said.

"All right. But don't get mad. Promise, okay?"

"Yes."

"Say it."

"I promise." Promises were supposed to be sacred, but he didn't know why. Giving his word meant nothing to him, but Dorothy didn't know that because it had never come up before.

"Okay," she said. "I can't do this with you anymore."

"You mean what we . . ."

"Yes," she said, cutting him off.

A sudden fury, that he'd felt once before, raged inside him.

"That's not all. I can't see you anymore."

He wanted to punch her. The desire didn't surprise him. He'd often felt like punching people. Especially girls. "Why?"

"Are you mad? I think you're mad."

"Why?" he asked again.

"You're mad, I can tell."

"I think you'd better tell me, Dorothy," he said flatly.

After she told him, he planned how and when he'd kill her. It never occurred to him that he wouldn't do it. He was as certain of that as he was of getting out of Grand Haven, having money and being looked up to, admired. Dorothy would have to die. No one could dump him like that and live to talk about it.

At Grand Central, he got off and walked over to the shuttle platform. A man in a gaudy green shirt and black jeans, with long hair dyed purple on its spiky crest, was singing a rock song into a standing microphone. He had an electric Casio keyboard slung over his chest, the drum and percussion booming from two small speakers behind him. As he sang, he gyrated to the beat. On the ground was an open box with change and bills in it.

Russ thought he was lousy. He looked in vain for a transit cop. A letter to the mayor might be in order. People were captive audiences in situations like this, and it didn't seem fair. Fortunately, the shuttle made its appearance, so he was able to get away from the singer.

Despite the anxiety about the police, he was excited about his plan. He didn't have all the kinks worked out, but he knew it would come to him. There was always a solution.

He thought about the apartment he was going to see. On the phone, the man had said it was a large one-room with a Pullman kitchen and a full bathroom.

When he got to the West Side, he took the train to Fourteenth and Seventh. Up on the street, he was glad to see that the rain had stopped. He walked west, then turned into a bar.

It was a sleazy place, smelling of smoke and stale beer with an overlay of disinfectant. The lighting was dim, and the television was a black-and-white with a raspy sound. Five men sat at the bar, one or two stools between them. The bartender was burly and needed a shave.

Russ ordered a Budweiser. When the bartender brought the

beer, he slammed it on the bar in front of Russ, and foam dribbled over the mouth of the bottle and down the side. Ordinarily, Russ would have said something—he didn't like to be treated that way— but he didn't want to be noticed. He drank the beer quickly and went into the men's room.

The stench made him gag. Thick grime covered the floor, and yellow stains surrounded the urinal. There was one stall. With the tip of one finger, he opened the door. The toilet was filthy, the seat missing. A metal hook was attached to a side wall. There was no lock on the door.

Russ unzipped his flight bag, withdrew a round mirror and a bottle, then hung both bag and mirror over the hook. He opened the bottle, removed the brush and applied the liquid above his lip. After returning the closed bottle to the bag, he extracted a plastic case, plucked out his new droopy, ginger-colored mustache and pressed it against the glue above his lip.

Satisfied, he threw the empty case into the bag and pulled out a red wig. When he'd positioned it and made adjustments, he put away the mirror, zipped up his bag, opened the stall door and quit the bathroom. Head down and walking on the side of the room away from the people, he left the bar.

Back on the street, he quickened his pace as he headed for Bank Street. The usual Fourteenth Street seedy-looking types passed by, but he kept his distance from them. At the corner of Fourteenth and Bank, a small shabby man, a dirty watch cap on his head, stepped in front of Russ.

"How about a buck?" he said.

Russ tried to move to the left, but the man moved with him, blocking his way.

"It's my birthday," the man said.

"It's not your birthday," Russ said, disgusted, and feinted to the left, then ducked right, passing the bum.

"You fucking bastard," the man yelled after him, "I hope you rot in hell."

The episode disturbed Russ. He felt it was a bad omen even though he didn't believe in those things. He turned down Bank and walked to Jane, where he made a left and crossed Hudson. The building he wanted was between Hudson and West streets and the number was 450. It was two houses in from the corner.

PIKE, B. was on the mailbox that also said 1A. The front door was unlocked. Russ was glad to see that the hall was dirty. If there was a super, he wasn't terribly conscientious. The less he was around, the better.

Apartment 1A was positioned perfectly for getting his next . . . friend to the street without prying eyes and ears. After Russ knocked and identified himself, he heard the pull and scrape of a police lock and the door opened.

Pike was in his early twenties. He had a long, narrow face with dispirited eyes and a matching mouth. He was wearing jeans and a blue turtleneck sweater with many holes, as if a moth had feasted on it.

The dingy room had one window protected by a gate. An easy chair, its stuffing erupting from the seat, a mattress on the floor and a small metal table were the only pieces of furniture. A typewriter was chained to the refrigerator door handle.

"Were you burglarized?" Russ asked, looking at it.

"Three times. It's been okay since I got the gate and police lock," he added hastily.

Russ didn't believe Pike, but it didn't matter. A burglar wasn't going to get anything from him.

Pike said, "What's your name again?"

"Kirk Leonard. How much do you want?"

"What I told you on the phone. Seven-fifty."

"That's robbery, you know."

"Don't take it then. I got plenty other people interested."

Russ knew he was being taken. Still, the place was just what he wanted. "What do I get for the seven-fifty?"

"You're looking at it. Shit, that window gate cost me two." He lit a cigarette.

"I'll pay you rent, and you'll pay the landlord?"

"Right."

The strong, sweet odor of marijuana filled the room. Russ saw then that what Pike was smoking was thin and homemade.

Pike said, "You want a toke?"

"No." He didn't approve of drugs. "When can I have it?"

Pike inhaled and held in the smoke as he spoke. It sounded as though he were choking. "In three days, on the fourteenth."

"Okay, I'll take it."

"All riiight." Pike held out his hand to shake.

Russ ignored him. With his gloved hand, he reached into the inside pocket of his Burberry raincoat and pulled out his wallet. He counted out seven hundreds and one fifty.

"I want the key tonight," Russ demanded.

"You got it." Pike dug into his pocket, gave him a key.

Russ handed him the money. "Don't try anything funny."

"Funny?"

"Like renting it to five other people. Because if you do, I'll find you, and you won't like it."

"Hey, this is on the level. And if there's any funny business going on . . . well, I got to tell you, Kirk, you don't look like somebody who'd want to live here."

"No? What do I look like then?" He didn't care for this. The kid was getting too personal.

"You just don't look like you'd live here. This a fuck pad for you or something?"

He stared at the kid for a few seconds, deciding whether to shut him up or be friendly. He elected to be a buddy, the way James Garner might. "You got it," he said and winked.

"You're married, huh?"

"I want to try the key," he said, cutting Pike off from asking another question.

"Shit, you really are suspicious. Be my guest."

Pike opened the door, and Russ stepped out in the hall. When the door was shut and locked, Russ tried the key. It worked.

"Okay," Russ said. He picked up his bag, then walked through the doorway again. "So long," Russ said.

"Can I ask you one thing?"

"What?"

"How come you're wearing a wig and a false mustache?"

Without thinking, Russ rushed back into the apartment, shoving Pike up against the wall, his forearm under the man's chin. Dropping his bag, he kicked the door shut. He should have made something up. But now it was too late.

Suddenly Pike pushed away from the wall and threw Russ off balance. He started for the door, but Russ regained his equilibrium and grabbed him around the waist. Pike pulled at Russ's hands, got under his middle finger and bent it back until, crying out, Russ let go.

Pike whirled around and threw a punch but missed. It gave Russ just enough time to recover. He hit Pike in the face with a straight overhand right, and Pike reeled backward but didn't go down. Automatically, his hands went to his face, leaving his body exposed. Russ swung a low left-hand punch to Pike's gut, and Pike doubled over.

Bringing his knee up under Pike's chin, Russ cracked him hard and Pike went down. Russ kicked him in the face twice, and then Pike was still, his face covered in blood from his broken nose and split lip.

Breathing hard, Russ locked the door. He picked up his bag, unzipped it, took out his boning knife, dropped to his knees, grabbed Pike by the hair and pulled back his head. Then moving himself away from the body as far as possible, he slit Pike's throat. There was a strange gurgling sound, as if Pike were trying to breathe through the slash. Russ watched the chest heave, and then the gurgling sound diminished, stopped. Russ stood up. He spotted the remainder of Pike's joint on the floor, crushed it with the heel of his shoe, picked it up and dropped it into his bag. For the next few moments, he stood there, staring at the dead man. And then he had a brilliant idea.

He reached into his bag and got out the meat cleaver. Kneeling next to Pike, he flattened the corpse's left hand against the floor, spread the fingers and, with one perfect stroke, severed his ring finger. Using a Kleenex, he pocketed it.

At the sink, he washed off the knife and cleaver, pulled a paper towel from the dispenser, dried them and returned the implements to his bag. He picked up the seven hundred and fifty dollars. Now he'd have to find another place. He remembered the bum who'd cursed him and how he'd felt it was a bad omen.

Stepping over Pike's feet, he cautiously opened the door a crack. There was no sound. Out in the hall, he locked the door, hurried to the front and down the steps. The street was empty except for one man walking away from him on the other side. Forcing himself not to run, Russ went in the opposite direction, toward Washington Street.

A fine rain had started again. Between Washington and Greenwich streets, he threw the key and the finger down a sewer, then continued to the corner of Jane and Hudson, where he took a right. Passing only two people, he hurried along, crossed West Twelfth, Bethune, Bank, West Eleventh, Perry, Charles and turned left at West Tenth.

Now that he was in a more populated area, it was essential that he appear casual, so he slowed his gait. Crossing Bleecker, he suddenly saw three cops standing in the middle of the block on his side. Instinctively, he wanted to cross back, run, but he knew he mustn't. The cops were in front of the Sixth Precinct. His heart slammed in his chest, but he continued on.

"Hey, cutie," one of the cops said, "your wig's slipping."

The others laughed.

"Better pin it up, tootsie," another cop said.

"You tell him, Cummings."

They laughed again.

Russ was furious. They thought he was a faggot. He knew he had to go along, do what they expected. He thought of Tony Curtis in *Some Like It Hot.*

"Thanks, honey," he said, smiling seductively.

The others started razzing Cummings, and Russ kept going.

The wig had to go. But what about the mustache? Well, maybe it was possible he could be a blond and have a red mustache. Right before he reached the corner of Waverly and Seventh Avenue, he surreptitiously slipped off the wig and tucked it in his belt under his coat.

At Seventh Avenue, he crossed the street and nonchalantly strolled to the subway. Once through the turnstile, he walked down the platform until he was alone, then opened his tote and slid the wig into the bag.

On the train he kept his head down so that no one could see the mustache too closely. He thought about what had happened and what he was going to do.

Fucking Pike. He'd spoiled everything. It was Pike's fault. He couldn't be blamed for it. Anybody would have done the same thing under those circumstances. Still, he should have been more careful, checked the wig and mustache to see if they looked all right. Now he'd have to find another place, read the goddamn *Voice,* make arrangements. Fucking Pike.

The train pulled into Times Square. He found a men's room. Holding his breath while he pulled off the mustache, he took a small bottle of alcohol and a cotton ball from his bag and wiped the glue from his upper lip. Returning the things to his bag, he dropped the cotton ball to the floor and left the bathroom.

Now he felt better, invulnerable and, unexpectedly, hungry. He stopped at a food stand and ordered a hot dog. The mustard dispenser was clogged; it made him mad. He wanted to throw it at the counterboy's pimply face, but he smiled instead, like Mickey Rooney, he thought, and asked if there was another. The boy gave him one, and Russ loaded the hot dog with the yellow mustard.

While he ate, he tried to decelerate his mind so he could formulate his plan, put the final pieces together, but he couldn't seem to calm down. His thoughts were fragmented: flashes of Sisters Honora,

Angelica, Bambi, and Pike. They tumbled through his mind like clips from a film.

The shuttle was in when he got to it. As he waited for the train to leave, he thought about Pike. Cutting off his finger had been a stroke of genius. The police would be totally confused. They'd see they weren't dealing with an ordinary man with *below-average intelligence.* Thinking about it, he almost laughed aloud.

The train pulled out. When he arrived at Grand Central, he went upstairs into the station and made his way over to the bank of lockers where he kept his things. He decided to keep his tote bag there as well.

Inside his locker was the suitcase that held his nun's outfit and his new police uniform. The next time he was going to be Officer Larson.

It had been a cinch buying the uniform. He'd checked out the store first by phone, saying he was a writer doing a book and needed to know if you had to have police ID to buy a uniform. The guy said anyone could buy one but not handcuffs, a nightstick or a badge. So he'd gotten a pair of kid's cuffs and a fake badge on Broadway. He had to skip the nightstick.

The best part was getting the gun. A year before all this had started he'd had the impulse to have a fake set of IDs. By reading a mystery novel, he found out how to go about it.

He'd driven upstate and gone to a cemetery in a town called Hudson, where he'd walked around until he'd found what he was looking for: the grave of a baby born the same year as he, with the initials K. L. Then he'd written to Albany asking for the birth certificate of Kenyon Larson. After it arrived, he'd taken a driving test and gotten a new license in the Larson name. Other credentials had been easy to come by after that. And then, without a hitch, he'd bought the Smith & Wesson .38. That had been prescient because now he needed to carry that gun when he was Officer Larson. He'd show them who had *below-average intelligence.*

He put the TWA bag into the locker, closed the door, fed it more money and pocketed the key. Back in the subway station, he boarded an uptown train.

The major part of his plan hadn't changed. He was still going to get one and bring her to his own building, put her in the freight elevator, then leave the elevator on his floor.

If the police wanted to think it was Lyle, that couldn't be helped, but he didn't think they would; why would Lyle be dumb enough to leave her there now that they suspected him? God, it gave him chills. The police would be swarming all over the place. And there he'd be answering questions, being cooperative.

He got off the subway, climbed the stairs and hit the street. As he was walking toward home, he began to fill in details.

The Greenwich Village apartment had to be scratched. He couldn't afford to go back to that neighborhood. It would be better to have a place closer to his building, but not too close. Some place in the Hundreds between Madison and Lex.

Then he'd have to find one who didn't wear a habit. But that wouldn't be hard. He could use his writer scam again and call places; he'd figure it out.

Dressed in uniform, he'd tell the nun her Mother Superior had asked him to pick her up because she was worried about the nun killer. Once he had her in the car, he'd have to use the gun, tell her he'd blow her brains out if she didn't come with him. She'd behave then, know who was in charge. He'd drive to his cozy place in Spanish Harlem, then tie her up and leave her there until later. After Andrea was asleep, he'd come back. Idly, he wondered if the nun would be glad to see him.

Afterward, if anyone saw them, he'd just be a cop taking in a drunken woman. Once they were in the car, he'd put her on the floor in back and remove his uniform. Then he'd drive to his building, into the garage where he'd put her on the freight elevator, hit the button for P and jump out. No one would be using the elevator at that time of night. He'd take the regular elevator up and sneak into his apartment. Andrea would never know what time he got in because he would have seen to that earlier.

When he reached his building, Marty, the evening doorman, smiled at him and asked him how his cold was.

"Much better, thanks, Marty," he said.

"Well, you look good, Mr. Lawrence."

"And I feel good. In fact, Marty, I think you could say I never felt better."

Twenty

"There had to be a leak somewhere," Dina said.

"You mean one of us?" Donato asked.

They were standing in front of 450 Jane Street. Barry Pike's body had been found around midnight by a woman in the building who had a key to his apartment.

"Not one of the task force necessarily," she said. "A uniformed cop, someone from the ME's office. But it's not a coincidence, and it's not our guy. It has to be a copycat."

"Maybe. But the apartment's like the last one. It's in a crummy, dingy building on the first floor, with no furniture to speak of. And then there's the finger."

"But the victim's a man."

"I admit that's a change in the MO. What do you think of this? Pike was trying to rent his apartment, and our guy came to see it. Then something went wrong, and bingo, he kills him."

Dina mulled it over. "That's a possibility. Who talked to the woman who found him?"

"Napier."

"Where is he?"

"Outside Pike's apartment."

"Let's talk to him."

Dina was worried about Donato. He didn't look well. But then neither did she. The case was getting to all of them. And they didn't have much time left.

Officer Napier had only questioned the witness about time of discovery and how and why she'd been in Pike's apartment, so they went to see her.

Her name was Sue Deakins. She was in her twenties and was dressed in a Royal Stewart plaid robe with brown and purple stains on the front. Her bleached blonde hair showed brown at the roots and hung limply around her face as if it had given up. A forgotten smudge of lipstick colored half of her bottom lip. Long nails painted scarlet were chipped. Everything about Sue Deakins seemed to need an overhauling.

Her apartment matched her perfectly. The living room needed painting, and the Danish modern furniture was exhausted. Yellow, cracked tiles covered the floor. There were no books, but a pile of magazines was stacked on a battered wooden coffee table.

"Excuse the way I look, okay? I work at night."

"What kind of work do you do?" Dina asked.

She hesitated, then said, "I work in a service industry."

That's a new euphemism, Dina thought.

"You wanna sit down?" She plopped into a shabby gray chair.

Dina and Donato sat on the foam rubber couch.

"Why did you have a key to Mr. Pike's apartment?"

"So I could get in," she said, as if Donato was one of the dumbest assholes she'd ever met. "We had each other's keys in case one of us needed something or locked ourselves out." Deakins shoved a cigarette in the corner of her mouth, lit it with a Cricket. "God, yer just not safe nowheres today. The city's run by animals."

Dina said, "Why did you go to Pike's apartment last night?"

"I run out of cigarettes and didn't feel like going out again. I just come home from work."

"Was Barry your boyfriend?" Donato asked.

"You kidding me? Barry didn't have a pot to piss in," she said, as though she were obviously used to luxury.

"How well did you know him?"

"Lemme think. Pretty good, I guess. He was like, 'Should I do this or that?' and I was like, 'Try this or that.' "

Donato sighed. "You mean he asked for your opinions?"

"Yeah." She exhaled smoke through her nostrils.

"Do you know if he was trying to rent his apartment?"

"Yeah, he was."

"Had he put an ad in the paper?"

"Yeah."

"Which paper?" Dina asked.

"Lemme think. When I saw him last week he's like, 'I can't wait to get out of this dump,' and I'm like, 'When are ya going?' and he's like, 'Soon as I rent the apartment. I put the ad in,' and I'm like, 'Where,' and he's like . . . and he's like . . . I can't remember, sorry."

"Was it the *Voice*?" Donato asked.

"Yeah, that's right," she said brightening. "The *Voice*."

"Do you know if anyone answered the ad?"

"Lemme think." After a long pause, she said, "Yeah, a couple people answered it, and when they saw it they didn't want it. And let's see . . . yeah. When he come over yesterday, he's like, 'I feel like shit, Sue. Nobody wants the place,' and I'm like, 'Don't give up, Barry, somebody'll take it,' and he's like, 'I got one guy coming about eight tonight.' "

"Did he tell you the name of the guy?" Dina asked hopefully.

"Lemme think." She scratched her chin, picked at her nail polish. "Yeah, he did because it was one of those names."

"One of what names?"

"Like one of those yuppie names. Justin or Tucker or something like that. Lemme think."

Dina glanced at Donato who was tapping his foot.

"I'm like, 'Hey, maybe this guy'll take it, Barry,' and he's like, 'He's got this yuppie name,' and I'm like . . . oh, shit . . . I don't remember."

"Try," Donato urged.

"Lemme think."

"Was it Keith Laine?" Dina asked.

Sue Deakins's eyes opened wide. "Yeah!" The eyes narrowed. "No. It wasn't that. But something like that. Lemme think."

There was a knock at the door, and Deakins said to come in. It was Napier.

"Sorry to bother you, Lieutenant, but there's been a development."

Dina handed her card to Deakins. "If you think of the name, or anything else, no matter how small, call me."

"Okay, I'll think on it."

"You do that," Donato said.

In the hall, Napier said to them, "We've found a finger."

Dina looked at the task force seated around the conference table. Bobby was smiling, his eyes reaching deep inside her. She felt like a teenager, and for one mad moment, she fantasized calling off the meeting, running home with Bobby, making love, hiding out. But instead she continued the meeting, filling in those who didn't know about the murder of Barry Pike.

"And a few hours ago, the finger, which is Pike's, according to a preliminary report, and the key to his apartment, were found in a sewer a few blocks away from Pike's place on Jane."

Lachman said, "Sounds like a copycat to me."

"Nobody knows about the fingers except us," Delgado added.

"Nobody's *supposed* to know," Keenan said. "But who does that cover? Not just us. Other cops, the Forensic people and the morgue crew. That's about fifty people."

"Yeah, but they know they're supposed to keep their fucking traps shut." Bobbin popped a piece of gum in his mouth.

"Shit. Knowing and doing are two different things," Pesetsky said.

"If there was a leak, it would've gotten in the press. Don't you think, Lieut?" Scott asked.

"Not necessarily," Dina answered.

"So, what are we talking here? Our killer's somebody we know or what?" Bobbin put in.

"Donato has a theory," Dina said.

He leaned forward, crossed his arms on the table. "I think it *is* our guy. A copycat would've picked a nun. Pike's apartment is the same type as the place where Sister Anne Marie was murdered.

"Pike was trying to rent his place, took an ad in the *Voice.* I think the Slasher went there to rent it, to set himself up with another slaughterhouse. Then something went wrong, maybe Pike made him as the nun killer. Anyway, our asshole panicked for some reason, and that's why he killed Pike."

Scott pulled on his ponytail. "If it was the Slasher, how come he left a finger close by for us to find?"

"Maybe he wasn't interested in keeping Pike's finger the way he is with the nuns'."

"Jesus Christ," Pesetsky muttered.

"So why'd he cut it off then?" Lachman asked.

"Maybe to confuse us."

Dina said, "Remember that besides wanting to kill nuns, he now has a vested interest in confounding us. The newspaper story about his intelligence may have gotten to him."

"Yeah, but, Lieutenant," Bobbin said, "there's nothing to prove it's not a copycat, is there? I mean, shit, with the amount of people knowing details it might've leaked."

"I think we have to assume that it's our guy. The cut of the finger is a match," she said, looking down at the report in front of her. "A cleaver-type instrument was used, just as it's been used in the nun killings. Donato's theory makes sense. Anyway, we have to operate as if it's our killer, eliminate suspects, go through the usual procedure.

"Pesetsky and Scott, get a rundown on Pike's friends and acquaintances. Bobbin and Lachman, interview as many people as you can on Jane Street between West and Hudson. See if somebody spotted him."

Lachman said, "It was rainin,' Lieut."

"Maybe somebody put out the garbage, walked a dog, something. Delgado, are you and Keenan still working on finding actors named Keith Laine?"

"He's not Equity and he's not SAG, but there are more non-Equity, non-SAG actors in this town than there are Chinese restaurants. We're checking theater companies and off-off-off Broadway shows."

"Keep on it."

Keenan said, "I have something else. The cabdriver who hit Sister Honora gave me a description of the passenger who split." He consulted his notes. "Male Caucasian, about six feet, one-forty-five to one-fifty, mid-thirties, blond. Very well dressed. He picked him up on Second Avenue and Seventy-third. Destination Grand Central."

"Goddam," Bobbin said, "that's gotta be Lyle."

"And it's right near his fucking building," Lachman added.

"Could he pick him out of a lineup?" Dina asked.

"He thought so."

"Good work, Keenan. Donato and I are going back to Pike's building. We want to talk to Sue Deakins again." It was rare to get the information you needed from a witness in the first interview.

As they rose, Keenan smiled at her, and her knees felt as if they were made of straw. She smiled back, wished she could touch him. Instead, she turned away and found Donato's eyes on her. Immediately, she got busy with some papers on the table.

When everyone was gone, she said to Donato, "Let's have some lunch before we try Deakins again, okay?"

"Fine by me," he said.

They went to Hunan Pan on the corner of Perry and Hudson. It was a large bright room strewn with plants, the walls painted red and black. They ate sweet and sour soup in silence.

Since Dina had told her mother about Rich's murder, her unease with Donato had grown. He hadn't asked her to keep it a secret from Renata, but she felt it was implicit. Keeping it to herself would have made her her father's accomplice, condoned his secretiveness. Still, she felt she'd betrayed him, something that would once have been impossible.

She remembered the closeness they'd once shared. Whenever he could, Donato had taken her to the movies. He'd knock on her bedroom door as if he were picking her up for a date.

"C'mon, kiddo, let's go," he'd say. "Got to make it to the first show."

She'd take his arm, and they'd walk up Broadway to the Loew's or to the Thalia, where they showed double bills. And afterward, they'd go for an ice cream soda or a big banana split. He'd always bet her she couldn't finish, but she always did.

"What's funny?" Donato asked. "You were smiling."

"I was thinking about all the banana splits I ate after you took me to the movies."

"You sure could put them away."

"Sometimes I wish I was that little girl again," she said.

"Sometimes I wish you were, too. We were all so happy then," he said wistfully.

"Except I was always afraid you wouldn't come home."

"And I was afraid I'd never see any of you again."

"I didn't know that."

"Don't you feel that about Cal? Didn't you with Liam?"

"Of course."

"Well, then," he said simply.

"I didn't think you felt that way."

"Sometimes I think you don't know me at all."

Dina wondered if that could be true. Was it possible to know a person all your life and not know what he was really like? Was her version of Donato a distortion? As she started to speak, her beeper sounded. She turned it off and went to the phone.

When they answered at the Thirteenth, she identified herself. They switched her call, and she swallowed hard when she heard Keenan's voice.

He was all business. "We've found Keith Laine, Lieutenant. Should I go ahead or do you want to question him?"

"I'll be there in ten minutes," she said and hung up.

Keith Laine was tall, handsome, had blue eyes and was terrified. After telling him his rights, and suggesting he call his lawyer, Dina had asked him if he would be in a lineup. He had no lawyer so they got him one, and even after Laine was told that he wasn't being charged with anything and didn't have to be in a lineup, he agreed to it. He said he had nothing to hide.

They'd driven downtown to 155 Leonard Street, where most lineups were held, then waited about an hour until Ellen Nehr, from Triangle Costumes, arrived. Her eyes were glittering, as if she were about to participate in something glamorous.

Nehr, along with Dina; Laine's lawyer, Elissa Rosner; and Chuck Mignon, an assistant DA, waited in the small, soundproof viewing room behind a one-way glass window for the lineup to begin. Donato and Keenan remained outside because the rules permitted only three people and the witness in the room.

Mignon was in his late thirties, had a fissured face and dark bushy eyebrows. "You're looking good, Dina," he said to her.

"Thanks." She didn't like Mignon, never had. He'd started off as a cop, graduating from the Academy with her class, gone to law school with her and then left the force for the DA's office. When they'd been rookies, he'd tried to date her, and when she'd spurned his advances for the tenth time, it had gotten back to her that he'd organized a pool betting on the size of her breasts. She'd always wondered how they'd determined a winner.

"You think you have something here?" Mignon asked her.

"Possibly."

"I understand you and Liam have split."

"That's right."

"How about dinner some night?"

"Still the consummate professional, aren't you, Mignon?"

"And you're still Miss Goody Two Shoes," he said sourly.

Dina turned to the witness. "Don't be nervous, Ms. Nehr."

"Nervous? I'm not nervous. He can't see me, right?"

"Right."

"So I don't see that there's anything to be nervous about." She patted her red hair.

Rosner said, "When they file in you take all the time you want. There's no hurry."

"I think either I'll know the guy right away or I won't," Nehr said.

"You might not find it that easy. Sometimes lineups can be confusing," Dina explained.

"That's enough talking about it," Laine's lawyer snapped.

Dina was annoyed. She didn't like Rosner's implication that she was trying to lead the witness.

Six men filed into the brightly lit lineup room. Each one, including Laine, wore a black mustache and a black wig like the ones Nehr had described. A number on a large white card was hung around each man's neck. Laine was number 4.

Through the intercom, Dina instructed the men.

"Turn to your left," she said, one eye on Nehr, who was scraping the polish from a nail with her front tooth. Dina told the men to turn to their right, then to face front. "What do you think?"

"I don't know," Nehr said, sounding less assured than she had before. "See, I can tell they're all wearing fake stuff."

"But you said Laine was."

"Yeah, I know. But now they all look alike to me."

Mignon said, "What's this about?"

"He was wearing a disguise when he came into the store," Dina explained.

"Number three," Nehr said suddenly. "Yes, I'm sure it's number three." She turned to Dina, smiling, waiting for praise.

Dina knew Laine was a longshot, but what worried her now was Nehr's witness potential. Sooner or later they'd get on to the real killer and need Nehr. If she'd been unable to pick anyone, it would have been all right. But insisting on 3 gave Dina real doubts. Number 3 was Detective Third Grade Bruce Taylor.

"You're positive?" Dina asked.

"I recognize the eyes. I'd know those ice eyes anywhere."

Rosner was smiling and Mignon was smirking.

"Well, it's him, isn't it?" Ellen Nehr asked, confused.

"I'm afraid not," Dina said.

"But those eyes," Nehr said.

"The man you picked is a detective," Mignon said snidely.

For a moment Nehr was silent. Then she brightened. "So what? I mean, so what he's a detective? Who says a detective wouldn't buy a nun's costume?"

"I really don't think he's our man."

"The hands. Tell them to put out their hands," Nehr insisted.

"This is ridiculous," Rosner said, shoving a pencil through her curly hair. "She's made her ID and it's not my client."

"Hold on," Dina said. "The witness has a right to ask for additional evidence." She turned back to the intercom. "Would you all hold both hands out in front of you."

Keith Laine and number 5 couldn't keep their hands from trembling. Dina thought Laine's tremor was from nerves, but number 5, who was also a detective, probably needed a drink.

Nehr moved closer to the window, her forehead touching the glass. "Okay," she finally said.

Dina told the men to put down their hands, turned to Nehr.

"I was wrong," she said sadly. "The man I picked, the detective, doesn't have the right hands. None of them do."

Dina was pleased. Nehr could still be a viable witness. "Don't worry about it, Ms. Nehr. You did fine."

"Fine? How could it be fine when I picked a detective?"

"You also disqualified him."

"After I *told* her he was a detective," Mignon said.

"He's right," Nehr agreed.

Dina dismissed the lineup, and they left the viewing room. Donato and Keenan were waiting expectantly. Dina shook her head.

"You can go now," Dina said to Ellen Nehr. "The officer who brought you here will take you back."

"That's all right. I'll hop a subway," she said dejectedly.

"Ms. Nehr," Dina said, "please don't feel badly. Picking someone out of a lineup is difficult. And you were nervous. You'll know what to expect the next time."

"You mean you'll give me another shot?"

"When we have a suspect."

"Oh, thanks, Lieutenant," Nehr said, "thanks a lot."

Dina watched the woman go, then turned back to Donato and Keenan. "She picked Taylor but then withdrew her ID when she got a look at his hands."

Mignon walked up to Dina. "Don't waste my time like this again, Lieutenant."

Dina bristled. "You know there's no way to know about an ID before the witness gets a look, Mignon."

"Nehr didn't know shit. Maybe *you* have time to kill, lady, but I don't." He glanced at Donato. "Jesus, what a combo." He whirled around and was gone before she could reply.

"What a guy!" Keenan said sarcastically.

"A swell fellow," Donato added.

"I turned down a dinner invitation," she said.

"Ahh," Keenan said, "the plot sickens."

"Are we going back to talk to Sue Deakins?" Donato asked.

"I think we should try," Dina said.

"Why don't you come along, Keenan?" Donato proposed.

Dina didn't like the idea of being with her father and Keenan at the same time, but the two men had already begun walking toward the stairs.

Deakins had still been unable to remember the name of Pike's potential tenant but assured them she'd keep trying. Then Donato had suggested they all have a drink and something to eat. Dina had had no ready excuse so she'd acquiesced.

They'd gone to Vincent's Clam Bar on the corner of Mott and Hester. The restaurant, known for having the best calamari in town, had three rooms. They took a table in the second one, where the lower half of the walls was dark wood and the rest was painted a sickly yellow. Fans hung from a painted tin ceiling. Red-and-white paper placemats were in front of each of them.

"This is what I call class," Donato said.

Dina and Keenan laughed.

"My mother's always hated this place," she said to Keenan.

"What's wrong with it?"

"Nothing," Donato said. "There's something wrong with her."

"C'mon now," Dina warned in a friendly tone.

He looked at her, smiled. "Let's just say, my wife has more refined tastes."

"I understand," Keenan said. "My mother's the same way."

Each of them ordered a beer and a plate of calamari.

"So what's next?" Donato said.

"We keep looking for the real Keith Laine, who isn't really named Keith Laine, and we hope that dimwit Deakins can remember the name, which probably isn't the real name, of the guy who was meeting with Pike," Dina said. "It'll be a snap."

Keenan said, "We're not much farther along than we were a week ago."

They were silent, depressed. Then the food came and they started eating. A piece of spicy calamari in her mouth, Dina looked up and met Keenan's eyes. She saw that Donato had caught their glance and, embarrassed, had turned away, back to his food.

The first time she'd introduced Liam to her father, he hadn't liked him. Over the years she'd brought other men home; some he'd liked. But Liam rubbed him the wrong way from the start. He was too possessive of Dina, too familiar with Donato and her mother. Donato wanted Liam to be a little awkward. Instead, he'd fitted in right away as if he'd grown up with Dina, known them all his life. Renata liked it but Donato didn't.

She wondered what he thought of Bobby. Did he think he was a good detective, at least? Or was the father in him still not objective?

Keenan interrupted her thoughts. "Any ideas, Mike?"

"Wish I did. I can't remember when I last felt so stymied."

"The Norton case," Dina supplied.

"That's right. But my God, Dina, you were only fourteen or fifteen then."

"I remember all your cases. I used to sit outside the living room listening when you'd tell Mom about them. I guess I was about six when I started hiding and listening."

"You told your wife about your cases?" Keenan asked.

"I never thought it was a good idea to keep my work separate. It makes for too much isolation . . . both ways. But she really didn't want to hear about it. Oh, maybe in the beginning she did. But after a while, she just tolerated my running cases by her. I pretended I didn't notice." He turned back to Dina. "So you remember the Norton case."

"You were stuck, just the way we are now. And then . . ." Dina's beeper went off. She silenced it and got up. "I'll be right back." She wasn't crazy about leaving her father alone with Bobby, but there was nothing to be done.

The call was to tell her that the previous night two uniformed cops had seen something odd on West Tenth Street that they thought might be related to the Pike homicide. Dina asked to have the cops meet them at Vincent's. She was damned if she was going to have another meal ruined.

When she came back to the table, she filled in the two men.

Keenan said, "I was just telling Mike that I agree with him about Pike. I think our guy did it. But what did Pike guess that made him kill him?"

"I don't see how Pike could have known he was the nun killer," Donato said. "But he had to have tipped his hand somehow. A knife that fell out of a pocket? A paper bag with a nun's habit in it that Pike saw?"

"Pike would be able to identify him," Keenan suggested.

"No more than Alby or Frank Lach," Dina said, reminding him about the fat man and the super of the building where Sister Anne Marie had been murdered. "He'd worn a disguise."

"And you can bet he wore a disguise to meet Pike, too."

"So why kill Pike if he was in disguise?" Keenan asked.

"Maybe Pike refused to rent to him," Donato suggested.

"But Deakins said he was desperate to rent it. I don't think Pike would have been too choosy about a tenant," Dina said.

"You're right," Donato agreed.

Dina said, "God, this calamari's good."

"Hot as hell," Keenan said.

"You should have asked for the milder sauce. The wimpy kind," she kidded and could see Donato processing her remark, chalking it up to intimacy.

"Real men eat *hot* sauce," Keenan said in a deep phony voice.

She smiled, glanced at Donato, who looked at her knowingly. Well, so what? He was going to know sooner or later. Anyway, the reason for this little get-together was because he *did* know and wanted to confirm his suspicions. She knew Donato's MO.

Then something occurred to her. "Maybe Pike saw that our guy was in disguise and made the mistake of letting him know."

"That has to be it," Donato said.

Keenan gave her a congratulatory smile. "I think she's got it."

"Being found out that way would enrage him," Dina said. "He prides himself on being superior, exceptionally clever. But he's getting overconfident. It's what we've been waiting for, and we didn't even know it," Dina said.

"But what good is it? Pike, our only witness, is dead," Keenan contended.

"Maybe he wasn't the only one," she said. "Maybe somebody else saw something. Maybe he made another mistake." She looked toward the door and saw the two cops come into the restaurant. "And maybe now we'll hear what that mistake was."

They introduced themselves as Officers Cummings and Arley. Cummings was the younger of the two, under twenty-five. He had a droopy mustache and bright brown eyes. Arley was short and broad. His eyes were set close together in a narrow face.

Dina told them to sit down.

Arley asked if he could smoke. She gave him permission.

"What do you have?" she asked.

Cummings looked at Arley and nodded for him to go ahead.

"Last night, about eight-thirty, we was in front of the precinct, me and Cummings here, and Blackburn. We was hanging out, kidding around and this jerk comes down the street."

"It was sort of raining," Cummings interjected. "Real fine, like a mist, so it seemed peculiar that this guy was walking real slow, like the sun was shining."

"When he got closer," Arley said, "we seen that he's wearing a wig."

Donato sat up in his chair, glanced at Keenan and Dina.

"Usually, we wouldn't think nothing of a guy in a wig on Tenth Street in the Village, right, Cummings?"

"Guys wearing wigs is commonplace over there. Wigs and costumes and all kinda weird shit," Cummings asserted.

"Makeup, jewelry, dresses," Arley added. "We don't bat an eye—we see it all the time. But the thing of it was, this bimbo's wig is almost falling off."

Cummings said, "Well, not really falling off, Leo. More like askew."

"Askew?" Arley said.

"Yeah, askew."

"What's askew?"

Cummings looked at the others and shook his head. Then to Arley he said, "Askew is outta line. Slightly off."

"Askew," Arley muttered. "Okay, it was askew then."

"What was so odd about that?" Dina asked.

"The guys in our part of town who dress up, wear wigs and things, wouldn't never have a wig be *askew*," Arley maintained.

Cummings elaborated. "Wearing a wig or a costume is very important to these guys, and everything has to be just so."

"I still don't get your point," Dina said.

The two cops glanced at each other, and some signal passed

between them. "Well, we was kidding around," Arley said, blowing smoke above his head, "and, well, Blackburn says to this guy, 'Hey, cutie, your wig's slipping.'"

Cummings looked down at the table.

"We were just fooling around," Arley illuminated.

"It's all right," Dina said. "Just tell us what happened."

Cummings picked it up. "Well, then I said something about pinning up his wig, and the guy gave this smile and said, 'Thanks, honey.' But it wasn't right. You know what I mean, Lieutenant?"

"What Jack means is that something was off about this guy. I don't think he was really a queen, and who the hell is going to pretend he's a queen if he ain't one? See?"

"Unless he wants you to *believe* he is," Dina observed.

"Right," Cummings said. "First off, a real queen wouldn't've had his wig askew and he wouldn't've said 'Thanks, honey' the way this guy did. And the smile. It was supposed to be, you know, sexy, but it wasn't. The thing of it was, we didn't pay no real attention to it, but when we come in today and hear about the homicide over on Jane, both me and Leo had the same thought. See, the guy was coming from the west and it was around the right time and all, so we just thought maybe you should know."

"Can you describe this man?"

"About six feet, wearing a tan raincoat and gloves."

"Black gloves," Arley added.

"And on his feet?"

"Sneakers."

"What kind?"

"Reeboks," Cummings said.

Arley looked at him, surprised at the detail.

"I just bought a pair so I noticed. They were black ones."

"What color were the wig and mustache?" Keenan asked.

"Red."

"Jesus," Donato said. "This guy's got a million of them."

"A red wig and mustache will be easier to track," Dina said. "What about his face?"

"There wasn't nothing unusual about him," Cummings said. "He didn't have a big nose or nothing like that."

"That was the thing," Arley said, "He was sort of ordinary-looking except for the wig and mustache."

"Good-looking?"

Cummings shrugged.

"Arley?" she asked.

"I don't know."

"Would you two be willing to be hypnotized to see if we can get a better description?"

"Yeah, why not?"

Dina stood up, said to Keenan, "Let's call Dr. Sherr, get her downtown. Can you guys reach Blackburn?"

"We can try."

She turned to Donato. "You don't have to come. I'll get in touch if we get anything. Where will you be later?"

"Mulberry."

They paid the check and walked out to the street. The cops had their car parked next to Vincent's, the front end on the sidewalk. Dina and Keenan got in hers.

As they pulled away, Dina watched Donato walking along Hester toward Mulberry. His loneliness showed in the droop of his shoulders. This man, her father, was going home to his mother, who could give him neither comfort nor joy. She wanted to cry, but as usual, this wasn't the place or the time. Big girls didn't cry, and neither did lieutenants in New York's Finest.

Twenty-one

The evening was warm, and people in Little Italy were on the streets: women sitting on stoops, sewing buttons on shirts, gossiping; men standing in small groups, drinking beer, talking baseball and horses; children skateboarding, matching pennies.

It made Donato recall his early childhood with longing: the days when his mother was normal and his father was kind to him, taking him to the Thompson Street Social Club. Fascinated, he'd watched the men playing pinochle and casino, and sometimes Papa would let him taste his wine. Even Steve loved him in those days, teaching him to throw a football, hit a baseball. He knew what was expected of him then, and it wasn't hard to comply. Life stretched ahead like a wonderful road of surprises. But now he was at the other end, the path shorter, the surprises unwanted.

A few buildings from his mother's, he thought he heard his name called but didn't turn around. He'd read somewhere that hearing your name called was your unconscious summoning your conscious self. He didn't feel like being fooled tonight.

And then it happened again: a woman's voice he recognized. When he turned, he saw Renata stepping out from a doorway across the street. A small hope, like a remote rush of wind, said she was there because she wanted him back. But he knew that was unlikely. Feeling uneasy, he crossed the street.

"I want to talk to you," she said.

She wore a pale yellow linen suit and a darker, yellow silk blouse. She looked lovely. "Is anything wrong?"

"I don't want to talk in the street. Let's go have a coffee." She started down the block from where he'd just come.

"Is something wrong, Renata?"

"Nobody's sick or dying, if that's what you mean," she said.

Donato recognized impatience and anger in her voice.

Once a drugstore, the Cafe Roma was on the corner of Mulberry and Broome. Marble tables, some square, some round, filled the place and only a few were unoccupied. Passing a display case filled with dozens of pastries and cookies, they chose a table in the back, near the espresso machine.

Renata put on her half-glasses, picked up the red menu, then shut it. "I don't know what I'm looking at this thing for, I know what I want. Do you want an eclair, cannoli?" she said absently, looking for a waitress.

Donato knew Renata would not tell him what was on her mind until they'd ordered. Finally, a young woman with a single long braid approached the table. Renata ordered a double espresso and a chocolate eclair. Donato wanted a decaffeinated cappuccino, but, as if that would make him seem unmanly in Renata's eyes, he ordered a regular one. He'd pay later for this stupid vanity.

"This is crazy," she said. "I haven't even had dinner."

"We could have dinner, if you like," he said automatically, then felt angry with himself for falling into old behavior.

"No. That wouldn't be a good idea."

They sat in uncomfortable silence, waiting for their order. Donato decided he wasn't going to ask her again what she wanted. Then suddenly he was certain he knew, and it made him feel sick. Renata was seeing another man.

He tried to gird himself for the revelation, determined not to show her his feelings. Imagining her with another man put him in a rage. Was it because he still loved her, or was it simply ego? The waitress came with their order. Donato emptied two packets of Sweet'n Low into his cappuccino, stirred it and licked the foam from his spoon.

Sipping her espresso, Renata stared at him over the rim of her cup. Then she said, "Dina told me the truth about Rich."

"Now listen, Renata," he said, "I know you're not going to understand why I kept it from you, but . . ."

"On the contrary," she said. "I understand perfectly. It's why I wanted to talk to you, Mike. I wanted you to know that I've been a hypocrite about this thing."

"I don't follow," he said.

"I haven't been completely honest with you."

It must be an affair. He wondered who the bastard was. As long as it wasn't anybody he knew, he thought he could handle it.

"I've been criticizing you for keeping things from me to protect me, when I've done the very same thing," she said, taking a bite of her eclair.

Maybe it wasn't a new affair. Maybe she'd been seeing some guy for years, even before things had gone sour with them. Hell, he had no right to complain, he'd had Sara, after all. Even so, if she'd been cheating and playing the saint, it pissed him off.

"What are you talking about?" he asked aggressively.

"I hope you'll understand. You should. I've kept this from you for the same reasons you kept things about Rich from me. I didn't want you to be hurt, Mike."

It had to be another man. Well, he was going to be the most sympathetic guy who ever lived. Not a negative word—nothing but patience and understanding.

"What is it?" he said more gently.

Renata took another bite of eclair and chewed, staring at him. When she'd swallowed, she wiped her mouth, took a sip of espresso, replaced her cup and said, "Rich wasn't your son."

Why was she saying this? Did she think it was funny? And then he knew it wasn't a joke. Renata was too angry for jokes. Her brown eyes were cold but honest. He hadn't spent a lifetime reading eyes not to know when someone was telling the truth.

"What are you talking about?" he asked flatly.

"Rich. And you. And me. He wasn't your son, Mike. I didn't know I was pregnant with him when we met, but I knew fairly soon after."

"Then who . . . ?"

"His name was Carmine Fugazo. I guess I had a thing for lower-class boys in those days."

He wanted to slap her.

"I really didn't have a choice," she went on. "There I was, twenty-two and pregnant, and there you were, eighteen and madly in love with me. Carmine wasn't about to marry me, that was for damned sure. You can imagine what my father would have done had he found out. It was bad enough that I married you and had Rich a month and a half before I should have."

"You never mentioned anybody named Carmine Fugazo," he said stupidly.

"Why would I?"

"You're lying." He felt as if he couldn't catch his breath.

"No, Mike, I'm finally telling the truth."

"Why now?"

"Because I realized that if I expected you to be honest with me, I should be honest with you." She finished her espresso.

He knew this was not her real reason for telling him now. She wanted to hurt him deeply, to destroy him. And she was succeeding.

"You never loved me," he stated.

"I didn't say that."

"Did you?"

She hesitated, looked down at her empty cup. "Yes. Yes, I did. For some crazy reason, I loved you right away. I wouldn't have married Carmine even if he'd wanted to marry me."

"Why are you doing this to me, Renata?"

"I told you, I just wanted . . ."

"Bullshit! Don't hand me that."

People at the table nearby looked over at them.

"I'd better go now." She tried to rise, but he put a hand on hers, kept her down.

"Tell me why," he repeated.

"All right. You want to know? I'll tell you. I'm getting even. I'm getting even for all the nights you kept me sitting up, waiting to see if you'd come home in one piece, or at all. And for all the hours you spent with your painting, the hours you wouldn't share with me. I could have lived with that. I understood that you needed to unwind. But then when we were together, you shut me out."

"I told you what was going on, told you everything."

"You told me facts, Mike. Facts about your cases. I never knew what was going on with you, *inside* you."

"What else?" he said, as if he wanted her to pile on the accusations.

"I'm getting even for the times you made me choose between you and my father, my family. And for all the hours you spent with Sara Nieminski that you didn't spend with me."

So she'd known about Sara. He thought he'd been so careful.

"And finally, Mike, I'm getting even because of what you did with Rich's death. For treating me like a child."

"Is that all?" he asked.

"It's all I can think of at the moment. May I go now?"

"You never said anything. You never told me how *you* felt."

"I didn't think you'd listen."

"That's not fair, Renata."

"What is?"

He didn't answer. After a few moments, she got up and left. He didn't watch her go. Unable to leave himself, he sat there staring at his glass as if it would give him answers, like a crystal ball.

Rich had not been his son. Was everything in his life something other than what it had seemed? There was no doubt in his mind that he'd loved Rich. He thought of the first time he'd seen him, the feeling of pure joy he'd experienced as he'd looked down at the wrinkled, red face, that monkeylike being. Would he have felt differently had he known that Rich wasn't his, didn't have his genes, his blood? At eighteen he probably would have.

But Dina was his. She was just like him. Stubborn and closed off, basically wanting to go it alone. People said they were alike, walked the same, had short tempers, loved being cops. But it was the inner core that counted, the little place deep within that no one else touched or knew. The hiding place.

Christ, who was he to hope she wouldn't get involved with Keenan or to criticize her for having a failed marriage, for not staying home with Cal? He hadn't made such a great job of it that he had the right to give her demerits or stars like he had with the old chart they'd made each year before Christmas when she'd been small.

She wasn't small anymore.

Dina.

His daughter.

His Lieutenant.

Ah, crap.

Donato paid the check, left Cafe Roma and headed up Mulberry. He passed his mother's house. Whatever shape she was in, he couldn't take the Contessa now. It seemed that his life was full of women he didn't want to see, couldn't deal with.

Walking west across Spring, he realized he was heading toward Barney's. Drinking was becoming a habit again. So what? His life felt like a barren place, and there seemed no other choice but to fill it up with booze. Besides, it would ease the pain.

When the phone rang on Monday morning, Donato was asleep on the couch. For the third night in a row he hadn't made it to bed, had slept in his shirt and pants. At least he'd removed his shoes.

It rang many times before he opened his eyes, knew where he was. And then it took another ten seconds to find the phone.

"Yeah?" Speaking hurt his head.

"Donato, it's Dina."

He looked at his watch. Six-forty-two. Something was wrong; she wouldn't have called him so early otherwise.

"Yeah?" he said again.

"We have another one."

He pulled himself up to a sitting position. His head ached, and his stomach felt sore. He wondered if he'd vomited.

"Where?" he asked.

"Six-three-six East Seventy-fifth. Kim Lyle's building."

Donato double-parked the Chevy a few doors away and threw his vehicle identification plate on the dashboard. He'd taken a quick shower, thrown on a fresh set of underwear and grabbed a pair of tan pants and a brown tweed jacket. His brown tie with thin yellow stripes was around his neck but untied. There hadn't been time to eat, and it was just as well. He wasn't sure he could hold anything down.

The cop at the door recognized him. "They're in the back, by the freight elevator."

A doorman Donato hadn't seen before was leaning against a marble column, his face white, like burnished bone. Donato nodded at him, held up his shield and turned right at the passenger elevators. He could hear the hum of the crowd coming from the back.

The view of the open elevator was blocked by the crush of people: Forensic and uniformed cops, the photographer, the ME. He spotted Dina, and they broke through the group.

The victim was in a green cotton dress; the skirt pulled up, bunched at her waist. White underpants were looped around one ankle. Her legs were bent at the knees and spread wide, as if she were

on display. The ubiquitous rosary, like an unwanted necklace, was wound round her neck, and the ring finger on the left hand was missing. As in the case of Sister Anne Marie, there was very little blood. She'd been killed elsewhere.

"Who found her?" Donato asked.

"One of the janitors."

They left the crowd and walked toward the passenger elevators.

"Do we have an ID?"

"Sister Mary Madeline. She teaches in Spanish Harlem at St. Boniface's but lives in an apartment with another nun. When she hadn't returned to the apartment by nine last night, the other nun called Missing Persons, who took down the information and said they'd have someone get in touch in the morning."

"And they didn't call you or . . ."

"It was a civilian employee who didn't put two and two together. Hard to believe but true."

"Where's Lyle now?"

"In his apartment. A cop's with him. I was waiting so we could question him together. I don't want Lyle to be able to make any of the task force if we have to set up surveillance."

"What else?"

"Two detectives from the One-Nine are checking the underground garage for unauthorized vehicles. Others are doing the usual, going over a ten-block radius for the weapon. Then they'll check every building and try to find his lair. He probably rented someplace nearby for his death house. After we talk with Lyle, Forensic will go through his place."

Donato pushed the up button. "What about the other tenants?"

"Everyone, except kids going to school, has been instructed to stay in their apartments. Cops are on every exit."

The elevator came and they got in. Donato said, "This is just what you and Dr. Stewart thought he'd do. Something outrageous, like putting a victim in an elevator where he lives."

"Not only where he lives. He left her in the elevator on his floor."

"Jesus Christ. Do you think it's Lyle?"

"I didn't, but this is too much of a coincidence. By the way, we can forget about the footprint being any help. Last night Lach, the super, admitted it was his. He went in there looking for booze, barefoot and drunk, just a few hours before we found the place."

"Are we sure he's not our guy?" Donato asked.

"Unfortunately, he checks out clean."

"Not smart enough anyway," Donato said. He pulled a handkerchief from his back pocket and wiped his face. The sweat kept pouring off him. Scotch sweat. He was swearing off.

The elevator opened its doors on P. Dina and Donato went into Lyle's apartment. A uniformed officer was sitting uncomfortably on one of the banquettes. He jumped to attention.

"Where's Lyle?" Dina asked.

"He went to the bathroom."

"Are you crazy?" she said, pulling her .38 from her leather bag. "Where is it?"

They all ran toward the back of the apartment, the cop in the lead. Donato's gun was drawn, too. He stood to one side of the door and banged on it with the side of his fist.

"Lyle, come out of there with your hands up."

The toilet flushed.

Donato tried the handle, but the door was locked. "Lyle, you hear me? Come out of there. Hands up."

They listened to the lock disengage, and the door slowly opened. Lyle, in pajamas and bathrobe, held his arms above his head. His upper lip was beaded with perspiration.

"What the hell's the matter?" he asked haltingly, looking at the three guns trained on him.

Donato put a hand on Lyle's shoulder and pulled him from the bathroom. He turned him around, pressed Lyle's hands against the wall, then patted him down.

"Okay," Donato said. "You can put your hands down."

They put their guns away.

Lyle turned around. His eyebrows creased across his brow in an angry line. "Just what the fuck do you people think you're doing? I mean, what the hell is going on here?" His abrasive voice rose and angled off into a squeal.

"Let's all sit down," Dina suggested.

"I want to call my lawyer," Lyle said.

Dina nodded. They filed back to the living room. "Officer," she said to the cop, "you can wait outside in the hall." She turned to Lyle. "Do you have any coffee?"

"Coffee? Coffee?" he asked, incredulous. "You have to be kidding."

"We haven't had breakfast yet," Donato said. He wondered if he'd be able to hold down coffee.

"You think I'm going to make you creeps coffee?"

"Mr. Lyle, you have to understand our position."

"Well, I don't," he said acidly.

"We didn't know what you might be doing in the bathroom."

"What the hell *would* I be doing? You shove guns in my face, search me and I'm supposed to understand *your* position. What about *my* position? First, you send that cretin cop in here and tell me I'm a prisoner in my own home, and then you practically kill me for taking a piss in my own john. Just what the fuck is going on, Lieutenant?"

"About that coffee, Kim." She gave him an engaging smile.

He stared at her for a few seconds. "I thought we went through all this the other day. Am I under arrest?"

"Of course not," she said. "We just want to talk."

"Look," Donato said, "you're not guilty of anything so you don't have anything to worry about, right?"

Lyle looked from Donato to Dina. She nodded in agreement. He pulled the belt tighter on his paisley robe, shrugged and led the way to the kitchen.

It was a fair-sized room with pine counters and cabinets. Lyle opened the refrigerator and took out a brown bag. He unfolded it and fished around inside, then dropped the bag on the counter, pulled out a drawer, felt around and finally freed a red measuring spoon from the back.

Donato moved closer to the opened drawer and scanned the contents. He reached in and took out a knife that had two steel studs in a polished wooden handle and a long, narrow blade, curved and sharp at the tip. He recognized it as a boning knife.

"You do a lot of cooking, Mr. Lyle?" Donato asked.

Lyle had his back to Donato while he filled up the container of a Braun coffee maker. "Some. Why?"

"My wife used to make a boned chicken. You ever try that?"

Lyle turned around and saw Donato leaning against the counter, the knife in his hand.

"What the fuck is this now?" Lyle asked. "What're you doing with that knife?"

"Funny," Donato said. "I was just going to ask you the same thing."

"I'm not allowed to have a goddamn knife in my knife drawer? Listen," he said, starting to push past Donato, "I'm calling my lawyer."

Donato put out his arm, stopped him. "You don't need your

lawyer, Mr. Lyle. Nobody's accusing you of anything. Why're you so jumpy?"

"I'm not jumpy. I just don't like what's going on here."

Dina put the container of coffee in the slot and then poured in the water. "Let's calm down, okay?"

Back in the living room, they sat on the gray banquettes, Dina and Donato across from Lyle. The coffee and blue willow cups were on a glass and chrome table between them. Lyle poured.

Donato drowned his coffee in milk and threw in two teaspoons of sugar. It wasn't his usual recipe, but it might sit better that way.

"Where were you last night, Kim?"

He looked at Dina, his brown eyes narrowed with suspicion. "Here. I was right here, working."

"All night?"

"All night."

Donato said, "Can you prove you were here all night, Kim?"

"Why should I have to prove I was in my own apartment?"

"Anybody call you?" Donato asked. The coffee was good, and it was staying down.

Dina's beeper went off. "Mind if I use your phone?"

"If you want privacy, there's one in the bedroom."

"Anybody call you last night, Mr. Lyle?" Donato asked.

Lyle took a swallow of his coffee. "I don't remember. Wait a minute. Yeah. A friend called."

Donato took out his memo pad. "Name?"

"Dolce Little."

"What time?"

"About eight-thirty."

"How long did you talk?"

"Ten, fifteen minutes."

"Anyone else call?"

"No."

"So after quarter to nine, you can't prove you were here."

"Look, I was here. I was working on a record cover."

"How late were you up?"

"Late. Five, five-thirty."

"You hear anything in the hall?"

"I had my radio on. Wait a minute. When I turned it off, I did hear something. At least I thought I did."

"What time was that?"

"It must have been about five-thirty, maybe quarter to six."

"And what exactly did you hear?"

"Just the sound of a door opening and closing."

"Could you tell what door it was?"

"It could only be one door. Lawrence's. I can't hear anything from the other two apartments on the floor."

Donato wrote the time and Lawrence's name in his notebook. "Can you hear the freight elevator when it opens?"

"No."

Dina returned to the room. "Message from Sue Deakins. She remembered the name of the prospective tenant for the Jane Street apartment." She handed Donato a piece of paper.

The name was Kirk Leonard. Another name with the initials K. L. "Would you mind if your apartment was searched?" Donato asked.

Lyle stood up, his face flushed with anger. "What the hell is going on here? You think I had something to do with those nun killings?"

"We'd like to search your apartment."

"You need a warrant for that, don't you?" His fists were balled at his sides.

"If you don't want to cooperate. But if you've nothing to hide . . ."

"Don't give me that shit. I know how you people operate. You could plant something here."

"I assure you we have no intention of planting anything in your apartment, Kim. What we want to do is eliminate you as a suspect," Dina explained.

"But why am I a suspect?" Perspiration dotted his face like beads of rain.

"A nun was found murdered on the freight elevator in this building early this morning. The elevator was on this floor."

"Jesus Christ."

They waited and watched while he took in this new information.

"Listen," he finally said, "who'd kill someone in an elevator in his own building? Do you really think I'd do that?"

"It seems unlikely," Donato said. "Unless the killer was taunting the police." Still, he didn't think Lyle was guilty. "Let us eliminate you, Mr. Lyle. Let Forensic in here to go over the place."

"Call your lawyer if you want, Kim."

"I don't have a lawyer," he said sheepishly. "Okay. They can come in. Can I get dressed?"

"Sure."

Donato went to the door and called in the cop; then he and Dina went out into the hall.

"Lyle heard Lawrence's door opening and closing at five-thirty this morning," he said.

"If it's true, that's very interesting. I didn't like Lawrence, did you?"

"No. And even if the K. L. initials don't fit, I have a gut feeling about him."

"So do I."

Donato knew that nine times out of ten gut feelings were right. And he also knew that five times out of ten gut feelings got you nowhere. Hard evidence is what you had to have. Still, something told him they'd never been closer.

He pushed the Lawrence bell.

Twenty-two

When the bell rang, Russ was shaving. He jumped and nicked his chin. While ripping a small piece of toilet paper from the roll, he admonished himself. He had to stay cool; it wasn't as though he hadn't been expecting the bell to ring. After all, everyone was under a kind of house arrest, and it only made sense that he'd be questioned. Especially since the elevator with the body had been found on his floor.

He stuck the toilet paper on the cut, then continued shaving. Andrea would answer the door. If she wasn't too groggy. He smiled at his image in the mirror. The night before he'd dosed her tea with a Seconal so she wouldn't hear him get up out of bed and leave the apartment.

By the time he got to the place he'd rented in Spanish Harlem, it was a little after eleven. Sister Mary Madeline had been tied up for seven hours. Being Officer Kenyon Larson had worked like a charm.

In the afternoon, he'd raped her and cut off her finger so he'd be able to put it with the others, knowing there wasn't going to be time to stash it away later. He would have preferred killing her then, but he couldn't have her going into rigor mortis. How would he have taken her out of the place stiff?

After killing her, he'd dressed her and covered her hands with gloves, then taken her out to the street, pulling his usual number, pretending she was drunk, in case anyone saw them. No one did.

He'd put her on the floor in the back of the rented car, stripped off his cop clothes for the ones he'd worn underneath and driven to his building. At that hour, there were no attendants in the garage. Luck on his side, he found the freight elevator on the garage level, so he put her inside, removed her gloves, arranged her and took off in the car again.

Earlier, he'd spotted a dumpster on One hundred and fourth Street between Lexington and Third, and he threw the uniform, which was in a brown paper bag, into it. Then he parked the car five blocks from his street and walked back. He went in through the garage and, in a change of plan, left the freight elevator on the G level. Fearing he might run into someone in the passenger elevator, he took the stairs all the way to his floor. It was good he was in such excellent shape.

Except for the sound of Kim Lyle's radio, which he could hear if he really listened, everything had been quiet. With his handkerchief over his finger, he'd pressed the button for the freight elevator. When he went back to his apartment, he noticed that Lyle's radio was off. He unlocked his door, shut it quietly and crept into the bedroom.

Andrea was lying on her back, snoring. He'd undressed, climbed into bed and gone to sleep. They'd both been awakened by a uniformed cop who'd told them they were to stay in their apartments but didn't say why.

Russ plucked the bloody piece of paper from his chin, washed his face, then dried it with a thick taupe towel. He ran a comb through his hair, sprayed it, put on a red polo shirt and tucked it into his tan pants. Looking down at his hands, he was dismayed by the sight of his nails. A stickler for detail, he'd let them go since he'd decided on the Officer Larson routine. It wouldn't look good for a cop to have buffed nails. The nails would have to wait, depending on whom he decided to be next. He couldn't help thinking that Dorothy would marvel at his performance. Too bad she'd never know. Her fault. The bitch.

That fucking lieutenant and that stupid sergeant he'd talked to the other day were sitting in his living room. Andrea was with them. He wondered why she hadn't come to get him. Were they asking her questions about him?

Smiling, he greeted each of the detectives, calling them by name. He could see that they were impressed by his memory.

The bitch was dressed in a slate-colored jumpsuit, the sleeves rolled up and buttoned back by a cloth tab, a maroon polo shirt underneath. On her feet were maroon leather small-heeled shoes. Her matching handbag was on the couch by her side. Russ thought she probably had a gun inside it.

Sergeant Donato's gun was holstered under his jacket. Russ could see it because Donato had his arm back, resting on a pillow. He sat in one of the easy chairs, glanced at Andrea, then turned toward the lieutenant and gave her a winning smile.

"So what's going on?" he asked. "Why are we being kept prisoners in our own apartments?" He thought it best to play it light at this stage, like Jack Lemmon.

Andrea said, "There's been a murder."

"A murder?" He sounded shocked, but the contrast from Lemmon he'd wanted just wasn't there.

The lieutenant said, "A murdered nun was found in the freight elevator early this morning by one of the janitors."

"My God, that's terrible," he said. He couldn't quite get a handle on who to be. All he could think of were people like Dan Duryea and Elisha Cook, Jr., for God's sake. Then he thought of Robert Taylor and tried to concentrate on him.

"Your wife was telling us that you both went to bed early last night."

"That's right." He looked at Andrea. "I think it was about ten, wasn't it, darling?"

Andrea gave him a strange look. "Yes."

"We've had the flu. Well, you remember. I was home sick the other day when you were trying to get in to see Kim Lyle."

"Did you sleep through the night, Mr. Lawrence?" the sergeant asked.

"Yes."

"So you didn't hear any strange noises?"

"No. Why would I?"

"The freight elevator was on our floor," Andrea said. "That's where the killer left it with the body in it."

"Really?" Robert Taylor was no good. He was angry at himself for not preparing better. "Well, it couldn't be anyone on our floor then. I mean, why would somebody put a body in an elevator and leave it on their own floor?" He noticed a muscle twitch in the lieutenant's jaw; the other one was chewing on his finger. He had them stymied. "If I were going to do something like that, I'd leave it on someone else's floor, wouldn't you?" He smiled at them, showing he was relaxed.

"Mr. Lawrence," the lieutenant said, "are you a Catholic?"

"No."

"Never have been?"

"No."

"Have you ever heard of anyone named Kirk Leonard?"

"No," he said. It felt as if his heart were pulsating irregularly, missing a beat. Somehow they'd found out that Pike's killer was named Kirk Leonard and suspected Leonard was also the nun killer. Bastards. Quickly, he reminded himself that they'd ask everyone in the building that question, that there was no way they could link Kirk Leonard to him.

"How about you, Mrs. Lawrence?"

"Kirk Leonard? No."

"Do the names Keith Laine or Kevin Lockwood sound familiar?"

Andrea said no and then they asked him.

He also said no, but their knowledge shook him. By dumb luck, they'd found the pieces, but did they have the pie?

"Where are you from, Mr. Lawrence?" the lieutenant asked.

"From?" He was still rattled.

"Where were you born, where did you grow up?"

Why did the cunt want to know that? Well, it didn't matter. This was all routine. He had to calm down, get more nonchalant, yet take it seriously. After all, they were talking about murder. "I'm from Michigan. I was born and brought up in a little town called Grand Haven. On the lake."

"Must have been nice," Donato said.

"It was all right." Why didn't they ask Andrea where she was from? But of course it was just men they were interested in.

"Have any brothers or sisters?"

"No."

"Your parents alive?"

If he were innocent, Russ knew he'd object to these questions, so he glanced at his watch, then said, "Forgive me, Lieutenant, but I can't see what bearing this can have on . . ."

"Just curious," Donato said.

Russ gave him a John Garfield smile. "Sergeant, what do you take me for? You people don't ask questions for no reason, just out of curiosity."

"Are your parents alive?" Dina asked again.

"My mother. She still lives in Grand Haven," he supplied.

"You see her often?"

"About once a year."

"Oh, Russ, we haven't been up to see your mother in at least three years."

He was furious. "Is it that long?" he said, trying to remain casual. "I didn't realize."

"Don't you get on?" Dina asked.

"I've been busy," he said, evading the question.

"You're a stockbroker, Mr. Lawrence?"

"And a financial consultant. Vice-president of my company."

"Which is?"

"Cornell/Pierce."

The lieutenant rose. "Well, I guess that's all, Mr. Lawrence, Mrs. Lawrence. Would you mind if we sent some people up to examine your apartment?"

"Examine?" Andrea asked apprehensively.

Laughing, trying for a little David Niven, nonchalant and in-the-know, Russ said, "Search, darling. That's what they mean. Don't you, Lieutenant?"

"What for?" Andrea asked, genuinely puzzled.

"It's one way of eliminating suspects."

"Suspects?" Now Andrea was appalled. "You don't honestly suspect *us* of this, do you?"

"They suspect everyone, don't you?" he said, wondering if he was sounding a touch too twinkly.

"That's right. Either you read a lot of mysteries, Mr. Lawrence, or you look at a lot of cop shows," Donato said. "You're well informed."

"I've read some nonfiction stuff. I don't watch television. I like to be up on things." He was pleased that they found him knowledgeable. "You can search the apartment if you want. We've nothing to hide." Cleverly, he'd moved the jar with the fingers out of the apartment two days before. There were no flies on him.

"Can we go to work now?" Russ asked.

"Yes," the lieutenant said.

Russ walked them to the door. "Is Kim Lyle a suspect?"

"As you said, Mr. Lawrence, everyone's a suspect," the sergeant answered.

He forced a chuckle. "Right. Well, I hope you get your man . . . or woman."

"We're fairly sure the killer's a man," the lieutenant said.

"And a pretty damn clever one, too," Russ added.

"Why's that?"

He looked straight in the detective's eyes. "Well, you haven't caught him, have you?" He hoped he hadn't gone too far.

Twenty-three

While waiting for the elevator, Dina said, "I want you to go to Grand Haven, Donato. We'll run a computer check on Lawrence before you go, but my bet is he'll be clean."

"No buffed nails," he said.

"Buffed nails can become unbuffed."

"True. What about Halliday? It's Monday." He ran a finger across his throat.

Dina smiled. "Funny thing, but old Hugh is out of town. He's in Denver. A convention. He won't be back for two days."

"I think they have phones in Denver."

"He won't do anything from there."

"Hope you're right. Grand Haven, huh? Talk to the mother, neighbors, check schools, that kind of thing?"

"Right."

"What about the way his wife looked at him when Lawrence called her *darling*?" Donato said.

"As if she'd never heard the word before. Not a happy marriage. Did you get the slip he made?"

"About putting the body in the elevator?"

"Lyle said, who'd *kill* someone in an elevator in his own building, but Lawrence said, who'd *put a body* in the elevator in his own building. Could just be a manner of speech, but I don't think so."

"Neither do I. This guy's slick, Dina."

"He thinks he's brilliant and we're dumb. He's everything Dr. Stewart said he'd be."

"But we need hard evidence."

"We'll get it."

The computer turned up nothing on Lawrence. He didn't even have an outstanding parking ticket. Dina was not surprised.

She sat at the head of the table, looked at her watch. Donato was at the airport now, about to leave for Michigan. She turned to Art Scott.

"We need to know where Lawrence was on the date of each murder. With the exception of Sister Honora, they all took place at night. Andrea Lawrence will probably alibi him for those, but see if you can pin down the afternoon of Sister Honora's murder."

Scott ran two fingers down each side of his generous mouth, as if smoothing a drooping mustache. "Should I check with his employer?"

"I'm going to interview Robert Cornell. Lawrence's secretary will know where he was at specific times. You see her."

"Or him," Scott corrected.

Dina looked Scott in the eye, smiled. "Or him," she repeated. If it was hard for her to keep politically correct, what could it be like for men? She'd have to go a little easier on them. She turned to Keenan.

"Detectives Kenin and Lewin, from the One-Nine, are on Lawrence now. I want you and Delgado to take over. Try not to let him make you. He's smart, and he'll probably be looking for a tail."

To Bobbin she said, "You and Lachman go home and get some rest because I want you to relieve Keenan and Delgado at midnight. Scott, you and Pesetsky take the eight-to-four tomorrow. Donato's out of town checking on Lawrence's background.

"Pesetsky, we need a picture of Lawrence. See if you can get one.

Try motor vehicle. He might not have one yet, depending on his expiration date."

"Are we going to get a surveillance truck?" Pesetsky asked.

"I've put in for one, but that may take a day. When we get it, we can take a picture from there, get copies made and take them around with other mug shots to the costume and makeup places. Ellen Nehr should see it first. And show it to the cab driver who hit Sister Honora.

"We're dumping the first composite drawing because of two cops from the Sixth, Cummings and Arley. I want them to get a look at Lawrence to see if he's the one they spotted in a mustache and wig the night of Pike's murder. They were hypnotized and came up with very detailed descriptions, but that doesn't mean they'll make him without his disguise. Same goes for Nehr. But let's try. Any questions?"

"Yeah," Delgado said. "What do we have on Lawrence? What makes you think it's him?"

"I'll be honest with you. We don't have anything hard. But the address Keith Laine gave when he rented the nun's costume was the same as Russ Lawrence's. Then, of course, this morning's murder happening in Lawrence's building. And—hold on to your hats, folks—a search of the Lawrence apartment turned up a can of Final Net hairspray."

"Puts his ass in the running," Bobbin said cheerfully.

Lachman said, "Let's take what we can fuckin' get."

"What about Kim Lyle?" Bobbin asked.

"Neither Donato nor I can see him as the killer, but we have some detectives from the One-Nine on him."

"How about Lyle's alibis for the dates in question?"

"The man never sees anyone. He works at home alone. We could book him on suspicion, but I think it's a waste of time." She wanted to say she *knew* it was Lawrence, but there was no percentage in pushing feelings when she didn't have facts to back them up.

"What about other people in the building?" Scott asked, snapping his gum.

"So far no one else is under suspicion."

Lachman said, "Basically, what you're sayin', Lieut, is that as far as Lawrence is concerned, it's circumstantial, huh?"

"That's right. But we'll *get* something on him. That's what this is all about. I won't kid you—it isn't going to be easy. And we don't have the rest of our lives. Halliday is out of town, but when he comes back he's going to take us off this case if we don't come up with the goods. Then somebody else will get the credit for the work we've put in." She knew how that would gall them.

"Fuck that," Pesetsky said.

"I'm not bustin' my balls so some jackoff can hot dog it around town," Scott said.

"Hey," Bobbin said, "your ass ain't even been on this case from the beginning."

"What the fuck's that mean?" Scott asked, irritated.

"Nothing," Bobbin said.

"Come on, man, spit it out."

"You don't have to get so fucking outraged when you're taking the place of somebody else who was in on it from the beginning. That's all it meant, friend."

"Listen, meatball, it ain't my fault that McCarthy got blown away, so don't go twisting things, okay?"

"That's enough," Dina said. "We don't need infighting here. We need to work together more than ever before. There isn't going to be any individual glory. We're a team and we've one aim in sight. We want to get this killer. That's all any of you should be thinking about. This bastard is smart, but we're going to stay on his ass until we have him. There's just not going to be another murder."

They mumbled agreement.

"That's it then. Report to me individually. You can get me through my beeper or at either of these two numbers." She gave them her home number and Renata's, then stood up, signaling the end of the meeting.

"Scott," she said, "I'll ride down to the Cornell/Pierce offices with you."

"You got it, Lieut."

"Keenan," she said, "I want to talk to you." She noticed Bobbin and Lachman exchange a knowing look and wondered if everyone on the task force knew. Did it matter? She was happier when people didn't know anything about her, but that was impossible in a situation like this. A task force was tight, like a family . . . like *some* families. "I'll catch up with you downstairs, Scott."

When the others had gone, Keenan took her in his arms and pulled her close. "I can't stop thinking about last night," he said.

She sucked in her breath. "Not now, Bobby."

"Now and all the time," he said.

She wanted to pull away, knew she should—this wasn't smart.

But she found she couldn't and moved in on his mouth, kissed him, her tongue feeling his.

He ran his hands down her sides, his fingers dancing over her breasts.

She pulled away. "I can't take this."

"Me either. When will I see you?"

"I don't know."

"Funny, that's what I thought you'd say. Midnight's too late, huh?"

"It is tonight. I promised I'd spend some time with my son. I'll be uptown at my mother's."

"I could pick you up."

"Don't tempt me, Bobby. We both need sleep."

"You're right." He touched her cheek, ran the back of his fingers over her skin. "Just know that whenever you think of me today, I'm thinking of you. And that I'm thinking the same thing you are."

"You sure know how to make a woman crazy."

"Good," he said.

They went downstairs together, through the muster room and out to the back, where they parted. Scott was leaning against a green Plymouth, clipping his nails.

"Who's driving, Lieut?"

"You," she said. She didn't want to think of anything except Keenan until she got to Cornell/Pierce. She was pretty sure it was the only luxury time she'd have all day.

The offices of Cornell/Pierce were on Pine Street in the financial district.

Robert Cornell's office was predictably masculine: walls of dark paneling, serious brown leather furniture, a massive walnut desk. He was in his mid-fifties, tall, trim and handsome with a shock of white hair. His eyes were a shrill blue. He wore a somber gray suit, a pale yellow shirt, a paisley tie and block-cut gold cufflinks in the shape of his initials.

"This morning," she began, "a body was found in Russ Lawrence's apartment building. I assume you're aware of the murders of nuns that have taken place in the last week or so?"

"Yes, I've read something about that." He opened a black leather box on his desk, took out a cigarette and lit it with a gold table lighter. He didn't offer her one. Smoke leaked from his nostrils.

"This was another one." She watched Cornell's eyes. Nothing registered.

"Forgive me if I'm a little slow, but I don't see where you're going. What has this to do with Russ?"

"That's what I'm trying to find out." She smiled sweetly at him, wondering what Donato would have said or done if he'd been here. "How long has Mr. Lawrence been with your firm?"

Leaning his head back against his leather chair, he closed his eyes as if he needed to concentrate, then slowly opened them. "About eight years."

"Do you know him well?"

"I think so."

"What kind of man is he?"

"Well, he's talented, industrious, honest . . . a worthwhile person."

"Do you like him?"

The question seemed to startle Cornell. "I . . . of course, I like him."

"Are you sure?"

He killed the cigarette in a large, oval glass ashtray. "What in hell does that mean?"

"Do you know his family?"

"Of course. Andrea's a charming and intelligent woman, and the girls are delightful." He appeared exasperated.

"Are you married, Mr. Cornell?"

"Yes."

"Do you have children?"

"Yes. Might I ask . . ."

"Do your two families get together?"

"Yes."

"Often?"

"It depends what you mean by often."

"Once a month?"

"Well, no. But we don't see anyone that frequently," he said defensively.

"How frequently do you see people? The same people, that is."

"What are you driving at, Miss . . ."

"Lieutenant Donato," she supplied.

"I'm a busy man . . ."

"I assure you, my questions are important," she said smoothly. "How about the other members of your staff, the other vice-presidents, let's say. Do you socialize with their families more frequently?"

"My wife doesn't care for Russ Lawrence," he said suddenly. "Is that what you want to know?"

"Why not?"

"She finds him . . . difficult."

"In what way?"

"I don't know. Ask her."

"I will. Where can I reach her?"

"In Italy," he said silkily. "She's in Palermo today." He smiled, as if he'd won a point.

Dina did not return the smile. "This isn't a game, Mr. Cornell. Why doesn't your wife like Russ Lawrence?"

He stared at her for a moment, his invasive blue eyes boring into hers. "She finds him cold."

"That's all?"

"He makes her uncomfortable."

"How?"

"She's never been able to explain it."

"And you, Mr. Cornell, do you find him cold?"

"I find him just fine. Men don't look for the same things in other men as women do."

"Do you know where Russ Lawrence was on the afternoon of April third?"

"If he wasn't here, I probably don't know where he was. He's not exactly an office boy, you know. He comes and goes, has his own clients."

"Would you know if he was here?"

"I might if we had a meeting or something."

"Could you check on that?"

Cornell leaned forward, snapped on his intercom. "Helen, where was I on April third in the afternoon, from . . ."

"Two to five."

"Two to five."

"Just a minute, Mr. Cornell," a nasal voice said.

Dina and Cornell waited, looking at each other warily.

Helen came back on the intercom. "You had a meeting at two with Mr. Baehr and Mr. Isaacs. It lasted until four-thirty. Then you left."

He snapped off the intercom without thanks. "So, I don't know where Russ was. Why don't you ask him?"

"I will. In the eight years that he's worked here, has there ever been any trouble, anything that bothered you about him?"

"No."

"You think he's a perfect business partner then?"

"No one's perfect, Miss Durato."

She didn't bother correcting him, sure he'd said it on purpose. "What would you say his faults are?"

"I'd have to think about that."

"Would you say you have a friendship with Mr. Lawrence?"

"Aside from our business, Russ Lawrence and I don't have that much in common. That doesn't make him a murderer."

"You seem very protective of him."

"I'd be the same about anyone you people were harassing."

"I'm not harassing Russ Lawrence. Every employer of every person in the Lawrence apartment building is being asked the same questions," she lied.

"Why don't I believe you, Miss Donato?"

"Only you can answer that." She stood up. "What I don't understand, Mr. Cornell, is why you've chosen to take such an aggressive tone with me? All you had to do was to answer a few questions, but you've made this interview difficult, and I don't know why."

"You're a detective, figure it out."

"I will." She held out her card. "If you think of anything else I should know."

He took it and, without glancing at it, set it on his desk.

Heading toward the elevator, Dina tried to understand Cornell's hostility. Her best guess was that he found Lawrence odd but didn't wish to reveal this.

She'd seen it over and over: the detective voicing what the interviewee feels, and the interviewee fearful of compromising the subject in some inadvertent way. It was impossible to believe that someone you knew could commit a murder. Even when the evidence was in, or the suspect had confessed, friends and family tried to find rationalizations.

As she waited for the elevator, Lawrence walked by, turned abruptly when he realized who she was and came back.

"What the hell are you doing here?" he said through his teeth.

"I was talking to Robert Cornell," she answered pleasantly.

The elevator arrived, and Lawrence got in with her. There were others in the car, so he said nothing. Dina watched the vein in his temple pulse as he stared straight ahead. When they reached the lobby, he took her roughly by the arm and led her off to the side.

She wrestled free. "Just what do you think you're doing?"

"I'd like to ask you the same thing?"

She faced him, her hand hovering near her handbag. It was unlikely that he'd do anything violent, but she preferred to be ready. "I could have you arrested for assault, Mr. Lawrence."

"Assault? I hardly call *that* assault." He raised his chin defiantly. "What were you doing talking to Cornell? You were talking about me, weren't you?"

"Yes," she said simply, hoping to upset him more.

"You have no right to do that."

"I have a right to interview anyone I wish. Why does it distress you so much?"

"This is harassment."

"If you haven't done anything, I don't understand why you'd be so disturbed by my talking to Mr. Cornell."

"Don't give me that haven't-done-anything routine, that if-you're-innocent business. What did you ask him?"

"Good-bye, Mr. Lawrence." She turned away.

He grabbed her by the shoulders and spun her around, clutching both her arms in viselike holds. "I demand to know what you said to him."

His strength surprised her, but she broke his grip with a backward swing of her arms, reached into her purse and withdrew her gun. "Make another move toward me, Mr. Lawrence, and you're a dead man."

Lawrence looked around frantically. "Put that away."

"I'm giving the orders. Not you. If you don't want me to arrest you for assaulting an officer, you'd better back off, get in the next elevator and disappear."

He stared at her, then slowly backed up. "You won't get away with this," he warned.

She returned the gun to her bag and watched him until the elevator doors closed. Smiling, she left the building. It was going to be easier than she'd thought. Russ Lawrence couldn't take pressure. If no hard evidence turned up, a war of nerves would do very nicely. He hadn't begun to know what harassment was. She couldn't wait to tell Donato.

Dina sat across from Cal at Burger King, his favorite restaurant. Sometimes just looking at him dazzled her and filled her with a joy that made her forget her problems. Loving a child was a special feeling, unlike any other. You couldn't fake it.

"You catch that bad guy yet, Mom?"

Talking about her work with Cal made her uncomfortable. She didn't want him to know how rotten the world could be, wanted to shield him as long as possible from ugliness. Shades of Donato.

"Not yet," she said.

"I wish you'd catch him soon."

"Me, too."

Cal stuck a french fry in a pool of ketchup, then shoved it in his mouth, leaving a whisper of red on his cheek. "Everybody says you're never going to."

"Who's everybody?"

"The kids at school. I told them you'd get him. I said you always get the bad guys."

Should she tell him that she *didn't* always get the bad guys? "You shouldn't dwell on this stuff, Cal."

He laughed. "But, Mom, it's on television and everything. Don't you want me to stick up for you?"

For a second, she was pleased that her son was defending her against her enemies, then realized they were other ten-year-olds. "I appreciate it, honey, but I'd just as soon you didn't get into discussions about that kind of thing."

"Yeah, okay." He drank some milk.

Dina wanted to scoop him up in her arms, hold him close.

"Want to know why else I wish you'd catch him?"

She'd just taken a bite of her burger so she waved her hand, indicating he should go on.

"I want to come home and live with you again."

"Don't you like being at Grandma's?"

"Sure. But it's not the same, know what I mean?"

"I do," she said. "It won't be too much longer."

"Like what?"

"You mean how long exactly?"

"Yeah."

"I don't know, honey. But you'll be back home soon." That much was true because Halliday would remove her from the case if she didn't break it.

"I get scared, Mom. Sometimes I think you're not ever coming back."

"Oh, Cal. You think I'd just leave you at Grandma's forever?"

"Mom, gimme a break, okay? I'm not a baby anymore. Don't you think I know you could get killed?"

When he was four, he'd had nightmares that she'd abandoned him somewhere, disappeared. Liam had insisted Cal was distressed because he knew she might die on the streets. The nightmares had stopped as suddenly as they'd begun. She hadn't realized Cal still suffered from this fear. But why wouldn't he? And why hadn't she known?

"I'm sorry, Cal. I didn't know you worried about that."

He shook his head as if she were hopeless. "Well, what do you think, Mom? Sure I worry. Who's going to worry if I don't?"

Dina understood. Besides the normal anxiety about his mother being a policewoman, he felt he should take on the extra burden of worry Liam would have had. It would be pointless to try and assure him nothing would happen to her. He was right—he wasn't a baby anymore.

"I'm so sorry you have to have these feelings, Cal. But I understand why you do. I had them about Grandpa."

"You did?"

"Sure. Sometimes when he'd say good-bye I'd wonder if I'd ever see him again."

"Me, too. You know that expression, here today, gone tomorrow? Well, that's what I feel about you. You're here today, but you could be gone tomorrow, just like that." He snapped his fingers and grinned. "You didn't know I could do that, did you?"

"No. That's great." She smiled.

He sobered immediately. "It's not funny, Mom. I don't know what I'd do without you."

"The case I'm working on now won't put me in any physical jeopardy."

"What about Judy?" he accused.

"Nothing like that is going to happen now. We know who the killer is and . . ." She hadn't meant to say that. "Cal, listen. I don't want you to tell anyone that, do you understand? It's very important that this is kept a secret."

"I won't say anything, Mom, honest. But who is it?"

Suddenly, there was something so familiar about this, and then she remembered a time when Donato had slipped in front of her, saying he had a case narrowed down to two suspects, refusing to tell anything more, no matter how she'd begged. She recalled how furious she'd been that he wouldn't confide in her, trust her.

"If I told you the name of the person," she said, "it wouldn't mean anything to you, Cal."

"So then why not tell me?"

She couldn't refute his logic and understood his need to know. "Do you promise you won't tell anyone, not even Tony."

"Not even Tony. I swear."

"I'm going to treat you just like you're one of the cops, okay?" She knew that would please him.

He smiled up at her, his bright brown eyes glistening with anticipation. "I cross my heart, Mom." And he did.

"His name is Keith Laine." It wasn't a total lie, and when the truth came out, she'd explain to him about Lawrence's aliases.

"Keith Laine," he whispered, as if it were a mantra. "How come you don't arrest him if you know it's him? Oh, I bet I know. You don't have any hard evidence, right?"

"Right." She couldn't help smiling.

"I've decided, Mom. I'm going to be a cop, too, when I grow up."

It hit her hard. The idea frightened her. She didn't want her son to be a cop. If he was, she knew she'd worry all the time. And now, she thought, we've come full circle. Thank God this wasn't something that had to be decided today.

"Great," she said, "that's a swell idea." Maybe if she pretended to approve, he'd have to rebel. It was worth a try.

After Cal had gone to bed, Dina and Renata sat in the dining room, having a cup of tea. They were talking about an opera Renata had seen recently, when she suddenly changed the subject.

"I told your father that I knew the truth about Rich's death." She held up her hand before Dina could object. "You never said it was a secret."

Dina wondered if she'd omitted the warning on purpose, so that her mother *would* tell him, hurt him.

"And I told him something else," Renata added. "I might as well tell you, too."

When Renata revealed that Rich was not Donato's son, and only her half-brother, Dina felt as if she were caught in the middle of someone else's life. Everything seemed so unreal. And then a great sorrow for Donato overwhelmed her.

"Didn't you *ever* love Daddy?" she asked.

"Oh, God, yes. I loved him right away. He made me realize how little I'd felt for Carmine. I loved your father more than you'll ever know."

She thought her mother's eyes were misty. "Then why can't you make it up? Don't you know how much he loves you?" She felt like Cal, pleading for her and Liam to stay together.

"There've been too many lies between us, Dina. Mine as well as his. You can't go on building a relationship when there are so many lies."

"All of a sudden it sounds like 'The Gift of the Magi' to me. Each of you lied to protect the other."

"Since when have you become so forgiving?"

Since I've fallen in love, she thought, and a stab of panic cut through her. "I don't know. It just seems that you had so much together. Why throw it away now? It's not as if there were another person involved. Do you know how unusual it is for a man to be faithful to his wife these days? Donato never even looks at another woman."

Renata was silent.

So there was yet another thing she didn't know about her parents. Whatever it was, she didn't need to know. "I guess if you could stay together you would. Liam and I would have, too. I'm sorry, Mom. I shouldn't push you."

Later, Dina sat in the living room, flipping the pages of *Newsweek*, not really reading anything. When the phone rang, she grabbed it.

"So here I am in the metropolis of Grand Haven, Michigan," Donato said. "I'm staying at a Howard Johnson's." He gave her the phone number. "They're congratulating Jim and Mary. It's up on the marquee. Wonder what Jim and Mary did? Probably stayed married. That's a real achievement these days."

"Are you okay?" she asked.

"Fine. Just dandy."

"What's your plan?" she asked.

"I'm seeing the principal of Lawrence's high school tomorrow morning, and then I'm going to drive out to the mother's house. She was in the phone book, but I decided not to call in advance. What have you got?"

She told him about Lawrence cracking when she was at his office.

"That's good news," he said. "That's real good news."

"I thought you'd like it."

"Well, I guess I'd better get some sleep. I should be back tomorrow night unless I turn up something that keeps me here longer. Where will you be?"

She knew she'd be with Bobby, but she didn't want to let Donato know. "You can try me here or at home, or Central will beep me."

"Well, I guess that's all," he said.

She wanted him to know about her talk with Renata, to tell him she knew how hurt he must be. She wanted to stop the polite performance they'd fallen into, constantly circling each other like two wary dancers. But they were frozen in their positions. When they said good-night, and Dina replaced the phone, she'd never felt so inadequate in all her life.

Twenty-four

Donato hated motel food, so he drove in his rented Ford to downtown Grand Haven. There was always at least one restaurant serving breakfast in small towns.

The main street, which had an island cutting through its center, like the one on Park Avenue, ran about eight blocks, and there were shops on the side streets as well. His jacket collar turned up against a brisk wind, he walked along, checking out the stores, looking for a place to eat. A sign reading The Bookman caught his eye, but it wasn't open yet. He'd come back later.

A few doors down he found a crowded place called Vivian's, a luncheonette with four booths, eight green vinyl stools and a counter. He took a seat at the end. A woman in her mid-forties, hair bleached the color of dandelions, a swatch of crimson on her lips, was taking the orders.

Donato glanced over the small menu and decided on pancakes. It had been a long time since he'd eaten them; he figured he might as well get something nice out of this trip. The woman took his order while she poured him a cup of coffee.

Russ Lawrence had probably left Grand Haven right after high school and wouldn't be remembered unless he'd done something worth remembering. Still, you never knew; some little thing could turn out to be important. That was why a trip like this had to be taken.

The counterwoman put a plate in front of Donato stacked with six large pancakes.

"I can't eat all that," he said automatically.

"Eat what you can, and what you can't eat we'll can," she replied and smiled at him. "My mother always used to say that."

"I've never seen so many pancakes," he said.

"You should've ordered a short stack then," she admonished gently. "Half as many. Just eat what you can . . . don't worry, I'm not going to say it again," she said in her midwestern twang, moving off to pick up two fried eggs with bacon.

Donato slid wedges of butter between the cakes, then soaked them with maple syrup. He remembered as a boy having pancakes at a friend's house, the mother asking which he wanted, butter or syrup? With seven children, they couldn't afford to serve both to each person. He'd chosen the syrup, but he'd only gotten one shot at it and hadn't enjoyed the breakfast.

Thinking of that now, he piled on three extra pats of butter and doused the cakes again until a pool of syrup collected around the edge of the plate. This was not, he reflected, any way to diet. He'd start again when he got back to New York.

As he made his way through the pancakes, the counterwoman refilled his coffee cup for the third time.

"Are you Vivian?" he asked.

"Yeah. How'd you know?" she said, seeming delighted.

"I just took a guess. Have you had the place long?"

"About fifteen years. Didn't like working for somebody else, so me and another girl opened up in 'seventy-two. It was called Carol and Vivian's then. But she got pregnant and couldn't handle it, so I bought her out. I like it even better without a partner. I have to make a decision, I make it."

"You grew up here?" Donato asked. "Went to the local high school?"

"Graduated, too, but I'm not telling what year," she said coquettishly.

She was older than Lawrence, but he tried the name on her. "It's sort of familiar, but I'm not sure. Why?"

"I'm trying to locate him. I owe him some money."

"Try Sparky Howard down the cigar store on the corner. He's about eighty-five, lived here all his life, knows everybody. He'll know your Russ Lawrence all right."

"Thanks," Donato said. "Nice talking with you, Vivian. Best pancakes I ever had." And they were.

"That's 'cause of the cinnamon Curly puts in the batter, but don't let him know I told you his secret."

"Mum's the word."

Outside, Donato glanced at his watch and saw that he had more than an hour until his appointment with the high school principal, so he decided to check out Sparky Howard.

The store had a black marble soda fountain and four metal stools with real leather seats. Magazines lined one wall, newspapers piled on a shelf below. Candy, gum, cough drops and cigarettes were stacked by the cash register. Paperback books revolved in a rack near the back, and other shelves held school supplies and stationery. A locked glass case displayed watches.

Sparky Howard was a big man who'd been well-built in his day, but now he was stooped, his enormous belly hanging over a pair of khaki pants held up with a peeling plastic belt. His head seemed too small for his body, and the fringe of white hair didn't help. He wore a faded Hawaiian shirt and a Saint Christopher's medal on a silver chain around his neck. His fingers were nicotine-stained by the unfiltered Camels he smoked, and he had a slight tremor in his hands and head.

"Sure do remember Russ Lawrence," he wheezed. "One of them loners 'til he got hisself a girlfriend senior year. Never could understand why she went with him. Not that she was no great beauty, you understand, but she was kinda pleasant-looking even if she did wear glasses. Anyways, that was the worst mistake that girl ever made." Smoke spewed from his mouth like fog.

Donato, sitting at the counter and drinking his fifth cup of coffee, felt a rush of adrenaline. "What kind of mistake?"

"She disappeared. Just went out one night to choir practice and never showed up, never come home."

"What happened to her?"

Sparky shrugged, his big shoulders hugging his long droopy earlobes. "Nobody knows. Just disappeared into thin air. 'Course I think he done it."

"Who?"

"Well, Lawrence, a course, ain't that who we're talking about here?" he said. "You sure you're a detective?"

"What is it you think he did?"

"Killed her. Killed her and buried her somewheres, or maybe weighted her down and rowed out onto the lake, dropped her in. Couldn't drag Lake Michigan, you know. It ain't no pissy little pond or nothing. Most people come here from New York, see the lake for the first time, they're real surprised. They ain't used to lakes that look like oceans."

"Why do you think he killed her?"

"First off, he was this weird sonofabitch. I never liked him coming in here, but I had no reason to keep him out, so I seen him enough to know something was wrong with him."

"Did the police think Lawrence killed her?"

"Sure did. But Chief Stone, he couldn't prove nothing. Boy's mom swore he was home with her the night Dorothy disappeared. That didn't hold no water with me. Lawrence and his mom were tight as two ticks. She thought the sun shone out of his asshole." He stubbed out his cigarette and lit a new one.

"What about Lawrence's father?"

"Ken?"

Donato felt his gut tighten. *Ken* Lawrence. K. L. Jesus! "So what about Ken Lawrence?"

"Died in a fire in his shop. Never did know what caused it. You ask me, I say Russ might've done that too. Wouldn't put nothing past that boy. He didn't get along with his dad. Didn't get along with nobody 'cept his mom and then Dorothy, leastways for a while."

"They never found Dorothy's body?"

"Nope."

"Were there any other suspects?"

"Well, they hauled in a few weirdos, checked out some bums from Muskegon and Grand Rapids, even looked into a few types down at Ann Arbor, but nothing ever come of it. Nothing would. They could look all their lives, all over America, and nothing would come of it 'cause Russ Lawrence done it and that's all there is to it. Hey, how come you're asking about him? He done something else?" His eyes kindled with interest.

"Maybe."

"Must be. I guess you wouldn't be asking questions about a guy who done nothing. I wasn't born yesterday, you know."

"Didn't think you were," Donato said affably. "What was Dorothy's last name?"

"Welles. Real nice family, too. Mrs. Welles never got over it. Wouldn't say the father did either, but he don't show it the same way the mother does. Then a man wouldn't, would he?"

"Do they still live here?"

"Sure do."

"Do you think they'd talk to me about Dorothy?"

"If I told 'em to."

"Could you do that?"

"Could. But the question is *would* I?"

Donato knew a hint when he heard one and reached for his wallet, put a ten on the counter. "Would you?"

"Why not?"

"I have a ten o'clock appointment with the principal of the high school. Maybe I could see the Welleses around eleven-thirty?"

"You're wasting your time with Ostrander. He's only been principal for about two years. Brought him in from Grand Rapids."

"There might be something in the records or a teacher who knew Lawrence."

"Only two teachers left there who would've known him. Raymond Lieberman teaches biology, and Penny Crawford, music teacher."

"I'll talk to them," Donato said. "I'd appreciate it if you'd call the Welleses, Mr. Howard."

"You can call me Sparky." Walking behind the counter, he ran his hand along it and scooped up the ten without stopping, heading for the phone booth at the back of the store.

If Donato could believe this man, and he tended to, Lawrence had killed before. Maybe twice. And if twice, maybe more. The excitement of finally getting close made him feel high.

He couldn't wait to tell Dina.

Sparky Howard had been right. Ostrander could tell him nothing. But Lieberman and Crawford both remembered Russ Lawrence clearly. The pictures they painted echoed Sparky's: Lawrence was weird, a loner, and might have killed Dorothy.

The photograph of Lawrence in the yearbook shocked Donato. The boy looked very little like the man he'd met. Pudgy and unattractive, he would have been called a drip in Donato's day. Underneath his picture, it said, *Remembered for his quiet manner, his interest in school and for being the first one in homeroom every day.* That wasn't much to say about someone, Donato thought.

After seeing Lawrence's photo, the one of Dorothy Welles didn't surprise him. She was a plain girl with steel-framed glasses and light-colored hair held back with a clasp. Underneath her picture, it said, *Remembered for her love of animals, her participation in Math Club and her nice smile.*

Donato was ten minutes late for his appointment with Mr. and Mrs. Welles. He'd gotten lost. They lived in a large house in a populated area near the lake. Sparky had told him it wasn't far from where Lawrence's mother lived.

George Welles greeted Donato and led him to a screened porch decorated in bright colors and crowded with plants.

Welles, in his late sixties, had a medium build without a dollop of fat. White hair stuck out in tufts over his ears, and his eyes, a dull, flat gray, were puckered at the corners. He wore neat brown slacks and a white sport shirt.

"Mother will be down in a moment," he said. "It's still hard for her to talk about Dorothy, so I hope you'll be gentle with her."

"Of course."

"It's been twenty years, twenty-one this summer. Probably seems to you like we should be over it by now, but you can't know what it's like to lose a child."

"I lost my son," he said. *My* son, he thought.

"Ahh. Then you do know. How old was he?"

"Twenty-three. He was a policeman, too."

"Ahh," Welles said again, nodding. "Well, it's the worst thing that can happen to you, losing your child. I can't think of anything worse, can you?"

For a moment, Donato thought that finding out your child is not your child might be worse, but then knew it wasn't. "Nothing worse," he agreed.

"We had eight children. People thought it would be easier for us because we had seven left." He laughed in hushed little pants. "How could people think that?"

Wondering if the Welleses were Catholics, Donato felt a flicker of excitement.

Welles went on. "Children aren't like tennis balls. You lose one, so what, you have seven more." He looked up toward the door. "Ahh, here's Mother."

Welles went to his wife and led the frail woman back to the

chintz-covered couch as though she were a delicate prize.

"This is my wife, Winifred," he said. "We call her Freddie, don't we, Mother?"

Mrs. Welles smiled wanly. Behind glasses, her glittering green eyes announced she was on medication. Arched eyebrows were thin and pale, and two tiny spots of color, as if she had a fever, highlighted her cheekbones. A white powder had collected in her wrinkles. Her gray hair was newly permed. She wore a pale pink polyester pantsuit, a white blouse and beige sandals. Sitting close to her husband, her small frame tucked under his arm, Donato thought she looked like a ventriloquist's puppet.

Trying to put her at ease, Donato smiled. She seemed not to notice. "I know this must be painful for you, Mrs. Welles, but it's important that I talk to you about Russ Lawrence."

She didn't acknowledge what he'd said in any way.

Uncomfortable, he continued. "Can you tell me what he was like?"

Welles said, "We never liked him. It wasn't just that he wasn't Catholic—we could have dealt with that. There was something else . . . something off about him. But he was Dorothy's first boyfriend, so we didn't want to put a damper on things. See, Dorothy wasn't a beauty like Anne—that's our third daughter. Anne had boys after her from the time she was eight. Isn't that right, Mother?"

Mrs. Welles nodded dutifully.

"Anne took after Freddie, but Dorothy looked like me, more's the pity. Still, she got my brains, too. Not that it would've been a bad thing to get Mother's brains," he quickly amended.

"Can you be more specific about Lawrence?"

"I wish I could," Welles said. "He was polite enough, always stood up when Mother came in the room. Had a good handshake. Did well in school. Never got into trouble like some of them. But there was just something about the boy . . ."

"He was a bastard," Mrs. Welles interrupted in a rasping voice.

Her outburst shocked Donato. She hadn't moved, still leaned against Welles, eyes sparkling but unseeing.

"Why do you say that, Mrs. Welles?"

Raising her head as if it were made of cement, her mouth trembled before she spoke. "Because . . . because he killed my Dorothy."

"How do you know?"

"I *know*," she said, tapping her heart with two fingers.

"We all knew," Welles said. "No one else could've done it."

Donato said, "But his mother swore he was home with her all that night."

"That was a pure and simple coverup," Welles replied. "I might have done the same myself in her shoes. You just don't know what you might do. We all want to protect our kids."

Welles's words hit home. Had he really been protecting Renata and Dina from the truth about Rich, or was it Rich he'd been shielding? "Yes," he said. "We all do."

Welles turned to his wife. "Sergeant Donato lost his boy, Mother. He was a policeman, killed when he was twenty-three."

Donato quickly brought the subject back to Lawrence. "So you believe his mother lied?"

"Absolutely."

"A lying bitch," Mrs. Welles snarled with that same shredded sound.

"Now, Mother. We have to be charitable."

She pulled away from him, her face contorting. "Why? Why do we have to be charitable? Russ Lawrence murdered our Dorothy, and his mother saved his neck by lying. Maybe you two would have done the same, but not me." She gave each of them a canny, merciless look. "I wouldn't lie to protect a murderer. She couldn't face that what she'd raised was a monster. A killer. She lied for herself as much as for him."

I raised a drug addict, Donato thought. It didn't matter whose blood son Rich was. I raised him, and when he went wrong, I guarded his image . . . and my own. His stomach heaved. Beads of sweat broke out across his face like hives. He gripped the sides of the chair and tried not to think about Rich.

"I was told that Dorothy was his first girlfriend and that he seemed to really care for her. Do you think that was true?"

"I suppose so," Welles said reluctantly.

"Then why would he have killed her? What was the motive?"

"She'd broken off with him," Mrs. Welles said.

"When?"

"A few days before . . . before he killed her," Welles supplied.

"Why did she break off with him?"

"Because of her decision," Mrs. Welles said. "Dorothy was going to be a nun."

Donato called Dina the moment he got to a phone, but he couldn't reach her. He left a message that he'd check in again or that she could try his motel later. It was already one o'clock, and he still had Lawrence's mother and the ex-chief of police to see. He didn't like being away from New York, but if he had to spend another night in Grand Haven he would.

Donato was convinced that Russ Lawrence was their man. But he was troubled by the fact that he'd gotten away with Dorothy's murder. If it was true that Lawrence couldn't take pressure, why hadn't they cracked him at the time of Dorothy's murder? That was one of the questions he wanted to ask ex-Chief Stone.

Turning into Holcomb Road, he climbed a hill and at its crest saw the name on the mailbox. The cedar-and-glass house was set back from the street and surrounded by trees. Farther up, Donato could see another house, and he assumed that the lake lay beyond. He'd drive down there after his meeting with Adele Lawrence. He didn't want to leave Michigan without seeing it.

As he walked up the drive, the sound of waves made him think of his childhood, days on the beach at Riis Park. Suddenly he felt old. In five years, he'd be sixty. He remembered he'd had a hard time turning forty, then the shock of becoming fifty. He hadn't realized how young he'd really been. But sixty. Jesus. He recalled what his old partner, Tom Bianchi, used to say: "If you're lucky, you grow old." Bianchi hadn't been lucky. He had. So what the hell was he grousing about?

Donato stood in front of the screen door looking into the house. The bright day precluded lights inside, and it was hard to see anything. He tried knocking on the door frame, but the sound was negligible. Then he spotted a set of reindeer bells hanging next to the door and rang them. After a few moments, he heard someone coming downstairs. And then a woman appeared.

"Mrs. Lawrence?"

"Yes."

"I'm Sergeant Donato from New York City and . . ."

"Has something happened to Russ?" Her hand flew to her mouth as if to cancel her question.

"No. Your son is fine."

"Oh, thank God." She let out a sigh. "Then what are you doing here?" she asked suspiciously.

"I'd like to talk to you." He held up his ID.

"Why?"

"I'd like to talk about your son."

"But you said . . ."

"He's a suspect in a case I'm working on."

"I see." If she was surprised, she didn't show it.

The downstairs was mostly open space, living and dining room combined. Off to the right was a kitchen, and beyond that the bedrooms. The walls were nearly all glass, and the feeling of being in the woods was overpowering. They sat opposite each other, he on a green couch, she on the edge of an easy chair.

Adele Lawrence was in her early sixties. She was a slim woman, and her skin stretched across the bones in her face like a canvas. She was heavily made up. Her eyebrows were penciled in, curving over sharp, indigo blue eyes, like her son's. A dark red lipstick was applied generously to her mouth, and rouge colored her cheeks. An ash blonde wig, styled short, cupped her ears. She wore tight lavender silky slacks and a bright blue blouse with a scooped neck that Donato thought was a bit too young for her. A lit cigarette burned between two fingers, each adorned by a ring. She was just this side of sleazy.

"Mrs. Lawrence, I'll get right to the point. I've been told that when Dorothy Welles disappeared your . . ."

"Oh, not that old saw," she said contemptuously. "Honest to God." She shook her head and reached for a glass on the table beside her. The contents were brown. Donato guessed rye.

"Your son was with you the night she disappeared?"

She downed the drink. "As I've said, perhaps one million times, yes, he was here. What's this have to do with Russ now?"

"I'll get to that. Mrs. Lawrence, I had a son who died under peculiar circumstances, and I lied about it because I didn't want it revealed that he was a drug addict. I understand lying for one's child."

"What's that supposed to mean?" she asked frostily.

"It means that I can understand why you lied about Russ being here that night."

"I don't think I have to listen to this, do I?"

"You can ask me to leave. But your son is in trouble, Mrs. Lawrence, and the more cooperative you are with me, the better it'll go for him," he lied.

She got up, walked to the kitchen, picked up a liquor bottle. "Want a drink?"

"No thanks. Tell me about Dorothy Welles."

She went to the refrigerator, got out some ice. Her back to Donato, she said, "Dorothy was a sweet girl." She slammed the door shut.

"You liked her?"

"Very much." She dropped the cubes in her glass and filled it, not bothering with water. "I was so happy for Russ."

Donato didn't believe her.

She sat back down in her chair. "She was his first girlfriend. He was very shy back then." The corners of her mouth twitched.

"How do you feel about Andrea?"

"A darling girl."

"When did you see your son last?"

"Four or five months ago, I think." She took a hefty swallow of her drink.

"He came here or you went there?"

"He came here. They all did. Have you met my granddaughters? Adorable," she said in a flat voice.

"Russ says he hasn't visited you in three years."

She blinked rapidly. "You must've misunderstood him."

"Your husband died in a fire, I understand."

"He was drunk, out in his workshop. He set himself on fire." She couldn't hide the loathing in her voice.

"Why did your son and Dorothy Welles break up?"

"They didn't. Where'd you get that?"

"Did you know she was going to become a nun?"

"That's absurd. She and Russ were going to be married after they graduated from college."

"She was going to become a nun. Everything was arranged."

"Who told you that?"

"Her parents."

"They're lying."

"Why would they do that?"

"They hated Russ."

"Why?"

"Because he wasn't Catholic."

"What do you think happened to Dorothy?"

"Someone must've gotten her."

"Gotten her?"

"Abducted her. Killed her. Why are we going over all this old ground? Why are you here?"

"Because your son has been killing nuns in New York City."

"How dare you say that? Russ wouldn't hurt anyone."

"He would and he has."

"I think you'd better leave."

"Your son has killed four nuns and a man in the last two weeks," Donato said bluntly.

"If that's true, why don't you arrest him?" she asked with a slight, insolent smile.

"We need your help, Mrs. Lawrence. Your admission of Russ's guilt in the Dorothy Welles murder would make it easier for us."

"In other words," she said, picking up her drink as if she were at a cocktail party, "you haven't got any evidence that Russ's done anything. It's the same thing all over again. A person like you can't stand a person of Russ's quality. You're jealous so you try to destroy him. It was the same thing with his father and Chief Stone. Small minds."

"Don't you care that he's killed all these people?"

"I'm sure none of them is worth one iota of what Russ's worth."

"And that would make it all right for him to kill?"

She cocked her head, smiled scornfully. "I wouldn't expect someone like you to understand."

"He did kill Dorothy Welles, didn't he?"

"Yes. At least I assume he did," she said, as if she were talking about an everyday occurrence.

Donato was surprised. He hadn't expected her to admit it.

"He went out that night at about seven-thirty and didn't come back until three in the morning. George Welles called about eleven to ask if Russ was home. He sounded distressed. I sensed I should say Russ was here asleep and hadn't been out. I wasn't about to let him get in trouble because of *her*.

"When he came home, I was waiting up for him. He told me that if anyone asked I should say he'd been home all evening. I told him I already had. He was pleased." She sipped her drink.

Donato waited for her to go on, and when she didn't, he said, "Did he say where he'd been?"

"No."

"You didn't ask?"

"No."

"Didn't you care that he'd killed an innocent young woman?"

"I wasn't about to have his life ruined."

"Jesus," Donato said. "Why did you tell me this?"

She shrugged. "Why not? What can *you* do?"

It would be her word against his. Useless.

"Now, will you please leave?"

At the door, he said, "Did Russ kill your husband, too?"

"Who knows?" she answered cavalierly.

Donato wheeled around and made a hasty retreat down the steps and across the driveway to his car. He backed out and headed toward the lake. There were a few houses on the water, but most of them, he remembered from a story in the *Times,* had been beaten down by the rising water level and fallen into the lake. He pulled up and turned off the motor.

He was shaking. Resting his head on the wheel, he thought that in all his career he'd never met anyone like Adele Lawrence. Her gelid core was frightening.

Lifting his head, he stared out through the windshield. It was big, all right. He watched the waves licking the sandy shore. So now he knew for sure. And he still had nothing. The case, like the lake, was deeper and crueler than it appeared on the surface.

There was still Chief Stone to see. He didn't expect much, but he couldn't go back to New York without talking to the man. And the sooner he found him the sooner he could leave. He wanted to get as far away from Adele Lawrence as fast as he could.

It had taken him the rest of the day to catch up with Stone. Wherever Donato went, Stone had just left, as if he were forewarned and running from him. Finally, Donato found him in a bowling alley.

Sitting on one of the benches, Donato nursed a Coors and watched Stone and his friends. The man had agreed to talk to him when he finished bowling. That was three games ago.

Stone was big, built like Donato. He was in his sixties, had thin white hair and a full white beard. Donato wondered if he ever played Santa Claus. His brick red face and the broken veins across his nose told Donato he was probably a drinker.

Finishing his beer, Donato placed the glass in a holder at the side of the bench and glanced at his watch. It was after nine. By five-thirty he'd faced spending another night in Grand Haven, re-engaged his room and spent an hour at the bookstore, buying a John le Carré. Now he was anxious to start reading it and wished to hell Stone would finish up.

He still hadn't reached Dina and that was driving him nuts. The information he'd gathered was too good not to share. He'd considered trying to contact another task force member, but then realized he wanted the kick of telling Dina himself.

Stone rolled a strike. There was a loud cheer from his team, some backslapping and handshaking, and then Stone announced the drinks were on him. He and his team went to the bar. When they'd all been served, a toast was made, and after they'd clicked glasses, Stone walked over.

"So what can I do for you, friend?"

"I'd like to talk to you about the Dorothy Welles case."

"So I heard." He sat down and smiled morosely. "News gets around quick in a town like this, especially when you talk to the human telegraph, Sparky Howard."

"Then you know I'm interested in what you can tell me about Russ Lawrence."

"A psychopath."

"No reservations about that?"

"None." He took a slug of his drink, looking as if he were tasting manna from heaven.

"You're convinced Lawrence killed Welles?"

"You bet. You?"

"I'm convinced. Adele Lawrence admitted to me that he wasn't home that night."

"Me, too. She's some piece of work, isn't she? She liked telling me he wasn't home the night Dorothy disappeared. Got a kick out of it. Later, I went back to her, tried to get her to say it all again because I was wired, but she was too smart for that. Acted like she was pure as the driven snow and that sonny boy's shit smelled like roses. God, what a fucking maniac. I think she's proud of him for doing it."

"You might be right. Why were you avoiding me today?"

Stone smiled. "Usual reason one person avoids another. I didn't want to talk to you."

"Why not?"

"It gives my ulcer babies when I got to think about Lawrence. That cocksucker cost me my job. Not to mention what he did. I knew Dorothy Welles. She was a real nice girl. Known the Welleses all my life." Stone raised his glass, which looked dwarfed in his huge hand. "So what's Lawrence done?"

"We think he's been killing nuns in New York City."

Stone's eyes opened wide, and he slammed his big hand on his thigh. "I'll be a goddamned asshole. You know, I saw something about that on TV, and I got this kind of nagging feeling inside, but I couldn't figure out why. Sure. That was it. Mr. Prick, plying his trade again. I'll be goddamned." He turned toward Donato. "You going to get him?"

"I hope so. Why didn't you?" He tried to keep any accusatory sound out of the question.

Stone slumped against the bench. "I didn't have a thing to bring the grand jury, friend. Not a fucking thing. No body. And he had his alibi. Then there was this one witness who claimed she saw Dorothy go walking off with an older guy who had a beard."

Donato told Stone about the disguises the killer had used. "Do you think he was wearing a fake beard even back then?"

"Why not? They got an MO, they got an MO. Never too young to start. At the time, I thought the witness saw wrong or was just trying for some publicity."

"Who was it?"

"Forget it. She died about five years ago. Burst appendix. Son of a bitch! It never occurred to me Lawrence might've been wearing a disguise. But listen, you get him, anything I can do to help, you just ask."

"Thanks. What did the Welleses say when you told them Adele Lawrence admitted Russ wasn't home?"

"I didn't tell them." He ran a hand over his beard, pulling it into a point. When he let go, it sprang back to its natural shape. "What the hell for? It would just make them more upset. Made me feel worse knowing that bitch lied and there was nothing I could do about it, so I figured it would make them feel worse. What'd they need to know that for on top of everything else? I didn't tell anybody."

Donato understood. "We have reason to believe that Lawrence might be sensitive to pressure. Did you try to crack him?"

"Yeah, sure. But I only had a week. He left for college a week after she disappeared. Went out to Harvard and that was that. Didn't even come home for vacations. I never saw the bastard again."

"Christ, what a lousy break."

Stone warmed to the sympathy. "You said it. After Lawrence left, I tried running down this and that, but everything was a dead end because Lawrence did it. There really wasn't anywhere for me to go. They 'removed me from my position' three months later."

"Lousy break," Donato said again. He wondered what would happen to him, and to Dina, if they couldn't crack Lawrence. "What do you think he did with the body?"

"Buried it. I looked for her but no dice. For years. Whenever I could, I went digging. 'Course there's the woods all around Adele Lawrence's place, which I couldn't hack up, but I don't think he buried her there. That would've been too risky. No. I think she's buried someplace else. Those first few years it wasn't so hard, but then this place started getting built up, all the new houses down by the lake and all. I had to quit it. Took up bowling instead." He smiled ironically. "That's about all I can tell you, friend."

"Think he might crack under pressure?" Donato stood.

Getting to his feet, he shrugged. "Might. I always felt if I'd had him longer I could've got to him."

Donato shook his hand and thanked him. "Do you ever play Santa Claus?" he asked, just before leaving.

"Every year since nineteen sixty-six."

Back at the motel, Donato stretched out on the bed and opened his book. Before he could begin, the phone rang. It was Dina. Excitedly, he told her what he'd learned. She responded as he'd known she would, and by the time they hung up, they were laughing together, filled with the possibility of victory, feeling like a real team.

He loved Dina deeply, though he'd sometimes denied it, turning her off to protect himself from her anger. The trouble was you couldn't be selective about something like that, so he'd shut down completely. But now life was slowly bubbling up inside him again, and he was beginning to take pleasure in things, like buying the book.

Donato thought of Renata. He'd walked away without a fight because he'd been dead inside. Now he felt differently. He couldn't wait to get home. He'd put his pride behind him and fight for his marriage, his wife, his beautiful Renata. And he'd talk to Dina again, tell her how much he loved her, how goddamn proud of her he was. And together, he and Dina would get Russ Lawrence. That came first.

Twenty-five

Pesetsky had taken a photograph of Lawrence from the surveillance truck, and the cabbie who'd hit Sister Honora picked out his picture from four others as the passenger who'd left the scene. It was not hard evidence, but it boosted the morale of the task force. Ellen Nehr had been unable to recognize Lawrence's photograph. After all, she said, he'd been wearing a mustache and wig. No one at any of the makeup houses was able to identify Lawrence.

The drawing the police artist made from the description Arley and Cummings had given was redone minus the beard and wig. The face he came up with was a very good likeness of Lawrence.

Art Scott reported that Andrea Lawrence definitely vouched for Lawrence's whereabouts on the nights of Sister Anne Marie's and Sister Mary Madeline's murders. She reiterated that Russ couldn't have left in the middle of the night because she was a light sleeper.

No one had seen Lawrence leave his building on either of those nights.

The Lawrence children and their mother had gone out to East Hampton on the Wednesday of Sister Honora's murder. The doorman remembered that Lawrence had come in about eight-thirty that night. According to him, and the doorman on the midnight-to-eight shift, Lawrence didn't leave again Wednesday night, which could rule him out for the murder of Sister Angelica.

Lawrence's secretary said that on the afternoon of Sister Honora's murder, he was lunching with a client at Fraunces Tavern and did not come back to the office that day. The client stated they parted around two-forty-five. His whereabouts between two-forty-five and eight-thirty were unaccounted for.

The night of Pike's murder, Andrea Lawrence said he had an appointment to go over accounts with a Howard Polk. Polk denied Lawrence was with him that night.

At last they had solid questions Lawrence would have to answer.

After her run-in with him at his office, Dina decided to make the appointment casual, giving him a choice of coming into the precinct or meeting elsewhere. She hoped that by adopting a laissez-faire attitude, she could lower his defenses and throw him off balance.

Lawrence chose the North Star Pub at the South Street Seaport. The place was a fairly good replica of an English pub: a dark wood bar with a brass foot rail running its length, Victorian ale pulls, ceiling lights, wainscoting, a tile floor, etched glass and the daily specials chalked on blackboards.

Dina, Donato and Lawrence sat at a wooden table near a window on the South Street side, drinking ale in imperial pints. It was two-thirty, and the lunch crowd had thinned.

"This place is a favorite of mine," Lawrence said. "It makes me feel like I'm back in England." He smiled at Dina, showing he'd forgiven her for the other day. "A lot of people don't like the Seaport. They think it's a ripoff. But I like going out on the pier and watching the water. Sometimes I go up on the second-floor deck, take a cup of coffee and sit for hours watching the boats in the harbor. I try to imagine what it must have been like a hundred years ago. Peaceful, don't you think?"

Dina had no intention of getting into a lyrical discussion of the nineteenth century with him. "Mr. Lawrence, on April third you had lunch with a client, a Mr. Trojan, at Fraunces Tavern."

"Was that April third? I can't keep track of dates." He sipped his ale.

Dina went on. "You parted at about quarter to three. Where did you go then?"

"I presume I went back to my office."

"But you didn't," she said.

"Really? Well, then I have no idea," he answered easily.

Looking into his eyes, she remembered Ellen Nehr's description of the eyes of the man who'd bought the nun's costume: *blue ice.* "How about later that night? Around midnight."

"I was probably sleeping. Check with my wife."

"We did."

Lawrence's mouth twitched. "What did she say?"

"She was away. In East Hampton."

"That's right. Well, then, you'll just have to take my word for it." He smiled unctuously.

Donato said, "How about the night you were going over accounts with Howard Polk?"

"What about it?"

"Mr. Polk says you weren't with him."

Lawrence took a sip of beer, patted his mouth with a cocktail napkin. "Howard must have forgotten."

Lawrence seemed to be enjoying himself. Dina wondered if she'd underestimated him.

"How did you feel when Dorothy Welles dumped you?" Donato asked.

There was only the slightest flicker in his eyes. "I see you've been checking on my background. If so, you know I've nothing to hide."

"Who said you did, Mr. Lawrence?" Donato wondered if his mother had warned him. "You were involved with Dorothy Welles in your senior year in high school, weren't you?"

"Yes. My heart was broken when she disappeared," he said.

"What do you suppose happened to her?"

He shook his head, looking sad. "I don't know. I suppose someone must have gotten her."

Donato was struck by Lawrence's expression, the same one Adele Lawrence had used. "Gotten her?"

"Killed her."

"And done what with her body?"

He shrugged. "How should I know? I suppose he buried her in the woods."

"Is that what you would have done?" Dina asked.

"What else could you do with a body? Either that or throw her

[311]

in the lake. But bodies usually surface in water, don't they?" he asked, unruffled.

Donato said again, "How did you feel when Dorothy broke up with you?"

"She didn't."

"How did you feel when she told you she was going to be a nun?"

"She didn't."

"How do you feel about nuns, Russ?" Donato said.

He sat up straighter in his chair, leaned toward them and spoke softly. "I'll tell you how I feel. I feel you're harassing me, and you don't have any right to do that."

This was more like it, Dina thought. "We're simply asking for your help with the case."

"I don't see how my feelings about nuns can help you."

"You're right," Donato said. "It's immaterial. Except that you might not feel too kindly toward them since Dorothy Welles broke off with you when she decided to become one."

"I suppose you got that nonsense from her parents. They might have believed Dorothy was going to become a nun, but trust me, she wasn't," he said lasciviously.

"Did you have sex with her?"

"Yes."

"Intercourse?"

"Naturally."

"The night you told your wife you were going to meet with Howard Polk, what did you really do?"

"Oh, well," he said lightly, "I guess I might as well tell you. This is a little embarrassing, but I have an enormous sexual appetite and my wife just isn't enough."

They said nothing.

"I had sex that night."

"And on the afternoon of the third?"

"Yes, then too."

Dina knew he was lying. "The same woman?"

"No."

"What were their names?"

"You can't expect me to tell you that."

"I think you'd better," Donato said.

"If I'm a suspect, then you'd better read me my rights," he cautioned coolly.

"We'll read you your rights," Donato said, "when we arrest you."

Lawrence's eyes flashed. "What do you mean, *when* you arrest me?"

Donato laughed. "Did I say *when*? Sorry. I meant *if.*"

"I think I'd better get in touch with my lawyer."

"By all means," Dina said.

"Then I *am* under suspicion?"

"We're trying to eliminate people from your building, Mr. Lawrence. If you can give us an alibi for the times we've mentioned, then . . ."

"What the hell were you doing checking into my past?" he asked abruptly. "Are you checking into the pasts of everyone in the goddamned building?"

Dina weighed it for a moment, then said, "Just key people."

He sat back in his chair, his head cocked to one side, eyeing her. "Truthfully, I don't give a damn what you investigate because I'm guilty of nothing. There's not a mark on my life anywhere. I loved Dorothy, and it damn near broke my heart when that little girl disappeared. Some people tried to make it look like I did something to her, but they couldn't prove a thing. When Dorothy disappeared, I was home asleep. You should ask my mother about it."

"I did," Donato said.

His face was impassive. "Well, then you know."

"Yes," Donato said smoothly. "I know."

The two men stared at each other; then Lawrence broke the gaze, saying, "And did you check on my record at Harvard, too?"

They had. His record there was perfect. And they'd learned that sometime during his sophomore year he'd changed, become more outgoing, lost weight, started dressing differently and turned into quite a ladies' man. But there was nothing else.

Donato said, "What were the names of the women you were with on April third and . . ."

"All right," Lawrence interrupted, "I don't like admitting this, but . . . I prefer whores."

Dina smiled. "So you can't identify the women."

"I only know that one called herself Mary and the other Betty."

Dina had to acknowledge he was quick. Mary and Betty were two of the most common names whores used.

"Do you remember where they took you, Russ?" Donato asked.

"No."

"What area were you in?" Dina asked.

"Eighth Avenue in the forties."

"Both times?"

"Yes." He glanced at his watch. "I'm running a little short of time."

"Would you be willing to take a lie detector test, Mr. Lawrence?"

"Of course not. Don't insult my intelligence. I'm not about to put myself in jeopardy for no reason. Everyone knows polygraphs aren't accurate." He finished his beer. "I really do have to leave now."

"Would you allow us to have a sample of your hair?"

"For what reason?"

"So we can eliminate you."

"I think I'd better speak to my lawyer."

"How about a lineup? Would you appear in one?"

He stood up. "I'm not discussing anything further until I speak to my lawyer." He started to walk away.

"Just a minute, Mr. Lawrence. I'd like to show you something." Dina reached in her bag and withdrew the composite drawing. She held it out to him. "I'd like you to look at it and tell me if you've ever seen this man before."

Hesitantly, he took it.

They watched as he stared at the excellent likeness of himself. Slowly, he lowered the drawing, stared at them.

"Is this a joke?"

"No joke," Donato said.

"Where did you get this? I mean, how was it done?"

"Various people who saw the killer described him to the police artist."

"People saw the killer?" he asked, his voice steady.

"Yes."

"You mean there were witnesses to the murders?"

"To other things." Dina noted a twitch in his cheek.

"Other things," he repeated. "Well, what do you expect me to say to this?" He waved the drawing in front of their faces.

"Can you identify the man?" Donato asked innocently.

"Don't be an ass. Do you think I don't recognize myself?"

"We thought it looked like you, too," Dina said.

Angrily, he balled up the drawing and threw it on the table. "I don't know what you're trying to do to me, but it's not going to work. I know my rights. You'd better back off or you're going to be in deep

[314]

shit." He turned on his heel and walked through the pub and out onto Fulton Street.

Keenan and Delgado were waiting outside, ready to stay with Lawrence until four, when Scott and Pesetsky would take over. They'd been instructed to let Lawrence make them. It was time to play on his nerves.

Russ called his lawyer. He told him that he was being followed and capsulized the meeting he'd had with the Donatos that afternoon. The lawyer told him to ignore what was happening, that if the suspect looked like Russ, they had to question him. He said the police were probably desperate and the composite drawing was all they had. When cops had hard evidence, they didn't play games, the lawyer said.

It didn't make Russ feel any better. What had that cunt meant when she'd said there were witnesses *to other things*? He felt sick. They knew it was him. Still, his lawyer was right. If they really had something, they wouldn't be fooling around. They'd arrest him.

But what were they doing talking to his mother and the Welleses? And probably that stupid cop, Stone. Well, they couldn't prove anything. No one could. No one would ever find Dorothy. And when his mother died, he'd keep the house. They'd use it once in a while so no one would become suspicious. There'd be no chance of anyone digging up Dorothy in the woods.

But that didn't change things now. Now he was being watched every minute. How long would they keep that up? It couldn't go on forever. Even so it made him nervous, edgy. He didn't like being watched.

When he'd left the pub, they'd followed him, the thin woman and the good-looking guy. And when he'd exited from the office that day, the man with the ponytail and the other one had been there. He knew them all by sight now. If he went out after midnight or before eight, it was the skinny guy with the red mustache and the black man. He didn't like it.

He called his lawyer the next day and complained again about being followed. The lawyer said he'd see what he could do. Russ wasn't sure how much longer he could take someone dogging his every move. And the worst part was that it was throwing off his schedule.

Sister Elizabeth, of St. Andrew's School, was supposed to be next. But how could he do it if he was never alone? And he needed to do it just like somebody else might need a drink. That was what it was like for him now. He hadn't thought it would become a compulsion, but it had, and it angered him that he was losing control. Nothing was more important than being in control of yourself, your situation. Now it was as if he had no choice.

Goddamn you, Dorothy Welles, he thought. It was all her fault. She'd killed the nuns and Pike as surely as if she'd stabbed them herself. If it hadn't been for her, none of this would have happened, and he wouldn't have a bunch of stupid cops watching him night and day.

Wait a minute. They *were* stupid. He could outwit them easily. What was he getting so worked up about? He'd shake them and go after Sister Elizabeth anyway. He had to or he was going to come apart.

Donato thought they should arrest him, put him in a lineup. Dina believed they should wait until they had more. They argued about it and finally Dina agreed, conceding that there might not be more.

Lawrence's lawyer, Manny Ghent, was livid. A youngish man of medium height, he wore a four-hundred-dollar suit, Bill Blass shirt, Yves Saint Laurent tie and Gucci shoes. Thick glasses sat precariously on a prominent nose. He used a Filofax organizer and sported a Movado watch.

Ghent, Donato, Dina and Ellen Nehr were waiting in the viewing room for the assistant district attorney. Nehr knew the drill now, but, having failed the last time, she was nervous.

"Your ass is going to be in a sling," Ghent said to Donato. "This is a respectable man you're picking on, not some junkie punk who's got nobody to protect him. I don't know what the fuck you people think you're doing."

"We'll see," Dina said.

He ignored her completely and kept addressing Donato. "You've been harassing my client. Following him. We could sue."

Donato wanted to tell him to go ahead but kept his mouth shut. "Why don't we see what happens in the lineup."

"The lineup," Ghent said, shaking his head. "This is outrageous. A man like my client in a lineup. You people must be crazy."

Donato knew Ghent was just making noise.

"What the hell are we waiting for?" Ghent asked, looking at the black-and-gold face of his watch. "Time is money, something you people don't seem to understand."

"We're waiting for the ADA," Dina said.

Still ignoring her, he said to Donato, "If the ADA can't get his ass here on time, then he shouldn't have the job."

Donato was pissed. "Mr. Ghent, why are you telling me about the ADA? I didn't say anything to you about the ADA."

"What?"

"Lieutenant Donato was the one who said we were waiting for the ADA."

"What?"

Donato sucked in air, took Ghent by the shoulders and turned him around to face Dina. "The lieutenant is the one to talk to if you have any complaints."

Ghent looked from Dina to Donato and back again. "What the hell are you talking about?"

"I'm telling you that I'm not in charge, Mr. Ghent. The lieutenant's in charge, and this is the lieutenant," he said, gesturing toward Dina.

Dina smiled sweetly at him. "Can I help you?"

Ghent was confused. "I . . . I . . . look, you shouldn't be putting Russ Lawrence in a lineup. You're making a mistake."

"We think not. Mr. Lawrence has no alibi for two occasions on which murders were committed."

"He was fucking hookers," he said, turning back to Donato.

"So he says," replied Dina.

"Do you honestly expect this man to be able to find these whores again?"

Donato pointed toward Dina.

"What? Oh." Ghent swung around to face her.

Dina shrugged. "If he can't, then he has no alibis."

"And what about when the other nuns were murdered? He has alibis for those. Doesn't that rule him out?"

"His wife gave those."

"Perfectly admissible in court."

It was true, and Donato knew the ground they were on was as shaky as the alibis themselves.

The door opened, and Chuck Mignon came in. "I hope you really have something this time, Lieutenant," he said nastily.

"I think we do," she said. "I'll go out, Donato."

"You sure?"

She nodded.

Donato ordered the lineup to begin, then turned to Nehr. "Take your time. Don't worry about anything."

The men filed in, all wearing black mustaches and black wigs. Lawrence was number 6. Nehr stood at the window, twisting a handkerchief in her hands. Time passed. Finally, she turned to Donato, tears in her eyes. His heart sank.

"I don't know. I'm sorry."

"That cuts it," Ghent said.

"Wait a minute." Donato put a hand on Nehr's arm. "Are you sure? Have you looked closely at their eyes?"

"They're so far away. And through the glass. You know what I mean, Mr. Donato?"

Mignon said, "This is untenable, Donato. I can't keep running over here for these stupid fuckups. I'm talking to Halliday." He slammed out.

Ghent said, "You'd better release my client."

Donato nodded. He felt as if he were going down the tubes.

Halliday was back. Dina decided that the only chance they had was to ignore him: not take calls, be hard to find. They had to put the pressure on Lawrence and do it fast and hard. But the extra help they needed would be blocked by Halliday. Dina called a meeting of the task force and told them the situation. They all agreed to stay on the case and remain incommunicado re Halliday. But they were still short of personnel.

Then Dina had an idea. "We all have snitches," she said. "How do you think they'd respond to working surveillance?"

"If the price is right," Pesetsky said.

Everyone knew the right price could be a little blackmail, a few promises and maybe a twenty.

They contacted their snitches and, except for Bobbin and Lachman, who had to stay on Lawrence, met them in Augie's bar. There were thirteen of them, including Florida Bob and Vinnie Sellito, all of them eager to do the job. Taking cars to chop shops, selling ludes and pot, duping marks and boosting TV's were one thing. Icing nuns was another. They had their standards.

Scott handed out Lawrence's photograph and his home and work addresses. Donato teamed them up. Keenan made out a time chart.

Fat Beauty, a two-hundred-twenty-pound check forger, had a brother-in-law who was in the electronics business. He outfitted them with walkie-talkies so they could stay in touch with each other and the task force.

Harry the Hat knew a guy in the used-car business who would lend them three cars. Dina and Donato asked no questions.

Dina advised the group that Lawrence was a killer but almost certainly not dangerous to them. And although they were to be careful, they were not to carry weapons. Each man and woman should make sure that Lawrence saw them, knew they were watching him, but they shouldn't get too close. The whole idea was to make the mark nervous. For most of them, this was exactly the opposite of their usual MO, which was to put the mark at ease.

Dina and Donato would be stationed in the surveillance truck. The snitches were to check in, reporting Lawrence's whereabouts, as often as possible. Finally, they were told that no one was interested in heroics should the occasion arise. Just do the job they were asked to do, nothing less, nothing more.

They broke up into two teams, the first team to go out at eight in the morning, the others from four P.M. until midnight, when the task force members would take over.

The whole thing was risky, and if anything happened to any of the snitches, Dina would be held responsible. She figured they had forty-eight hours at the most. After that, there would be no way to avoid Halliday. And the snitches couldn't be expected to stay on the job longer than that, even if they did have a little moral outrage going for them. But Dina felt sure that if they did it right, Lawrence would crack before time ran out.

Just before she and Donato were leaving to go to the surveillance truck, the first call came in from Halliday. She informed the cop who took the call to say she was gone. He smiled and did as he was told.

When Russ left his apartment building, he looked both ways and across the street. He didn't see any cops, but that didn't mean they weren't there. Still, Manny had assured him the surveillance would end. At the corner he turned south.

He hated being watched more than anything. Adele and Ken had watched him all his life in Grand Haven. No matter what he'd been doing, they were watching. Even when he ate. When he'd come home for lunch, his mother sat across from him and watched each bite he took as if it were an incredible feat. And they'd watched him playing, looking at television, doing his homework. There'd been no locks on the doors, no privacy anywhere. They'd even watched him take a bath until he was ten. Finally, he'd made such a scene they allowed him in the bathroom by himself. But the watching went on. Even when he couldn't see them looking, he knew they were there. That was one of the reasons he'd had to get rid of Ken. His father had brought it on himself.

And now there were these cops watching every move he made. He stopped and turned suddenly. Behind him were a woman with a child, two men carrying briefcases, and a very fat woman with short, black hair. But no one he could identify as police.

Glancing across the street, he saw a stream of people going to work. And then he spotted it. A blue car moving very slowly in the same direction he was going. A man wearing a cowboy hat was driving. Russ had never seen him, but maybe they'd changed personnel to confuse him.

He stepped into the street and raised his hand to hail a cab. Three occupied ones passed him by. The blue car was idling at the curb, the driver watching him. Russ felt frightened. He turned to look behind him. The fat woman was leaning against a building, watching. And then he saw another one: a man sporting a deep tan, wearing black jeans and a black T-shirt, was propped against a parked car, watching.

He was short of breath and dizzy. He felt as if a vise were crushing his chest, sending waves of pain through him, and he wondered if he were going to have a heart attack.

At last a cab stopped. When the driver took off, Russ looked out the window at the fat woman. She smiled at him, and he immediately turned away. Passing the tan man leaning against the parked car, Russ saw him take something out of his pocket and raise it to his mouth. As he looked back through the rearview window, he saw the blue car pull out and get behind the cab.

They had definitely changed personnel. Furious, he tried to think what to do. He would call Manny with their descriptions and the license plate number of the blue car. And if Manny couldn't do anything, he'd get Cornell to use his influence. These bastards didn't know whom they were dealing with. But he had to stay composed. He couldn't let them get to him.

He wouldn't turn around again, to see if the car was still following. Leaning his head back against the seat, he tried to muster some self-possession. And then the blue car pulled even with the cab. A woman in the passenger seat, with long red hair, heavily made up, put her head out the window and winked at him.

He shot up, hurled himself forward against the front seat. "Driver, do you see that car next to us?"

"Yeah?"

"I have twenty dollars for you if you lose it."

"I'm outta here," the cabbie said.

The driver gunned the motor and swung away. Smiling, Russ closed his eyes and gripped the seat. They were just stupid cops, and no one could get to him if he kept his head. From now on, he wasn't going to let anything bother him. He didn't have to panic if they were watching him . . . he just had to keep under control . . . in charge. And fuck Adele and Ken.

By the end of the first day, they could see that the plan was working. Earlier that day Lawrence had taken a client to lunch, and Donato and Dina had occupied a table two away from his. Lawrence had come over to them, his face flushed with rage.

"What the hell do you people think you're doing?" he'd asked in a low, strangled voice.

"Having lunch," Donato said, popping a piece of bread in his mouth. "Nice place, don't you think?"

"I'm going to sue you for harassment if you don't get the fuck out of here."

Dina said, "We're having lunch, Mr. Lawrence."

His eyes bulged. "I have a client at my table, and I want you people out of here, do you understand?"

"We're having lunch," Donato repeated. "Linguine with clam sauce and a side order of sauteed escarole. I recommend it."

"Are you going to leave here or am I?" he asked, shaking.

"We're not leaving."

"Goddamn you to hell," he said and walked away.

They watched him standing at his table, saying something to the client. And then the man rose and they both left.

Lawrence had next taken his client to a fish restaurant, where two of the more respectable-looking snitches sat at a table near them, watching Lawrence's every move until he'd spilled his wine and run from the place, leaving a confused client behind.

But even though the war of nerves was working, they were no closer to an arrest. And Halliday was, according to reliable sources, on the warpath, ready to fry their asses. They kept on ducking him, hoping they'd get a break. An arrest, especially a confession, would soothe Halliday completely and give him a good case of amnesia about the preceding days.

Then early on the second day, Donato got a message to call Chief Stone in Grand Haven.

"I thought you'd like to know," Stone said, "Adele Lawrence is on her way to New York. Wired up, I went out to see her last night, thinking I'd try once more. She was a mess. Been crying, and she'd had a few, too. I asked her again to tell me the truth about Dorothy, but she wouldn't. She kept asking me questions about the nun killings, and finally she said she had to go to Russ. If the police were persecuting him, he'd need her. Said Andrea wouldn't be any help. Anyway, she should be arriving about ten at Kennedy. United flight 312."

Donato thanked him and looked at his watch. There wasn't time to meet the plane. But maybe his mother's appearance would push Russ Lawrence closer to the edge.

At nine-twenty, they got word that Lawrence had come running out of his office building, grabbed a cab and headed uptown. Pretty Boy Alan and Vinnie Sellito were right behind him.

Russ jumped from the cab in front of his apartment building and paid the driver through the window. As he turned away, he saw a big, white-haired man in his sixties with a horrible scar on his face and a younger one who was so pretty he thought for a moment he was a girl get out of a car and start walking his way. He didn't wait to see if the men were going to speak to him, but ran into his building and back to the elevators.

He couldn't understand it. Manny had checked out the license plate Russ had given him and learned that the car was not police property. And the people were not police. So who were they and why were they watching him? He could lose them any time he wanted to, but what would be the point? Whenever he came home or went to work, it would start again.

But nothing mattered now except getting his keys, including the one to the Grand Central locker. He couldn't believe he'd left them on the dresser. It was the fault of that stupid lieutenant and sergeant. If they hadn't begun following him, upsetting him, he would never have gotten into this condition. And he knew they must have something to do with those awful people who were following him now.

The elevator finally came. When he got to his floor, he ran down the hall, and then he realized that he couldn't get in. He didn't have his keys.

Maybe she hadn't left yet. He rang the bell several times. Nothing. Back at the elevator, he pushed the buzzer.

If Andrea had found the keys, surely she would have called him at work, asked what he wanted her to do with them. Or perhaps she would have left them with Charlie. But Charlie hadn't said anything when he'd come in. Did that mean she hadn't found them?

The elevator doors yawned open, Russ got in and pushed L. The car stopped at 10 and two women got on. He nodded, recognizing one as a tenant, and she smiled. The women chattered on, irritating him.

But what if Andrea *had* found them and had *not* tried to reach him and had not left the keys with the doorman? What would that mean? He couldn't allow himself to think about it. Most likely, she hadn't even noticed them.

The car stopped at 8, 7, 5, 3 and 2. He couldn't remember when he'd felt this anxious. At last the elevator hit the lobby and he got out, pushing by an older man. He could hear some grumbles behind him, but he didn't care.

"Charlie," he said, approaching the doorman, "Charlie, did Mrs. Lawrence leave my keys with you?"

"Morning, Miss Von Nardroff," Charlie said, touching the brim of his hat. " 'Nother beautiful day. Be right with you, Mr. Lawrence," he said, opening the door for the woman and those who followed. When they were gone, he turned back to Russ. "Now, what can I do for you, Mr. Lawrence?"

Russ wanted to smash his stupid face. He asked again about the keys.

"Nope. Saw her this morning, but she didn't say nothing about no keys. You locked out?"

"Yes."

"Well, hey, I'll ring Fred for you. He's got keys."

"Don't you have them?"

"Ever since the murder, Fred's been in charge of them. Don't ask me why. Not like somebody got into one of the apartments and bashed somebody's skull in or anything, is it?" He moved closer to him, whispering. "See that man out there, across the street near the corner?"

Russ saw the man in the cowboy hat.

"That's a plainclotheser. Seen him around here lots, watching this building."

"Could you ring Fred?" he said curtly.

"Sure. Sorry, Mr. Lawrence." Charlie sounded miffed. He

picked up the house phone and pushed a button. After a few moments, he hung up. "He's not there. Probably working around the building somewhere."

"I've got to get into my apartment," Lawrence said desperately.

"You wanna wait I'll try him again in a little while. Or you could go down to the basement and take a look for him. Maybe one of the other janitors is around and'll know where he is."

"I'll do that." He rushed back through the lobby to the elevator again.

But once he was inside he remembered that Kim Lyle had a set of keys. They'd exchanged them years ago for just such an eventuality as this. He pressed P.

Lyle was probably still asleep. He recalled the day the police had come looking for him. Goddamn Lyle. It was his fault that the police were on to him. If Lyle hadn't attracted their attention, if he'd been up at a decent hour like any normal person, the police would have never noticed him. He got off the elevator and ran down the hall. He pressed Lyle's bell, keeping his finger on it.

Minutes passed. Russ's finger hurt; the muscle in his arm was sore. Tension, he told himself and tried to breathe deeply, to calm down. At last he heard the locks being tumbled, and then Lyle stood there in a robe, hair mussed, the pattern of a crumpled sheet creased into his cheek.

"What the fuck do you want in the middle of the night?"

"I'm locked out. I need my keys."

"Huh?"

"Jesus, Lyle, are you deaf? I need my keys. You have a set, remember?"

"Oh, yeah." He led Russ down the hall, through the living room and into the kitchen, where he opened a cabinet. Several sets of keys were hanging on hooks on the inside of the door.

Russ saw his name on a label under one and grabbed for it. "Thanks," he called, running back through the apartment and out into the hall.

He shoved the key in the lock and entered. In a moment, he was in the bedroom. His keyring was gone. And so was the locker key under it. The bitch must have taken them. He called her at work, and her secretary said she hadn't come in yet, that she'd called at nine-thirty to say she'd be late. Russ looked at his watch. It was ten-fifteen.

What the hell was she up to? And then he knew. For a long time, she had believed he was having an affair. He knew how her mind worked. She'd found the locker key and assumed he stored love letters or something incriminating there. She'd try Grand Central first. It was closest.

He left the bedroom and went to his study, where he opened his closet. From a top shelf, behind some books, he grabbed the box, brought it down, flipped off the lid and reached inside. Thank God he hadn't put the gun in the locker. Opening the chamber, he dropped in the bullets one by one, shut the chamber and put the gun in his pocket.

He'd have to go to Grand Central. If Andrea had gone there and opened the locker, the place would be swarming with police. And then he'd know what he had to do.

The word around the department was that Dina and Donato were on the run from Halliday, trying to crack the nun case. There was no love lost between most detectives and Halliday, so he wasn't getting any help from them. But Donato and Dina were.

Two airport detectives had met Adele Lawrence's plane and were bringing her into the city. And Alan Verber, an old partner of Donato's, assigned to Grand Central, called him in the surveillance truck when the shit hit the fan at Grand Central. Despite his efforts, Donato couldn't stop Verber from giving him every particular.

"Now picture this, okay. It's ten after ten, and the rush hour crowd's gone, but there's still a bunch a clowns going here, going there. Walking past the bank of lockers, you see it, Donato, you get the drill?"

"What's the point, Verber?" Donato asked impatiently.

"Hold on, I'm telling you, you'll just listen. There was this old broad, from some jerkwater town in Iowa or some fucking place. She's standing next to Lawrence's wife, trying to lift her suitcase up, put it in her locker . . ."

"Come on, come on."

Verber continued to savor each detail.

"Some dude comes along, asks the old biddy she needs help? Naturally she says yes. So now we got two people on the left of the Lawrence dame."

"Al," Donato threatened.

"Wait a minute, it gets better. On the other side of Lawrence, two schoolgirls, thirteen and fourteen, it turns out later they're gypping school, are taking a locker to stash their books and junk. Now get this . . ."

"What I want to get," Donato yelled over the wire, "is what the fuck happened?"

"I'm telling you, you just pay attention," Verber answered. "So this being not enough, just as Andrea Lawrence sticks the key in the locker and the door pops open, a bunch a second graders going on a field trip with their teachers are walking by." He sighed, as if the picture he'd created was a thing of beauty. "So you got the idea, you see it?"

Through clenched teeth, Donato said he did.

"Lady Lawrence screams. The guy helping the old dame drops the suitcase on his foot. The old broad stumbles back against the lockers. The two schoolgirls grab each other, and the entire second grade of P.S. Eleven stops in their tracks. First Lawrence pulls out this boning knife and everybody backs off, like maybe she's gonna slice somebody up or take it in the chest herself. But she don't. She drops it on the floor. Then she pulls out this nun's costume, which she also drops. You're wondering what she screamed about, right, Donato?"

"Right."

"The Lawrence broad is shaking all over, I mean like she's got St. Vitus Dance or something. So one of the teachers with the second graders comes over, asks her what it is. But she don't answer because she's like in shock and she's staring into the locker. Being a bright jomoke, this teacher gently moves Mrs. L. out of the way and looks in the locker himself. Know what happens?"

"What?"

"The guy takes a good long look and then he loses it. I mean really. He pukes all over himself, and by now the old broad is screaming, the schoolgirls are screaming, they don't even know why, but it's like mass hysteria, and all the second graders are screaming, and a course now other people are piling up, rubbernecking like they do. Finally somebody's smart enough to get a cop. You wanna guess what's in the locker, makes Mrs. Lawrence go crazy, the guy puke?"

"I want you to tell me, Verber."

"Besides the nun's costume, the knife and a cleaver stashed inside the locker, there was a fucking jar with four fucking fingers in it."

They had him now. Or almost. Nobody had called in since Lawrence had grabbed the cab. Dina figured he was still en route somewhere, and they'd hear as soon as he landed. It was time to call Halliday.

"Sorry I haven't gotten back to you, sir, but this case has had me on the run," she said.

"Lieutenant, I'm going to assume you're telling me the truth, and I'm going to forget about you not calling me back. So where is this bastard?"

"My people have had Lawrence under surveillance every minute for the last few days. We'll be taking him into custody immediately, Chief." As soon as they learned where Lawrence was, she'd call off the snitches, and the task force would move in and take him. It was going to end much more simply than she'd anticipated.

"All right," Halliday said. "Take this fucker alive. We don't want the goddamn media down our necks any more than they have been. Keep me informed."

A moment later the call came in from Florida Bob.

"We lost him," he said.

Dina sat down. "Where?"

"Grand Central."

"Why didn't somebody call before this?"

"The walkie-talkies got fucked up."

"What happened at Grand Central?"

"We followed him in from the main Forty-second Street entrance. He goes through the waiting room into the big ticket area, then hangs a left past the ticket booths, goes by Zaro's bakery, the newsstand and toward the turn for the Oyster Bar. Then he stops and looks down the ramp at some lockers. Cops was piled up like some grifter's just scored off Ronald Reagan. Lawrence hightails it out of there and heads for the subway. Me and Fat Beauty is right behind him. First he's there and then he ain't. The guy disappeared like in a magic trick. What d'ya want us to do?"

"Nothing. It's over for all of you. You did good work. We'll be in touch."

"I'm sorry, Lieut," he said, sounding genuinely sad.

"Don't worry about it. We'll get him."

"Good luck."

"Thanks." They could use it. Hanging up, she turned to Donato. "They lost him."

"Christ."

She related the gist of Florida Bob's call.

"So he knows we have him. If he saw the cops by the lockers, he knows."

"He must have gone home for his keys. I think we really shook him up, Donato."

"That's why he forgot his keys. Verber told me his wife said he'd never left them behind before. At least we know he won't go back to his office. We have to remember the man's crazy. He's probably not going to do anything logical like try to get out of New York. Still, we better have the airports, train and bus stations blocked."

Donato called Al Verber and asked him to take care of it, but not to blast it around that they'd lost Lawrence. When he hung up, he said to Dina, "We've got to find him before anyone else does, kiddo. If somebody else picks him up . . . well, I'd hate to think where Halliday might transfer you to."

She felt touched by Donato's concern for her career. "Might send me to the Ninth," she said, trying for a smile from him.

He bought it. "Yeah, might be as bad as that."

She was fresh out of ideas. "Got any suggestions?"

"You know," he said, "I think I do. I think I know where the bastard'll go."

Russ was furious that events kept forcing him to take subways. He stood, holding on to a center post, one hand in his pocket touching the gun. They thought they were so smart. He'd figured out that the people who'd been following him were part of some group headed by that cunt lieutenant. Well, he'd shown them who was smart. Looking around the car, he checked once more to make sure none of the tails was with him. He was alone.

And after all, that was the only thing he wanted. To be alone. That was what he'd always wanted after Dorothy left him. But you couldn't be alone. They wouldn't let you. You had to have friends and a wife and children. You had to show them who was smarter, and you couldn't do that alone.

The subway stopped at Chambers Street. He clamped his hand around the gun, but no one suspicious got on. The one thing he was determined about now was to do this his way. People were always trying to get you to do things their way. But this time they wouldn't have a chance. Because he was smarter than all of them.

When the train stopped at Fulton, Russ Lawrence got out.

As Donato and Dina were pulling out, they were stopped by a siren wailing nearby. A faded green Plymouth, flashing light on the roof, drew up next to them. A detective jumped out from each side. The one on the passenger side opened the back door and out stepped Adele Lawrence.

She looked older than she had in Grand Haven. She wasn't

wearing her wig, and wisps of gray hair had sprung from the bun on the back of her head.

Donato approached her. "We have proof, Mrs. Lawrence, that your son's the nun killer."

"Where is he?" she asked in a whisper.

"We're not sure, but we've got an idea. Want to come?"

"Yes. Please."

Donato opened the door of the Chevy and helped her in. Dina drove, and he sat in back with Mrs. Lawrence.

Adele Lawrence turned to Donato. "Will you kill him?" she asked.

Donato felt for her. Whatever kind of monster her son was, he was still her son. "We don't want to kill him. It will depend on him. Maybe you can help."

"How?"

"I'm not sure yet."

"I'll do anything," she said pitifully.

He knew she would. Anything to keep her son alive.

Neither of them spoke again. Donato watched Dina skillfully maneuver the car through traffic. He felt filled with love for her, grateful that he wasn't in Adele Lawrence's shoes, contemplating the death of her child.

And then it hit him that Dina's life was in jeopardy too. Just because Lawrence's murders had been psychosexual, just because he'd always used a knife and strangled, didn't mean that he might not change his MO if he was cornered. Remember Pike, Donato told himself. Pike hadn't been in Lawrence's plan, but he'd gotten in his way. Anything could happen.

Of course, Lawrence might not be there at all. But Donato trusted his hunch, and he wanted to go out with this thing neatly tucked under his belt. He'd made up his mind. He'd retire when this was over. And he was going to make one last try for his wife . . . his life.

Dina cut the siren and turned onto South Street. At Fulton she pulled up on the sidewalk in front of the closed fish markets. It was twenty after eleven. The day was beautiful, the tourists in full swing; but the lunch crowd, from the surrounding offices, had not yet descended. Crowded as it was, it was going to get worse. If Lawrence was here, they had to move quickly.

"Where are we?" Mrs. Lawrence asked.

"South Street Seaport," Donato said. "I want you to wait here.

Don't get out of the car. It could mean your son's life." So it wasn't true. Still, it was important that she stay where they could find her.

The other members of the task force had been notified of the operation, and they were all to meet at the bar at the Fulton Street Market Restaurant. Dina and Donato hurried down the cobblestoned street.

Most of the tables in front of the restaurant were empty now. Soon there'd be a long line waiting for one to open up. The bar inside was a mixture of wood and green tile. Flowing green plants hung from the ceiling. Waiters in green shirts and tan pants were readying for the lunch crush. Standing at the bar, sipping Cokes and club soda, were the six task force members. Excitement showed in their eyes.

Dina said, "We're not sure he's here, but there's a good chance of it. We'll try the pier first. He likes it there. If he's not there, we'll go up Fulton, through the shops one by one.

"We think he's on one of the mall decks. Let's try to take him by surprise. He may come quietly. On the other hand, it could be a trap. Don't forget who we're dealing with."

"Ain't about to forget that," Bobbin said.

"And the sucker could also be in Canada, right?" Lachman asked.

"Doubtful," Donato said. "We've blocked all the exits."

"We've got his mother with us," Dina continued. "But we don't want to use her unless we have to. Whatever happens, be very careful. The place is swarming with tourists. Don't use your guns unless absolutely necessary. Now let me explain how we're going to approach this."

Five minutes later, Dina and Donato were carefully making their way up the boardwalk of Pier 17. The others would follow at one-minute intervals.

On the pier, the large steel structure that housed shops and the decks was painted maroon. Across from the mall building, on the other side of the boardwalk, the big schooner *Peking* rested in the water, and further up, the paddlewheel boat.

Keeping close to the building, Dina and Donato passed some empty stores. To get to the next level without being seen from any of the decks, Donato followed Dina and pulled himself up by holding on to a railing. He felt his joints creaking. What the hell was he doing this for when he could be painting or reading a book in an easy chair? Soon.

At the end of the walk where they turned the corner, they kept close to the building, and passed under the outside stairs that led to the decks. There were two of these, and Bobbin and Lachman would be watching them. When they reached the main entrance, Donato waited while Dina continued down the length of the building to the end, hand in her bag on her gun. She turned the corner. In a moment she was back, shaking her head.

Inside the mall, there were stores on either side of a ramp that led to the main area. They gave the glass-enclosed stores a quick once-over. Looking back, Donato saw Keenan and Delgado enter the front door. He presumed that Bobbin and Lachman were in their places; Pesetsky and Scott were stationed at each end of the pier.

At the end of the ramp, the first floor opened up into a large rectangle, stores lining the sides. In the center were the stairs and escalator leading up to the next level. And to the right was another ramp to the colonnade area, which had a staircase to the second floor. Earlier, Dina had made the decision to skip the stores and go directly up to the decks.

Keenan and Delgado took the stairs in the colonnade, and Dina and Donato went to the second floor by stairs and escalator. Had Dina taken the stairs out of deference to his age? He removed his gun from his shoulder holster and shoved it into his pants.

As he rode up, his hand on the butt of his gun, Donato prayed his kidneys wouldn't act up. He always felt like he had to pee at just the wrong time. He wondered if that ever happened to Dina.

Suddenly, he was thinking of a million things he hadn't asked her: What did she think of the latest John Updike? Had she seen the current Woody Allen film? Did she still like the Mets? He'd have to ask later and silently prayed he'd have the chance.

When they reached the second level, Keenan and Delgado stationed themselves at the staircases to the next level, and Dina and Donato went toward the doors that led to the outside decks at either end of the floor.

To get to the deck, Donato had to walk past the bar of Flutie's. Even at this hour, the place was filling up, and the cacophony that came from the restaurant reminded him of the innocent people whose lives might soon be at risk. Maybe Lawrence wouldn't put up a fight.

At the double doors, he could see several benches on the deck, all of them filled, but no Lawrence. He pushed through the doors, his hand still on his gun. A warm breeze fluttered across his face. At either end of the deck were the outside staircases.

He walked toward the left end of the deck, keeping close to the wall, his gun in both hands, held in front of him pointed at the ground. When he reached the corner, he raised the gun and made the turn in a combat stance.

The deck was empty. He went back across the front deck and repeated the procedure on the right.

Nothing.

He walked to the railing, looking both ways. Across from him was the *Peking,* people milling about on its deck. He started to turn when he thought he heard his name called. Was *this* that phenomenon, his unconscious calling to him, or was it real? He gazed down at the crowd. Hundreds of people were on the gray boardwalk below, but no one stood out. Then he heard it again.

"Do-na-to."

This time the call seemed to come from beyond the boardwalk, out on the water. Sound could be deceptive when water was involved. He scanned the shoreline. Nothing.

"Do-na-to."

And then he saw a man on the deck of the *Peking,* one arm around a woman, a glint of metal in the other hand, which he held against her head. The boat was a tourist attraction, and Donato could see that the people cruising the deck were looking in the direction of the man standing near one of the four yellow masts, shouting Donato's name. He was too far away to make out the man's features, but Donato knew it was Lawrence.

"Do-na-to," it came again.

Below, Lachman and Bobbin headed toward the boat. Donato pulled open the door and yelled to Dina and the others to follow. He ran out to the deck again and started down the outside stairs.

When he reached the boardwalk, he ran across it toward the *Peking,* trying to avoid people but bumping into them, knocking over a man. To get to the boat, he could take the long way around or vault over an iron gate. There was no contest. He had at least one more leap left in him. He scaled the three-barred railing in what felt like an effortless jump. As he ducked under the heavy rope tying up the red-and-white *Ambrose Lightship,* he saw a woman running up the gangplank toward the deck of the *Peking,* heard Bobbin calling for her to stop.

They were both too late. Adele Lawrence had made it to the deck of the boat.

"Sorry," Bobbin said. "She got past me."

"Clear the area," Donato said.

Below the *Peking*, they stared up at Lawrence, who stood at the top of the gangplank, holding a gun to a woman's head. Two gangplanks led to the deck. Lawrence stood near the one used for the tourists; the other was near the bow of the boat, unused.

Keenan said to Dina, "Should we try and get up the other gangplank, Lieutenant?"

"Not as long as he has a hostage. Lachman, secure the other gangplank." She turned to Delgado. "Call for backup and an ambulance. And let Halliday know what's going down."

Suddenly, Lawrence backed up, and they were unable to see him or his hostage.

"What now?" Pesetsky asked.

"We wait for his next move. A lot of lives are at stake," Dina said.

Donato was fearful for the people aboard. He cupped his mouth and shouted to them to stay put, warning them against any heroics. But he wasn't sure that the wind hadn't carried his instructions out to sea.

"Why the hell did he call attention to himself?" Donato asked Dina. "He could have gotten away."

"Maybe he doesn't want to."

Then Lawrence reappeared at the top of the gangplank, his mother in front of him, one arm around her neck, his gun at her right temple.

"You see this woman?" Lawrence shouted. "I'm going to blow her brains out."

Adele Lawrence's face was impassive, as if she'd always known that this was how her life would end.

"Don't do it," Donato said. "You've killed enough people."

"Not quite," he said. "I want everybody off this boat."

"All right. Send them down," Dina agreed.

Lawrence stepped back, dragging his mother with him, the gun still at her head. He ordered the frightened tourists off the boat. The exodus took almost two minutes. When they were all safely down, Pesetsky cleared them from the area. Donato looked around. Behind them the boardwalk was jammed, even though the other members of the task force were holding people at bay. In the distance, he heard sirens.

"Why did you call me?" Donato yelled to Lawrence, hoping to distract him.

"Because I wanted to see you when I do what I have to do."

"What's that?"

"I just told you. I'm going to kill her. Unless," he smiled, "you help me not to."

"I'll do whatever you say," Donato said.

"Good. Send up the lieutenant."

Donato thought again that the wind might be playing tricks, but then he knew he'd heard correctly.

"What for?" he asked.

"Because if you don't send her up, I'm going to blow this bitch's brains all over the boardwalk."

The words hung in the air like a cloud of noxious gas.

"And if I come up?" Dina shouted.

"I'll release her."

Dina touched Donato's arm. "I have to," she said.

"The hell you do." He couldn't recall feeling more frightened than he did now. All his protection over the years, meaningless, useless. This madman wanted his child, his only child, and she was in charge, ready to go. He was helpless.

"Donato, I can't let him kill an innocent woman."

"She's not so innocent," he said, grasping at straws.

"You know what I mean," Dina said.

Keenan came over to them. "What are you going to do?"

"I have to go up."

"No," Keenan said.

Lawrence yelled, "I'm waiting, Donato."

"How will we work it, Lawrence?" Donato called, stalling.

"When she gets up here, I'll send this one down."

"How can I believe you?"

"You'll have to trust me."

Halliday appeared, demanding to be told what was happening. They filled him in as quickly as possible.

Keenan said, "You can't go up there, Dina. He'll kill you."

"I don't think so," she said. "He'll probably use me as a hostage, to get out of here."

"*If* he wants to get out of here," Donato put in. "He could have left before all this."

"Donato's right," Keenan said.

"He's a showman, don't forget. Leaving the city quietly wouldn't satisfy that enormous ego. He has to prove to us how smart he is, make us jump through hoops, do his bidding."

Halliday said, "She has a point. I don't think he'll harm her."

Donato whirled on him. "You don't *think*," he snapped. "What the hell do you know about it?"

Dina stepped between them. "It doesn't matter what either of you thinks," she said. She turned to Donato and Keenan. "I have to go up. If he wanted you, you'd go."

The two men looked at each other. They knew it was true.

Halliday said, "We have no choice." His eyes challenged Donato.

Donato wanted to offer himself in place of Dina, but he knew it wouldn't do. Not for Lawrence. Not for Dina.

"All right, she's going to come up," Donato yelled.

"I want her to give her handbag to you and to take off her jacket," Lawrence directed.

Dina did as he asked.

"Now come up," Lawrence said.

Donato could see that Keenan wanted to reach out for her but resisted. She smiled at him, then turned toward Donato.

"It'll be okay, kiddo," he said, wishing he believed it.

"I know." She touched him lightly on the arm and started up the stairs.

Donato's insides had turned to soup. He watched, powerless, as she climbed the steps, moving away from him toward peril.

When she reached the top, Lawrence grabbed her by the arm and pulled her roughly to one side. Then he fired the gun into his mother's head. As bits of brain and bone flew into the air, he wrapped his arm around Dina's neck and they lunged backward, disappearing from view.

Russ's face and clothes were covered with his mother's blood. Her body had fallen sideways and lay heaped at the top of the gangplank. He told Dina to sit down on a hatch cover while he pulled a handkerchief from his pants pocket and wiped what he could from his face and gun hand. When he'd cleaned himself as much as possible, he looked at Dina. There were streaks of blood on her face and clothes. He didn't offer to wipe them off.

"Get up," he commanded.

She rose.

Moving behind her, he placed his arm around her neck, the gun at the back of her head. "They know I mean business," he said. "And you do, too. So don't try anything. We're going down now." He thought he sounded like Bogart.

They walked to the edge of the deck. He looked down. Donato and the others were standing in place, waiting. Donato looked mad. Well, hell. This wasn't his fault. If they hadn't come after him, he wouldn't have had to kill Adele. They'd better not try to blame him. The responsibility for this was theirs.

"We're coming down now," he shouted. "Step away from the bottom of the stairs. When we get down, all of you back off. You've seen what you've forced me to do, don't make me do it again." To Dina he said, "Take it easy going down. I wouldn't want you to fall."

Adele Lawrence's body was in the way. Dina watched while Lawrence gave it a kick and it slowly thumped down the gangplank, stopping on the metal platform as if she were resting there.

"Okay," Lawrence said. "Let's go."

Dina put a foot on the first cleat. Lawrence's arm around her throat hurt. She felt his body close up against hers, his breath in her ear, on her neck. And the gun hard against the side of her head. She couldn't allow herself to believe that her life would end like this.

"Again," he said.

Carefully, she took another step, reached the next cleat. Below, she saw her father. The agony on his face echoed what she felt. She knew his impotence in this situation was killing him.

She took a third step, Lawrence right with her. Next to her father, Keenan, his jaw set, hands balled into fists at his sides, never took his eyes from her. Even at this distance, she could sense his intensity. Behind them was Halliday, arms akimbo, his face an unreadable mask.

"A little faster," Lawrence said.

"I can't because of the way you're holding me around my neck."

"Okay." He loosened up, held on to her by her shoulder. "Don't try anything because this gun is still ready to blow you apart."

Slowly, they continued down until they reached the platform and Adele Lawrence's body. Dina had to step over it and almost slipped in the blood. There was one small step from the platform to five more metal steps.

Dina had been frightened before but never like this. Looking to the left, she saw below the two men she loved, standing side by side. What had been wrong with her? Why hadn't she known that independence didn't have to mean going it alone, that being competent could nestle nicely next to vulnerability and that loving Keenan didn't mean she had to lose her identity? Why hadn't she realized that she could be mad at Donato and still love and respect him? All sorts of feelings could co-exist.

As she reached the bottom step, she looked again at Donato and Keenan and gave them the best smile she could. Cops to the end, they returned her smile through their eyes.

"All right," Lawrence said to the group. "We're leaving here. You've seen what I can do. You know who I am and . . ."

"Who are you?" Donato interrupted.

Dina knew he was stalling, hoping to come up with something, some way to get her away from Lawrence.

"What do you mean, who am I?" Lawrence asked suspiciously.

"You said, we know who you are. I assumed you meant someone other than Russ Lawrence. Someone special. Someone unlike any other person."

"How did you know?"

Dina felt Lawrence's attention directed toward Donato. He loosened his grip on her shoulder, his hand sliding forward and hovering over her breast.

"You've made it very obvious that you're no ordinary man, Lawrence," Donato said.

"I'm surprised you know that, Donato. I have . . ."

Dina grabbed the carelessly dangling hand, thrust her left elbow backward hard into his gut, dropping to one knee and simultaneously flipping Lawrence over her shoulder onto his back. She heard the gun go off, the report so loud she knew she was alive. She wouldn't have heard it had he killed her.

Keenan, Bobbin and Delgado were piled on top of Lawrence. Halliday held the gun in his hand. But where was Donato? Whirling around, she saw Lachman and Scott kneeling by him on the ground. Blood seeped from his chest. She knelt down and grabbed his hand.

"Oh, Daddy, my God, Daddy, no."

His eyes flickered open. "You got him," he said.

"*We* got him."

"You knew what I was doing . . . trying to distract him."

"Of course I did. We're a team," she said.

"You bet."

He coughed, and Dina could see the pain in his face. "You'll be okay." But she wasn't sure.

An ambulance had been standing by, and now the attendants ran to them and set down the gurney. Carefully, they lifted Donato onto it. As the wheels sprang open, the gurney rose. They began rolling him away.

"Hey," Donato called weakly.

Dina, running alongside, held his hand. "What is it?"

"Just wanted to tell you . . . I love you, kiddo." Slowly, he closed his eyes.

Twenty-six

When Donato opened his eyes, he saw faces but couldn't make them out. They were blurred, fuzzy. And he didn't know where he was, but he was damned if he was going to ask anyone. His chest hurt. He figured the hell with it—the whole thing was too much trouble—so he closed his eyes again.

The next time he opened them the faces were still there, but this time he could see who they were.

Dina.

Cal.

Renata.

The three people he loved most in this world. Now he realized he was in the hospital and slowly began to remember the events that had gotten him there.

"Jesus, Dina," he said. "You took one helluva chance. What a crazy thing to do."

"Thanks, Donato," she said. "Now I can leave. I can tell you're going to be just fine."

"Wait a minute. What about Lawrence?"

"Padded cell at Matawan."

"The others? Keenan?" He could see the red begin to flood her cheeks. "You know, it doesn't look right for a lieutenant to go around blushing."

"You really are a . . ."

"Don't say it . . . there's a child present." He reached out and took hold of Cal's hand. "So, how's Keenan?"

"He's fine. Everybody's okay. You were the only dope who got hurt."

"Just lucky I guess. The damn gun went off in his hand, and I was in the right spot at the right time."

Cal said, "Don't you mean the *wrong* spot at the *wrong* time, Grandpa?"

"Yeah, that's what I meant to say."

"We'd better let you get some rest," Renata said.

"Wait, I'm not finished. What about Halliday?" As weak as his voice was, it still had venom in it.

"Halliday was very pleased," Dina said. "You're out of the Ninth."

"Yeah? Where's he sending me, Fort Apache?"

"With me, if you want. I'd like it."

"We'll talk," he said.

"Fine. We'd better go now." She leaned down and kissed him on the cheek. "Be nice," she whispered.

After Cal kissed him good-bye, they left, and he and Renata were alone. He didn't know what to say to her, and then she reached out and took his hand.

"Don't make a big thing out of this, Mike," she warned.

"Who me?" he said. He thought she looked beautiful.

"It scared me to death when I heard. This thing I've been fearing for thirty-three years finally happening. God, I thought I was going to die myself."

He couldn't believe how happy it made him to hear that she still cared. He kept quiet.

"Well, they say lightning doesn't strike twice, so I guess we're safe. I mean, *you* are."

He smiled.

"Don't give me that look. *If* . . . and I mean *if* we get back together, there have to be a lot of changes."

He nodded.

"You'd better get some rest," she said and ran a hand over his forehead.

Donato thought he ought to tell her about his decision to retire . . . but . . . you never knew what might happen.

He went to sleep instead.